Shadow

of

Perception

KRISTINE MASON

ISBN: 0989479021
ISBN-13: 978-0-9894790-2-8

For one of my dearest friends, Mary Gardner.
Whether I'm right or wrong, you always have my back. When I
get a little crazy, you encourage me to get crazier. When I need
someone to lean on, you've never let me down.
Thank you for your support and friendship.
Life just wouldn't be the same without you in it.

ACKNOWLEDGMENTS

Special thanks to Jamie Denton, Christy Esau and Mary Ann Chulick for their help with this book. Another big thanks to my cover artist Kim Van Meter, KD Designs.

PROLOGUE

"LOOK AT ME, Daddy."

Michael Morrison ignored the howling wind lashing against the metal building and concentrated on the old TV. A slow, bitter smile pulled at the corner of his mouth as his daughter moved across the screen. She'd just turned five and had looked so adorable and proud dancing and twirling for the camera in her lavender taffeta dress.

"Do you think I'll win, Daddy?" she asked as she paused to admire herself in the mirror. "Mommy says I'm sure to be crowned Little Miss Hanover." She frowned at her reflection and plucked at the puffy lace capping her slender shoulders. "But I saw the other girls during rehearsal and—"

"Don't you worry about those other girls," he reassured her as he'd held the camera steady. "And even if you don't win, no matter what, I think you're the most beautiful girl in the world."

He still did.

His eyes misted, with grief, with regret, with overwhelming sadness.

Another strong gust swept against the building. Howling and protesting, the wind angrily pelted the metal walls. Almost as if nature, the universe, God, or whatever higher powers there may be, understood and shared his pain. Approved of what he was about to do.

He wiped a hand across his damp forehead, a huff escaping from between his dry lips. If anyone had heard his inner thoughts they'd think he was crazy. Hell, if anyone had a clue of what he'd planned they'd lock him in a padded cell until his body rotted to dust and his soul slid to the bowels of hell. But he wasn't crazy. Angry, yes. Vindictive, you bet your ass.

Hardening his jaw, he returned his focus to the TV, where the DVD he'd created from old home movies segued to the next scene. The crowning of Little Miss Hanover. As her mother had predicted, Eliza had won. While the crowd had cheered and the judge placed a bejeweled crown on her head, Eliza had smiled for the camera, mouthing "I love you, Daddy" as she'd smoothed her tiny hands over the full skirt of that lavender dress.

Her proud, innocent smile faded from the screen as the film moved forward. Images of Eliza's many other beauty pageants—that she'd ultimately won or placed—flew by almost as quickly as her short life.

The wind barraged the building again, the TV screen suddenly flipped, blurring the frames into a Technicolor nightmare. The old picture tube protesting its use, he supposed as he stood and gave the top of the box a slap. After a second, the screen burst to life again, but in slapping the TV, he must have accidently rattled the DVD player, too. The images jerked to a screeching halt before jumping ahead. Past Eliza's cheerleading years, the night she'd been crowned homecoming queen, her first modeling shoot, and straight to the final scene.

He hit PAUSE and froze the image. No. Not a scene or a segment from the old home movie collection, but a still shot of his daughter lying on her bed.

Naked. Dead. Unrecognizable.

His throat thickened and his eyes filled with tears he couldn't afford to shed at the moment. Holding his grief at bay, he focused on the anger. And as he leaned forward and traced his fingers along the TV screen, along the gaping slashes across her wrists to the blood pooling at her sides, he allowed that anger to take root. Let the hatred numb his heart and blacken the soul that would eventually belong to the devil. The devil could have him. He could give a shit if he burned in hell for an eternity so long as he took the men who had destroyed his daughter along for the ride.

He would have added her mother, the woman he'd once loved fiercely, to what he liked to refer to as his "death wish list." But Sarah had scratched herself off his list before he'd written a single name by putting a bullet through her head at their daughter's funeral. Not even in death could Sarah allow Eliza a moment to shine. No, the narcissistic bitch had to blow her brains all over the metal casket, making it about her. Always about her.

Now it was about Eliza. As it should have been from the beginning, as it would be now, and ever shall be, world without end. A-fucking-men.

The alarm on his watch beeped, reminding him what he'd already known. His patient would be waking soon, and by the low moan from the other room, Michael would have to act fast before the bastard regained full consciousness. Sure, he'd strapped the man down, but he didn't want to miss the look on the shithead's face when his eyes fluttered open, only to discover he'd just woken up in hell.

As he was about to exit the office, though, shame suddenly clouded his judgment. What he'd spent seven long years preparing for went beyond immoral and had his conscience battling with his anger and need for revenge. Sweat coated his skin and trickled down his back. His heart quickened and his head grew dizzy with the onslaught of a panic attack. Until he glanced at the letter he had framed and hung on the wall. The final contact he would ever have from his beloved daughter. While he'd memorized Eliza's words, each bold and bubbly stroke of her script, he honed in on one line in particular for encouragement.

Make them listen, Daddy.

Another moan, this time even louder, filtered into the office. His head cleared, his heart slowed to normal, and an eerie calm settled over him.

"They'll do more than listen, baby," he whispered, rage suddenly sweeping away any thoughts of immorality or ethics or principles. Screw those things. Screw those quacks who had destroyed his daughter's life.

Without hesitation he left the office and entered the main section of the thirty-by-fifty steel garage. He hadn't needed the entire space and had chosen to fulfill his plans in the west corner of the building, where the lighting was best and the bathroom and utility sink were closest. Things would become messy, after all.

When he reached the corner that housed his private operating room he couldn't help a stab of pride. He'd worked half his life in the medical field and knew the space he'd created here rivaled most hospitals. Although, his OR did lack a heart monitor, he amended with a grin as he rounded the operating table and stared at the man strapped to it. His patients were here to suffer, not survive.

As he reached for his scrubs, the man on the table lolled his head and his eyes began to flutter. Grabbing a water bottle from the bench next to him, Michael opened it then splashed water on Doctor Thomas Elliot's face.

Coughing and sputtering, Elliot widened his eyes. Before the man could release a word, Michael pierced the doctor with a syringe, sending a paralytic rushing through the man's veins.

Elliot's eyes drifted shut and his body stilled. If someone were to walk into the room, they'd think he was dead. The drug paralyzed the body, but not the mind, or hearing, or...

Michael used masking tape to force the doctor's eyelids to remain open. "Can't let you off that easy, can I?" he asked Elliot, then turned the man's head toward the bench that held the medical instruments. He wanted him to see the tools. He wanted him scared out of his mind. Helpless and at his mercy.

Make them listen, Daddy.

Immobile and paralyzed, the bastard would listen to him now. He had no choice.

"Good evening, Dr. Elliot. I'll be handling your surgery," he said as he shed his own clothes and reached for the scrubs again. Once dressed he pointed to the instruments on the bench.

"I'm sure these items are familiar to you considering you're a doctor. As you can see, I have everything needed to perform your procedure. I wouldn't want you to think I was a quack or anything."

He glanced at his watch. The paralytic would wear off in less than a minute. He'd love to give the good doc another dose, but didn't want to risk killing him before he had a chance to perform the surgery.

"I've got a schedule to meet, so let's get this show on the road." After slipping on his surgical cap and gloves, Michael reached for the Ziploc bags lying on the bench. He pretended to weigh the bags in his hands, fighting a grimace as the maggots inside moved. "Like you tend to do for your own patients, I took it upon myself to choose just the right size for you. With your height and build, I thought a D-cup would be perfect. Don't you think?"

He dangled the bags in front of Elliot's face. "No? Yes?" With an exasperated sigh, he set the bags on the man's bare chest. "I have to admit, I *am* a bit nervous. After all, you've performed hundreds of breast augmentations and this is my first." He shrugged. "But, gotta start somewhere, right? I just hope I don't botch this up. Not that you would know anything about botching up a surgery. I mean, you *are* the expert."

Michael noticed the bags on the man's chest begin to move, and it had nothing to do with the contents. The drug had started to wear off and within seconds, Elliot would regain control of his body. He leaned closer to the man's still paralyzed face. "This is truly an honor, Doctor. One I know I won't regret. Oh, and thanks so much for agreeing to do the surgery without anesthetic. It really saves on time and money, don't you think?"

Elliot answered with an audible wheeze. As he dragged in a deep breath, his eyes widened. He shifted and circled his gaze, the muscles around his eyes fighting against the tape holding his lids in place. "W-why...?"

Michael slapped a piece of duct tape over the doctor's mouth. "Really, Doc. You know how tight surgery schedules can be. But because you asked so nicely and you've been such a good patient so far, I'll give you a hint. Eliza Morrison. Ring a bell?"

Elliot groaned and shook his head. If he could have spoken, Michael suspected the doctor would have spewed lies to save his sorry ass. The bastard had known how Eliza had died. He'd known why. Abiding by his daughter's last wishes, Daddy had told them and tried to make them listen. They hadn't, though. Holding the scalpel high, Michael would bet his own sorry ass Elliot was ready to listen now.

Too little, too late.

Elliot screamed from beneath the duct tape, raised his head from the table and fought the straps holding his shoulders, waist and legs. He would need more restraints, Michael realized. But as he'd told the good doc, this was his first surgery. He'd just have to make note to purchase more restraints for his future patients.

"Hold still and we'll be done before you know it," Michael said as he hovered above the doctor, whose watery gaze darted from the metal blade to the bags. "Wait. You're not worried I'm going to screw up your breast implants like you did my daughter's, are you?"

Elliot groaned, his breath quickening through his nostrils, tears and sweat coating his face.

"Or maybe you're worried about the implants themselves. If you are, don't be." Michael leaned closer, relishing the fear in the man's eyes, and whispered, "The coyotes will have torn the limbs from your body before the maggots ever have a chance to fester in your flesh."

Elliot screamed against the duct tape. Eyes bulging with terror, he pulled and thrashed against his bindings with renewed vigor.

Michael straightened. With a satisfied sigh, he tied his surgical mask, then turned and flipped the video camera he'd stationed in front of the operating table to RECORD.

Setting the disgusting bags aside, Michael raised the scalpel and smiled. "Let's begin. Shall we?"

KRISTINE MASON

CHAPTER 1

Two days later...

A MUFFLED SCREAM poured from the surround sound of the office, amplifying the horror on the big screen TV. Hudson Patterson shifted in his chair when another wail tore through the room. "Snuff film?" he asked, keeping his gaze on the screen.

"Not in the way you're thinking," Ian Scott said in a flat tone. "Keep watching."

Frowning, Hudson did as he'd been told, albeit reluctantly. What he'd started watching less than two minutes ago first reminded him of a low budget horror film. One of those slasher types with a psychotic villain who preyed on horny teenagers.

Only the man on the screen, strapped to a table in some sort of makeshift operating room, wasn't a horny teenager. While his facial features were indiscernible due to the angle of the camera, he had enough silver and dark brown hair covering his chest, arms and legs to rival an old Grizzly.

Another man suddenly filled the TV. He wore hospital scrubs, cap and surgical mask. The mask had been graffitied with black marker, a bubbly smile and bucked teeth drawn across the front. The doctor's hair color—not that Hudson truly believed the man was a doctor—was indeterminable thanks to the cap. His eyes blue, maybe gray and his skin bone white beneath the bright florescent light hanging over the operating table.

"As you know," the doctor began in a mild, easygoing tone that Hudson suspected belied his true sentiments. "I'll need to remove your chest hair before we proceed."

The man on the table screamed and twisted, but both had been in vain. The duct tape pressed against his mouth kept his screams muted, and the series of restraints around his body kept him prone.

"There, there," the doctor crooned as he slapped some sort of gooey substance on the man's chest, then coated it with a couple of strips of cloth. "Quick and painless. I promise it'll be like yanking off a Band-Aid."

Before the man could protest, the doctor tore first one, then the other strip. The man's flabby pectorals instantly dotted with beads of blood.

"See, told you it wouldn't be so bad," the doctor said as he placed two Ziploc bags on the man's heaving, hairy stomach. "Now let's move on to the fun stuff."

"What's in the bags?" Hudson asked, knowing Ian had already viewed the DVD.

"Maggots. I had to rewind several times to figure it out, and when I did...just watch."

Hudson stole a glance at his boss, but then the doctor spoke and forced his attention back to the flat screen. He regretted looking the moment he did.

"Let me see," the doctor said, waving a scalpel in the air. "Like I told you, I've never really done this, but how hard can it be? I guess if I just make an incision...here."

The duct tape binding the man's lips couldn't drown out the agonizing pain ripping through him as the doctor proceeded. Blood oozed down the side of his body, pooling on the table and when the doctor raised the thick slab of tissue he'd cut, Hudson had to turn away.

"Christ Almighty." He leaned forward and pressed his thumb and index finger to his eyes, wishing he could blot the image from his mind.

"It gets worse," Ian said in a clinical tone that set Hudson on edge.

"If you've already seen the goddamn thing, just tell me the gory details instead of making me watch them. After spending a month on the job you had me working in Detroit, I've seen enough blood."

"You've never seen anything like this, though." Ian turned his head and gave him a thoughtful, almost pondering look before returning his gaze to the screen. "Then again, maybe you have."

As founder and owner of the Chicago-based agency CORE (Criminal Observation Resolution Evidence) Ian Scott knew Hudson's history, his time spent in the Marines and the declassified missions while he'd worked for the CIA. Not the assignments or unsanctioned activities that had remained buried or likely destroyed by his CIA handlers. Yet Ian's cryptic remark made Hudson wonder where his boss's knowledge about him stopped. It also brought back memories he'd thought he'd purged.

The room tilted as the torturous scene continued to play out on the flat screen. Screams filled the room and his head. His mind drifted. For a moment, the florescent light on the screen turned white-hot, blinding, glaring. He forced himself not to squint, forced his body to remain rigid and his heart rate level. They might be able to see the sweat, the blood coating his body, but he couldn't allow them access to his mind. His fears. His—

A low, keening cry pierced his ears. Hudson blinked and brought the glass he'd been holding to his lips, forcing the memories that had nearly killed him from his mind and focusing on the TV. He wasn't the one enduring the torture. The man on the screen played that role today, fighting against his bonds with each slice of the doctor's scalpel.

In one gulp, he drank the whiskey Ian had given him when he'd first arrived. The burn along his throat knocked back the rising bile, until the doctor stuffed one of the bags beneath the man's loose skin.

Hudson shoved off the chair, taking his glass with him. "Enough, dammit," he said, and helped himself to Ian's liquor cabinet.

"We're almost to the end anyway," Ian said. "Let me fast forward to...here."

Fresh drink in hand, Hudson moved back to his seat and faced the flat screen again with disgust. For Ian, for the unwanted memories, for the psycho playing doctor.

The man on the table no longer fought, and Hudson suspected he'd likely passed out from the pain. His skin gleamed with sweat and blood beneath the florescent light. Only instead of gaping holes in his chest, his pectorals were now fat and plump. Crudely sewn, lumpy and...moving.

"Oh my God," he said the moment a bubbly, bucked toothed smile filled the camera.

"Did I get your attention?" the doctor asked as he moved next to his patient. He gave one newly filled breast a Pillsbury Doughboy press. "Bet I finally got his."

He drew closer to the camera again. "Now, I could go on like some bleeding heart with a cause, but I'll spare you the agony. After what you've just viewed, I think that's the least I can do. So here's the bottom line, Eden."

Hudson sat straighter and glanced at Ian. "Eden?"

"Eden Risk," Ian said, and nodded back to the screen as the doctor continued.

Hudson hadn't seen Eden Risk live and in person for over two years. Hearing her name, though, brought memories he didn't mind. Her scent, her taste, the smoothness of her skin. Too bad he'd screwed things up with her. They might have had something good. If she hadn't been so damned hardheaded and he hadn't been such an ass.

"I've been planning this for a long time," the doctor continued. "But I wasn't sure how to get my message out there for the world to see. When I saw your investigative series on beauty pageant kids and their moms, I realized you understood a part of what I've been grappling with for too many years.

Now I want you to be my voice. I want you to make sure this DVD is aired. If it's not on tomorrow's six o'clock news, plan on receiving another."

He moved closer to the camera, close enough so that Hudson realized his eyes were blue, not gray, lined with crow's feet and weariness. "I didn't want to do this. I doubt I'll ever sleep right. But they wouldn't listen and they've left me no other choice. Last year over four hundred thousand women had breast implants. Fifteen years ago that number was only thirty thousand. What does that tell you? We are being poisoned by airbrushed images of magazine models. There's no such thing as perfect, only perception. Isn't that right, Eden?"

Hudson frowned and rubbed his temple. He didn't understand what the doctor had meant. Eden was a beautiful woman. Perfect teeth, nose, eyes, hair. Her body could rival the models the nut job referred to. But what had he meant by "only perception?" Did this man know Eden? Did her perception of perfection somehow connect her to this man or even the one lying on the table with new breasts?

Pulling a syringe from a nearby table, the doctor looked to the man. "I need to tend to my patient now. Do as I've instructed." He raised his arm as if to turn off the camera, then stopped. "Eden, take care of yourself," he said, his eyes sincere, almost worried. "While I've been watching you, someone else has been, too."

The flat screen went black.

Hudson stared at the darkened TV and wondered how Eden had managed to tangle herself in another bad situation. "I take it you got the DVD from Eden."

Ian nodded.

"Okay. So what do you want from me?" He didn't bother hiding the contempt from his voice. Ian had a reason for everything he did. He also knew about his blow-out with Eden Risk.

"Your thoughts."

"My thoughts? Is that all?" he asked not believing Ian one

bit. Ian had been behind the scenes when the FBI had begun its profiling unit. He didn't need Hudson's opinion, not on something like this.

"For now."

"Okay." He shrugged. "Guy's a sick bastard. Uses torture to send a message rather than gain information. Reminds me of..." Reminded him of another sick bastard who had tried to do the same to him.

"Reminds you of?"

He ignored the prompt and continued. "I think he's using this message he's sending as an excuse for revenge."

"Interesting. Why do you say that?"

"He said he'd been planning this. Then there's the comment about the child beauty pageants. This is personal to him. And the guy on the table with the new...chest? I wouldn't be surprised if he's a plastic surgeon. Maybe implants were his specialty."

"Excellent," Ian said with a smile. "My thoughts exactly."

A throb built behind his eye. Releasing a frustrated sigh, he sagged in the chair. "If you already suspected as much, I'm gonna ask again. What do you want from me?"

"I want you to find him." Ian pointed to the darkened TV. "And protect Eden."

"I'm not a profiler, or criminalist or even an investigator. And I'm sure as hell not a babysitter. You've got plenty of those guys on the payroll to handle this."

Ian stroked the side of his glass with a finger. "True. You hunt, you find, you capture. That's your specialty. Unfortunately, I don't have anyone else to cover this."

"What about John? I heard he's—"

"Busy at the moment."

Hudson set his glass on the table beside him. He didn't need the whiskey spiking his temper any higher. While he'd been stuck in Detroit, dealing with gangbangers with an affinity for slitting the throats of their enemies and prostituting kids, he'd learned some interesting gossip from CORE's forensic computer analyst, Rachel Davis.

The eyes and ears of the company, Rachel had told him how John Kain had met and fallen for Ian's daughter while working a case in Wisconsin. No one who'd worked for Ian even knew he'd had a daughter. From what Rachel had said, it appeared the daughter had had no idea Ian was her father. It all sounded like a shitty soap opera, and Hudson had let most of it in one ear and straight out the other.

"Busy my ass," Hudson said. "I heard the whole story. Congratulations on being a father, by the way."

Ian nodded, yet remained somber. "I know you're not usually on the investigative end. But you did a lot of investigating with the CIA, and were very good at your job."

"*Were* being the operative word."

Ian shook his head. "Hunting and tracking criminals are just different facets of investigating and you know it." When Ian appeared to realize he still hadn't convinced him, he said, "Look, I need you on this. John's working something else for me. Owen's in California for at least another two weeks. Russo won't be back from Texas until later next week."

"So I get screwed babysitting." Damn it. And to Eden Risk of all people.

"Investigating," Ian corrected, then took a long gulp of his Scotch. After setting the glass aside he folded his hands. "I know you and Eden had a falling out a few years ago."

"That's putting it mildly." She'd ripped his head off for outing her source, a source who had been under investigation by CORE as a serial rapist. A source that had been feeding her false information in order to make her his next victim. Even now his stomach seized and knotted when he thought of what could have happened had the bastard been given the opportunity to find himself alone with her.

Ian's smile didn't reach his eyes. "I've known Eden for years. There's been a few times when her investigative reporting skills, and even her sources, have helped CORE. I also know she's not the easiest person to understand or even like. But you've watched the film, you've heard what the man said." Ian's voice rose with irritation. "She has one man sending her DVDs and allegedly another stalking her. Set your ego aside."

Hudson ignored the jab and searched for another out. Not because he'd been reduced to babysitter, but because of the DVD. Like a divining rod, the film found a way to tap into memories he hadn't thought of in nearly four years. "Let the Chicago PD handle this."

"The instructions to stated no police."

"Since when do you obey the rules?" Hudson rose and reached for his coat. "Sorry to bolt on you. But I've been up since four AM and haven't been home in over a month. I'm not saying yes to anything without a clear head."

"Eden needs immediate protection."

Guilt gave a sharp stab to his conscience. Eden might irritate the hell out of him, but he didn't want to see anything happen to her, either. He slapped his leather gloves against his hand. "Fine," he snapped. "I'll do it."

"You'll go now?"

Hudson shrugged. "Sure." He began counting off on his fingers. "First a psycho, then a stalker, it's not like my night could get any worse. Why not a little reunion with a woman who thinks I'm a total asshole?"

CHAPTER 2

FOR SOMETHING TO do, Eden Risk sipped the lukewarm coffee. She grimaced at the taste, then set the mug on the kitchen table with an impatient sigh. "You two really don't need to babysit me."

"Boss's orders," John Kain, CORE's criminalist and her sister's fiancé said with a shrug.

Boss? More like tyrant. When she'd called Ian Scott about the DVD, she'd been a little—okay a lot—hysterical. At the time, she'd figured Ian would try to talk her down, give her direction. Instead, he'd sent some huge, blond haired, blue-eyed guy—who could have been the Nazi poster child for the Aryan race—to collect the DVD, and before she could close the door behind him, her babysitters had swept into her townhouse.

Eden looked to her sister for support, but received a shrug identical to John's. "Sorry. I'm with him," Celeste said, then pushed her coffee mug aside and twined her fingers with John's.

Eden stared at their joined hands and then at the two lovebirds. They made quite a striking couple. Celeste with her blond hair curling softly around her peaches-and-cream cheeks, and John with his dark GQ looks. Her sister appeared happy, content. She'd found a good man to love, and by the adoration in her future brother-in-law's eyes, Celeste found a man who loved her equally.

Eden couldn't help the resentment.

Not for Celeste's love life. Eden had no fairytale fantasies of Prince Charmings or white picket fences. Most men were intimidated by her career, her fame, her income. Those who weren't served one purpose to her and love had nothing to do with it.

The resentment had begun during childhood, but remained buried deep in the pit of her adult belly. She'd always hid the bitterness well, but occasionally had a hard time ignoring it when Celeste called or, like now, sat in front her.

Celeste, the golden child.

Celeste, the natural nurturer.

Celeste, who had shared a unique bond with their mom. A bond, a special love Eden in no way shape or form could have competed against. Even as a child Eden had seen the way her mom's gaze would touch on Celeste. The wonder, the awe, the unconditional love. And when Mom had been diagnosed with cancer, and their dad and brother had needed help taking care of her, who had come to the rescue?

Eden toyed with the mug handle while guilt toyed with her conscience. God, she was becoming a true bitch. If it hadn't been for Celeste their family would have fallen apart after Mom died. She'd sacrificed so much for them all, and had helped their dad keep the family diner afloat while he'd dealt with his grief.

Now her sister sacrificed her sleep by playing babysitter along with her fiancé. Damn Ian and his big mouth. Celeste had come running the moment she'd thought Eden had been in trouble.

And instead of gratitude, all Eden had offered was attitude. She couldn't help herself. She wanted John and Celeste to leave and give her a chance to come to terms with the events of the day now that her head and fears had cleared.

Eden slid the mug back and forth between her hands and forced a smile. "Well, your *boss* is being overly dramatic," she said to John, then looked to her sister. "I hate keeping you here this late. Aren't you bakers supposed to be up by four in

21

the morning?"

Celeste looked away for a second, but Eden noticed John squeeze her hand. "The Sugar Shack hasn't had its grand opening yet. Remember?"

"Oh, sorry." Eden frowned. She should probably know this. "I've been so busy lately I guess I must have forgotten."

"Must have forgotten?" John shoved away from the table when his cell phone rang. "Celeste sat here and told you about the bakery less than thirty minutes ago. Right after you two discussed the weather and right before you talked about your dad's new girlfriend."

Little snippets of their earlier conversation began to filter through her head as John left the room. "Damn." She shook her head. "I'm sorry." She offered Celeste an apologetic smile.

"Seems like you're always sorry for something lately," Celeste said as she reached across the table and took her hand. "What's going on, Eden? I swear we talked more when I was still living in Wisconsin. At first I thought it was just me. That maybe you were upset about Ian being my father and us ending up as half-sisters. But you don't return Dad's calls or Will's, either. And Lloyd said you'd acted like you'd never seen him before."

With her free hand, Eden rubbed her temple where a headache had begun to build. She could care less that Celeste didn't share a biological father with her and their brother Will. Their dad, Hugh Risinski, had adopted Celeste upon her birth, and to Eden, that made her a Risinski no matter what. Hell, considering she'd changed her name from Risinski to Risk the moment she'd left home, and that she hadn't been the most family-oriented daughter, Eden had no room to judge. Rather than grapple with that issue—a discussion which they'd yet to share—she asked, "Lloyd who?"

"Lloyd Nelson. He was the big blond guy who'd picked up the DVD five minutes before we showed. Don't you remember him?"

"No, should I?"

"Yeah, considering he's Will's partner. Oh wait. Let me

guess, you forgot our brother was gay, too."

Ouch. "No. I guess I just didn't—"

"Care enough to return his phone calls. Or take half an hour out of your busy schedule to stop by his new apartment, not to mention the art gallery."

"I was at the gallery when Will had his opening," she said defensively and tore her hand away. She had been at the gallery and had never been more proud of her brother and his accomplishments. Just because she wasn't all sugar and spice like Celeste, expressing her emotions with an added fluffy dollop of whipped cream and a cherry on top, didn't mean she didn't care.

"For ten minutes. God, Eden. I swear I feel like I don't know you anymore."

Here we go again.

And Celeste wondered why she wasn't interested in talking. Their conversations always boiled down to what was wrong with her. "Probably because you never really did."

Celeste released a sarcastic half-laugh. "And you're full of it. I know you. And I know that your need to control every aspect of your life is destroying you."

Eden shoved away from the table and shot out of the chair. "Get all that out of your crystal ball?" she asked just as John stepped back into the room.

He looked at her first, then to Celeste. She hadn't missed the accusation and contempt in his gaze, and she could care less. Let him—let Celeste—think what they wanted. Because neither of them, nor the rest of her family included, knew the entire truth.

"Ian has someone on the way," John said to Celeste. "He should be here any minute."

"Good," Celeste said, and patted his arm. "Could you give us a sec?"

He smiled at her sister, then sent her an "eat shit" glare. "I'll grab our coats."

When he was in the next room, Celeste turned to her. "I don't want to fight with you. The way you looked when we

23

first got here...you scared the crap out of me. What was on that DVD Lloyd picked up for Ian?"

Gruesome violence. Mutilation. Inhumanity.

The memory of the images she'd witnessed on the DVD and the worry in her sister's eyes took the fight out of her. She slumped back in the kitchen chair and shook her head. "I'm not exactly sure myself."

"Okay. Well, what if I touch the DVD or the jewel case it came in. You know, try to get a reading."

Eden rubbed her chin, then pressed her knuckles to her mouth to keep from saying what she knew would cause a swift end to their slight truce. Both her mom and Celeste claimed to have a psychic gift. At one time she'd believed in them and their powers, but that belief had gone the way of Santa Claus, the Easter Bunny and the Tooth Fairy. If the two of them had truly been able to predict the future then they could have warned her. They could have made sure a sixteen-year-old girl never had to understand true terror and pain so early in life...if at all.

A knock at the door saved her from having to answer Celeste. Before she had a chance to stand and check the door's peephole, John moved from the living room. "Our replacement is here," he said over his shoulder to Celeste.

Replacement? God, was she exchanging one set of babysitters for another?

"Think about what I suggested," Celeste said, as she stood. "I know how you feel about my abilities, but if I can help—"

Eden rose, too, taking the coffee mugs with her. "Thanks. I'll call you."

"I won't hold my breath."

With a deep sigh, she dumped the mugs in the sink, then faced her sister. The hurt and anger in Celeste's eyes tugged at her again. "Look, you know how I feel about your psychic stuff. But, I *will* call you. And Will. Maybe we can meet for lunch..."

A familiar, masculine voice from the foyer made her pause. She moved passed the kitchen island and peered around the corner, then froze.

"Hey, Eden," Hudson Patterson said as he shrugged out of his leather coat and pierced her with his steely blue gaze. "I see you got yourself into another mess."

The room shrank and her sole focus remained on the one man who had stirred more emotions in her than all the other men before and after him combined. Two years ago, he'd lit a fire inside her, and within months, he'd smothered the flames with his arrogance and bullheaded attitude.

Based on the condescending remark he'd just made, she doubted his opinion of her had changed. His appearance had, though. Harder, darker, more dangerous. His brown, wavy hair now reached his shoulders and he needed a shave. Even without the worn, black leather jacket, which now hung on the coat rack, he looked thuggish in a tattered charcoal gray thermal shirt, low-riding jeans and black Doc Marten boots. The whole badass biker look shouldn't have appealed to her, but Hudson owned it and wore it well.

When he said something she couldn't hear to John, she glanced at his mouth, then immediately regretted it. Lust slammed into her belly as wicked memories of what his firm lips had done to her surfaced. Those unwanted memories collided into a kaleidoscope of naked skin, harsh moans and multiple orgasms. Even now, she swore she could still feel his rough hands urging her hips, spreading her legs, gripping her bottom. Could imagine his mouth on hers, or better yet, between her thighs.

"Then you two know each other?" John asked.

"You can say that," Hudson replied with a smile. A smug, satisfying smile that snapped her out of her sexual spell and reminded her exactly why breaking things off with him had been the right decision. Her body might not have thought so at the time, and those urges to have him in her bed right now might still be strong, but her head knew better. Hudson was an arrogant jerk who exuded less emotion than she did.

After she'd slipped on her coat, Celeste squeezed her hand. "Think about what I said. If I can help—"

She tore her gaze from Hudson's and looked to her sister. "I'll call you. For lunch," she added to make her stance regarding the psychic reading crystal clear.

With a tired smile, Celeste nodded, then she and John left the townhouse. Hudson followed them out to the front stoop, giving her a chance to gain some composure.

First she'd find out what Hudson had to say on Ian's behalf, then she'd kick his ass out the door. She wouldn't have to tiptoe around him like she had with her sister and John. Niceties weren't necessary with Hudson. He'd never expected them and besides, she'd given up playing nice the night he'd treated her as if she were a rotten, spoiled brat. The fact that they'd had sex only hours before didn't help his cause, either.

"Callous, crass bastard," she said as she finished cleaning the kitchen.

"And who might that be?"

She jumped, splashing running water over the sleeves of her sweatshirt. Swearing under her breath, she shut off the water and reached for a towel. "Don't sneak up on me like that."

"Don't avoid the question. Am I the callous, crass bastard? 'Cause if that's the case, then that makes me think you're still mad at me."

She shrugged. "I'd have to care, which I don't."

The corner of his mouth slid up in a slow smirk. "Suppose not, and I wouldn't be surprised if you ever did." He gave her a once over. "You look pretty good."

Pretty good? Had she known Ian planned to send Hudson tonight, she would have made sure she'd looked damn good. She might not want anything to do with him—relationship wise—but no woman wants an ex-whatever to see them at their worst, either. "And you look as if you're a front for some eighties big hair band," she shot back with a raised brow, quite proud of her comeback even if it was immature.

His smirk slid into a sexy smile. "Then that explains all those hot groupies following me around and throwing their g-strings at me."

"You wish," she said, and dropped the kitchen towel on the

counter. "Look, I've had a bad day. Let's put aside all the bullshit baggage and get to the point of why you're here."

"Good enough," he said, and headed into the living room. He plopped himself on the center of the couch, forcing her to sit on the oversized chair in the corner. "Did you watch the entire DVD?"

She shuddered and hugged herself. "Unfortunately."

"Why call Ian and not the cops?"

"There was a note with the DVD that said no police."

"What about that homicide detective, Mallory? Are you still chummy with him?"

She rubbed the back of her neck. Until today, Bob Mallory had not only been her source with the Chicago PD, he'd been her friend. "I'm not sure," she began, fighting the hurt tightening her throat. "He said some pretty harsh things to me tonight and accused me of leaking information that shouldn't have been made public."

"What about?"

"Last week a nurse was killed in her apartment. Today, another woman…another nurse, was found dead in her condo. The media are calling the killer Dr. Dread."

"Stupid name."

"No kidding. Anyway, Bob had confided the details of both murders to me and asked that I keep the information confidential. I did. Went to Buckstown where the latest murder occurred, and reported what I could about the case. Unfortunately, Kyle one-upped me and went ahead and revealed every gory detail about both murders on live TV."

"Kyle Edwards, the anchor?"

"You got it," she confirmed.

"That doesn't make any sense. Don't you two work for the same TV station?"

Ever since Network had offered her a contract to host her own investigative reporting show, out of childish rivalry, Kyle had been finding ways to make her life miserable. She wasn't about to tell Hudson this, though. She'd been taking care of herself for a long time and had learned the hard way that she didn't need to lean on him, or anyone else, for support. Besides, she'd only have to endure Kyle until the end of the month, then she'd leave for New York and begin the next level of her career.

"Yeah," she answered. "Although you wouldn't know it with the way he acted on air. What he did was reckless. I mean, he might have jeopardized a murder investigation." She shook her head, still stunned by the entire situation. "What's crazy is that Kyle has writers who are paid to give him the news to read, not sources with inside information. He hasn't done beat reporting in the ten years since becoming lead anchor and yet he somehow knew details only the homicide detectives or the ME would know. And what's even crazier is that both nurses had been killed with surgical instruments and tonight I wind up with a DVD showing..." She waved her hand. "I'm assuming you saw it for yourself."

"Unfortunately."

"Well? Don't you think it's possible this so-called doctor in the DVD and the guy who murdered the nurses are one and the same?"

"It's possible," he replied, but she caught the doubt in his eyes.

"But you don't think so."

"Mallory's worked both crime scenes and knows how the victims were killed. Let's let him decide if they're related."

"The note said no police," she reminded him.

He shrugged. "I'm not suggesting we waltz into the police station where everyone will notice the famous Eden Risk. Call Mallory in the morning and ask him to come here."

"I'm not sure if he's taking my calls. You'd better do it."

"Done."

"What about airing the DVD on tomorrow's six o'clock news? There's no way in hell the station manager would allow it. *I* certainly wouldn't want to see that aired, either. Otherwise every idiot with a cause will think it's—"

"Other than Mallory, I don't want you telling anyone else about this."

She shivered when the image of the mocking buck-toothed smile drawn on the surgical mask mingled with the poor man strapped to the operating table. She'd never seen anything so grotesque or cruel in her entire life and wanted to do everything possible to prevent another person from having to endure such horrors. "But that...doctor. He said that if the DVD wasn't aired, to expect another. I can't, as a responsible journalist, justify airing the DVD, but I don't want to be the reason another person...dies."

"Doesn't matter what you do," he said with a shrug. "This guy's going to keep on keepin' on regardless of what he says. I'm guessing he didn't go through all the trouble to build himself an operating room for just one *surgery*. I'm thinking this thing is bigger than that and driven by revenge."

She wiped a hand over her face, then rested her chin in her palm. "Maybe I should watch it again. I...it was hard to take in every nuance when—"

"I've got a copy with me, but let's watch it tomorrow. I can't stomach another viewing tonight," he said with disgust. "Ian's having the original and the case it came in dusted for prints. He's also having our computer geek go through the DVD to see if she can pick up any additional information about the victim, his tormentor and where this had taken place."

Although she doubted they'd find any prints, Ian putting his team to work gave her a sense of relief. Because his agency was privately owned, and Ian had more money than God, his resources were limitless.

Hudson shifted and leaned forward, drawing her attention. "How well do you know your neighbors?" he asked.

She frowned and shrugged at his sudden change of subject. "The guy who lives in the townhouse to the right has a condo in Naples and left a few weeks ago for the winter."

"On the left?"

"A young couple. Both are attorneys, I think." She shook her head. "I don't know any of the other neighbors."

"Why doesn't that surprise me?"

She didn't miss the sarcasm and laid on her own. "And how often are *your* neighbors stopping by and borrowing a cup of sugar? Pardon me for liking my privacy."

He raised his hands as if surrendering, but she knew this man better than that. He never surrendered to anyone and was the type who had to come out the victor no matter what the cost. She knew this above all else considering his need to win was what had ended their relationship.

"I'm just wondering if we should bother asking your neighbors if they've seen anyone hanging out around your townhouse. I noticed none of these places have security cameras, so that's a wash. And while we're on the subject of security, I also noticed your system sucks."

"Excuse me? I'll have you know that I paid top dollar—"

"For a piece of crap. I'll take care of it myself in the morning." He glanced at his watch, then rubbed a hand along his face. When he finally looked at her she realized his exhaustion mirrored her own.

"How late is it?" she asked.

"One and I've been up since four this morning," he said, then propped his boots—his scuffed up, filthy boots—on her suede couch and laid back. "Go get some sleep. We'll talk more about this in the morning."

She knocked one Doc Marten off the couch. "And what do you think you're doing?"

Sitting up, he reached down and unlaced his boots. "Sorry. After a month in Detroit, I've gotten into the habit of wearing my shit kickers to bed."

She refused to allow sympathy and worry to rule her mind. If Hudson wanted to take on dangerous assignments that could possibly send him to the morgue, it was none of her business. Not that it had ever been. He'd made his feelings abundantly clear years ago. He'd been with her for the sex. Nothing more.

"So wear them to bed, just do it at *your* place."

He set the boots aside, then lay back on the couch again. Resting his head on the crook of his arm, he closed his eyes and said, "Not gonna happen tonight."

She fisted her hands. "I can't have you sleeping here. What will the neighbors think?"

"More importantly, what will your stalker think?"

From the darkened family room the TV blared an old rerun of *Three's Company.* Considering the lazy bitch detested Don Knotts, that meant she was likely asleep. Good. Maybe tonight there could be a moment of peace.

Time to think. Time to create a new plan. Time to remove the wig, make-up, and evidence.

With a smile and a gentle push, the door closed with the softest click.

"That you, Pudge?"

Damn it. The bitch was up after all. Frustration and anger slithered slowly inside. "Yeah, Mama."

dont let her call you that

Ignoring the seductive whisper, Pudge slipped down the short hall of the dilapidated, small ranch to the only bathroom in the house.

"Wait. Where you off to?" Mama shouted with alarm. "And why don't I smell no Happy Jax's? I told you to pick me up two double bacon cheeseburgers and them hand cut fries I love."

"They were closed by the time I got off work," Pudge replied from the threshold of the bathroom.

"Then put a frozen pizza in the oven. I'm starving. And when you're done, I need you to get a new battery for the remote. I've been stuck watchin' this stupid show for twenty minutes. Can't stand that goddamn Mr. Furley and his—"

Pudge closed the bathroom door drowning out anything else Mama had to say, then quickly moved to the sink. The putty needed to be removed, along with the make-up, wig and clothes. Mama couldn't suspect. She couldn't know.

so what if she does so what so what so what

"Because," Pudge said, and tossed the putty in a protective case to keep it from hardening. "Just leave me alone until I take care of Mama."

i know the perfect way to take care of mama just let me just let me just let me show you how good it can be

"No," Pudge whispered while applying cold cream. "I've told you before. I can't kill her."

you didnt have a problem killing daddy

"I wasn't the one who killed him."

no you only helped hide the body

Pudge stripped off the bloodied clothes, then shoved them into a garbage bag. "It doesn't matter. Once the bitch dies, of *natural* causes, we'll inherit half a mil and will be able to leave this dump. Maybe even Chicago."

why would we leave when theres so many opportunities here for us youre not giving up on us yet are you are you

"No. But you saw what happened tonight. This plan of yours isn't going to work."

but i sure had fun slicing up that nurse didnt you doctor dread

Playing Dread had been powerful, invigorating, freeing. Pudge stared at the mirror, at the high-wattage smile reflecting back. "Oh yeah." The smile faded. "But killing didn't help us any. Instead it only made *her* look better."

but the killing was fun fun fun

"Yes."

then maybe we should just kill her

"What?" Skeptical, Pudge gaped at the mirror. "No way. She's too high profile."

scare her

"We tried that before."

not hard enough try harder

"She went to the cops before for help. What if they linked those calls back to—"

they didnt they wont because they wont help her anymore remember

"Yes." Pudge nodded. "Thank you for helping me with that."

my pleasure always my pleasure i love you precious

Precious, not Pudge. The name stroked over the senses like a lover's caress. "I love you, too."

will you let me love you touch you taste you

"Yes," Pudge hissed and pinched a nipple. Loving the pain and anticipating the pleasure to come.

will you take care of her for me

"Mama? Yes. Just give me a half hour." Feeding Mama's fat face and changing her colostomy bag normally brought the gag-reflex into full force. But the desire overrode the disgust.

not mama youre right she must die naturally

"Then who?"

eden risk

CHAPTER 3

SMOTHERED.

His chest heavy, his arms numb, a blanket of weight pushed the air from his lungs, while the tickling under his nose drove him bat shit. Orlov, the crazy Russian, had proven to be unpredictable and full of surprises over the days he'd held him captive, introducing new torture techniques that had made him wish he was dead.

His nose twitched. Whatever the hell Orlov was doing to him made him want to scream. He'd never experienced anything like this, the infuriating, irritating tickle, and wished to God for the chance to rub the itch from his nose.

Something rough and wet suddenly swept across his cheek, followed by that maddening tickle. He cringed and when he shifted his head, sharp, tiny daggers pinched his nose. He couldn't take it anymore. He had to fight. He had to keep his control. He had to—

Hudson snapped open his eyes, then froze.

Memories of last night hit him full force. He was in Eden's townhouse, not a cavern basement in the jungles of Columbia. His arms weren't tied behind his back, but sleep numb. And the weight on his chest wasn't some sort of torture device but a...cat.

A very large, very menacing looking cat.

As big as a dog, with long yellow hair, the cat sized him up with one eye. The other looked as if it had been sewn shut. A scar ran from the damaged eye to the top of its head were there should have been an ear.

Damn the thing was ugly. And heavy as hell.

"Shoo," he whispered, his nose still itchy, likely from the cat's fur brushing against his face. And to think he'd been having a nightmare about Orlov. It had been years since the Russian had invaded his sleep.

The images from the DVD he'd watched last night with Ian ran front and center through his head. The torture, the cruelty. No wonder the Russian had come for a visit. Now he had to deal with another nightmare. Some crazed doctor who was into slicing and dicing, and...Eden Risk.

Last night he'd told her she looked pretty good, but that had been a lie. Just a way to needle her, and maybe crawl under her skin. Her looks were important to her. She wasn't the type to flaunt them, and she wasn't vain. But she always had to look perfect. How he'd ended up in bed with her he'd never understood. She was class, and he was...crass. Hell, last night was the first time he'd ever seen her in a pair of sweatpants. Given the choice, he'd live in them or jeans every day.

She had looked kinda cute, though. All rumpled...sexy.

Shit. He had to focus. Not on her, but on whoever had been behind that DVD. Christ, then there's the potential stalker, which they'd never discussed. Tired as he'd been, he'd wanted to, but he'd seen the strain, the shock of the evening's events etched on her face. Seen how hard it had been for her to maintain control. And control was something she lived for.

They'd talk soon enough. About the stalker, about a few rules he expected her to follow while he was stuck on this case. But first he had to find a way to remove the lion cub from his chest without it clawing off his face.

The cat winked its golden eye, then yawned, revealing a hell of a set of sharp teeth.

Yeah, easier said than done.

"Okay, big guy, I need to move. So why don't you—"

Slippered feet shuffled against the wood floor. "Fabio,

where are you?" Eden sang—terribly—as she entered the living room. The cat raised its head and purred.

The shuffling suddenly stopped and Eden burst out laughing.

"Funny," he said, eyeing the cat. "I take it you know Baby Huey?"

"Duh. He lives here," she said as she leaned over the couch and looked down at first him, then the cat. Instead of shooing the thing off, she stroked its yellow hair.

"I didn't see him last night."

"Fabio's a big baby and doesn't like strangers."

"You don't say. How 'bout getting him off me before he takes off my face."

She came around the front of the couch, wearing a too big plaid, flannel robe and clashing baggie pajama bottoms, then sat on the edge of the coffee table. "He wouldn't do that. First, he's declawed. Second he's a sweetie. Aren't you, baby? Come to mama," she coaxed and patted her thigh. The cat jumped on her lap with surprising grace.

With the weight literally off his chest, Hudson shoved off the couch and stared at her. Last night's sweatpants had been one thing, all that flannel, well, who didn't like flannel when the weather turned to shit? But he'd never seen her so...comfortable. Normally her hair was styled perfectly. Hell, even after a session of hot sex, she'd walked from his bed looking just as good as she had when she'd climbed in with him. This morning, though, her straight, dark hair had been pulled back in a slack, messy ponytail. He'd never seen her without make-up and he thought she still looked gorgeous. Soft. Inviting.

He cleared his throat. "I've only seen cats that size at the zoo or in the jungle. What the hell is it? Besides big and ugly."

"Don't talk like that." She cupped Fabio's only ear. "He's sensitive."

Eden had to have snapped at some point during the past two years. Literally. Since when did this woman, this no bullshit, headstrong woman, become all sensitive?

"Whatever, Dr. Dolittle," he said, hiding his irritation. She could let her guard down, shed her hard as nails persona for a frickin' cat, but she'd never bothered to make the effort with him. During those months they'd been together, she'd come willingly to his bed, or she'd invite him to hers. Their pillow talk had been fun and sexy. They had exchanged stories, but never secrets. And after a while, that had bothered him. For the first time…ever, he'd been intrigued by a woman and he'd begun to trust enough to want to give more of himself than he'd ever been willing to in the past. Unfortunately, despite the intimate moments they'd shared, she had kept herself guarded. Instead of trying to find a way to break through her barriers, he'd gone and screwed everything up with her. He'd regretted that night for over two years. And the mistake she'd promised him she would never forgive.

A noise at his feet distracted him from the memories of the hurt and betrayal that had clouded her eyes when she'd told him to go to hell. Which had probably been for the best. Eden was chaos. Her career kept her on the go and in the limelight. Traipsing around the world, first as a Marine, then for the CIA, he'd experienced enough chaos. He wanted normalcy. A house in the burbs, a lawn to mow, bushes to trim. Hell, maybe he'd even take up golf.

He glanced down, then at the last second controlled the urge to kick. What he'd initially thought was a large rat dry heaving at his feet was a small dog attempting to bark. With ears bigger than its head, and huge brown eyes that took up most of its face, the thing was uglier than the cat, and about a quarter of the size.

"I don't know why, but I think he likes you, too." She set the cat on the floor. "He's usually a better judge of character."

Ah, there's the Eden he knew. The animals hadn't brainwashed her yet.

She scooped up the rat dog and kissed its head. "This is Brutal. And I'm betting he has to go potty. Don't you, boy?"

Brutal dry-heaved a response as he squirmed out of her hold. When she set him down, the dog teetered on three legs.

He glanced between the two animals. "Must have been one hell of a fight."

"Not with each other. Fabio's original owner had sold him to some jackass who thought it would be cool to see how a Maine Coon cat would hold up to a Pit Bull."

Her face hardened with anger and disgust as she lovingly stroked the cat's fur. "I happened to be working a story near the local animal shelter when one of their employees approached me and told me about Fabio. I'd been ready to give her the brush off because I'm constantly approached by people who think they've got something hot for me to investigate. For some reason I didn't."

She bent and kissed the top of the cat's head, then stood. "Brutal had been brought in that same day. His throat torn and his leg mangled by only God knows what." She moved to the hall closet, then pulled out a heavy winter coat.

"So you saved them."

She shrugged. "Sometimes I think it's the other way around."

Before he could analyze that remark, she'd unlocked the front door. "Where are you going?" He shoved his feet into his boots.

"To take Brutal potty before his little bladder explodes."

He looked to the three-legged dog. God, the thing was ugly. "I'll do it," he growled as he moved past her to grab his coat off the rack. If the dog was a German Shepherd, he wouldn't have cared. But this...rat. Not so manly.

She half-laughed, half-snorted. "Did you just growl at me?"

He zipped his coat and reached for the dog's leash. "Yeah, so? You just snorted. What's the difference?"

She shoved the leash behind her back. "It's my dog. I'll take him outside."

"No. I'll take the damned dog out." He reached behind her, but she shifted and slipped the leash into her other hand. Pressing against her bulky coat, he reached again. Only she'd slipped the leash back causing him to fumble and twine his fingers over hers.

Even though her coat's thickness rivaled a fluffy pillow, and she wore ugly, baggy clothes beneath, the faint traces of her citrusy perfume made his mouth water and drove him crazy. With memories. Eden naked, hot and willing, offering him the sweetest pleasure. Those memories also spurred his anger. He didn't want to want her. Even if she'd decided to forgive him, she'd played with his head before and he wouldn't allow it to happen again. She was an assignment. Protecting her and finding a killer were his only concerns.

He pinned her wrists behind her back. "Use your head. You've been sent a sick DVD and might have a stalker. Either I take the rat out to go *potty*, or he pisses all over your floor."

"Fine," she said and released the leash. "But don't you dare think you can waltz into my house and tell me...are you even listening?"

"Nope. Didn't quite hear anything after fine," he said and scooped up the dog. Without another word, he slammed the door behind him, then stomped down the front steps. When he reached a small grassy spot in front of her townhouse, he carefully set the rat down, attached the leash to his collar then drew in a deep breath.

Well, so much for thinking she'd changed. Her way or no way. Always was, always will be.

Not this time.

If he had to babysit her while trying to figure out who had sent the DVD, they'd play by his rules. She'd watched the DVD and should be scared out of her mind. She should be hiding in her townhouse with the doors bolted and the alarm set to DEFCON one. Maximum readiness.

Which reminded him...

While Brutal—such a stupid name for a five-pound Chihuahua—sniffed for a spot to do his business, Hudson called Ian. After telling him what he needed to rig Eden's security system to his liking, he then called Detective Bob Mallory. By the time he'd ended the call, Brutal stood at the bottom of the steps, tugging at the leash and staring at him expectantly. "C'mon," Hudson said as he picked up the dog.

"Let's go see if your mama made some coffee."

Brutal licked his face, then nuzzled his cold wet nose into the collar of his coat. "Cut it out," Hudson half-laughed as he opened the door, then caught himself actually enjoying the way the little rat had cuddled against him and set him on the floor.

The aroma of coffee hit him as he shrugged out of his jacket. After he'd placed it on the coat rack, he headed for the kitchen with a plan of attack.

When he rounded the corner, he realized Eden had other ideas of how the morning would go. Tying her tennis shoe, and dressed in tight spandex leggings and a hooded sweatshirt, she looked ready to go for a run. "What are you doing?"

She stood and propped her hands on her hips.

And what the hell had happened to all of her curves? Last night she'd worn baggy sweats. This morning she'd been bundled in loose flannel. He'd assumed the big clothes were what had made her appear so skinny, but he'd been wrong. There was nothing to her. Her legs and hips had lost their sexy curves. Her ass...he'd loved holding her sweetly rounded ass when he'd drove himself deep inside, but he doubted he'd find an ounce of flesh to hang onto now. Not that she was offering. And not that he'd be interested if she did offer.

Liar.

He'd never forgotten the slide of her soft body against his. How she'd wrapped her legs around his back, dug her nails into his shoulders, cried out his name as she came.

"I'm going to get in a quick workout," she said as she drew a water bottle from the refrigerator. "Coffee's brewing. Help yourself."

She started for the hallway, refocusing his attention to the present, not the past. In a few strides, he blocked her. "Your workout can wait. We need to talk."

With a quick glance to the kitchen clock, she released a breath. "Fine, but I'm on a time crunch. I need to be at the station—"

"Screw that, your workouts, and everything else. We're on my time now."

She crossed her arms and cocked a dark brow. "Is that so?"

"Yeah, and we're not going anywhere for a while. I got a guy dropping off what I need to beef up your security and Mallory will be here around eight-thirty."

"And how is it you have his number?"

He leaned closer, torturing himself and likely irritating her. "From when you and I were...ah...what were we doing anyway?"

She shoved at his chest. "Making a big mistake."

He followed her into the kitchen. "Glad we cleared that up," he said even though he'd never considered what they'd had a mistake. How he'd handled the situation with her source? Yeah, that had been bad. But everything before that night had been more than good, and definitely not a *mistake*. "Now let's talk about your stalker."

With an exasperated sigh, she opened a cupboard, then slid a mug across the counter. "I don't have a stalker."

He caught the mug, then poured himself a cup of coffee. "Mallory says you had a bunch of crank calls and text messages last month." He leaned against the counter next to her. "They bothered you enough to turn to him."

"They *bothered* me. They didn't scare me. Plus, they weren't the first I've ever received, and I doubt they'll be the last."

He supposed plenty of celebrities, local and otherwise, had their share of screwy fans, but he'd never considered Eden a celebrity. Maybe because she'd never acted like one, or at least his perception of one. Perception. There was that word again. He'd bring up what the doctor from the DVD had said about perfection and perception later, though. Right now, he wanted to discuss the leads on the possible stalker.

"Did Mallory find out who was making the calls and texts?"

She shook her head. "They came from two different cell phones. Both had been reported stolen. Then one day they just stopped."

"Tell me about them."

"Not much to tell," she said, looked to the clock again, then fidgeted with what he figured was a heart rate monitor around her wrist. Man, she must be itching for that workout.

"There were only four voicemails. The voice was weird, kind of reminded me of Yoda, you know, from *Star Wars*. And the messages the old Jedi left were all pretty much the same. 'You think you're so pretty, but you're not' or 'Chicago can't wait for you to leave, I know I can't'." She shook her head. "Harmless really and the three texts were basically the same thing. Telling me I should leave town, do everyone a favor and never show my face on TV again."

"Did you save the messages?"

"I just deleted them last week. There didn't seem a point in saving them. They weren't threatening and the last time he'd contacted me was almost four weeks ago."

A knock came at the door. Probably Lloyd with the equipment he'd requested. When she moved to answer, he stopped her. "Look," he began. "Until we have a better idea of what we're dealing with, consider yourself in danger."

"Really, Hudson. I think you're being—"

"Careful." He tucked a loose strand that had slipped from her ponytail behind her ear. "Just being careful."

Eden kept her gaze on him as he walked to the door, and swore her skin still tingled from where his fingers had lingered. She pushed away the sudden, sharp longing and looked to the clock for the umpteenth time. Damn. She only had an hour before Bob showed, which meant she'd have no time to squeeze in a workout. It also meant she'd have to cut back her calorie intake today.

She put the water bottle back in the fridge, then poured a cup of coffee. The door slammed, followed by heavy footsteps. She'd know that walk anywhere. Hudson had a certain swagger, a walk that demanded respect and oozed confidence.

"I'm gonna get to work on your security system," he called from the hallway. "Do you have another monitor anywhere else besides the front foyer?"

"Bedroom," she answered, then cringed. "But I'm going to take a shower, so you'll have to wait."

He rounded the corner wearing a cocky grin. "Nothin' I

ain't seen, but lock the bathroom door if you're worried I can't control myself."

Without a word, because for once she couldn't think of a snappy comeback, she took her mug and made her way to the bedroom. Fabio and Brutal were curled up on her bed together, sleeping. How she'd love to join them, and sleep through the day. She wasn't ready to face Bob yet and she wasn't sure how to handle the demand the man on the DVD had made. Even if the station manager, Rodger Jeffries, would let her use airtime to send the man a message, what would she say? And although the DVD held the utmost priority, she still had to finish the final episode of her series.

Then there was Hudson.

Climbing into the shower, she let the hot spray wash over her. But she couldn't wash away the longing or regret.

She'd stupidly fallen for Hudson, only he hadn't been the man she'd thought...steady, worthy of her trust. He'd made her want to lose control and live up to her pseudonym. Risk her heart for something other than her lonely career.

Thank God she'd been too scared to admit that she'd cared about him. The blow he'd dealt to her heart and ego had been bad enough. The betrayal, the way he'd used her.

Fucking *used* her.

She'd do well to remember the anger, because just being near him now brought back too many other memories. The good times, the sexy times. God, she was such a hypocrite. The guilt, the regret. The way she'd taken advantage of his screw-up to end things fast and furious when deep down, she'd understood and had forgiven him.

A hard rap at the bathroom door had her shutting off the water.

"Just wanted to let you know I've already finished with your bedroom monitor," Hudson said from the other side of the door. "And Mallory'll be here in less than thirty."

"Thanks." She reached for the towel hanging over the stall and wrapped it around her body. After she heard the outer door click shut, she wiped steam from the mirror, then moved through the motions of fixing her hair and applying her make-up. All the while, her thoughts strayed to Hudson, to the lies between them. And of course...the DVD. The reason he'd blown back into her life.

Despite his "rules" she dressed in a suit, prepared to go into the station, talk with Jeffries about what had happened with Kyle and hopefully work on the final segment of her series. Of course, after Bob reviewed the DVD.

Her stomach flipped. She didn't want to watch the DVD again and she wasn't ready to face Bob yet. She'd hoped the next time they talked, that she'd be armed with information. Like who was Kyle Edwards's source.

As she exited the bedroom, steam from the guest bathroom lingered in the hallway. A quick glance to the right, and she noticed a small suitcase sitting in the guest bedroom which actually held no bed, but served as her personal gym. She remembered Hudson mentioning last night that he'd been up since four in the morning and that he'd just spent a month in Detroit. He must have gone from the airport, to CORE, then straight to her place.

She closed the guestroom door, then moved down the hall. As she neared the living room, muffled screams echoed off the vaulted ceilings. Cold dread sprinted up her spine. Even without seeing it, she knew Hudson was watching the DVD. She'd never forget those sounds or the images that had come with them. Avoiding the TV, she glanced around the room and caught Hudson's concerned gaze. When he jerked his head, she followed the motion then sucked in a breath.

"Bob, hi. I—"

"Turn that thing off," he ordered Hudson, and the muffled screams abruptly stopped. He wiped a hand over his balding head, then released a deep sigh. "Not the way I wanted to start my morning. Especially after how I ended my night."

She didn't miss the irritation in his gaze when he glanced at her. "I told you I had no idea Edwards knew anything about the murders," she said defensively. "I'm going to visit Jeffries when we're through here and see if I can get information on

Edwards's source."

He shook his head and offered her a sympathetic smile. "It won't matter. I've been told—ordered, actually—to no longer speak with you or anyone from your station. Sorry, kiddo, you've been blackballed." He blew out a deep breath. "I shouldn't even be here right now."

Reeling in her shock, she gripped the back of the couch. "Let me talk to your captain. Maybe if I explain…You know I'd never betray—"

"I knew that last night even when I was poppin' off on you. Sorry about that by the way. I knew how things would end up going down and I was angry." His expression somber, Bob pulled his keys from his pocket. "I know you had nothing to do with any of this, but Edwards revealed information that could compromise my case and he works with *you*. On top of that, he leaked the name of the victim before we even had a chance to notify her family. This has become a PR nightmare." He moved toward the door. "I've gotta go."

"What about the DVD? You obviously haven't finished watching it. Did Hudson tell you what was on the rest?"

"He did, but you have no body. Hell, you don't even know if this guy's dead." Thumbing toward the TV he looked to Hudson. "I can take a copy and have it checked, but I'm guessing you've already got someone at CORE working on it. Better equipment, too."

"We do."

"Well, if it turns out this thing isn't a hoax, and you find a dead body, you know the drill."

"A hoax," she echoed with shock. "I can't believe you'd even think…What about the two murdered nurses? Maybe there's a connection between them and this." She motioned to the darkened TV.

"We found evidence last night that would suggest otherwise." Bob held up a hand. "And don't even bother asking. I'm not supposed to be talking to you, remember?"

"I understand." She rubbed the tension tightening the back of her neck. "If I find anything out about Edwards's source, can I at least call you?"

"Have Hudson do it. Maybe after things calm down..." Bob stared at her for a moment, then glanced at Hudson. "Keep her safe."

The door quietly clicked shut, leaving her alone with Hudson again. "So I guess we're on our own." She moved toward the kitchen, furious with Kyle Edwards for screwing up her relationship with the Chicago PD. Before last night, she could have turned to Bob for help. Now she had to depend on Hudson.

"Hey," Hudson murmured and snagged her hand. "At least you know Mallory isn't holding anything against you."

"Right. Just the rest of the CPD. And let's not forget my station manager, either. He's going to go ballistic when he finds out we've been blackballed." She tightened her hold on his hand. Not only could Jeffries make her last month at WBDJ-TV a living hell, but more importantly, word of what had happened could reach Network and damage her upcoming contract.

When Hudson threaded their fingers together the rough texture of his hand against hers gave her what his touch had always done in the past. Comfort.

Until she met his gaze.

His eyes burned with deep concern, and her comfort morphed to something stronger, darker. Carnal. Scary.

He still cared.

Jerking free from him and the crazy thought, she tucked her hand in her pocket and moved past him.

"Eden," he said, and reached for her. "I—"

His cell phone rang. Muttering a curse of some sort, he turned and answered the call. She stared at his broad back, the way his shoulders and arms filled out his black t-shirt. He ran a hand through his long hair, then held it bunched at the base of his neck. "Okay," he said. "We'll see you soon."

When he turned, the concern that had darkened his eyes moments ago gave way to excitement. Forgetting about Bob, Jeffries and Network, she stepped forward and gripped his arm. "What is it?"

"We got ourselves a lead."

Michael Morrison emerged from the century-old farmhouse for the first time in two days. His head ached. Hell, even his teeth ached. His stomach still churned with nausea, but he moved across the field anyway.

The cool wind didn't help the hangover like he'd hoped. Instead, the morning air stung his sensitive skin and dry eyes, and the chills that had been running through him since he'd awakened only worsened with each step through the frost laden leaves.

The binge had been necessary, though. The bottles of booze—Wild Turkey, Evan Williams, Black Velvet—were used to forget. The blood, the yellow fatty tissue oozing from rubbery flesh. The screams.

Oh God, the screams.

With a shiver, he rested the varmint rifle against his leg, then reached inside his heavy Carhart coat. The rough material snagged against his chapped hand and drew blood from the cracks in his skin. Although he'd worn Latex gloves when he'd performed the *surgery*, he'd scrubbed his hands raw. No amount of soap or scalding water could seem to make him feel clean again.

He pulled the flask he'd filled before leaving the house and took a long swig.

After what he'd done to the doctor, he'd never be *clean* again.

But he'd started something. Something he'd planned for too many years to quit. Besides, he'd made a promise. To himself. To Eliza. Those men would pay and they would pay dearly, even if their payment shredded the last remnants of the man he'd once been...God fearing. Moral. Just.

Human.

The whiskey burned his throat, but soothed his queasy

47

stomach. Although tempted to drain the flask, he shoved it back inside his coat. He had work to do.

Picking up the varmint rifle, he continued deeper into the one hundred and forty acre property. He paused fifteen minutes later to regain his bearings, then moved northwest. Seventy-five steps would take him to where he'd dumped Dr. Thomas Elliot's body two nights ago.

Rifle ready, he counted as he walked, shifting his gaze from the ground to the overgrown brush. Although they didn't come out much during the day, the coyotes were in a bad way at this time of year. Starving, desperate. And he'd given them Thanksgiving dinner, with extra plump breasts.

Fifteen, sixteen, seventeen—

He stopped. Raised his rifle and looked around the area. A squirrel skittered up a tree and he continued moving.

Eighteen, nineteen, twenty, twenty—

Michael turned and retched. The acid from his stomach, mixed with the booze, burned his throat as he vomited on the ground. Drawing in deep, steadying breaths, he wiped his mouth with his sleeve. Once the dizziness passed, and his stomach no longer protested, he looked over his shoulder.

He wouldn't have to walk the full seventy-five steps. The coyotes had dragged Elliot's body—or what was left of it—and saved him the trip. He should have expected as much. The coyotes had been feasting for two days. Tearing off bits and pieces of the doctor and scattering the bones. By this time tomorrow, other than the head and maybe a few scraps— inedible for even a starving coyote—he doubted he'd find any other traces of Elliot.

The coyotes wouldn't have to worry, though. By this time tomorrow he planned to have their next meal prepared.

Then the feeding frenzy would begin again.

CHAPTER 4

BEFORE HUDSON PARKED the car, Eden had her seatbelt undone and her hand on the door handle. She needed space. She needed a moment alone. Being near Hudson brought back too many memories, and she'd realized she wasn't as immune to him as she'd hoped.

"You planning on waiting until I stop or are you gonna do some sort of tuck and roll onto the concrete?" he asked as he veered the Trans Am into a parking space.

"It's already close to ten, and I need to make it into the station before noon." *And being near you is driving me crazy.*

"I told you—"

"Yeah, yeah." She sighed. "Your rules. No workout, no work, no anything else."

He parked the car, then turned off the ignition. "I didn't mean that you couldn't work or anything else. I just...this case is priority."

Of course.

The sarcastic barb sat at the tip of her tongue.

Hudson's job, his cases, had *always* been top priority. Not her, and she'd do well to remember that, even if a small part of her—the part that still held a little something for this ruggedly handsome and somewhat broken warrior—wished otherwise. Men like Hudson would never change, and she wouldn't expect him to. Her career gave her identity, and she suspected it was the same for him.

Rather than give him the reply she'd wanted and start an argument, she climbed out of the car. Besides, if she said anything, it might come across bitter. Always perceptive when it came to people, Hudson might misconstrue and think she still harbored feelings for him. And while she did—on a very small level—she figured those feelings bent more toward lust than anything else.

Lust she could handle. The anything else? She pulled her purse strap over her shoulder and crossed her arms. She'd do her damnedest to keep reminding herself he'd broken her heart once and avoid *anything else* that might make her look like a fool a second time around.

When he rounded the car, though, desire pulled deep in her belly. Although she wasn't a fan of his shaggy hair, the man still did a number on her hormones. His walk alone conjured images of his powerful body above hers. Hovering between her spread thighs. His lips a hair's breadth from hers.

She cleared her throat and her mind, then looked to his Trans Am. Black, with the classic gold firebird painted on the hood, the car could have been used as a double in the movie *Smokey and the Bandit.* "What happened to the El Camino you used to drive?" she asked to divert her thoughts from him, his body, his rough calloused hands and all the things she knew he could do with them.

He pointed to the corner of the parking garage. "She's right over there. I sold her to Rachel, the woman we're meeting, about six months ago."

She'd remembered how much he'd loved that car. One warm spring night after they'd made love—sex, they'd had sex—he'd told her that after he'd left the CIA and joined CORE, he'd begun refurbishing the El Camino. Therapy, he'd said, a way to help stop the nightmares.

She hadn't pried or asked what those nightmares entailed. Based on the scars that had marred his body, she'd figured the emotional and mental scars were probably much worse. Instead of going into reporter mode and drilling him, she'd run her fingers through the soft hair lining his chest and had rested her head on his shoulder. And listened. To how he'd overcome the nightmares, then later, to his breathing as he'd drifted off to sleep.

That night, his trust had opened up a part of her she'd been too afraid to tap, and she'd realized she was half in love with Hudson. Or maybe all the way. But he'd destroyed those feelings along with any fairy tale thoughts of love five days later.

And she hadn't been in love since. Because of her job, there'd been no time for romance. Occasional, bland sex to scratch the itch, yes. But love? She'd learned her lesson. Once bitten, twice shy.

Still, Hudson had loved that El Camino. Although only a car, it had represented his triumph over emotional pain and had helped him heal.

"How could you sell the car?" she asked, unable to hide the accusation and bitterness from her voice. It bugged the hell out of her that he'd tossed the car aside just as easily as he'd tossed away their relationship.

He shrugged and ran a finger along the Trans Am's back fender, then turned toward the elevators. "The Camino's in good hands now. Besides, I get to see her or drive her when I want. Rachel's good like that."

A stab of ridiculous jealousy pierced and pricked. They'd been apart for over two years. Almost two and a half, really. She'd been with other men. Okay, two. Of course Hudson would see other women. Still. "Is she now?"

"Jealous?"

Yes, damn it. "Hardly."

"Well, just in case you are, Rachel's a good kid and friend. Nothing more."

She quickened her pace toward the parking garage elevators with sick satisfaction tingling her fingers and toes. "I'll sleep so much better tonight."

He half-laughed and pressed the button for the elevator. "I just bet."

"Mmmm." She slid her gaze to his strong profile and realized he still hadn't answered her question. And she wanted an answer. The night he'd told her the story about the El Camino had been one of her favorite memories of them. She'd felt close to him then, and sure that they had something good going. "So why did you sell the car?"

Keeping his gaze on the elevator, he shoved his hands into his pockets. "Enquiring minds want to know?"

"Something like that."

"You sure?"

He made the sale of the car sound like a dirty, dark secret, which of course made her even more curious. "I wouldn't have asked."

"It was time for a new project."

The elevator dinged and the doors slid open. "The Trans Am?" she asked as she stepped inside. "You remodeled that car, too? When?"

Regret, guilt, and need darkened his eyes as he moved into the elevator. "The day after you left me."

"Wow. Look at me hobnobbing with a celebrity," Rachel Davis said as she pumped Eden's hand and flashed a big smile. "So refreshing after having to deal with Neanderthals like this guy day in and day out."

"Ugh," Hudson grunted, then pretended to take offense. "Someone steal your secret stash of Special K this morning?"

"I couldn't eat a bowl if you tried to force feed me," Rachel replied as she led them into CORE's evidence and evaluation room. State of the art, large TV screens lined one wall, several computers sat stationed in the opposite corner, and an enormous metal table filled the middle of the room. A white erase board took up the other wall and he noticed Rachel's bubbly scribble, written in black marker, already filled one side of the board.

Thankfully, Eden kept her gaze on everything but him, just

as she had during the elevator ride to the fourteenth floor, one of the two floors CORE leased at the Becker Building. Why he'd sabotaged himself and opened his big mouth about the Trans Am he didn't know. From the moment he'd realized he'd be forced to work with her, he'd told himself he wouldn't allow old feelings to interfere with the case. Less than twelve hours later, they had anyway. Because they hadn't disappeared?

He shoved a hand through his hair and focused on Rachel. Terrible with emotions and relationships, he'd rather put his mind to use on what he was good at. Hunting.

"Stuff's gross anyway," he said to Rachel. "Oatmeal's what you need. It'll put hair on your chest."

Rachel walked to one of the computers, then hit a key. A TV screen jerked to life showing the victim from the DVD lying on the operating table. "Hair's not what I need. And if your theory on oatmeal is true, this guy must have eaten it by the barrel."

She hit a few more keys and the other TVs, one by one, came to life, each with a different still shot. "Okay, show time," she said, then began punching more buttons. "Watch screen number one."

He moved closer to the screen and tried to ignore Eden's coaxing scent as she stood next to him. "What am I looking at besides a foot?"

The keyboard tapped behind him, then the screen enlarged. "See anything interesting?" Rachel asked.

He shook his head and started to say no. Then he saw it. A tattoo, buried beneath thick black hair and just above the victim's ankle. "Wait. Got it."

Eden pointed to the markings on the screen. "I see it, too. Letters?"

"Greek actually," Rachel clarified. "Sigma Alpha Mu."

"Do you think he was a Sammy?" Eden asked Rachel.

"Makes sense to me."

"Hold up. A whatty?" They might as well have been speaking Greek at the moment. Hudson had no idea what the hell they were talking about.

Rachel hit a few more keys and the screen changed to a website. "The Sammys, or Sigma Alpha Mus, are a fraternity."

"Jewish," Eden added.

"Yes. And according to their main website, currently fifty-four chapters are recognized in universities across the country."

"Currently," he echoed. "This guy's gotta be somewhere in his mid to late forties."

Rachel switched from the website's home page to its alumni page. "That's my guess. So figure this guy was in college twenty plus years ago."

Eden leaned against the metal table. "Not to sound negative, but without a name or a...body, this isn't going to help us right now."

"True. But it's given us a few leads. The vic is Jewish and had at one time belonged to a fraternity."

Hudson nodded to the Sammy alumni page on the TV screen. "I'd be interested to know how many alumni in the vic's age group ended up as plastic surgeons."

"Plastic surgeons?" Eden repeated.

"Think about it." He pointed to one of the still shots on the other TV screens. "The guy doing the slicing wasn't torturing our vic to gain information, but to send a message. He gave him breast implants, then went on about how we're all being poisoned by airbrushed images."

"There's no such thing as perfect, only perception," Eden quoted the doctor.

"Right." He moved a finger over the screen. "Look at the operating room. This guy did some serious planning. I doubt our vic will be the last, even if you were to somehow air this DVD or found a way to let him know you'd received it and *can't* air it."

Her knuckles grew white as she grabbed the metal table. "I worried about the same thing, especially when he made the comment about my beauty pageant series." She looked at him, her green eyes forlorn, distressed. "This is personal, isn't?"

"It's revenge."

"Dun, dun, dun," Rachel mumbled, and pulled a pencil from behind her ear. "Are we done with the melodramatics? Because I have something else I want to show you."

"I'm not being melodramatic," he countered. "I'm being realistic. This *is* a plain old case of revenge."

"Just a cut above the rest?" Rachel tapped the pencil eraser against her chin and pursed her lips.

"Smart ass. Do you think you could somehow, preferably legally—"

"Search the Sammy data base for any males who would have graduated twenty to twenty-five years ago with a degree in medicine."

The corner of Eden's mouth tilted and the anxiety in her eyes momentarily disappeared. "I think Rachel pretty much has it covered."

Puffing his cheeks, he looked away.

"He hates when I finish his sentences for him," Rachel said as she moved back to the computer. "They all do. Which is why I do it. Okay, keep your eyes on screen two."

The TV didn't show the man being tortured on the table, or even the doctor with the bucktoothed surgical mask. Instead, Rachel had blown up an image of the back of the operating room. A few strokes to the keyboard and the still shot moved. He watched, then smiled when a clap of thunder, chased by lightening illuminated a small window.

"Did you see that?" Eden asked. "Those were trees, right?"

"Sure did look like it. Rachel, can you replay that?"

She did, this time in slow motion. Sure enough, the split second of lightening revealed trees outside the operating room window.

"We can eliminate some sorta basement torture chamber," Rachel said. "And I highly doubt this is someplace in the city."

"He'd want privacy," Hudson confirmed. "Neighbors nearby wouldn't do. Not for this guy. So we can likely eliminate the suburbs, too."

"So he's out in the country?" Eden suggested.

He shrugged. "Hard to tell. Either way, he'd have to be

within driving distance to *your* townhouse." When he chanced a glance at her, he noticed the worry in her eyes again and cleared his throat. "I mean—"

"I know what you meant. He's obviously been at my place, he knows where I live."

"He's also been watching you enough to know someone else is, too," Rachel added, her tone holding a hint of apology. "In a way, that might not be such a bad thing. Maybe this guy isn't a threat to you, but just looking at you as his media outlet. Why else would he warn you about a potential stalker?"

Hudson had given that possibility a quick thought, too. He'd just as quickly dismissed it, though. In his experience, there was no such thing as a killer with a heart of gold.

"Is there anything else?" he asked Rachel.

"I was able to enlarge some of the equipment's make, model and even a few serial numbers. After you leave, and after I look for our frat boy, I'll see what I can find. I'm not hopeful, though. This guy probably bought the equipment secondhand. Paid in cash."

"What about this?" Eden asked, and pointed to the third screen where vials of medicine sat on a small table. "Were you able to get a name off the drugs he used? If they're pharmaceutical—"

"I've already tried enlarging the vials, but the angle of the image gave me nothing. Hopefully we'll have a better view next time."

"Next time," Eden echoed, then drew in a deep breath and looked away from the TV screens. Fear, despondence and worry hollowed her too thin face. For a strong woman, she appeared breakable. He didn't like her sudden vulnerability, or the urge to wrap his arms around her and give her comfort. He'd already screwed up once today. Revealing that he'd needed "car therapy" to overcome their break-up had been a mistake. Offering physical comfort would be catastrophic. In a matter of twelve hours, old wounds had been reopened and old feelings had emerged. Or maybe they'd never gone away in the first place. Whatever the case, he had to keep his focus sharp.

Another DVD would be coming their way.

Using the side rail remote, Dorothy Long raised the bed for a better view of the old, thirty-six inch Sony TV. The channel guide promised a marathon of *Mama's Family* reruns on TV Land today and she'd intended to watch every episode. She loved the show, and how Vicky Lawrence played the character of Thelma "Mama" Crowley Harper. All that sass and the way she'd run the family reminded Dorothy of herself. Not that she had much of a family anymore, but she still had Pudge.

Where the hell was that child anyway?

Lowering the volume, she shifted her head toward Pudge's room. Half past ten, she needed her pills, her colostomy bag changed and her bed sores treated. She also needed her breakfast. Lord she was starving. That frozen pizza Pudge had baked last night hadn't even come close to satisfying her. But Pudge had disappeared into the bedroom before she'd had the chance to ask for anything else to eat. And when she'd called out, she'd been ignored. She should punish the ungrateful shit for that one. What if there had been an emergency? What then?

With disgust, she set the remote on the bed tray. Lately, her sweet child had been acting like a spoiled, ungrateful brat. Pudge needed to learn a lesson. If she could climb out of this bed she'd wallop Pudge's ass so goddamn hard the ingrate wouldn't be able to sit for a week. Yes. That's what was needed around here. A good old-fashioned reminder about respect.

But the bed had become her self-imposed asylum. Her legs could no longer hold her body weight. Hell, she'd become so blessedly huge she couldn't even wipe her own ass anymore. Roles had been reversed.

Aside from Pudge's strange mood swings, Dorothy loved how life had turned out for her. She ate, slept and watched TV whenever she wanted, as much as she wanted, without having to answer to a pig bastard of a husband who'd expected nothing but perfection. She'd shown Rick, though. If only he wasn't dead—at least for just a couple of minutes—she'd love for him to gaze upon his wife now.

"Fuck you and a dress size number 2," Dorothy sang to her dead husband, then reached for the remote. She'd blast Pudge's ass out of bed. When the volume had been raised to the point Dorothy worried she'd blow the old TV's speakers, Pudge finally opened the bedroom door.

Dorothy hit the MUTE button, drowning out a commercial for feminine hygiene. "There you are. I've been waiting on you all morning. I'm hungry. But I need you to change my bag and the gauze on my sores first."

Instead of answering, Pudge went to the kitchen.

"Son of a..." Dorothy muttered, then reached for the remote again. She thought about giving the room another sound blast as a way of showing her irritation, but lowered the volume instead. Why ruin the TV? Besides, she thought she heard Pudge rummaging around the fridge.

Minutes later, Pudge pushed through the kitchen door and stood at the threshold holding a glass of orange juice. Anticipating the sugary sweet burst of flavor on her tongue and how delicious bacon and eggs would taste with the cold juice, Dorothy licked her lips. "I'll have my eggs scrambled, today. Four should do it, along with three pieces of toast and six slices of bacon." When Pudge didn't move, she motioned impatiently toward the bed tray. "Come on now. Gimme the juice before it turns warm, then get to work on my breakfast. I'm so damn hungry, changing the bag and gauze can wait."

Pudge moved into the shadows of what had once been the dining room. Years ago, the room had been used for parties and holiday celebrations, but now served as storage space for medical supplies and food. Not that Dorothy cared. She'd hated all that celebrating and holiday nonsense. The extra work, the extra mouths to feed...the extra beatings.

Her left eye twitched—an infuriating reflex she hadn't been able to shake over the past fourteen years. Not when the memories tried to settle in and take over like they were now. Not even when she knew, personally, that Rick was dead and buried. All over the place.

"Bring me my goddamn juice," she demanded while rubbing her eye with the back of her hand, and at the same time rubbing the old phantom bruises from her face. There had been so many. Cuts, broken bones, black and blue marks. She raised both hands and no longer rubbed, but scrubbed. She scrubbed the memories, the filthy images, the face of the man she'd once called husband. Breathing hard, her cheeks overflowed into her palms reminding her that she wasn't his skinny punching bag anymore.

Rick rested in pieces, while she remained alive. Living the way she wanted, the way she'd chosen.

"You shouldn't talk to me that way," Pudge said in a tone so quiet and menacing Dorothy dropped her hands and stared across the room. Fear caused by the memories of her dead husband had nothing to do with the tremors of dread rippling through her body and lodging in her gut. The midmorning sun shone through a small slit in the ripped dining room curtain. The thin stream of light played with the features on Pudge's face.

For a moment, her once adorable child resembled the monster Dorothy had married and buried. Pudge's normally bright blue eyes had darkened to black, the whites surrounding were yellowed and bloodshot. Deep scowl lines around the mouth bracketed lips too thin. Smudges under the eyes gave Pudge's face a hollow, gaunt look of emaciation. But it was in the smile where Dorothy's fears festered. Pudge wore a grin similar to Rick's when he'd been ready to mete out punishment. Deviant, malicious, hateful.

"What's the matter, *Dot*?" Pudge asked and moved toward the living room. "You look like you've seen a ghost."

A cold prickle of unease raced along her skin. Rick had called her Dot before he'd beaten or raped her. Hearing the name from Pudge's mouth sickened and frightened her. What if Pudge became a cruel sadist like Rick? Finding pleasure in abuse and suffering. Unsure if drugs played any role in Pudge's change, Dorothy decided to tow a fine line. And although afraid, she shrugged. "Just thirsty is all, honey. Tired, too." She shifted and gripped the bedrail. "Didn't sleep well on account of heartburn and these bedsores." Holding tight to the rail, she used her upper body strength to attempt a slight roll hoping to emphasize her pain and elicit sympathy.

"Maybe if you weren't so fucking fat you wouldn't have them."

"Pudge," Dorothy said on a gasp and with genuine hurt. Of all people, Pudge had always understood the weight gain. "How could you say something like that to me? Besides, you know I have thyroid issues and—"

"People with thyroid problems don't blow up to six hundred pounds. No. Your issue isn't medical. It's called gluttony. You eat more food in one day than a normal person would eat in a week."

"You make me sound like a—"

"Pig? Just calling it like I see it."

The glint in Pudge's eyes resembled Rick's menacing glare. Uncannily so. And just like her dead husband who had held power over her all those years ago, Dorothy realized that by allowing herself to become morbidly obese, unable to walk and tend to her own needs, she'd given Pudge power over her, too. With that realization, her fear morphed to utter dread. What if Pudge forced her into a nursing home? No more frozen pizzas or Happy Jax burgers and fries. The doctors would limit her food intake not to mention the amount of TV she watched. Hell, did nursing homes even have cable?

Then she remembered the nurse who visited every other week. She also remembered her will and her life insurance. Pudge might scare her lately and hold *some* control over her, but Dorothy knew who really held the cards. And it was time Pudge had a healthy reminder.

Releasing the bedrail, she rolled flat on her back. "A pig, huh? Is that what you think of your mother? After all that I've done for you? After all that I've saved you from. I might be fat, but so are my benefits. You'll receive what? Over four hundred grand when I'm dead? Unless..."

A small smirk played at Pudge's mouth. But it was the eyes Dorothy couldn't look away from. Defiant, dark, unearthly. "Are you threatening me, *Mama*?"

"Do I need to?"

Body rigid, face expressionless, Pudge's eyes became deadpan, blank.

Minutes passed.

The laugh track from Mama's Family sounded off in the background. A car's engine revved somewhere down the street.

And Pudge hadn't blinked let alone answered or moved.

Swallowing hard, Dorothy held out a shaky hand. "Pudge? Honey, you okay? You're scaring me."

When she received no response, she slapped both hands together and screamed as loud as she could.

Pudge jumped. The juice glass shattered on the floor. Pudge looked to the mess, then to Dorothy. "I'm sorry, Mama. I'm such a klutz. I'll get you another glass of juice. Then we'll take care of your bag and gauze. How did you say you wanted your eggs?"

Confused, Dorothy continued to stare at her child. The dark defiance in Pudge's gaze had disappeared. Eyes that had seemed unearthly moments ago now sparkled blue. The resemblance to Rick had also vanished.

But for Dorothy, the fear remained.

Something was wrong with her Pudge.

CHAPTER 5

HUDSON KEPT PACE with Eden as she led him through the corridors of WBDJ-TV's offices.

"Hurry," she said and grabbed his arm. "I need to find David."

"Who?"

"My cameraman. I want to catch him before he goes to lunch."

Hudson's stomach grumbled, a reminder he hadn't eaten since yesterday evening. When he'd raided Eden's fridge and cabinets this morning, he'd come up empty. Brown, squishy bananas, yogurt and protein bars did not constitute food in his opinion. "Lunch isn't a bad idea," he said, hoping she'd take the hint.

"No time. I need to finish this last segment for the Sunday evening news. And I hate having to rush or be crunched for time." She stopped and asked a security guard if he'd seen the cameraman. The guard pointed to the left and she took off again. "Besides," she began, "I thought you wanted to review my beauty pageant series that's been airing over the past few weeks."

He did, but while eating a Big Mac and fries. Before he could respond, though, she stopped dead.

"Oh good, you're still here," she said to the large Asian

man approaching them. Wearing a long, leather duster, boots, flannel shirt and carrying a cowboy hat, he looked as if he'd stepped off the set of an old spaghetti western film.

"And a good afternoon to you too," the man replied with a thick Southern drawl.

Hudson suppressed a smile. He'd met all sorts of people in his life. An Asian man dressed as a cowboy, and sporting a deep, baritone twang that rivaled Johnny Cash's, was a first.

"Sorry," Eden said, then looked to the ceiling. "Hello, David. How are you today?"

"Fine, ma'am." David smiled. "Now that wasn't so bad, was it?"

She turned to Hudson. "David's been trying to turn me into a Southern Belle."

"Just 'cause you were born a Yankee doesn't mean you hafta act like one," David responded and offered Hudson his hand. "David Ito. Cameraman extraordinaire and Eden's personal lackey."

"Professional consultant," she corrected. "This is Hudson Patterson."

"Nice to meetcha," David said, then turned to Eden. "Now, why are you so happy to see me?"

"I was hoping you'd work with me on the last segment for my series."

"You don't need me. You're better off with Rusty."

"No. I mean, Rusty is good, but you've been with me on every interview and had taken every shot. It's your opinion I need. You're the reason this series has been so successful."

David looked at him and shook his head. "Does she get all sweet and lay on the sugar when she wants something from you, too?"

Sweet wasn't a word he'd ever use to describe Eden. Stubborn. Yes. Sexy. Hell yes. He cleared his throat before his thoughts jumped on the train to depravity.

"Well?" Eden asked before Hudson could form a response. "Are you free this afternoon?"

"He's taken." A tall, leggy blond said as she rounded the

corner and placed a hand on David's arm. "Sorry, Eden. You can't keep him to yourself all of the time."

"Tabitha," Eden said, and from her pinched expression Hudson suspected she was holding back her surprise. "You're going on assignment?"

"Don't sound so shocked." Tabitha narrowed her eyes and gave her curly hair a fluff. "While you've been busy rubbing asses with Network, I've been working some hardcore stories."

"That's right." Eden nodded. "I saw your piece on the teachers union. You did a great job."

"I...thank you." Tabitha blinked several times, as if confused or shocked by Eden's compliment, then lifted a vibrating cell phone from her suit coat pocket. "I have to answer this. David, I'll wait for you in the van."

Hudson noticed David staring at her ass as she walked away. When she was no longer in sight, the cowboy cameraman released a deep sigh. "I think I'm in love," he drawled and held his hat over his chest.

"Just be careful about mixing business with pleasure."

Wondering if Eden was sending *him* the warning, Hudson shifted his gaze to her. She had her eyes on David.

"Okay, traitor," she began. "Go chase after your latest conquest. I'll see if Rusty's around to help me."

"He is and he will. Check for him in Production Room C."

Two hours later, Hudson turned off the TV Rusty Jones had supplied. While Eden and Rusty had worked on her report, he'd sat in a small conference room and watched Eden's series "Beauty Pageant Queen Bees."

Although Eden's reporting and interviewing were excellent, and David had captured the essence of the child beauty pageants with his camera skills, the series left him with more questions. Like how did the crazy ass doctor make the leap from beauty pageant kids and their moms, to society being poisoned by perception, to mutilating a man in order to send a message? And where exactly did Eden fit with the doctor's plans? He had to know she wouldn't be able to air the gruesome DVD, which made Hudson wonder why the doctor had bothered involving her at all.

As it had for the past few hours, his stomach protested lack of sustenance and he regretted not taking Rusty up on his offer of Slim Jims and Funyuns. Deciding to hit the vending machine he'd passed earlier, Hudson left the conference room and ran into Eden and Rusty in the hallway.

"I was just coming to get you," she said. "I'm finished for the day, unless you're still watching the shows."

"No, I'm good."

"I'm not," Rusty griped and held his stomach. "I'm grabbing some lunch."

Eden winced. "Sorry, Russ, I'll make it up to you. How about I bring donuts with me tomorrow?"

"Make 'em apple fritters and you'll be back on my good side."

After Rusty rounded the corner, Hudson turned to her. "Rusty's got the right idea. Let's go grab a bite."

"I'm not hungry," she said as she led him through the halls and toward the exit. "I'd rather go home."

When he held the glass door open for her, the cold November wind swept passed them. "Okay, that'll work. But let's at least stop at the grocery store on our way. I think a mouse could starve at your place."

"I have plenty of things to eat at my house."

"Let me rephrase, you don't have anything *good* to eat." He flipped his coat collar up to combat the wind and followed her brisk pace to the parking lot. Once in the Trans Am, he pulled off his gloves and started the ignition. "If you don't want to stop at the store, then I'm at least going to grab some take-out."

She rubbed her gloved hands together, then held them in front of the heat vents. "Do it on your way home."

"Isn't that what I just said?"

"No. I meant after you drop me off at *my* place and you go home to *yours*."

"Subtle."

She shrugged. "One of my strong points." Looking out the

window, she shook her head. "Anyway, what did you think of the series?"

"Fishing for compliments?"

She whipped her head toward him and narrowed her eyes. "You know damn well I'm not like—"

Chuckling he held up a hand. "Easy. I'm just blowing you crap. I thought it was good. A little shocking, though. I had no idea those things were so popular."

"Oh yeah," she said with a sarcastic huff. "You remember the JonBenét Ramsey case?"

"Sure."

"The media had a field day with that one, not only focusing on every move the police and family had made, but the Ramseys' participation with the pageant scene. I honestly think that, for most Americans, it was the first time people were exposed to the child beauty pageant phenomenon."

"It was a first for me. I remember wondering why any parent would purposefully try to make their six-year-old daughter look like she was sixteen."

Eden shrugged. "You're not a mom or a little girl."

"Observant. And your point?"

"Lots of little girls love to play dress-up. Wear pretty princess dresses. Play with their mom's make-up and nail polish. I know I did. My sister and I used to do it all the time."

Eden had a sister? He'd assumed she was an only child, but now that he thought about it, he'd never asked her anything about her family when they'd been…dating. Okay, they'd been beyond dating when things had ended. He'd considered what they'd had a relationship. A partnership.

Then why did you lie to her?

Now wasn't the right time to dissect all of that bullshit, or even drill her about her family. Keeping his focus to the case, he said, "I get that. But according to your series, it seemed to me that the moms were the ones pushing their daughters. And it wasn't for fun." The car had warmed up enough Hudson could turn down the heater.

"True," she replied as she pulled off her gloves. "From

what I witnessed, I'd say maybe eighty percent of the girls competing were there because they wanted to win. The rest..." She let out a long sigh. "During one pageant, I had been backstage with David. We'd just finished filming an interview with a mom and her thirteen-year-old daughter. After David and I walked away, I realized I'd left my notes behind in their dressing room. When I went back, I overheard the girl we'd interviewed telling her mom she felt sick she was so hungry. Her mom told her she could eat after the pageant ended—two hours from that point by the way—and that she needed to be able to fit into all of her dresses. I also heard her say that if her daughter didn't at least place in the competition that she'd make her sit in the learning room and write 'I will be talented and beautiful' a thousand times."

Hudson released a low whistle. "I could only imagine what mommy dearest meant by the learning room."

"Me too. Especially when the mom realized I had been listening. She had an absolute conniption and threatened to sue me and the TV station if I mentioned anything about what I'd overheard. She did, of course, insist that I still use their interview. She wanted TV exposure for her daughter. After all, mom was convinced her daughter would wind up a model."

"You'd interviewed a lot of moms and daughters. Which episode were these two in?"

"They weren't. I decided not to use their interview and instead called a woman I know from child services."

"Nice," he chuckled. "When are people going to learn not to mess with you?"

"What can I say? I'm a sucker for kids, old people and animals."

"And the rest of us can kiss your ass?"

She sent him a big grin. "Don't go putting words in my mouth. Anyway, nothing came of it. The girl said she loved her mom and that everything was hunky-dory. My friend with child services made the visit herself and said everything checked out. No signs of abuse or neglect. She did say her gut told her the mom wasn't as sweet as she'd come off during their meeting.

But, because she hadn't found anything, and the girl refused to admit to any abuse, she had to close the case file."

"And you think twenty percent of these girls might be in similar situations?"

"I'm not suggesting abuse." She held up her hand and shook her head. "I'm saying that some of these girls aren't competing in pageants because they want to, but because their moms want them to. And these moms are living vicariously through their daughters. Look at a lot of child movie stars. Those kids want to play and go to school like others their age, but mom and dad only see dollar signs."

"Not that you're grouping every parent with a famous kid into the same money grubbing category."

"Of course not, but...okay, do you remember the interview with the mom from Calumet Park? She was in the third episode."

"Lived in a trailer? Daughter was about three?"

"That's the one. Now, her husband earns thirty-three thousand a year. She spends fourteen thousand a year on these pageants."

"Ho-lee. It costs that much to enter these things?"

"No, but the clothes are expensive, then there's the travel expense. Food, hotel room, gas money."

"All of this for a three-year-old? That's nuts."

"To you. Well, and to me. But to that mother, her little girl is her ticket out of the trailer. She's already had offers for her daughter to do a few local TV commercials and department store ads. Next stop. Hollywood." She shrugged. "What these beauty pageant moms are doing isn't any different from dads who push their sons into sports. But society doesn't seem to be bothered by a four-year-old linebacker."

He thought about his own childhood. How his father had pushed him to be better, tougher, stronger. Hudson hadn't been as interested in all of the sports programs his dad had shoved him into, but remembered how good it had made him feel when he saw his dad cheering from the sidelines. Later, he and his dad would sit for hours in their small family room where they'd discuss his game. Most times though, that discussion would end with his father drunk on gin, yelling and bitching about his own sorry experiences with sports. How, if he hadn't knocked up his mom and been forced to take a shit job and skip college, his dad could have been...something. "You won't get any arguments from me."

"That's a first," she said with a half-laugh.

"Not really. The only time we argued, and I mean really argued, was—"

"I don't want to go there. It's over and there's no point in bringing it up now."

"I never liked the way things between us ended," he said even though he knew she was right. He supposed a part of him resented her for not allowing him the chance to fully apologize and explain himself. Or maybe he resented her for not caring enough about him as he had for her. She hadn't even cared enough to tell him she had a sister.

Remember, you didn't ask.

"Please. Let it go."

He didn't want to, and couldn't understand why. She kept giving him easy ways to avoid their past and for some reason, he kept pushing to rip open old wounds.

"Um..." She cleared her throat. "Did you come up with any ideas as to why the doctor from the DVD might have associated my series with what he'd done to his victim?"

Back to business. He should be ecstatic, grateful that Eden was the type of woman who didn't bitch about the past. If she'd complained about what had happened between them, though, it might have been a sign that she'd given a rat's ass about him—at least when it had counted, or even now. He'd fallen hard for her, and yeah, he'd screwed up big time. But knowing she'd felt even an inkling of what he had for her meant that someone finally had cared about him. His mom had walked when he was a kid, his dad had been a narcissistic drunk, his ex-wife...

He gripped the steering wheel and refocused. Now wasn't the time to give himself a mini therapy session. He'd save that for when the case ended. The old Stingray Corvette sitting in the garage he'd rented would make for great therapy. When he walked away from Eden again, and he knew he would because he also knew the woman, he'd need it.

"I'm still not sure why this guy's pegged you to be his outlet. Maybe he had a daughter who'd been in beauty pageants?" he asked controlling his irritation for both her and himself. He wasn't so sure he would want to walk away, or have her throw him out again. Being around her again...damn she stirred too many memories, of what they'd had between them and what they'd lost when he'd lied to her.

"Maybe. But that will do us little good without a name or a face." She blew out a deep breath. "If he did have a kid on the pageant circuit, why torture a plastic surgeon?"

"If the guy was a plastic surgeon."

"You said yourself that—"

"I know what I said." He slowed and parked on the street in front of her townhouse. "Look, I do believe this is a case of plain old revenge. But the guy running the torture chamber might be using the beauty pageant, society being poisoned by the perception of perfection crap as a way to throw us off his trail."

"I don't believe that. I don't think you do, either."

"Doesn't matter until he makes another move or Rachel ID's the victim. What does matter is my need for food. Let's order a pizza before I starve to death." He opened his car door and rounded the front end of the Trans Am. "I'm even willing to sacrifice sausage and pepperoni and go all veggie for you," he said as he helped her from the car.

When she unlocked the front door to the townhouse, they were greeted by raspy barks and meowing. He asked her to place the order while he took the Chihuahua out to take care of business. While Brutal searched for the perfect spot, Hudson wondered, once again, what the hell was wrong with him? Last night, even this morning, he'd dreaded working in close proximity with Eden. Now, though, he looked forward to spending time with her. Although she was still a little icy, he'd noticed a thaw that hadn't been there two years ago. Maybe, despite her reluctance in the car, given time, she'd be willing to...to what? Get back together? Jump into bed and have hours of hot sex? Picturing her naked, imagining the ways they could spend the rest of the afternoon sent blood rushing to his dick. At this point, though, he'd enjoy hanging out with her. Eating pizza and watching a movie. Things normal people did. Things they'd never done. Between his job and hers, normalcy hadn't been an option. With Eden's career, he wondered if it ever would.

Hudson scooped up the dog and headed into the townhouse. He needed to shut down the part of his brain that kept going back to all of those emotions he hadn't and didn't want to deal with now if ever. Rather than dwell on her and him, he'd finish the case and simply enjoy whatever might happen between them...well, if it happened.

Looking forward to a quiet afternoon, he hung his jacket on the coat rack, then rubbed his rumbling stomach. "What time will the pizza be here?"

"I...uh, I didn't order it," she said, avoiding eye contact as she gave the dog a treat.

Leaning against the kitchen island, he crossed his arms and fought his irritation. Her apparent obsession with weight was beyond ridiculous. Didn't she realize she'd become too skinny? Didn't she realize other people, namely him, actually enjoyed eating and not starving?

"You don't have to eat pizza," he said and retrieved his cell phone. If she wouldn't call it in, then he would. "I'll order a salad if you're worried about the calories or carbs or whatever's the latest thing to avoid."

"I have stuff for a salad here," she said, not meeting his gaze and busying herself with filling the dog and cat's water dishes. "And I already told you, if you plan on ordering anything, have it delivered to *your* place. Not mine."

He slipped his cell phone back into his pocket. "Why?"

"Why what?"

"Why are you kicking me out? Aren't you worried that—"

"I'm going to get another DVD?" Still not looking at him, she released a deep sigh. "We don't even know if there will be another one. And if there is, it probably won't happen tonight. Remember, the threat was for another person to die if the DVD didn't air on today's six o'clock news."

"So you think you'll be safe here? Alone?" He shoved off the wall and approached her. "You don't think it's possible that this guy's anticipated that you *won't* be able to air his horror flick and already has his next victim on the operating table? Oh, and let's not forget your possible stalker."

She flinched and when she finally met his gaze, he moved closer, fighting the urge to reach for her and smooth away the worry creasing her forehead, to hold her and assure her he'd never let anything happen to her. He fisted his hands instead. The wariness in her eyes, the rigidness of her body told him what he needed to know. She wasn't ready for what he was willing to offer. Not just sex, but comfort, familiarity, and maybe this time around more of himself.

"I'm not trying to scare you. I want you to be realistic. I want you safe."

Gripping the edge of the kitchen counter, reminding him he'd unintentionally crowded her, she leaned back. "I appreciate your concern. But I'll be well protected tonight. *All* night."

Unconvinced he said, "The security system is good, I've seen to it myself, but having me here—just in case—is an even better security measure."

"Sorry, but three's a crowd. I doubt my date will appreciate my babysitter hanging around while we're...dating."

She had a fucking date?

"Cancel," he said, hoping he'd kept the resentment from his voice. Of course he shouldn't have expected her to remain celibate since they'd broken up. He'd had his share of "dates" too. But knowing another man would be here, in her townhouse, in her bed, had his empty stomach churning with jealousy. The way his emotions were hitting him like a barrage of bullets today, he realized he'd never gotten over the loss of what could have been between them.

No other woman before or after Eden had stirred his gut with thoughts of love and all that other stuff he didn't have the vocabulary to name.

"I'm not canceling. I refuse to allow a bunch of what ifs to rule my life." She straightened and met his gaze. The fierce determination in her eyes made him take a step back and give her space. "I have the security system, my animals and my *date* to protect me. If I need anything else, I'll give you a call."

She moved to sidestep him and he grabbed her arm. Unable to resist her tempting scent and equally tempting body, or the jealousy raging through him, he drew her close until his lips were inches from hers. "I still remember everything. How you felt. How you reacted to my touch." He shoved a hand into her thick, black hair and gripped her scalp. "How you cried out my name when you came."

A slow, sexy smile curved her lip. "If your memory's so good then you should also remember what an asshole you were, too." She pushed past him and moved toward the front door, grabbing his jacket along the way. "Time for you to go," she said and tossed him his coat.

"Good afternoon, I have an appointment with Dr. Westly."

"Your name?"

"Jim Robinson." The lie rolled smoothly off Michael Morrison's tongue as he looked around the dental office. He'd stolen a blueprint of the building eighteen months ago, when some of the offices were being remodeled, and he knew there were two exits from this particular office. One through the reception area and another from the hallway flanked with several rooms used by either the dental hygienists or the dentist himself. That exit had a security camera watching the employees as they'd come and go.

After searching for dental equipment for his personal use, he understood why the dentist had added the extra security. A used, refurbished dental drill sold for nearly fifteen hundred dollars, which was why Michael decided to stick with his old Black & Decker. After all, he was concerned with results, not his patient's comfort.

"Have you been here before, Mr. Robinson?"

His daughter had...too many times. "No. This is my first visit. A family member recommended Dr. Westly." He shrugged and offered a sheepish smile. "It's been a while since I've been to the dentist."

"Before I started working here, I used to avoid the dentist, too," the receptionist returned with a smile of her own.

"Can you hear the drill from your desk?" he asked and, using his acting skills, shivered. "That's gotta be like nails on a chalkboard."

"You get used to it." She laughed and looked at her schedule. "Okay, Mr. Robinson, I have you down for a cleaning, x-rays, and exam."

"I won't be doing any x-rays today. If Dr. Westly finds something, then maybe." Leaving dental records behind would be suicide. Once the authorities realized the dentist was missing they'd likely look at Westly's patients, connect the dots, and discover his true identity.

"Well, that'll save you a pretty penny. I see you don't have dental insurance."

"No." Another lie, but another way to avoid leaving behind a paper trail. "I'd still like to discuss cosmetic options with Dr. Westly, though. Veneers in particular."

The receptionist raised a brow. She looked over her shoulder, then back to him. Lowering her voice she said, "But you have such lovely teeth."

"Thank you, ma'am. But they're not for me." Michael paused when a sharp bark of laughter caught his attention. He peered around the corner and immediately recognized Dr. Brian Westly from his website photo.

Dressed in a lab coat, button down shirt and corduroy trousers, Dr. Westly escorted a patient toward them. The dentist nodded to the receptionist. "Linda, Mr. Bailey got off easy today. Two fillings. I still want to see him in six months. Got it, Frank?" he asked his patient and softened the harshness of his tone with a wink.

When Frank Bailey leaned over the receptionist desk and peered at her calendar, Dr. Westly turned to Michael. "New patient?" He offered his hand, then a conspiratorial grin. "Or latest victim?"

The irony of the dentist's words made him laugh out loud. Michael wiped his sweaty palm on his jeans, then shook the man's hand. "I'll stick with patient, Dr. Westly."

And leave being the victim up to you.

CHAPTER 6

"WHAT THE HELL are you doing here?" Hudson asked Owen Malcolm as he entered CORE headquarters.

"Good to see you, too, bro," the former Secret Service agent replied with the hint of a smile. "Haven't seen you in months, but I'm glad to see you haven't lost that sparkling personality I've always admired."

Hudson brushed past him and headed to the evidence and evaluation room. "Whatever."

Owen caught up with him and fell into step. "You're being a serious dick here."

"Not just a dick, but a serious one? Interesting."

Owen chuckled. "Annoying, more like it. What's with the attitude?"

Hudson pushed open the door and immediately noticed Rachel, perched over a computer keyboard and gnawing on a pencil. "Why aren't you in California?" he asked with more vehemence than he'd intended. Everyone who worked at CORE knew Ian Scott was a calculating son of a bitch. Hudson knew it wasn't Owen's fault that Ian had lied about the other man's current case or whereabouts. Still chapped his ass anyway. Owen could have been assigned to babysit Eden and deal with the sick bastard making DVDs. Instead, Ian, once again, manipulated the situation knowing he and Eden had had a relationship with a bad ending. Why? He hadn't a clue. Since he'd joined CORE, Hudson hadn't been able to gain a good read on his boss.

"Just got back. But I won't be staying long." Owen looked to Rachel as he started to follow him into the room. "Hey, Beav, that pencil taste good? I think I've got a wooden ruler in my desk drawer if you're interested. Better yet, I'll just pry off the leg of a chair and—"

"What the hell are you doing here?"

Owen looked between Hudson and Rachel. "I'm starting to get a complex."

Rachel dropped her chewed pencil on the desk and stood. She shot her lower lip out in a pout. "So sorry if I hurt your widdle feewings," she mocked Owen, then gave him the finger.

"A serious complex," Owen said. "You two mind explaining the problem? Hopefully it won't take too long. I'm leaving for Nevada in about four hours."

"What happened to California?" Hudson asked.

"Slight detour. Guy I'm investigating is heading for Vegas. I needed to lie low and go in a different direction."

Hudson realized he'd been wrong to jump to conclusions about Ian. At least this time. "Thought I'd head here," Owen continued. "Gather a few things—"

"Like the plane?"

Owen smiled at Rachel. "Yes, Sunshine, I wanted to use CORE's plane because I didn't think O'Hare's airport security would appreciate the small arsenal of weapons I'd planned on stowing in my carryon."

"How thoughtful," she said and looked to Hudson. "Now that we know why the golden boy is here, what about you? Because if you dropped by to see if I have any leads for you...wait a sec, where's Eden?"

"Eden, who?" Owen asked.

"Risk," Rachel responded. "You know, the TV chick who does the investigative reports for Channel 5 News."

Owen released a low whistle and looked to him. "Now I know why you're pissed."

"What's G.B. talking about?" Rachel asked him.

"G.B.?" Hudson echoed.

"Golden Boy," Owen answered for her. "It's better than her last nickname, D.B."

"D.B.?" Hudson repeated, not able to keep up with their nonsense.

"Douche Bag," Rachel said as she sat on the edge of the desk. "My personal favorite, but apparently Owen's ego couldn't handle it so...anyway, where's Eden?"

Hudson shook his head and now wished he'd gone to his apartment instead of CORE. He'd hoped to maybe bounce some ideas off Rachel, take another look at what she'd found earlier, anything to keep his mind off Eden and her *date*. Not deal with Owen and Rachel's grade school crap.

"She's at home."

"Who's watching her? I thought Ian said you were to provide her with twenty-four/seven protection."

"She...ah." Hudson fumbled with his words. Now he really wished he'd gone home. To admit that Eden had kicked him out so she could screw another guy, plain sucked. Especially in front of Owen, who knew the entire story behind the original Eden Risk fiasco.

"She kicked your ass to the curb again," Owen said with a shake of his head. "Sucks, man."

"What do you mean by again?" Rachel asked.

"Me first," Owen said. "Why are you supposed to be watching Eden in the first place?"

Hudson filled him in on the details. Rachel helped by showing Owen bits and pieces from the DVD. When they'd concluded, Owen no longer wore his trademark grin that usually had the ladies slipping off their panties, well, except for Rachel. Somehow she was the only woman Hudson knew who was immune to Owen's charms. Instead, Owen's California tan had momentarily paled and he held his lips in a grim line.

"I guess I shouldn't bitch about having to go to Vegas tonight, huh?" Owen finally responded as he turned away from the TV screens on the wall. "I hate to see what that doc does to the next vic. 'Cause you know there's going to be another."

Hudson nodded. "That's what my gut's telling me. But without any more leads, we wait."

Rachel cleared her throat and gained both he and Owen's attention. "Now that the G.B. has been informed, don't leave me hanging. What did Owen mean by Eden kicking your ass to the curb...again? And don't you dare try to get out of telling me, because if you don't, I'll do some serious snooping, which means I won't be able to worry about your case. You know how I get when I'm on a mission of discovery."

"You mean when you're clearly being nosey," Owen said with sarcasm.

"Hey, being nosey is what makes me excellent at my job." She looked to him. "Well, Hud, gonna spill it?"

Hudson glanced to Owen, then back to Rachel and shrugged. "I used Eden as bait to catch a serial rapist."

"Bastard," Eden muttered and tossed the throw pillow across the room. Hudson's scent still lingered on her couch, though. She should light some candles to remove the enticing odor. But Fabio hated fire.

She leaned into the sofa and reached for the remote, then decided she wasn't in the mood to watch TV. Resting her head on the arm of the sofa, she closed her eyes and instead of denying herself the pleasure, she gave in and relished the comfort Hudson's scent brought her. After not seeing him for over two years, then spending last night and most of today with him, she couldn't help herself. Her body hummed with the memories of his touch.

But comfort wasn't the right word. His lingering presence reminded her body of more than comfort, it reminded her of skin on skin, hot kisses, slow kisses, wet kisses. With sex suddenly on the brain, she almost regretted making him leave earlier. Actually, when he'd run his hands through her hair, brought their lips close together, and told her how he'd remembered how she'd felt, how she'd reacted to him, how she'd cried out his name as she came...

She pressed her legs together and curled them to her chest. Making him leave had been a good decision. If she hadn't, she'd probably end up with his scent on her body rather than the couch or throw pillow. Like him, she remembered everything, too. His touch, the way his hard muscles bunched beneath her hands as she gripped his chest and rode him. Yes, and the way she'd scream his name as she came.

A wave of lust caused her face to heat, and the dull ache between her legs became a full throb. She still wanted him. Bad. Just for sex, of course.

"Of course," she echoed out loud. Sex had never been an issue. In fact, the sex had been beyond excellent. Unfortunately, the sex had morphed her emotions beyond her comprehension. Before Hudson, she'd never been in love. Not that she'd been in love with him. She'd liked him a lot. A very strong like. But would she want to marry a man like him? Raise babies?

"Whoa, whoa, whoa," she said, and launched off the couch. Fabio and Brutal both raised their heads, and stared at her as she paced.

"I never wanted to marry him," she announced to her cat and dog. "And babies...I'll leave that up to my sister. I mean, I'm lucky I can take care of you two. Right?"

Not really expecting an answer from her animals, she stomped to the kitchen, then opened the fridge. Hudson was right. She didn't have anything good to eat. As she was about to slam the door shut, she reached back inside and pulled out a beer.

"Screw the calories," she mumbled as she opened the beer and took a long swallow. The carbonation tickled her throat. She released a sigh, then took another sip, then another, and another until she drained the bottle.

"Damn, that was good." She reached into the fridge and pulled out another beer. This time she decided not to chug it like a kid at a fraternity party, but savor the empty calories. As she sat on the couch though, slightly buzzed, surrounded by her animals and the scent of her former lover, she couldn't help think that maybe she'd handled the Hudson situation all wrong.

Two beers later she decided she'd definitely handled things with Hudson just fine.

"The rat bastard," she hiccupped, and looked to Brutal and Fabio. "Do you know what he did to me? Well, it wasn't pretty. In fact, it was downright ugly."

She took another swig and leaned closer to the animals. "He used me to get to my source." She nodded. "That's right. He *used* me. And get this, the guy, ya know, the source, he was a friggin' rapist. My darling lover allowed me to cavort with a rapist so that he could nail the bastard. And he didn't even bother to tell me. I mean, I was gang raped when I was a kid and he didn't think I should know who I was dealing with?"

You never told him.

"Oh my God." The bottle hit the floor with a thud, and she quickly bent to retrieve it. Thankfully she'd swallowed the last drop of beer, because she didn't have it in her to clean up the mess. Four beers on an empty stomach had been a stupid idea. Being angry with Hudson was foolish as well. How could she be mad at him for using her as bait—for a serial rapist—when she hadn't bothered to open up to him about her past?

But he could have at least told her that she'd become part of his plan to catch Mason Winters. They'd been partners in bed, hadn't they? Why couldn't they have been partners for life?

No. That's the beer talking.

Was it? She'd fallen hard for Hudson, and honestly believed he'd cared about her, too. Other than the whole Winters debacle, he'd treated her with respect, compassion and love? Maybe?

Officially drunk, her head hurting from too many beers and too many thoughts about the past, she decided to go to bed. But as she lay on the mattress, fully clothed and her head spinning in time with the ceiling fan, she wondered if maybe she should...try. Hudson had made it crystal clear that he still wanted her. In what capacity her muddled, mushy, beer-filled head couldn't decipher. All day he'd kept trying to bring up the past, so maybe—

She bolted upright, and gripped the comforter. Did she set the alarm? Did she even know how to set the alarm? She glanced at the clock. Only half past eight, she could call Hudson and ask him.

But she was drunk.

Shit. She couldn't call him. He'd find out she'd lied about her *date*.

Plus, she was horny.

"Damn it," she muttered, and reached for the cell phone she'd left on the nightstand.

Dressed in his scrubs, Michael Morrison stepped back to admire his handiwork. No sense of satisfaction ensued, though. The sight before him caused his hands to shake and his mouth to turn dry.

What the hell was he doing?

Knowing his patient would remain immobile, due to the drug he'd used to knock him out, he rushed from his OR and didn't stop until he'd reached the solitude of his office. He grabbed the open bottle of Wild Turkey and took several long swallows. Wiping his mouth with the back of his hand, he blinked his watery eyes.

"This is wrong," he whispered. "All wrong."

Did Dr. Westly deserve the punishment for his crime against Eliza? The man had been his daughter's dentist. He'd pulled a bunch of teeth out of her head, given her veneers...all of which Michael had thought unnecessary. Eliza's smile had been beautiful before the dentist had even touched her. She'd worn braces for two years while in high school, and the orthodontist had said her teeth were perfect. Not Dr. Westly, though. He'd convinced Eliza and her bitch of a mother that investing twenty grand for veneers was necessary if Eliza was to have a *perfect* smile.

Michael clenched his jaw as he remembered how Eliza had told him what the dentist had said about the veneers. The bastard had told his beautiful daughter that her smile, her teeth, were "just okay." Just okay hadn't settled well with his daughter, who had obvious self-confidence issues. Thanks to her mother, Eliza had become convinced she needed to take any measure, no matter how extreme, to make herself perfect. Or rather her mother's perception of perfect.

He brought the Wild Turkey to his lips again, and drank. As the whiskey traveled down his throat he looked to the still shot on the old TV. Michael had decided watching the DVD he'd created of Eliza would become part of each operation. The string of old home movies fueled his anger and grief. Especially this final still shot of Eliza lying on her bed, the razor wounds to her fragile wrists open and weeping with blood.

He then looked to the final letter she'd written to him before she'd taken her life.

Make them pay, Daddy.

After taking a final swig, he slammed the bottle of whiskey onto the desk. He would make them pay. Elliot paid for the botched up breast implants he'd given his daughter. He'd paid severely. Now, Dr. Brian Westly would pay. Yes, he might have simply been Eliza's dentist, but Westly had been involved with the group of plastic surgeons who had manipulated and mutilated his daughter. After Eliza had died, and he'd investigated the surgeons, Michael had learned that Westly enjoyed fat kickbacks for every patient he'd sent to the group.

The thought of Westly making money off the insecurities of his daughter and other naïve, young women, lavishing himself with expensive cars, vacation homes and exotic trips, made him physically sick. Bile rose in his throat, but he bit his lip and swallowed. The acidic burn from the Wild Turkey would serve as a reminder. Westly, and the others, would pay for their crimes.

With renewed determination and rage, he left the office and moved quickly into the OR. Westly still hadn't awakened, and remained restrained in the barber's chair Michael had bought at a garage sale. A slow smile tugged at his mouth as Michael anticipated Westly's reaction when he suddenly woke and realized he was in hell.

Michael grabbed a syringe from the nearby workbench and double-checked the amount of paralytic he would soon administer. He then made sure the video camera had been set properly. After a few quick adjustments, Michael approached his patient, then gave his bony face a hard slap.

Westly jerked, but remained immobile due to the duct tape Michael had wrapped around the man's head, hands, and ankles. Panic shone bright in Westly's eyes as he darted his gaze first at him, then around the room.

"Oh my God," the man yelled. "What the hell is this? Where am I?"

"Hell is exactly where you are, Dr. Westly. Welcome."

Westly rapidly blinked his eyes several times. "Wait, you're my…new patient. I checked your teeth today."

"That's right," Michael said as he raised the syringe. "What did you say when we were introduced? Ah…that's right. New patient or latest victim."

Westly stared at the syringe Michael held in front of him. His overlarge Adam's apple bobbed as he opened his mouth. "I…what did I do to you? Whatever it was, I'm sorry. I'm fucking sorry," he screamed and tried to kick his legs.

"There's no use in exerting your energy, Dr. Westly. You're fully restrained and will remain so until we've completed your procedure."

"What the hell are you talking about?" Westly darted his eyes from the syringe and then to the workbench. "Oh no. No, no, no, no. You can't be serious. You can't," he finished with a shout as he kept his gaze riveted on the Black and Decker drill.

"As a heart attack. Sorry, that was a bit clichéd," Michael said with a smile. "Now I suggest you calm down and relax."

"Calm down? Do you know who I am? I—"

Michael backhanded the dentist, then leaned into his face. "Make no mistake, I know exactly who you are, *Doctor* Brian Westly. You prey on naïve, young women with fragile egos and zero self-confidence. You make them feel bad about themselves in order to make a buck...or in my daughter's case, twenty thousand of them."

Tears streamed down Westly's face. "I don't know what you're talking about. Honestly. Please, if it's money you want..."

"I don't want your money."

"Then what? I'll give you anything you want."

"What I want you can't give me, unless you can raise people from the dead. Which I doubt, considering you can't figure a way out of this chair." Michael slapped the armrest, then raised the syringe again. "What I really want at the moment is for you to shut the hell up. I noticed earlier today, during my check-up in your office, that you talk too much. This will help."

Westly squirmed his ass against the chair.

"Calm down. This is a paralytic. It will only last for a minute, just long enough to keep you still while I ready you for your procedure. Don't worry, though, you'll be able to see, hear and *feel* everything I'm doing to you."

"Please...what procedure?"

Michael jabbed the man's arm and released the drug. "You ask too many questions." He turned and grabbed the thin metal chains he'd manipulated specifically for Westly's benefit. Each chain had been fashioned with two large, razor-sharp hooks. Knowing he had to work quickly before the drug wore off, he took one of the chains, pierced the inside of Westly's cheek with the hook, then gave it a tug. Blood, mingling with saliva, oozed from the corner of the dentist's mouth. Michael ignored the mess as he pulled the chain taut, and pierced the other hook through the man's ear. Certain the chain would hold, he hurriedly fastened the second chain to the other side of Westly's mouth.

Michael checked his watch. He only had fifteen to twenty seconds before the dentist would regain use of his body again.

Strips of duct tape, which he'd cut from the roll earlier, hung from the workbench. He pushed Westly's chin down in order to use the duct tape to keep his jaw from closing. Unfortunately, he hadn't anticipated the lack of mobility the hooks would cause.

"Well, Dr. Westly, I hadn't planned on adding this to your procedure, but I'm afraid we'll have to improvise."

He grabbed a hammer off the bench, then smacked the dentist's jaw until it dangled. With Westly's jaw hanging in a permanent yawn, Michael decided the duct tape wasn't necessary after all, which happened to be a good thing considering the paralytic would begin to wear off in a matter of seconds.

At that moment, Westly began to groan and his eyes rolled. Tears started to stream down his cheeks and fall into his perma-grin.

"Shh," Michael hissed. "Talking will only force the hooks deeper into your flesh. Trust me, what I have in store for you will be enough pain. You don't want to add any more."

Moaning and now fully alert, his eyes bright with fear and pain, Westly stared at him.

"I'll admit I know my way around surgery, just not *this* kind of surgery. But I did look it up on You Tube, so I feel confident that I'll do right by you."

Westly widened his eyes and tried to talk. More blood oozed from his mouth as the chains tightened.

"I told you not to try and speak." Michael reached for the Black and Decker, then set it on the man's lap. He then tied the surgical mask at the nape of his neck. "But I see you're uneasy. Maybe if you know what I'm going to do, that'll help you relax."

He moved to the video camera, checked the focus then said, "Do you remember your patient, Eliza Morrison? Blink once for yes, two for no."

One blink.

"Good. You see, she was my daughter. You convinced her to have teeth removed and replaced, and also talked her into veneers. You then sent her to the bastards who proceeded to talk my daughter into unnecessary surgeries. You know, breast implants, liposuction, nose job...understand?"

Two blinks.

"No? Hmm. You don't remember receiving money for patients you sent to Cosmetic Solutions and Med Spa?"

Tears filled Westly's eyes as he blinked twice.

"Tsk, tsk, Doctor. You're lying. Now tell the truth. Did you receive money for sending patients to those butchers at Med Spa?"

Westly blinked once and released a low, guttural moan.

"See, now doesn't it feel good to tell the truth? Here's the real truth behind your buddies at Cosmetic Solutions and Med Spa. They're all quacks. They talked not only my daughter, but as I've discovered during my research, many, many others just like her, into unnecessary surgeries. Some of those girls turned out okay, others are in therapy. Guess where my daughter is, Dr. Westly? Six feet under."

The dentist closed his eyes and groaned again.

"My sentiments exactly. Now, enough chit chat."

Michael turned on the video recorder, then moved toward his patient, and retrieved the drill from the man's lap.

"Open wide and say, ahh."

"That you, Pudge?"

"Yes," Pudge responded and slammed the door shut.

"You remember my Happy Jax this time?"

"Yes, you fat bitch," Pudge mumbled, then said loud enough for Mama to hear, "I'll bring it to you in a minute. Just let me change."

"Well, you better hurry on up, I'm starving. You can't expect me to—"

Mama's words fell on deaf ears as Pudge slammed the bathroom door shut. "I hate her," Pudge whispered.

me too me too kill her

"Don't start that again. Especially after what you did this morning to Mama."

so sorry precious dont be mad at me i love you

Pudge released a sigh and reached for the cold cream to remove the make-up. "I'm not mad at you. I can never stay mad at you. I love you, too. But I'm worried you might have caused a problem with Mama."

i told her i was sorry and made the bitch her breakfast

"I know you did, but remember what she said about the inheritance?"

yes yes we should kill her now kill her before she takes the money away

Pudge stopped, stared at the mirror and smiled. "She can't take the money away. Without me, she has no contact to the outside world. All I have to do is take the phone away and she's completely isolated."

wrong wrong wrong the visiting nurse the nurse remember the nurse

Pudge frowned. The inheritance could be in jeopardy. "Shit, the nurse. You're right. Mama could get the nurse to help her draw new papers changing her will."

cant happen cant cant kill her

"Damn it, I'm not killing Mama. I already told you—"

hello doctor dread hello

Grinning again, Pudge looked to the mirror. "You're so bad, and brilliant. That's why I love you so much." Pudge released a sigh. "Let's talk more about this in the morning. I don't want to think about Mama, I'd rather think about how much fun we had tonight."

so much fun so much

"And you didn't think it was a good idea."

sorry precious i shouldnt have doubted you youre so smart and sexy

Pudge's smile grew at the compliment. Only recently were people beginning to see Pudge as someone to admire and respect. Not a pudgy punching bag. Except for Mama. But Mama would be put in her place. Pudge would see to it. No one would interfere with the plan. Too much was at stake.

i enjoyed our lover enjoyed enjoyed

Naked, Pudge sniffed the clothes recently removed. After inhaling the strong scent of semen still lingering on the clothes, Pudge released another sigh. "I enjoyed myself immensely. But not as much as my time with you." Pudge giggled. "Or what we'd done afterward."

yes yes but we should have killed her

"You have a two track mind," Pudge scolded, but with a slight smile to lessen the blow. "Sex and murder."

money fame fortune money fame fortune

"Okay, so more than a two track mind," Pudge chuckled. "Don't worry, we'll kill her. When the time is right."

tonight was right tonight tonight

Pudge finished dressing, then checked the mirror for any remnants of the disguise. "Tonight wasn't the right time. You know as well as I do that we weren't prepared. We have to stick with the plan. Plus, it looks like she has a new boy toy. We have to be cautious and make sure she's alone…all night." When Pudge had lurked around Eden Risk's townhouse, an alarm had been raised. Not literally, but figuratively. The woman was alone, but without knowing the depth of her relationship with tall, dark and sexy, Pudge didn't want to take any chances. Plus, Pudge had noticed a small change to Eden's townhouse. A security camera.

the man would be fun fun fun

"Mmm," Pudge hummed. "He would. Very sexy."

kill eden kill her make him our boy toy please please

A loud crash splintered from the living room, drawing Pudge's attention away from the mirror. "I better go see what that dumb bitch did now."

attention thats what she wants and her happy jax stuff it down her throat stuff it down make her choke

Pudge smiled and reached for the door knob. "You really are bad."

yes yes very bad very bad lets be bad together

"We have been, and we will be again. Patience, honey," Pudge said to the mirror, then opened the door and turned off the light. After Mama had fed her face, Pudge would retreat to the bedroom and formulate a plan. If everything worked as anticipated, Eden would be dead by the end of the week. As for Mama…Pudge had suffered the woman's abuse for over twenty-five years, a few more months was manageable. Mama's nurse would be, too.

CHAPTER 7

"DID YOU SLEEP here?"

Hudson jolted in the chair, reached for the gun strapped to his ankle then aimed.

"Damn it, Rachel," he said as he replaced the weapon. "Don't do that to me."

Rachel stood in the doorway of CORE's evidence and evaluation room, her big green eyes taking up most of her face as she stared at him. "You? How about me? A simple 'good morning' would have been nice."

While she acted as if being threatened with a gun at six in the morning was an everyday occurrence, her labored breathing said otherwise. He'd scared the shit out of her.

He rubbed his eyes, then stretched. "Sorry. Good morning. And yes, I did sleep here."

Eyeing him with caution, she turned and peered at his laptop's screen. "Who you spying on?"

"I wasn't spying on anybody. Just watching."

"Eden?"

"No, her townhouse."

"What does her *date* look like? Cute?"

He cracked his neck and tried to tamp down his irritation. While he wasn't necessarily irked with Rachel, he didn't need the reminder that Eden had kicked him out of her house for another man. And lied about it.

"Her date never showed. And even if he had…I highly doubt I'd ever use the word 'cute' to describe any man."

Rachel raised her eyebrows. "No date? Hmm."

"Hmm," Hudson echoed. "What's that supposed to mean?"

She shrugged. "Whatever you want it to, I suppose. Not that it's any of my business, but I guess I'd be wondering why she'd lie and put herself at risk rather than be alone with you."

Hudson stood, then moved to the coffee pot and filled two mugs. After he offered one to Rachel, he sat at the edge of the desk. "I know," he said with a deep sigh. "She's still pissed at me for what I did during the Winters case, but that's no reason to put herself in a potentially bad situation."

"So you sat here all night watching. How do you think she'll feel about that?"

He winced. Knowing Eden, and how she liked her privacy, she'd be doubly pissed. "She doesn't have to know."

"Huh," Rachel grunted as she stared at his laptop. "Then how are you going to explain knowing about the guy dropping a package at her front door?"

Hudson rushed to the computer and squinted at the screen. "Holy shit. I gotta go." He grabbed his jacket and keys, then reached for the computer.

Rachel stopped him. "Leave the laptop. I'll see if I can find out who this guy is."

Five minutes later, he drove the Trans Am out of the parking garage. After making a quick turn, he pulled his cell phone out of his pocket. As he was about to call Eden, the phone rang. He checked the screen. Eden.

"Morning," he answered, trying to keep his tone light, even as his heart raced.

"Hudson, thank God," she said in a rush. "There was a man at my door just a second ago."

"I'm on my way, and will be there in less than fifteen. Don't answer the door until I get there."

"I won't. I didn't. When I was going to take Brutal out to go potty, I checked the peephole first and saw him. Scared the shit out of me."

Damn, there was a lot of shit scaring going on this morning. Not knowing the identity of the man or his intentions, and that Eden was alone and unprotected, scared the shit out of him, too. He might have used her as bait during the Winters case, but she'd been surrounded by CORE agents and never in a position where harm would come to her. This time around though...this time there were too many uncertainties.

He decided then and there that under no circumstance would she be allowed to remain alone. At any time. Screw her dates, real or imagined. He refused to lose her twice. Being near her again had solidified what he'd known all along...he'd never stopped caring.

Hudson remained on the phone with her, listening to Eden's nervous babbling about the poor rat dog's bitty bladder, until he reached her townhouse. He ended the call and raced up the steps. A newspaper sat at the front door.

The door swung open as he was about to pick up the paper. "Is it another DVD?" Eden asked in a hushed, conspiratorial tone.

"Looks like your morning paper."

"I don't get the paper."

He looked up at her, took in the fear brightening her puffy eyes, then glanced back to the paper. With the cuff of his jacket, he gave the folded paper a shove. A blur of black and white opened, revealing a familiar manila envelope.

"Oh my God," she whispered. "He's killed again."

Eden's stomach cramped as she sat inside CORE's evidence and evaluation room. The DVD jacket had been checked for fingerprints, but as before, nothing had been found.

While Rachel readied the DVD for viewing and Hudson

finished talking with Ian in the hallway, she waited with nervous anticipation and morbid curiosity. Maybe the doctor hadn't killed someone this time, or maybe, if he had murdered another victim, they'd find new clues to help them stop him from killing again.

She clutched her churning belly and wished for the umpteenth time that she hadn't drank all those beers last night. What had she been thinking? And when she'd woken up and found her cell phone lying next to her with Hudson's number on the screen, she'd panicked. In her drunken stupor, she'd almost called him. Thank God she'd passed out before that mistake had happened. With the mood she'd been in last night, she might have thrown herself at him.

And if they'd had sex, what then? Would they fall back into their old pattern of having mind-blowing sex on a regular basis while tiptoeing around their emotions? She honestly didn't think she could handle another relationship with Hudson on those terms. But she also wasn't sure she could expose her emotions, her reasons for having been so disgusted and angry with him after the Winters debacle, either. Even her family had no clue what had happened to her when she'd been in high school, or how that event had shaped her—good and bad—into the person she'd ultimately become...an obsessive-compulsive, introverted loner. No one had needed to know how she'd made a fool of herself, or how she continued to let that night rule her existence. Her family had always admired her strength—why disappoint them, or herself, again?

She smoothed her hair, then tightened her ponytail. Besides, what would be the point of telling Hudson anything? By the end of the month she'd move to New York to take the Network job. When that happened, there would be no future with Hudson. He was just as married to his career as she was to hers.

The door to the evidence and evaluation room opened, and Hudson entered. Wearing his ugly shit kickers, jeans and another thermal shirt—this one a lighter shade of gray—he made her heart jump and her stomach coil with something other than hangover nausea.

She tamped down the lust coursing through her veins and shifted in her chair. "Is Ian joining us?"

"No, he's heading to D.C. for business and doesn't have time."

"Poo," Rachel said. "He's going to miss the early morning matinée."

Hudson cracked a small smile. "Bummer for him." He looked to Eden. "Ah...you don't have to watch this. Actually, Ian suggested you use his office while we review the DVD."

She folded her hands and let them rest in her lap. A part of her wanted to jump at Ian's offer, but the investigative reporter in her demanded she sit through the damned thing. Besides, the killer had sent the DVD to her house. He'd targeted her. And this time, she wanted to be part of the team that stopped him. Not the bait.

"I appreciate the offer, but I'd rather stay."

With his mouth set in a grim line, he stared at her for a moment, then said, "Suit yourself. Ready, Rachel."

With a nod, Rachel hit PLAY, and within seconds, the TV screen came to life.

"Oh my God," Rachel murmured, and without looking, slumped into a chair.

Eden suppressed a gasp while a cold shiver momentarily shook her body.

"Damn," Hudson muttered with disgust. "Pause it."

Rachel hit a button on the remote and the TV went still. A man, grotesquely bound to a chair, filled the screen and Eden suddenly wished she'd taken Ian's offer. Her empty stomach rolled and sweat beaded along her upper lip. She swiped at her mouth, then looked away.

"Do you think there's any way to ID him?" she asked, trying to take her mind off the inevitable. Barfing in CORE's evidence and evaluation room, in front of Rachel and Hudson, was out of the question. She was Eden Risk, damn it. Hard core. Tough as frozen dog shit. She'd seen dozens of horrific crime scenes and had earned the respect of Chicagoans along with CPD and other law enforcement agencies. She wasn't a puker unless it was purposeful. And she'd stopped shoving her fingers down her throat years ago when her dentist told her the enamel on her teeth had begun to wear due to acidity.

Dentist.

She shifted her gaze back to the screen. "Wait, the victim's a dentist."

"You took the words right out of my mouth," Rachel said, then winced. "Bad word choice." She stood and approached the screen with a pointer. "We've got a drill in his lap, his head is taped to the chair and his mouth...God, this is like something out of the movie *Hellraiser.*"

Hudson crossed his arms and rested his ass on the edge of the desk next to her. "Okay, so first he gives a guy, who we're thinking is a plastic surgeon, breast implants, now he's performing dental surgery? I'm wondering if there's a connection between the two men or if he's choosing them at random."

"If that's the case, then there goes your theory about vengeance," Rachel said.

"Unless he knows them somehow," Eden countered. "Based on the OR this guy's created, his equipment, the drugs...maybe he's in the medical field and that's how he knows the victims."

"Maybe. Makes sense. But without a body or ID..." He trailed off, then nodded to Rachel. "Start it up again."

Once more, the screen came to life. Low, painful moans filled the room. Silver tape wrapped the victim's head. His cheeks were bloodied and swollen, and in the shape of a gruesome grin. His jaw dangled at such an odd angle, she couldn't tell what the man looked like before the killer had tortured him. She touched her own cheeks, unable to imagine the pain the man must have endured.

"Open wide and say, ahh," the killer said as he took the drill from the man's lap. "I'm not going to lie. You're *definitely* going to feel some pain."

Anticipating what the doctor had in store for his victim,

Eden's skin crawled as the drill came alive, whirring and humming. "God, no," she whispered, then clapped a hand over her mouth in horror.

The man strapped to the chair released a high-pitched, painful scream as he raised his torso and tensed the rest of his body. Blood poured from the holes in his cheeks and ears. With each touch of the drill, more blood oozed from his dangling jaw.

The scene ended as quickly as it had started. But, based on the tools lying on the workbench next to the chair, she suspected the killer was far from finished.

The doctor set the drill back in the man's lap. With his back still to the camera, he reached for a pair of pliers. "This won't do." He shook his head. "Looks like we're going to have to extract a few of your teeth before we can proceed with the veneers."

"No way," Rachel said on a gasp.

More screams rocked the room as the doctor ripped a tooth from the man's head.

Eden's stomach flipped. She looked away, and caught Hudson's gaze.

"Doing okay?" he asked, and reached for her hand.

She didn't pull away. Instead, she held onto him, seeking his comfort and strength. Not a fan of the dentist to begin with, she doubted she'd enter a dental office of her own free will again.

Nodding, she held onto his hand, then turned her attention back to the TV just as the doctor dropped the tooth into a bag. He reached for the pliers again and, while the man released a painful scream, pulled another tooth free.

"There, that wasn't too bad," the doctor said as he placed the next tooth into the bag. "I think we're ready to prep your teeth for the veneers now."

He withdrew a large, metal file from the workbench, then paused. "Like I said, I Googled veneers and saw an entire procedure on You Tube. So I've got a pretty good idea how to do right by you. Unfortunately," he said as he waved the file. "I don't exactly have the proper equipment. For our purposes though, this should do the trick."

Eden tightened her grip on Hudson's hand. She couldn't begin to imagine the pain the victim had endured as the doctor proceeded to file the man's teeth. With each scrape of the file, she winced and fought the acidy bile burning her throat. After what seemed like an eternity, but according to the timer on the DVD player had only been about a minute, the doctor stopped.

He dropped the file on the man's lap, then rubbed his chin with the back of a Latex gloved hand. After a few seconds, he flicked the victim's nose. The man didn't make a sound or flinch.

"Holy crap," Rachel said, and leaned closer to the screen. "I think he's dead."

Eden looked to Hudson. "We didn't see him kill the last victim. We only assumed he was dead. This time, we have him torturing a man to the point where his body gave out and he died."

"That's felony murder. After what this guy's done, it's too bad Illinois doesn't have the death penalty anymore," he said.

Rachel paused the DVD and turned to them. "Doesn't matter. We still don't have a body, and without physical evidence…" She shrugged, then said, "I can understand why your cop friend suggested the first DVD might be a hoax. First, no one wants to believe anyone could be capable of such atrocities. Second, with the way they can do special effects, who's to say this isn't fake?"

"You don't seriously believe that, do you?" Eden asked, shocked Rachel would even suggest what they'd witnessed wasn't real. Sure, she agreed that the special effects shown in movies had become eerily realistic, but would an amateur be able to create a film like this, or the one with the breast implants? When she realized the answer was "yes," a seed of doubt took root. Maybe the whole thing was a hoax used to gain her attention, or better yet, gain the attention of someone in Hollywood.

"I'm not saying I do," Rachel responded with a shake of her head. "I don't know what to think. Maybe——"

"Let's just finish the damned thing," Hudson interrupted. "We'll discuss all of this afterward."

Rachel raised an auburn eyebrow. "As you wish," she said, and hit PLAY.

The doctor released a deep sigh, and with a shake of his capped head, he turned to face the camera.

"God, this guy is creepy," Rachel said with a shiver. "Just looking at him gives me the heebie jeebies."

Eden agreed. During the last film, the doctor had drawn a bucktoothed smile on his surgical mask. This time he'd gone with a similar theme, giving the mask a jagged, Jack O' Lantern smile...minus several teeth.

Folding his arms across his chest, the doctor approached the camera. With the cap and mask, Eden couldn't tell what the man looked like, except for his eyes. Bright blue and lined with crow's feet, she swore his eyes spoke of sadness and grief. For the man in the chair, or for something else? Maybe the reason he'd begun this torturous murder spree in the first place?

"Well, that didn't go as I'd expected." The doctor shrugged. "Win some, lose some, I suppose."

He suddenly turned, and retrieved something she couldn't see from the workbench. "While I didn't quite finish filing his teeth, I can't let him leave without at least finishing what I've started."

The doctor moved to the dead man, then shoved something into his mouth. After a few adjustments, he stepped back and nodded. "That's better, don't you think?"

"*Fucking* creepy," Rachel muttered.

Eden couldn't agree more. With the way the man's face had been hooked and forced into a grin, the fake, overlarge, crooked teeth the doctor had placed in the man's mouth gave him an eerie, and yes, fucking creepy smile.

"We'll just slip these in here..." The doctor tucked the small bag filled with the victim's teeth into the man's bloodied shirt. "You know, for the Tooth Fairy."

He stepped back, then approached the camera again. "Hello, Eden," he said as he began plucking off a Latex glove. "Thank you for not going to the police, but I am disappointed you didn't air my last DVD. I guess I understand, though. I wish we could talk, because I'd love to know if *you* understand."

"What does he mean by that?" Rachel asked.

"Shh," Hudson hissed.

"This…" The doctor motioned to the man strapped to the chair. "This is a tragedy that could have been stopped. If only *he* had stopped when I asked him. If only *he* had done the right thing. But he didn't. None of them did. Now they pay."

He dropped the bloodied glove on the workbench, then began removing the other. "I'd told you that I wanted you to be my voice, but I now realize my error. I can't expect you to air these DVDs. I know that now. But I do expect you to watch them and learn from them. When I've finished what I've started, you will have one hell of a story for your new investigative show."

"Oh my God, he knows about my Network contract," Eden said, and tightened her hold on Hudson's hand. When he squeezed back, she glanced at him. The reassurance in his eyes gave her little strength. They didn't know who the killer was, who his next victim would be, and he seemed to know way too much about her.

"I know you'll tell my story when the time's right. Then, and only then, will people begin to understand. I told you before, there's no such thing as perfect, only perception. What we perceive as perfect is mere opinion. Yours. Mine. We've all seen ugly kids. Do the parents of those kids see them as ugly?" He shrugged and dropped the glove. "When you look at that scarred cat and three-legged dog of yours, do you see them as ugly?"

Eden sucked in a deep breath. He knew about her animals, too. Had he been in her house? Did she actually *know* him?

"I'm guessing you don't. I believe that you look at them

and don't even see their flaws. Because you love them. Don't deny it," he said, and wagged his finger. "I've seen the way your face lights up when you're with them. It amazes me, though. You demand perfection from yourself, yet surround yourself with flawed people and animals. And yes, I realize you have flaws of your own, but you don't let anyone else see them, do you? You're tough, but a body can only take so much. Of this I know too well. It's also the reason why I'm here." He raised his hands and slowly spun in a circle. "In my private OR."

He shook his head. "I'm not going to expect you to air this DVD. But you can expect to receive another. I'm sure they're difficult to watch, but I assure you there is not only a method to my...madness, but only two more to go."

"He's being generous with clues this time," Rachel commented.

"In the meantime, I want you to know that I'm pleased with your new security system. After I picked up my patient this evening, I drove by your townhouse and noticed the security cameras. I also noticed you had a visitor. I couldn't exactly get out of my car and go after that person." He jerked his thumb toward the dead man. "After all I had a procedure to perform. But given the chance, I'd take care of whoever it is watching you. I don't want anything to happen to you, Eden. No matter how things may appear, I mean that. I—"

The doctor stopped as a noise, reminding her of baying wolves, permeated the surround sound in the evidence and evaluation room.

"Rachel," Hudson said.

"On it," she replied, and raised the volume.

"I have to go now," the doctor said. "It's time for dinner." As he reached for the camera, he paused. "No deadlines this time. After tonight, I'm going to need to take a few days off. Be safe, Eden."

The TV screen went black.

"Those were dogs in the background," Rachel said as she began to rewind the DVD. "I'm going to filter out the sound and run it against different breeds. Maybe this guy raises dogs. Which would make sense. He's obviously not in the city, and I highly doubt he's in the Burbs. The building isn't sound proof enough, considering we heard the dogs."

Hudson shook his head. "Run it against coyotes first, before you waste time on other breeds."

Rachel looked at him. "Huh. Look at you. Badass agent *and* coyote expert."

"When I was a kid I used to hunt with my dad. Coyotes have a distinct sound, that's all."

Eden stared at Hudson and tried to imagine him as a kid. She had a hard time looking past the rugged, sexy adult, not to mention the five o'clock shadow.

"Let's review the DVD again," Rachel suggested. "Our doctor seemed more relaxed this time, and definitely more forthcoming. Don't you think?"

Hudson nodded. "Agreed. But right now I'm more interested in the guy who delivered the DVD. Were you able to ID him?"

"Yep. Guessing he was over sixteen, I ran his picture against driver's license photos from the Illinois DMV." She looked to Eden. "Shh, don't tell. The DMV wouldn't be happy if they knew about this."

Eden nodded. Even the investigative reporter inside of her wouldn't tell a soul. She could care less how Rachel or any member of CORE received their information on this case, so long as they stopped the killer.

"And," Rachel continued as she grabbed a sheet of paper off of her desk, then handed it to Hudson. "We got a hit. Meet Evan Pope . Seventeen. Lives in Lincoln Park with his folks and is a senior at Douglas High School."

"He made the drop at Eden's at six A.M. School doesn't start that early, so maybe he's a carrier for the Chicago Tribune," Hudson suggested as he looked at Evan Pope's picture.

"How did you get a picture...?" Eden pulled her hand away from Hudson's, then hugged herself. "Never mind," she said, and fought the urge to storm out of the room. How could she have been so blind? Even the killer commented on the security cameras. With everything that had been happening, she hadn't noticed the devices or where Hudson had installed them.

Stupid. Stupid. Stupid.

Although the cameras were able to give them the ID of the kid who'd dropped the DVD at her front door, the damn things also gave away her secret. Hudson had worn an excellent poker face this morning. She'd bet anything that he knew there was no date last night and that she'd slept alone.

Fine with her.

She didn't care what he thought either way. He should have told her about the cameras. Just as he should have told her about Winters.

"We need to talk with him," Eden said as she checked her watch. "But he's probably in school now. Let's go over the DVD again, then I need to head back to my townhouse to change. I'd like to make it into the station for a few hours today. *If* that's okay with you."

Hudson eyed Eden, who had turned her back to him. He hadn't missed the sarcasm, and was thankful Rachel was in the room. Maybe by the time they left CORE, Eden would have calmed down enough about the security camera—or the fact that she'd been caught in a lie—to not start another argument. He didn't want to fight with her. While he hated watching the DVD, he'd loved holding her hand. Such a simple thing, yet the act had spoken volumes.

She trusted him.

Maybe.

He didn't know and had no business analyzing the reasons behind the hand holding phenomenon. All he knew was that he loved touching her again, he didn't want to fight, and that they had another sick DVD to dissect.

"That's fine," he answered. "Going to the station will kill time before we find Pope. Hopefully he can describe our killer."

"If not, maybe he saw the car he was driving," Rachel

added, then waved the remote. "Are we ready to do this again?"

"No," he and Eden said simultaneously.

He glanced at Eden and realized she looked like hell. Purple smudges marred her tired, puffy eyes, and her face appeared almost ashen.

"Why don't you sit this one out," he suggested to her. "There's some breakfast sandwiches in the lunchroom freezer or you can help yourself to—"

She shook her head and sat. "I'm fine. Let's just get this over with."

He didn't think she looked fine. But he couldn't stop her from viewing the DVD again. Well, he could. He just didn't want to add another item to her bitch list. The arguing had grown old. He wanted to start fresh, and this time, do things right. While it still pissed him off that she'd lied to him about her date, a part of him couldn't be happier. No date meant no other man was sleeping in her bed.

He nodded to Rachel. "Fire it up."

Thirty minutes later, the dry erase board had been filled with a list of clues to investigate.

"Okay," Rachel began. "We suspect the latest victim is a dentist, the previous one a plastic surgeon. We think the killer has his OR in the country, but within driving distance to Chicago."

She tapped a few buttons on her keyboard. A map of Illinois and the surrounding states popped up on one of the screens. "So if our victims are from Chicago and the killer is doing his dirty work in the country..."

"From what he said on the DVD, it sounds as if he picked up the dentist, drove past my townhouse last night, then drove to his OR and completed his...surgery. Considering the DVD was placed at my door at six this morning, I don't think he could have driven more than four hours round trip."

"Maybe even less than that," Hudson said. "We also have to consider the time it took for him to prep the vic and dispose of the body."

"It's time for dinner," Rachel mimicked the killer. "That line bothers me. Do you think he's disposing the bodies via dog?"

Eden's body shuddered. "That's a disgusting thought."

"No kidding," Rachel agreed. "Think about it, though. If we can't ID the victims or the killer, and the dogs…eat the bodies, what do we have?"

"Shit," he grunted.

"Exactly," Rachel said.

"No, I'm saying we have shit. Dog shit. Coyote shit. Ask that lab guy who does our DNA stuff if it's possible to extract DNA from shit or stomach contents."

Both women cringed when they looked at him.

He shrugged. "Just a thought."

"A gross one," Eden mumbled. "Can we go back to the driving distance thing?"

"After you two leave, I'll check the areas in Illinois and Indiana that are within two hours driving distance from Chicago."

"What about Wisconsin?" he asked.

"It's close to three hours from here."

"Good enough. Look for farming communities, anything rural. With the amount of screaming we heard on both DVDs, this guy's got to live on a bunch of acres."

"Unless he killed the neighbors and fed them to the dogs," Rachel said as she jotted notes.

"Really, Rachel," Eden said with disgust.

Rachel reached for a pencil and brought it to her lips. "Just saying."

He rubbed his hand along his forehead. Although good at her job, sometimes Rachel's mind went to the macabre. "Anyway," he said to end the discussion of dogs eating people. "I know this isn't going to get us any closer to finding our guy, but as clues add up, it may help. Now back to a few other things on our list. Actually, two glaring things. The first, he told us that there will be only two more DVDs, which means two more victims."

"He also said that he planned to take a few days off," Eden reminded him.

"Right," he began. "So we need to—"

Eden held up her hand. "If I may, I suggest we keep our focus on the victims. The killer has made it clear that this is about revenge. During this DVD he said that the victim didn't listen to him, that this was a tragedy that could have been stopped. That none of them had listened and now they have to pay. There's *got* to be a connection to the victims and to the killer." She turned to Rachel. "Can you pull up any missing persons reports for the Chicago area?"

"Promise you won't tell?" Rachel asked with a conspiratorial wink.

"I take that as a yes."

"Uh-huh. The problem with that is we don't have a good description of the vics."

"But we suspect what they do for a living," he added.

"Still," she countered. "These are grown men. Unless the killer left behind evidence of foul play, their families might not even report them missing. Maybe they think they've gone on vacation or on a business trip." She tapped the pencil against her chin. "On the bright side, I do have data to go through from our first vic. I've got a list of plastic surgeons who live in Illinois and Indiana, and were members of the Sigma Alpha Mu fraternity. I'll do what I did with Evan Pope, pull up their driver's licenses and see if any of the men even come close to the hairy guy on the first DVD."

"Good. Call if you come up with anything," Hudson said, and reached for his jacket. He needed to take Eden to her townhouse, and then to the station. As a senior, Pope might finish school early, and he wanted to catch up with the kid as quickly as possible. Right now, he was their only link to the killer.

Eden grabbed his arm as she rose. "Wait. What was the second thing?"

"Your stalker's back.

CHAPTER 8

HUMMING, PUDGE LEFT the uniform store. Thanks to the new purchases, phase one of their plans would begin tonight, then it was off to phase two. After that, they would have only one more thing to take care of...Eden Risk.

yes yes kill her take her boy toy take her life her life

Pudge smiled. They would take her life, literally. Pudge would become the next Eden Risk. Only better. After a few months, Chicagoans would have forgotten all about Eden. Mama would hopefully be dead, and Dr. Dread would have become an unsolved mystery.

Standing on the curb of the busy street, Pudge waved at a passing taxi. The car came to a stop, and after entering, Pudge set the packages and backpack on the seat.

"Where to?" the cabbie asked as he looked in the rearview mirror.

Phase one wouldn't begin until later, but plans for phase two needed to be set in motion. For that, Pudge needed to do some serious recon. If they screwed up...

wont happen wont happen youre too smart too smart

Pudge stuffed the packages into the backpack, then looked at the window. Not even Mama would recognize the person in the reflection. Neither would Eden.

"Take me to WBDJ, Channel 5 news station on Clark

Street."

"Yes, sir," the cabbie said as he shifted the car into drive, and pulled away from the curb.

Eden hugged the toilet bowl as her stomach revolted again. Over the years, she'd learned to become a quiet puker. A talent, an extreme necessity, and the only way she'd been able to keep her bulimia a secret from her family, former roommates and co-workers. While she'd controlled those barf sessions, she couldn't control this one. Maybe she had the flu. She'd drunk four beers—if not more—in the past, and had never felt this shitty.

With nothing left in her stomach, she clutched the toilet and now endured painful dry heaves. Because she hadn't had a chance to exercise yesterday, she hadn't bothered to eat. Because she'd felt like crap when she'd woken up today, she hadn't touched a morsel of food. Now that she thought about it, she couldn't remember the last time she sat and ate a meal. Two days ago? Maybe?

Sweating and shivering at the same time, she used the hand towel to wipe her mouth. A few minutes later, she dragged herself off the tile floor, then started the shower. Although lethargic and achy, she moved through her toiletries. Since her series aired on Sundays, she needed to give the last segment of Beauty Pageant Queen Bees a few final touches before her station manager could review it for approval. God, she really didn't want to talk with Rodger Jeffries. She hadn't seen the station manager since the on-air debacle with Kyle Edwards had happened two nights ago. She'd tried calling Jeffries, and had also approached his office yesterday. But her calls had gone into voice mail and his secretary had told her he was too busy to see her.

"Bullshit," she muttered as she dressed. She'd heard Jeffries in his office, and had also heard Kyle's distinctive voice. Since accepting the Network job, she'd noticed that the anchor and station manager had become quite chummy. What did she care? In a matter of weeks, she'd leave them in the dust.

After checking her reflection, she shook her head. Damn, she looked terrible. Even the extra make-up couldn't hide the bags under her eyes or brighten her ashen complexion. But she had a job to do, and an infuriating man waiting for her in the living room.

Leaving the bedroom, she forced her achy legs to move. Flats would have been the way to go today, except she needed the height of the three-inch heels to elongate her legs. While vanity could be an ugly thing, on her, stubby legs were uglier.

"Feeling any better?" Hudson asked as he wadded a wrapper from the fast food breakfast sandwich he'd just eaten.

The thought of the sausage and egg concoction made her stomach queasy. She pressed on her belly, and quickly moved into the living room to avoid the lingering, greasy odor.

"I'm fine," she answered when he entered the room.

"You sure?" he asked. "No offense, but you don't look fine."

"I think I have the flu. What's your excuse?"

He chuckled. "I'm suddenly starting to miss the silent treatment you gave me in the car."

She hadn't meant to keep quiet during the ride from CORE to her townhouse. Actually, she'd wanted to go off on him about a few things. The only reason she'd kept her mouth shut was to avoid puking all over the Trans Am's upholstery.

"Sorry if I'm not looking dapper enough for you. I had a long night at the office," he said, then looked to the floor where Brutal pawed at his pant leg. When he picked up the dog and stroked him behind the ears, she nearly melted.

She must be sick—in the head. The little cuddling he gave her dog shouldn't have any effect on her. Damn it, he'd tricked her again. Yesterday, even when she'd been spouting off about her *date* spending all night with her, he'd probably been scheming. Thinking he'd spy on her and her date with his stupid security cameras. Instead, he'd caught her in a lie.

"Yeah, I know. Spying on me," she blurted, then instantly

regretted her words. First the vomiting, now she had diarrhea of the mouth. While showering, she'd sworn she wasn't going to bring up anything about the security cameras. She didn't want Hudson to know how he'd upset her, even if the drunk girl from last night thought they were made for each other. Maybe that drunken girl had been right, but it didn't matter. Too much had happened between them in the past to consider a future. He hadn't changed, she knew she certainly hadn't, and she was leaving for New York in a few weeks. Period. End of story. Enough said.

After Brutal gave his stubbled cheek a lick, he set the dog on the floor. "I wasn't spying. I was looking over information for the case."

Keep your mouth shut, she reminded herself. *Don't let him goad you.*

"Hmm," she grunted while gathering her computer case.

"It's true. The only time I bothered to look at the security camera feed was when you walked into your bedroom. Alone."

She dropped the case on the couch. "You son of a bitch," she shouted. "You spied on me in my bedroom?"

"I didn't—"

"Pig."

"Any other names you want to call me, or are you going to let me explain?"

"There's nothing to explain. Actually, it all makes sense to me now."

He folded his arms across his chest. "How's that?"

"I should have known you were up to something. After the he-man, 'I remember how you screamed my name' crap, I figured you would have called at some point last night to interrupt my date. But, you didn't need to because you already knew there wasn't a date."

He shoved his hands in the pockets of his jeans, and nodded. "True."

"True? That's all you have to say?"

"Make it easy on me. Tell me what you want me to say."

"Sorry would be a start."

He shrugged. "Okay, sorry."

"Like you mean it."

Narrowing his eyes, he pulled his hands from his pockets and took a step forward. "That's all you're going to get from me."

Shaking her head she glanced to the ceiling. "Why doesn't that surprise me?" she asked then looked at him. "God forbid if you actually own up to something when you're wrong."

"Back atcha."

"Really," she began, and took a step toward him. "I love how you're turning this around on me. *I* didn't do anything wrong. Then or now."

"Oh, here we go," he said, and threw his hands in the air. "You never do anything wrong. You don't lie. And you sure as hell don't avoid the truth."

"I only lied last night because I wanted you out of my house. You, on the other hand, have a lot of room to talk. You spent the entire time we were together avoiding the truth...and lying."

He took another step forward. "Bullshit. You were the one who couldn't handle it."

"It? What do you mean?"

Another step and he invaded her space. "Me." He reached and tucked a lock of her hair behind her ear. "Us."

"I handled you and us just fine," she murmured, and fought the urge to rest her cheek in his strong palm. She felt like crap and until she had time to consider the truth behind his words, she needed to keep herself guarded. She refused to allow him to hurt her again.

"Yeah, the moment you found a chance to run, you did."

Damn the man was perceptive. Here she'd thought she'd been so smart, and he'd been onto her the whole time.

"That's not true," she lied. Again. "I—"

He rested his hands on her shoulders. "Stop. Please. Just stop. I screwed up during the Winters case. I should have kept you in the loop. But Winters was your source and you'd become tight with him. I couldn't risk...I couldn't let anything happen to you. I apologized to you then, and I'm apologizing to you now. I should have treated you better. I should have trusted my gut and told you everything." He gave her shoulders a squeeze. "Now, trust me when I tell you that I've been regretting my actions for two long years."

Thank God he held her shoulders. Otherwise she might have dropped to the floor in a puddle of mush. His words, his apology… Damn, the shame, the pain, and the longing in his eyes. She'd never meant to hurt him. She'd honestly thought ending their relationship before it became ugly had been a smart move. In her heart, she'd truly believed things between them would grow ugly. They were too alike to make it as a couple. Both married to their careers, both hardheaded, both ready to step on anyone's toes to achieve their goals. And neither one of them could admit to their feelings. Yet, Hudson had changed since they'd been together. He seemed determine to break past both his and her emotional barriers. Was she ready for that?

She needed time to think. She needed space.

God, she needed to puke.

"Hud, I've got to—"

"Let me finish. I need to tell you the truth about something," he said, and cupped her face. "Holy shit, Eden. You're burning up."

Clapping a hand over her mouth, she shoved past him and ran for the bathroom. His shit kickers made a racket against the hardwood floor as he followed her.

"Go away," she shouted as she reached the toilet. "I need to be—"

Unable to fight the urge, she retched.

Instead of leaving the bathroom, Hudson stayed and held her hair away from her face. When her stomach settled, he released her hair, then ran a washcloth under the faucet. He flushed the toilet, then gently dabbed her mouth and forehead.

"Do you have a thermometer?" he asked.

"No. I'm sure my temperature is fine. My face is probably hot from…exerting myself."

"Too much of a lady to say puking?" he teased as he soaked the washcloth again.

She cracked a smile, then released a deep sigh when he rubbed the cool material against her face. "Yeah, I'm the picture of a proper lady right now." She grabbed his wrist. Their gazes collided. "Thank you. And...I'm sorry, too."

He set the washcloth on the counter, then began to help her stand. "Shh, not now. Let's get you out of these clothes and into bed."

"Where have I heard that line before?" she asked with a grin, then stopped him. "I'm fine. Really. Besides, I have to get to the station. My show airs Sunday. If I don't go today, and Rusty has to help me over the weekend, I'll have to buy him a dozen donuts for the rest of my life."

"Make him work the weekend or give him the flu. Tough choice," he said as he forced her to sit on the edge of the bed. "Which do you think he'd prefer?"

Too weak to argue, she let him remove her heels. If she weren't sick, she'd have been completely turned on right now. Watching this sexy, badass man cup her foot with his big hands made her temperature rise. The flu bug didn't help, either.

Knowing he was right, and too exhausted to change her clothes, she lay back on the mattress and closed her eyes. "You're right. I'll just doze off for a few hours, then see how I feel. If I owe Rusty a lifetime's worth of donuts..."

He smoothed the hair away from her face. "Don't worry about Rusty," he said, and pulled the comforter over her. "Remember the blonde who was here with John Kain the other night? She's his fiancé and, according to Rachel, is about to open up a bakery. Maybe she'll extend the CORE discount to you. Anyway, get some rest."

When the door clicked shut, she opened her eyes. "Damn it," she mumbled.

Time to quit avoiding the truth.

****

Michael Morrison clutched the varmint rifle and dropped to his knees. When the wave of nausea passed, he stood and looked at the mess the coyotes had made of Dr. Brian Westly.

When he'd checked on what the animals had done to his first patient, Michael had just emerged from the farmhouse after a two day drinking binge. The coyotes had left next to nothing of Dr. Thomas Elliot. Apparently the beasts had discovered a taste for humans, though. Westly had only been in the wooded field for about eight hours, and the animals had wasted no time stripping the flesh, muscle and bone from the doctor's body.

As he stared at Westly's remains, a warm tear slid down his cold cheek and a sob tore through him. Why hadn't they listened?

"Look what you've made me do," he accused the dismembered corpse. The coyotes had torn the skin from the man's face, and even without the chains and hooks drawing his cheeks back, Westly grinned at him.

The eerie, toothless smile infuriated him. If they'd only listened, none of this would have happened. Eliza might still be alive. His precious baby would have been twenty-five next week. She'd been robbed of her life. Her future. As he stared at what remained of Westly, he imagined those milestone moments he'd never experience. Eliza's college graduation, her wedding day, his grandchildren.

Raw fury climbed inside and fueled him with uncontrollable rage. "Why didn't you just listen?"

He smashed the butt of the rifle against Westly's head. Over and over until the skull split into pieces and gray matter covered his rifle and gloves. Panting, he looked to the gun, then to what was left of the head. Horrified at the sight, horrified by what he'd become, he stumbled back, tripped and fell on his ass.

Stunned, he glanced to the ground, then scrambled to his feet. Bits of flesh and sinew clung to the dead man's femur. And he'd tripped over it. Disgusted with Westly, with all of them, and himself, he raced back to the barn. To his OR.

He rushed inside and headed straight for the office. Ripping the filthy gloves from his hands, he stared at the wall, at his daughter's last letter to him.

Tears blurred his vision. A sob tore through him and he reached for the bottle of whiskey on the desk.

Empty.

"Fuck," he shouted and threw the bottle against the wall. Made of plastic, it rebounded off the metal and bounced onto the cement floor. "Damn it." He kicked the bottle as tears streamed down his cheeks.

Exhausted after no sleep, emotionally and physically drained, he dropped to the floor and wept. "What have I done?" he sobbed. "What have I done?"

Gravel churned along the driveway leading to the house. Michael jumped to his feet and peered out the window. "Not now." He stripped out of the Carhart coat, then ran to the bathroom to wash his hands and make sure Westly's remains weren't splattered on his face. After scrubbing his hands and face, and blowing his nose, he ran back to the office. As he was about to leave, he glanced at Eliza's letter.

Make them pay, Daddy.

"I am, sweetie," he murmured, and fighting the tears clouding his eyes, he drew in a deep breath, then left the barn.

"There you are," neighboring farmer, Larry Hollister said as he rounded the front of his old Ford pick-up truck. "I just tried the front door. How've you been?"

Michael shook the other man's hand. "Good. Real good. Just working on the tractor I'd bought at the auction this past summer."

"How's it coming? Need any help? The wife says if I don't get outta the house she's gonna put me to work. And I don't do women's work," Larry finished with a chuckle.

Michael mustered a smile. "I know what you mean," he said, then motioned him toward the house and away from the barn. "I've got to head out in a few hours, but if you have time for coffee..." He hoped Larry declined. Exhausted and emotionally raw, he wasn't in the mood for company.

"Not allowed unless it's decaf. And what's the point of that?"

"Right." He stopped at Larry's Ford. "So, what brings you by?"

"Couple of things. I heard Joe Decker is looking for a temporary place for his horses. You got a lot of land they could run on, and he'll pay you for the use. And don't worry, Joe don't expect you to feed 'em or nothing. He said he'd come by daily and take care of things."

No way in hell. The last thing Michael needed was horse and people traffic on his property. He'd stick with the coyotes for now. They served a purpose.

"Sorry, Larry. I'm not interested. Why doesn't he try Ruth Gardener's place?"

Larry grinned. "Cuz that woman's a bit...crazy," he answered, and to emphasize, circled his index finger around the side of his head.

Michael laughed. "Yeah, I guess she is a little eccentric. Anyway, what else do you have for me?"

Larry moved toward the driver's side of the truck, then opened the door. "You know Sal Cooper? Lives about a mile down the road."

"Yeah, we met at the auction when I bought the tractor. He's the one that had recommended I buy it."

"Mmm," Larry grunted. "He knows tractors. Any who, Ol' Coop tends to be a bit bat shit crazy, too. He and Ruthy oughta get together, if you catch my meaning."

Michael nodded and wished Larry would shut up and leave. Considering he'd been up all night dealing with his...patient, he had to catch some sleep before his shift started at St. Mary's Medical Center. He faced a ninety minute commute, and couldn't risk falling asleep at the wheel. While he hadn't had anything to drink since he'd begun Westly's surgery, he couldn't afford a run-in with the police or highway patrol. He was only halfway finished with his death wish list, after all.

"So," Larry continued. "Coop was telling me he's been

havin' some coyote problems."

Maintaining his perfected poker face, Michael shrugged. "'Tis the season."

"No kidding. Only Coop says these scavengers have been bad. Real bad."

"How do you mean?"

Larry climbed into the truck, turned the ignition, then rolled down the window. "I guess those nasty fuckers went after his dogs. He's got these little prissy mutts that he spent a fortune on for his ex-wife, got stuck with 'em after they split…any who, ripped one of 'em to shreds."

"How's this unusual? I've heard about coyotes going after livestock before, why not a dog?"

"I hear ya. Only, when Coop went out to stop 'em, those damned coyotes circled *him*. Thank Christ he had his rifle with him. Otherwise…" He trailed off with a shrug. "If those coyotes start giving you a hard time, call the sheriff. If enough of us do, maybe they'll send out the animal warden to kill 'em."

Maintaining his poker face, Michael nodded his head. "Absolutely. I've been thinking about getting a dog," he lied. "But maybe I'll reconsider…"

"Might wanna. All right, Mick, I'll let you get back at it. If you change your mind over the next few days about them horses, let me know."

Michael gave the Ford a light rap. "Will do. Sorry I can't help with Joe's horses, but thanks for thinking of me."

Larry waved as he backed the Ford down the driveway. When he'd turned onto the county road, Michael released a deep breath.

"Fucking coyotes," he muttered. He'd have to feed them sooner than he'd planned, otherwise they might cause a problem for him.

"Is Eden Risk available?" Pudge asked WBDJ-TV's pretty receptionist, Carla.

"Your name?"

"Murugan Punjab," Pudge said, quite pleased with the new identity and that Carla had been fooled by the disguise. Experimenting with other cultures had been fun. But actually deceiving people who knew the real Pudge? An extreme necessity for their plans to come to fruition.

"Do you have an appointment, Mr. Punjab?"

"No, but I had a story idea for her," Pudge said with a well-practiced Indian accent. "She's proven to be such an excellent investigative reporter..." Pudge trailed, and hoped the compliments helped gain entry into the station as Murugan Punjab. While Eden knew Pudge in another capacity, being able to talk with her as a stranger, and watch her at work in her office, might help them gain a better understanding of her schedule and this new man in her life. Did she have a picture of him on her desk? Dates scribbled on her calendar? Before they could make a move, they needed to make certain no one would be there to save her.

"Well," Carla began as she looked at the computer screen. "It looks as if Ms. Risk hasn't come into the station yet today."

Disappointed, Pudge clutched the backpack. After all the effort put into the disguise, of course the bitch didn't have the decency to show up to work. "That's too bad. Do you know when she'll be in?"

"No, I'm sorry I don't. But, if Ryan Anders is available, I'm sure he'd be happy to talk with you."

the rumors the rumors all true kill anders kill him

Pudge ignored the voice, and asked, "Is this...Mr. Anders an investigative reporter, too?"

Carla smiled. "Yes. A very good one. Would you like me to check his availability?"

This had to be a joke. The prick from Cleveland had only been working for WBDJ for a month and Jeffries was giving him the opportunity Pudge had never been given. Eden's job.

make him disappear mama taught you how taught you well

Covering up a murder had been the only good thing Pudge had learned from Mama. Well, the only useful thing. But to kill two people from the same TV station? Too risky. They would have to deal with Anders another way.

To maintain the charade, Pudge nodded. "Yes. I would like to meet with this Mr. Anders."

we must learn more about him we must must

They would, in time. If Anders thought he could waltz into Chicago and steal Pudge's job…the arrogant bastard had another thing coming.

slice of a scalpel slice dice slice dice

Carla hung up the phone. "I'm sorry Mr. Punjab. Mr. Anders is also unavailable. If you leave your contact information, he'll call you at his earliest convenience."

His earliest convenience. How nice of him.

Still, Pudge's latest charade might prove useful when the time was right to rid Chicago of Ryan Anders. As Murugan Punjab, Pudge could escape detection while probing into the new investigative reporter's life. And if Anders or anyone else suspected Murugan Punjab to be a fake, Pudge could simply flush evidence of the Indian man down the toilet.

Pudge wrote down the number of one of the several prepaid, disposable cell phones hidden at the house. After Eden had gone to the cops last month, *caution* had become one of Pudge's new buzzwords.

"Here you go." Pudge handed the phone number to Carla. "I look forward to hearing from Mr. Anders."

Backpack in hand, Pudge left the station, then hailed another taxi. Although Pudge didn't want to go home, it was necessary. Murugan Punjab needed to disappear for a while.

After all, Dr. Dread had to make a final appearance.

CHAPTER 9

HUDSON GLANCED AT the clock on the laptop's screen, scrubbed a hand over his face, then leaned into the sofa. After spending the past hour looking at the driver's license photos Rachel had sent him to compare to the computer composite she'd created of the first victim, his eyes had grown tired.

Needing a break, he turned to the rat dog lying next to him. "Wanna go potty?"

The ugly Chihuahua stared at him, then dry heaved.

"I'll take that as a yes. Okay then, let's go."

Hoping the cold air would wake him, he didn't bother with a coat as he left the townhouse. He set the dog on the ground, then sat on the front step and thought about the sick woman lying in bed.

Even while reviewing the photos, he couldn't take his mind off of Eden, or their argument. He never did have a chance to tell her there wasn't a security camera in her bedroom. He'd only said there had been to goad her. He didn't know why. Maybe because she'd lied to him? Or maybe because she looked sexy when she was all fired up. Hell, even green around the gills, she still managed to make him want her...

Them. Naked. Together in her bed.

Her looks, he realized, had nothing to do with wanting her.

After she'd dumped him years ago, he'd convinced himself that their relationship had been purely physical. Eden had been right, though. When they'd been together, he'd been lying, not to her, but to himself. He'd avoided the truth, too. About his past and his feelings for her. A not so charming childhood hadn't helped. A failed marriage hadn't made opening up and spilling his guts any easier, either.

Over the years, he'd often wondered if things between them would have been different had he simply sat down and told her all about himself, about his true feelings for her. He shook his head. If he had talked, would she have, too? After all, he and Eden were a lot alike. She'd been tightlipped when it had come to discussing the past. As for her feelings for him? Aside from telling him she didn't want to see him anymore, she'd never once said anything about their relationship. At the time, her reluctance to discuss her feelings hadn't bothered him much. He knew she'd enjoying being with him, and not because of the many orgasms he'd given her. They'd actually gone on dates, rented movies, hung out as a couple. Yes, while skirting the truth.

Brutal pawed at his boot. He looked at the dog, at his missing leg, and then thought about her cat. Their killer had known about Eden's animals, which bothered him. Had the man been in her house? How long had he been watching her? Aside from that, what about this stalker?

Before scanning through driver's license photos, he'd reviewed the security camera feed again. This time he'd honed in on the approximate time he'd figured the killer and stalker had been at the townhouse last night. He'd found nothing. Not a car. Not a person. If the killer had noticed the addition of the security camera, had the stalker, too?

He scooped up the dog, then headed into the townhouse. After he set Brutal onto the floor, the dog walked toward his little doggy bed. Hudson stared at the Chihuahua's three legs, and remembered what the killer had said about Eden demanding perfection from herself, and yet she surrounded herself with flawed people and animals. That she had flaws, but never let anyone see them. She was tough, but a body could only take so much.

He shook his head. How were Eden's flaws related to the reasons behind killing the two men? Sitting in front of the laptop again, Hudson stared at the photos on the screen. And what in the hell did the sick bastard mean by *there's no such thing as perfect, only perception?*

Fifteen minutes later, Hudson stood, then headed for the kitchen in search of a soda. Tired of looking at the driver's license photos, and nearing the time their only link to the killer would be leaving school, he decided to call Lloyd Nelson. New to CORE, Hudson hadn't had a chance to learn much about the former deputy. But he trusted, albeit reluctantly sometimes, Ian's judgment. Hudson swore Ian had a sixth sense about people and situations. If Lloyd was good enough for Ian, for CORE, he'd work out fine as Eden's babysitter.

He winced as he drank the diet soda. Too skinny, and obsessed with her workouts and strict eating habits, of course Eden would have nothing but diet crap in her house. As he dialed Lloyd's number, then waited for him to answer, Hudson realized that in the two days he'd been with her, Eden hadn't eaten a thing. Who the hell did that?

Lloyd answered, forcing Hudson to shift gears. He explained to the other man the equipment he needed for the extra security camera Hudson had decided to hide on the property, and then the situation.

Within thirty minutes, Lloyd arrived. "That was quick," Hudson said as he opened the door to the townhouse. "I hate to stick you on babysitting duty, but Eden's sick and I don't want to wake her up for this."

Lloyd shrugged his massive shoulders. "I don't mind at all."

As Hudson put on his coat, he watched the other man. At six foot, two inches, Hudson had never considered himself short, until he'd met Lloyd. The guy had at least five inches and fifty pounds on him. With his ridiculous muscles, and long, white hair, Lloyd reminded him of Thor, minus the hammer.

Yeah, Lloyd would serve well as Eden's babysitter. Intimidating, even with a three-legged Chihuahua sitting on his lap, Hudson couldn't imagine anyone willing to mess with Lloyd. Then again, a pissed-off Eden could be just as intimidating.

"Don't I know it," Hudson mumbled as he shoved his hands into his gloves and thought back to how she'd berated him over the Winters case.

"Sorry, what did you say?" Lloyd asked from across the room.

"Nothing." Hudson headed for the door. "Call if you need anything. "

"If Eden wakes up while you're gone, do you want me to give her a message?"

Hudson stopped, then glanced down the hallway to Eden's bedroom door. Knowing Eden, and how she needed to be fully immersed in anything she was involved with, he realized no message would help save his ass.

Hoping Mama had opted for an early afternoon catnap, Pudge quietly slipped inside the house. After all, they had an appointment to make.

"That you, Pudge?" Mama asked over the blaring TV.

hate her hate her cant let her see you hate her

"Yes, Mama," Pudge said. "Give me a minute. I have to use the bathroom, then I'll make you lunch."

Pudge reached the bathroom, then closed the door. Needing to remove any evidence of Murugan Punjab, Pudge quickly went to work.

"I need to leave soon, but Mama…"

sleep put her to sleep

"Damn it," Pudge whispered, and stared at the mirror. "I told you I'm not killing Mama."

sleep didnt say kill sleep

Face now cleaned, Pudge said, "You're right. She needs to

123

go to sleep. And I have just the thing to help."

Minutes later, Pudge entered the kitchen. Dirty plates filled the sink and table, stale food covered the counter, and dirt tarnished the floor. Pudge ignored the mess and rummaged through the cabinet that held Mama's medications. After finding and crushing the pills that would put the fat bitch to sleep, Pudge opened the refrigerator and pulled out the mayonnaise. Once the crushed pills were mixed with the mayo, Pudge made Mama a sandwich, grabbed a bag of barbeque chips and a grape soda, then headed for the living room.

"Here's your lunch," Pudge said, and set the food on the tray.

Mama frowned. "No snack cakes? What's a meal without dessert?"

Pudge eyed the half dozen empty boxes of brownies, Swiss rolls, Twinkies and cakes. "Go ahead and eat. I'll bring you one."

"Don't be stingy," Mama said over a mouthful. "Bring the whole box. And some ibuprofen, three of them. My ass is hurtin' today."

more give mama more

Pudge entered the kitchen, opened the cabinet, then pulled out the bottle of ibuprofen.

sleep give mama more sleep

Pudge considered the amount of crushed pills in Mama's mayonnaise and the amount of time before the medication would take effect. Directly ingested, the sleeping pills would knock Mama out fast, but would that be too many pills at once?

do it do it mama wont know wont know do it now now

"Shh," Pudge hissed, then opened the bottle of sleeping pills. "You better hope this doesn't hurt her. We can't afford for Mama to die of an overdose. The police might start looking into what we've been up to, and that can't happen. Not when we're so close."

too fat mama too fat to die from pills needs elephant tranquilizer too fat

Pudge smothered a chuckle. "You're so bad."

With three sleeping pills in one hand, a box of snack cakes in the other, Pudge walked back into the living room and nearly gagged. "Here you go, Mama. Smells like your colostomy bag needs to be changed. Why don't I move your tray aside and do that before you finish your lunch?"

"Smell don't bother me. Now hush up," Mama ordered, and raised the volume on the TV. "I'm trying to hear this. You can change my bag after I'm done with my lunch and the show's over."

"Yes, Mama," Pudge said, and with disgust and anticipation, watched Mama swallow the sleeping pills. Unable to watch Mama eat, or endure the vile odor, Pudge left the living room for the privacy of the bedroom. Once the door had clicked shut, Pudge looked in the mirror.

soon slice dice slice dice

Pudge opened the closet and pulled out an old suitcase. After opening it, and staring at the disguise, Pudge smiled.

welcome back doctor dread welcome back

Hudson climbed out of the Trans Am the second Evan Pope exited the school bus. He waited a moment until the bus had turned the corner, then followed the kid up the walkway to his house.

"Hey, gotta minute?" Hudson asked.

Evan shifted the backpack to his other shoulder and flipped his long, straight bangs out of his eyes. "Who are you?" he asked, then looked to his house.

"I'm a private investigator."

Evan glanced at the house again, then took a few steps toward him. "No shit?"

"Yeah, no shit," Hudson said. "I have a feeling you know what this is about. Don't you?"

"Look. I didn't know what was in the package. This guy just, like, told me to deliver it. He said it wasn't anything bad, ya know, like drugs or a gun or something."

Nothing bad. Only the filming of a man's torture and death. "I know," Hudson assured the kid. "But what was in that package could have an impact on the case I'm working. Did you see the man who gave you the package?"

Evan shook his head, causing his bangs to fall forward again and reminding Hudson that he too could use a haircut. "Naw, it was dark. I was on my route, delivering papers and, like, the guy just came out of nowhere. Scared the crap out of me."

"What was he wearing?"

"Am I gonna get in trouble for this? I promise I'll give back the money. I just can't afford to have an issue with the cops. I'm a senior and applying to colleges. If I end up with a record, I—"

Hudson held up a hand. "You're not in trouble. Just tell me everything you can about the man and was this the first time you've done a delivery for him."

"Wait—there's other packages?"

Hudson shrugged. "I'll take that as a no."

"Take it as a hell no. As for the guy, he was about as tall as you. He had on a big coat so I couldn't guess his weight. He had on a baseball cap, black, and a scarf pulled up high around his neck, almost to his mouth." Evan knocked the hair out of his eyes. "Like I said, it was dark, so I couldn't see his face."

"What about a car?"

"There were cars parked on the street, but there's always cars parked on the street. I couldn't tell you what kind or color." Evan shrugged. "I never pay attention to that kinda stuff. I just wanna finish my route so I can get home and eat before school."

Dead end. Not that Hudson had high hopes the kid would have pertinent information which would help them find the killer. Their doctor had already proven to be adept at covering his tracks.

"Thanks for your time, Evan," Hudson said, then pulled out a small notepad from his jacket pocket and wrote down his cell phone number. "Call me if this guy asks you to make any other deliveries."

Evan stuffed the paper into his back pocket. "So you're not going to say anything to my parents about this?"

Hudson didn't see the point of involving the kid's folks. He hadn't done anything wrong, and he hadn't seen anything of any value. Then a thought occurred to him.

"How much did the guy pay you?"

"Two hundred dollars."

"That's probably a nice chunk of change for you. And you didn't question this…delivery?"

Evan held up both of his hands. "Are you kidding me? Of course I did. I asked him about the drugs and guns thing, and like I said, he told me it wasn't anything illegal. Then I asked him what it was and he was like, just a DVD for a friend. He said it was one of those extreme makeover shows, ya know where they take ugly people and make them perfect." He flipped his bangs. "I was like, why don't you take it to her yourself? And he was like, because I wanna surprise her. Sounded like a stupid surprise, but for two hundred bucks, what do I care? Right?"

Dizzy from the hair flipping and all the "likes," Hudson nodded. "I get it, kid." He walked to the driver's side of the Trans Am. "Just call if this guy approaches you again," he said before climbing into the car.

"Wait," Evan shouted, and ran to Trans Am. "I did feel the package, and it did feel like a DVD. Did you see what was on it? Was it one of those makeover shows?"

Without answering, Hudson closed the car door, turned the ignition, then pulled the Trans Am into the street. What would he say to the kid anyway? Yeah, it was an extreme makeover.

Extreme in that the doctor tortures his patients until they die.

Eden woke, then snuggled next to Fabio. As the big cat purred, she reached to stroke Brutal. She felt around the comforter and realized the dog had probably followed Hudson from the bedroom earlier. The little traitor had taken an obvious liking to Hudson, which didn't bother her. She loved that her dog had finally become a little more social. After he'd been attacked, he'd shied away from strangers, and sometimes piddled on the floor when someone came to the house. What bothered her though, was that she more than liked Hudson.

She had to admit to herself that she'd never gotten over him. She also had to face the fact that he was right. When she'd had the opportunity to run from their relationship, she'd taken it. When there had been a prime opportunity to talk about her past, and their future, she'd avoided it. She'd only lied to him once, and that had been about her phantom date, but she *had* skirted the truth over and over.

Her past had never been something she'd been interested in sharing. With anyone. Her family had never known what had happened to her, and to tell them now would break their hearts. She'd been on the investigating circuit for too long not to understand the human psyche. She'd seen families destroyed when secrets had been disclosed. Her secrets wouldn't destroy her family, but she hated the thought of her father or sister blaming themselves for something they couldn't have controlled. Or beating themselves up because they hadn't had the chance to help her through the after affects of the rape. Will would have been too young to understand, but as an adult and a sensitive soul, she knew he'd have a hard time grasping at the thought that his sister had been gang raped.

Yawning, she stretched. Every part of her body still ached, but at least she didn't have the urge to puke. She glanced at the clock. Just past three, she could still make it into the station. She shifted and pulled her legs over the side of the bed. Blinked several times to ward off the dizziness, then placed her feet on the floor.

Her mind still a little foggy, she tried to remember what else she'd planned to do today. Exercise was obviously out of the question. Was she supposed to go to the grocery store and pick up more dog and cat food? Wait, the high school kid. They were supposed to interview the high school kid.

Anxious to tell Hudson she was ready to meet the boy who had delivered the DVD, she stood, then wobbled. She reached for the nightstand to steady herself. A wave of blinding dizziness knocked her off her feet. The nightstand and its contents crashed to the floor. She tripped on the clock, then landed on her ass.

Seconds later, the Aryan from the other night scooped her off the floor, then set her on the bed. "Are you okay? What happened?"

She had to be hallucinating. Why else would this man be in her bedroom. Unless…

"Where's Hudson?" she asked.

"He had to leave. Now answer me. Are you all right?"

Tucking a lock of hair behind her ear, she nodded. "Just lost my balance. Have you seen my dog?"

"He's in his bed," the Aryan said as he righted the nightstand. "Rest here and I'll go grab you some water."

Confused and suddenly overheated, she started to unbutton her blouse. "It's hot in here. I need something cold."

"Ah, okay," the Aryan said, then looked away. "I'll make sure it's cold water."

"No. Make it a frozen daiquiri. Wait. A Pina Colada. Do you like Pina Coladas?" she sang, then giggled. "I love that song. Don't you? I don't really like Pina Coladas though. Or getting caught in the rain? If some guy asked me that I'd think he was an ass. Who wants to stand in the rain? Makes your makeup run, messes up your hair…" She lay back on the pillow, closed her eyes and thought about dancing in the rain with Hudson. Actually, that might be fun. But she'd have to do it without makeup. "Don't want to have raccoon eyes."

"I'm sorry, what was that?" the Aryan asked.

"Lloyd?" a familiar voice said from the bedroom door.

She opened her eyes and smiled. "Hey, you. I was just getting ready to go for Pina Coladas."

"What's she talking about?" Hudson asked the Aryan.

Wait. Dumbass. The Aryan was Lloyd, Will's partner. And why the hell was she suddenly talking about Pina Coladas?

"I don't know," Lloyd answered. "She woke up, fell and has been...out of it."

She frowned. "I'm not out of it. I'm totally with it. You know, hip, happening, Superfly."

Hudson felt her forehead. She closed her eyes and smiled, relished the caress of his warm hand.

"Mmm, you always did have a nice touch," she murmured, and tried to move closer to him.

"Something's not right." Hudson said, his voice tinny, muffled.

As he left the room, she shook her head hoping to clear her clogged ears. They must be clogged, why else had Hudson and Lloyd sounded as if they were the teacher from the Charlie Brown cartoons? She always liked Charlie Brown.

"We used to call Will, Pig Pen, when he was a baby." She giggled, then curled on her side and looked at Lloyd. Will had been such a cute, chubby toddler who had made sure no rock had been unturned, and no worm left alone. "And now you're banging my baby brother," she whispered, and winked at Lloyd.

Lloyd smiled. "So you do remember me."

"Don't let her move," Hudson said as he entered the room carrying a duffle bag.

"Where we going?" she asked, and tried to rise. The moment her head lifted from the pillow, her stomach lurched and she gripped Lloyd's arm. "Puke. Gonna puke."

Within seconds Lloyd had the trashcan from the bathroom in front of her. Thank God. Who wants to sleep in vomit?

Hudson zipped the bag. "She okay?"

Lloyd smoothed her hair. "I think she's finished. What next?"

Hudson tossed the bag to Lloyd, then scooped her in his strong arms. If she hadn't been so damned confused and felt as if someone had run her over, she'd have loved this moment. She'd missed having him hold her. Anyone who knew her assumed she was strong, and they were right. Badass. Hardcore. With Hudson though, she didn't always have to be strong. She could take a mini vacation from being a badass and simply be herself. Well, minus all that truth-telling crap Hudson had harped about earlier.

She touched his cheek. "I hope I don't stink," she said as he carried her from the bedroom.

He kissed the top of her head. "You don't," he said with a small smile. "Lloyd, her coat."

As she clung to Hudson's neck, Lloyd draped the coat around her. When she realized they were leaving, she squirmed in his arms. "Where are you taking me?"

He held her firm and steady as they exited the townhouse. Once they reached the Trans Am and she'd been stowed into the backseat, Hudson handed Lloyd the keys and joined her. "You drive," he said to Lloyd.

"Where am I heading?"

"St. Mary's Medical Center."

"May I help you?" Gretchen Meyer asked as she opened the door.

Pudge smiled and touched the bill of the baseball cap worn to keep the wig in place. "Evening, Ma'am. I hope this isn't a bad time, but we're checking the building for potential gas leaks. Your apartment is next on my list." Pudge jangled the tool belt for effect.

"Oh my, that sounds serious. Should I be worried?" Gretchen asked as she let Pudge into the apartment.

"No, Ma'am. Just a precaution. With the weather getting colder by the day, and everyone cranking up the heat, Management wants to make sure all of the apartments are safe." Pudge sniffed, and caught the scent of spaghetti sauce. "This won't take long. I'll be long gone before you have a chance to eat your dinner. Now, if you could direct me to where your hot water tank is stored..."

131

Gretchen lead Pudge down the hallway, then pointed to a closet. "It's in here with my washer and dryer."

Pudge eyed the scrubs hanging to dry. "Are you a doctor?"

Gretchen laughed. "Hardly. I'm a nurse. I usually take care of patients at their homes."

Because of their low income, Mama rarely allowed Pudge to call upon a professional to fix things around their home. Over the years, Pudge had become quite adept at fixing leaks and simple electrical issues. Falling into the role of a maintenance worker hadn't been difficult, plus the tool belt gave Pudge a place to store the necessary equipment to take care of Nurse Gretchen.

"I bet you meet some real characters in your line of work," Pudge said, and pulled out a long, heavy-duty flashlight. Holding it high and leaning into the crevice behind the hot water tank, Pudge pretend to search the water and gas lines.

waiting waiting stop waiting

Gretchen laughed. "You have no idea. But I love my job. I'm not stuck in a hospital all day working a twelve hour shift. Instead I get to go to different places and meet all kinds of *characters*."

kill her dr dread kill her waiting waiting

Pudge ignored the taunt. The space in the hallway and closet were too small for what they'd planned. The kitchen would provide the room needed to take care of Nurse Gretchen.

"Gotta love what you do for a living," Pudge said, then stepped back and closed the door. "Everything looks good here. Let's check the kitchen."

Once inside the small room, Pudge inhaled. "Smells delicious. I hope I'm not interrupting a dinner party."

"Yeah, a party of one," Gretchen said with a smile.

alone all alone kill her kill her now now

"More for you," Pudge said, then frowned. "I don't know much about cooking, and I don't want to screw up your sauce. But I'll need you to take the pots off the stove so I can pull this thing out and check the gas line."

now dr dread now kill her kill her

Gretchen nodded, and moved past Pudge to the stove. "Not a problem. I was just warming the sauce while I was waiting for the noodles to boil."

now now kill now now

"Shut the fuck up," Pudge muttered.

The pots on the stove left untouched, Gretchen turned. "I'm sorry, what did you say?" she asked, her boney face contorting in confusion and alarm.

"Mind your business, bitch." Before the nurse had a chance to react, Pudge swung the heavy flashlight. As metal connected with bone, the light died, and Gretchen crumpled to the floor. "I was having a private conversation," Pudge finished, then gave the woman a kick.

When Nurse Gretchen didn't move, Pudge checked her pulse. Alive. Bummer. While playing Dr. Dread had been fun, cleaning off the blood had been a pain in the ass.

sorry so sorry are you mad at me sorry

"I can't stay mad at you," Pudge said, and slipped the flashlight back into the tool belt. "But you have to be patient. I know what I'm doing."

yes yes so smart precious so smart

Pudge smiled. "*We're* smart. Together we can accomplish anything." Pudge pulled out the scalpel hidden next to the pliers in the tool belt pocket.

slice dice slice dice

"Yes, my love. We'll slice and dice this bitch, and consider what we do here today..." Pudge slit the nurse's throat. "Practice for what's to come."

CHAPTER 10

"MS. RISK HAS a moderate case of dehydration," the E.R. doctor said as she closed the curtain surrounding Eden's hospital bed. "The fluids we're running into her system now should improve her condition, but if she remains dehydrated, feverish, confused, I'll admit her."

Hudson sucked in a deep breath. While he wanted Eden healthy, he worried about her staying at the hospital unprotected. Then again, the hospital might be the perfect place for her to remain until they discovered more about the killer and her stalker. Right now, there were too many uncertainties in the case.

"Is she awake?" Hudson asked.

"No. I gave her something to help her sleep. She was extremely confused when she first arrived and I worried she might pull out the I.V."

Nodding, Hudson pulled the curtain slightly aside and peeked at Eden. She lay in the hospital bed, sound asleep. Color had already begun to infuse her pale cheeks, but her face held a gauntness that unsettled him.

"She'd been vomiting all day, but would that have caused the dehydration?"

The doctor checked something off on her chart, then rested

it on her hip. "I asked Ms. Risk about her eating habits prior to catching the flu. Again, she was disoriented, but she told me she couldn't remember the last time she'd had anything to eat. She also said she drank alcohol last night. Alcohol will dehydrate you, too. Tack on the flu..." The doctor shrugged. "And you have a recipe for moderate dehydration."

A nurse approach, then whispered something to the doctor. "I have to go. Are you Ms. Risk's spouse?" she asked.

Knowing he truly had no right, legal or otherwise to remain by Eden's bedside, he decided a small lie was in order. "Her fiancé," he said.

Lloyd, who had been standing next to him the entire time, coughed.

"Well, Mr. Patterson, if you'd like, you can sit with your fiancée until she wakes. We'll check her vitals when that happens and decide whether to admit her or not."

When the doctor left, Hudson turned to Lloyd. "I've got to call Rachel and let her know we're at the hospital. If I'm going to be here for a while I'll need my laptop. Can you go back to Eden's townhouse, let the dog out, feed him and Fabio, then bring me my laptop?"

"Who's Fabio?" Lloyd asked.

Hudson released an impatient sigh. "Tell me you didn't see the enormous cat lying on Eden's bed."

"I thought it was a stuffed animal." Lloyd shrugged. "The damn thing didn't move once."

"Then make sure it's not dead when you go back there," Hudson said. "Stay with Eden while I call Rachel, and when I get back you can head over to the townhouse."

"In case another DVD arrives or the stalker tries to make contact, do you want me to stay at her place until she comes home?"

Hudson scrubbed a hand down his face. "Shit. The extra security camera you brought me is still sitting in Eden's hallway." He'd planned on installing the camera after his interview with Evan Pope, but he hadn't planned on Eden taking a trip to the E.R.

"No problem. I'm handy with electronics and will have it up and running for you before I head back with your laptop." Lloyd checked his watch. "Make your call fast so I can leave. I don't mind working at dusk, but if it gets any darker…besides I have some calls to make, too."

"Sorry, man. I didn't mean to boss your ass around. I'm sure you have other assignments—"

Lloyd held up his hand. "No, we're good. I just want to make sure Eden's sister and brother know she's in the hospital. Knowing them, they'll want to come see her. I'll give them a head's up on your upcoming nuptials, though," Lloyd finished with a grin.

"They're both in Chicago?"

Lloyd nodded. "Have been for a few months."

"And how do you know her brother and sister?" Hudson asked, beyond confused as to how Lloyd could possibly be connected to Eden's family. A family he hadn't realized existed. Well, the sister he knew about only because she'd mentioned her in passing, but she had a brother, too? Why hadn't she bothered to mention either of them when they'd been together?

"Long story," Lloyd said, then moved the curtain and entered Eden's makeshift room.

Once Hudson found a private area in the hallway off the waiting room, he called Rachel. After giving her an update, he asked if she knew how Lloyd was acquainted with Eden's family.

"Oh, that's right," she began. "You were gone when everything happened with Celeste and John."

"Kain? Yeah you told me they'd met while he was working a murder case in Wisconsin." Then it hit him. After putting sixteen and twenty-four together he said, "Holy shit, Celeste is Ian's daughter."

"That's right, super sleuth. And Eden and Celeste are sisters."

****

With the scent of fresh blood lingering on the maintenance uniform, Pudge entered the house as quietly as possible. Light from the TV screen flickered on the darkened wall of the family room. Uncertain as whether or not Mama still slept, and not in the mood to have the glorious kill ruined by her bitching, Pudge slipped down the hallway to the bathroom.

Once the door had been locked, Pudge dropped the backpack, shrugged off the heavy wool coat that hid the bloodied uniform, then stared at the reflection in the mirror. Twisting from side to side, Pudge smiled. "We made more of a mess than I'd planned."

worth it worth it slice dice worth it

"Yes, and when the agency calls to replace Nurse Gretchen, I'll tell them we've already found a new nurse."

good good good bye dr dread hello nurse nancy hello

"Nurse Nancy?" Pudge grinned. "Clichéd, but the name does have a nice ring to it. Nurse Nancy it is," Pudge finished, and began removing the uniform. Once naked, Pudge eyed the mirror. "I had fun with you this evening."

fun i want to have fun with you tonight pinch your nipple pinch

Pudge did as ordered, and sucked in a deep breath. "So good. So *very* good."

more more harder more harder

Pinching harder, Pudge's knees buckled with arousal. "I need sex," Pudge groaned.

Killing excited Pudge. More than an adrenaline rush, feeling the life seep from their victims' bodies had become an aphrodisiac.

Foreplay.

With each cut made into Nurse Gretchen, Pudge's body had throbbed with the need for sexual release. Her blood had reminded Pudge of a lubricant, the knife's blade, the way it slid in and out of Gretchen's flesh, of a sexual tool.

bend bend over bend over and show your ass

Pudge's face grew warm at the seductive command. "Let me finish cleaning myself first. Then I have to check on

Mama."

sleep sleep let mama sleep let me love you

Arousal coiled through Pudge's core. Need and desire fueled Pudge to work quickly. Within minutes, any remnants of the maintenance worker had been washed away. Pudge left the bathroom wearing a towel and, carrying the bloodied clothes, quietly headed for the bedroom. After stowing the clothes in the "Dr. Dread suitcase," Pudge slipped into a pair of flannel pajamas, then tiptoed to the family room to check on Mama.

Mouth dangling open, Mama lay on the hospital bed, snoring. The entire room reeked of shit, which meant Mama's colostomy bag needed another changing.

Pudge didn't want to clean up shit, not now, not when they could disappear into the bedroom and have sex. "Damn her. Damn the helpless bitch."

leave her come with me come for me

"In a minute," Pudge whispered. "Let me take care of Mama. If she wakes up, I don't want any interruptions."

mmm so smart so smart

Ten minutes later, Pudge had changed Mama's colostomy bag, and had even left a fresh sandwich, new bag of chips, can of soda, and more snack cakes on her tray. Now in the bedroom, Pudge undressed, then, propped on elbows, lay on the bed in front of the mirror. Legs spread, sex reflecting back, Pudge shivered with arousal.

sexy so sexy let me love you love you

"Mmm," Pudge moaned. "Too bad it's just you and me. I wouldn't mind trying a threesome again."

toy edens boy toy play with boy toy

Positioning to all fours, Pudge turned and eyed the mirror again. Ass high, Pudge imagined Eden Risk's sexy boyfriend naked and in bed with them, and groaned with pleasure. "Yes," Pudge hissed. "Even if we have to strap him down, we'll make him ours."

now now make him ours now

Pudge rolled from the bed, then retrieved the dildo hidden between the mattress and box spring. "Soon," Pudge began, and climbed onto the bed again. "I promise you Eden will be dead by the end of the week, and my gift to you will be her boy toy."

promise promise precious promise

Pudge inserted the dildo and released a low groan. "Mmm, yes. I promise. Now hush and love me."

"Did you hear who was admitted tonight?" Laurie, the receptionist from the OR, asked.

Michael Morrison continued to review the chart the on-duty anesthesiologist had given him. He could care less which celebrity had been admitted to St. Mary's. Located in the heart of Chicago, the hospital was no stranger to local politicians, actors or sports legends.

"No, but I have no doubt you'll tell me," Michael said with a smile. While he had no interest in hospital gossip, he'd worked at St. Mary's Medical Center for fifteen years, first as a nurse, then as a nurse anesthetist, and genuinely liked his coworkers. Laurie, like many others from the hospital, had attended his daughter's funeral. These people had also been staunch supporters afterward, when the heads of the hospital had tried to make him take a leave of absence. He'd understood why the administration had suggested he take time off of work. Hell, even some of his coworkers had needed counseling after they'd witnessed his ex-wife blowing her brains all over his daughter's casket.

Because of his superb record with the hospital, and a glowing report from one of St. Mary's lead psychologists, he'd remained on duty. Months after Eliza had committed suicide though, and after Michael had lost his fight against the plastic surgeon group from Cosmetic Solutions and Med Spa, he'd realized he'd need to take justice into his own hands. He'd needed a plan to execute the punishment no court system in this country would ever allow. As a means to his revenge, he'd decided to become a nurse anesthetist. With the slight career change, he'd been able to remain at St. Mary's, had been allowed access to the necessary drugs, and given the opportunity to view multiple surgeries. His coworkers would never suspect that while he'd viewed surgeries, he'd created new means of torture to practice on the patients who would eventually visit his private OR. Not that he'd needed new ideas. He'd discovered through his plan of vengeance that he had quite the imagination.

Laurie held the coffee mug between her hands. "Well, if you don't want to know…" She shrugged.

"You're not going to bait me this time," Michael said with a wag of his finger.

"Fine," she began, "Then I guess I won't tell you that one of Chicago's hottest reporters was admitted earlier this evening."

While his heart rate skyrocketed, he pretended to go back to reading the chart. "I guess you won't," he said, playing along. He could easily check the hospital records to discover if the reporter happened to be Eden, but he'd rather have Laurie give him the information. If all hell broke loose, and people began checking, they would be able to see his computer activity. No paper trails, real or electronic. He hadn't finished with his death wish list.

He just hoped to God nothing had happened to Eden. The unknown person he'd seen lingering around her townhouse had him worried. No one lurks around another person's home—cloaked by darkness and dressed like a burglar—unless they're up to no good. Besides, he liked Eden. In some ways she reminded him of Eliza. Always pushing to be perfect, and unwilling to accept her own personal flaws. When she'd caught his attention with her Beauty Pageant Queen Bees series, she'd gained his respect. He'd witnessed her kindness. Watched her work hard to serve justice for the little guy. Hell, she even rescued disfigured animals. Anybody who liked animals was cool in his book. After all, look how he'd been taking care of the coyotes.

"Right." She tapped her nails on the coffee mug. "So I

guess I won't tell you that Eden Risk is on the third floor recovering from dehydration."

He stopped and looked at her. "Eden Risk?" he asked, playing dumb. No one needed to know he'd researched her, and knew her better than she knew herself.

"You know. The investigative reporter on Channel 5 News."

"Oh, that's right. I've heard of her. Sorry, I usually watch Channel 3," he said.

"Well, you're missing out. Eden is awesome."

"Hmm, you don't say?" Michael hid his relief and pretended to review the chart. While dehydration could be bad, and lead to complications, being a victim of an unknown assailant would be worse. If his *patients* hadn't been ripped to shreds by coyotes, they could certainly vouch for that fact. "Well, I have to run. Try not to gossip too much," he said to Laurie. "I've got a surgery in an hour and need to check on a few patients before I begin prepping. Page me if you need me."

Leaving Laurie behind, he made his way to the break room. Blessedly alone, he allowed his thoughts to race.

Eden Risk.

In the hospital.

On many occasions, he'd been very close to Eden without her knowing. He could do this again. After all, she lay in a hospital bed on the floor below. Drumming his fingers on the table, he considered his options, then came up with a plan.

After slipping on a pair of Latex gloves, he tore a piece of paper from a notepad lying on the table, then began to write. Minutes later, he folded the paper, then slipped it into his pocket. He poured coffee into a Styrofoam cup, grabbed his chart, then left the room. As he traveled down the hallway, he nodded to coworkers he knew, then once alone, opened the door to the stairwell. No one would think anything of him traveling to other floors. Side effects from anesthetics were not uncommon, and part of his job was to check on patients recovering from surgery.

When he reached the third floor, he made his first stop. A

woman in her mid-forties lay sleeping in the hospital bed. He checked her vitals, reviewed notes on her chart, then turned to leave. The flower arrangements lining the window caught his attention and he stopped.

With an idea in his head, he left the room, and continued to make his rounds. Twenty minutes later, he collided with a man, who looked like a biker, exiting a patient's room.

"I'm sorry," Michael said with a smile.

"No problem," the man responded, and continued down the hall.

Michael continued as well, then stopped short when he chanced a glance into the room the man had just exited.

Eden.

Now he knew which room was hers.

Now he could carry out his plan.

Minutes later, with a small bouquet he'd stolen from another sleeping patient's room, he checked the hallway, waited a moment to make sure all was clear, then slipped into Eden's room. She remained sound asleep. He set the bouquet on the window ledge, withdrew the note from his pocket, then tucked the paper between the flowers.

When he exited the room, he quickly made his way down the hallway. The elevator next to the stairwell entrance chimed. As he entered the stairwell, he saw the man he'd run into earlier exit the elevator. Michael closed the door, waited a few seconds then opened it, and peered down the hallway…just as the man entered Eden's room.

The humming and beeping drove her crazy.

Groggy, but annoyed, Eden yawned and opened her eyes. Alarmed, she pushed herself up, and scooted her legs to her chest. A pinch to the top of her hand forced her to stop. She glanced at her hand, at the I.V., then looked around the room.

Hudson sat in a chair in the corner, sleeping, his laptop closed and resting on his thighs. As she continued to gaze around the room a rush of memories filled her mind. Throwing up, Pina Coladas, the Aryan, and the E.R. doctor. The way Hudson had held her in the car during the drive to the hospital, and the sweet kiss he'd given the top of her head.

Considering she hadn't vomited in a while, she assumed the flu bug had finally completed its mission. Although weak, and a little tired, she felt good. Not good enough to plow through a sixty minute workout, but good enough to leave and enjoy the comfort of her own bed.

With the blinds drawn, she couldn't tell whether it was morning or night. Had she spent the night in the hospital? She glanced at the clock on the wall. Was it nine in the evening or in the morning? Her poor babies. Brutal probably needed to go potty, and both animals would need to be fed.

Before she threw herself into a panic attack over the dog and cat, she shook her head and thought long and hard. Hudson would have made arrangement for the animals. He knew how important they were to her, and whether he'd admit it or not, she suspected he liked them, too. She leaned back into the pillows and smiled as she remembered thinking the same thing before falling on her ass and Lloyd coming into her bedroom.

Wait, why had Lloyd been in her bedroom? Where had Hudson…?

Knowing exactly where he'd been, she eyed the sleeping man. She'd bet anything that Hudson had gone to see Evan Pope, and had left Lloyd to babysit her. God, and she'd made such an ass of herself in front of Lloyd. She didn't care about looking like a fool in front of Hudson. He'd never been the judgmental type, especially with her. Well, except when they were discussing—or rather, arguing—their relationship. Then he had no problem telling her where she'd gone wrong. Now that she thought about it, just before her last major puke session and her nap, he'd told her he had needed to tell her the truth about… something. Their past relationship? Himself?

He's right there. Ask him.

But did she want to know? Did she really want to know

how he felt about her? Before the DVD arrived, she had her life in order. The Network job was hers. All she had left was to sign the contract, which she'd planned on doing next week. Damn, she'd almost forgotten about the trip she'd scheduled to New York City. She'd also forgotten about the realtor she'd planned to use to sell the townhouse. Shit, Celeste had planned the grand opening of her new bakery next week, too.

Considering she had a sudden case of the stupids, she realized she needed her smart phone to review the following week's upcoming events. With the killer sending her DVDs, the last segment of her series coming up in a few days, becoming sick, and…Hudson, she hadn't been as on top of things as she liked. Probably because all she kept thinking about the past couple of days was having Hudson on top of her.

In her.

Behind her.

Between her legs.

"You're awake," Hudson said.

Cheeks burning from Hudson catching her deep in wicked thoughts, she mustered a smile. "Finally," she responded. "How long have I been here?"

"Not long. We brought you in around four this afternoon. How do you feel?" He set the laptop on a nearby table, then stood.

"Good," she said, and watched him approach. Even with all that hair, and dressed like a thug, she couldn't help herself from wanting him.

Naked.

In her bed.

Sliding into her body.

He touched her cheek. "You look good. I'm glad to see color returning to your cheeks."

If only he knew why. What would he say, or do, if she told him this particular truth? That she'd been blushing because instead of worrying about her health, or the case for that matter, she'd been thinking about sex?

"What did the doctor say? I can't believe I've been admitted for a flu bug."

"The flu wasn't the problem. Well, it didn't help." He shrugged. "The real problem is that you don't eat."

Her face grew hot again. This time it had nothing to do with thoughts of sex. Only moments ago she'd considered Hudson a nonjudgmental person. She suspected that was about to change. He'd brought up her eating habits before. Even when they'd been dating he'd commented on how little she had eaten. In her opinion, strict eating habits were better than bulimia. She controlled what she ate, and control had always been important to her. At one time in her life, during a long ago night she'd spent half her life trying to forget, she'd been left without the power to control what happened to her body. Never again.

"My eating habits are none of your business."

"Yeah, they are."

The I.V. pinched her skin as she crossed her arms over her chest. "What I put between my lips is not your concern."

He dropped his gaze to her mouth. "I can suggest something you could put between your lips."

Thoughts of taking him into her mouth caused a throb between her legs. "Pig," she muttered, despite her desires. Until she knew where they stood, she refused to let him know how much she—or rather, her body—had missed him. "I can't believe you would even think about sex when I'm lying in a hospital bed."

"Dirty girl," he said, and sat on the edge of the bed, his hip touching hers through the blanket. "I never said anything about sex."

True. Damn it. "You insinuated it, though."

He shook his head. "Nope. But sex with me is obviously on your mind, considering where *your* thoughts went." He reached across the bed and took her hand off her chest. With a gentle caress, he stroked the pad of his thumb near the I.V. "What I was going to suggest is that if you're going to deny yourself meals, at least find a supplement you can take. You need something to help make sure you're getting the proper nutrition."

"Badass investigator turned nutritionist? What an interesting combination."

Smiling, he stroked her cheek. "Before I joined CORE I was with the CIA. During my last mission, I ended up being held prisoner by this Russian jackass. Before the Marines came in and helped me escape, the Russian kept me locked in a basement cell for weeks. During that time, my daily ration was a shitty bowl of broth and, believe it or not, one of those milkshake supplements you can buy at the grocery store."

He held her hand again, and looked to where their fingers twined. "I was in the middle of a Columbian jungle, and this crazy Russian somehow has a lifetime supply of these milkshake things? I'm not saying they taste all that great, but I will tell you that if he hadn't been feeding them to me…things might have ended different." He looked at her now, the pain and anguish in his eyes reflecting the memory of his experience in the jungle.

She tightened her grip on his hand, then reached to smooth his rough cheek. "Is this where we stop avoiding the past and tiptoeing around the truth?" she asked, nervous and yet excited at the prospect of finally having something real with Hudson. Although the move to New York loomed in the back of her mind, she wanted something real. Even for a short period of time. The memories they could make would last her a lifetime, and maybe erase those lingering, terrifying memories that still gave her nightmares.

He turned his face, kissed her palm, then cupped her cheek. "I just don't want to ever bring you to the E.R. again. You scared me today." He sighed, then smiled. "I just tiptoed, didn't I?"

"A little bit."

"Okay, then. Yes."

"Yes, we're going to actually start talking?"

"We've never had a problem talking."

She gave his cheek a soft pinch. "Talking about our past."

"I'm game," he said, then kissed her forehead. "I want to know you, Eden. I always have."

She wished she'd had an opportunity to brush her teeth. Right now, all she wanted to do was kiss him. Yes, she'd talk. But damn, it had been way too long since she'd had his lips on hers.

He pulled away, and held both of her hands. "I told you a little bit about me, now it's your turn. Those flowers on the window ledge..."

"Yes. I saw those. Thanks for being sweet, but you didn't have—"

"I didn't. I assumed they were from your brother, Will, or maybe your sister, Celeste. You know, Ian's daughter."

She winced. "I guess I kind of tiptoed around that one, didn't I?"

"I'll admit I was disappointed when I realized you hadn't bothered to tell me that you have a brother and sister. I mean, c'mon, Eden. Your sister was actually in your townhouse the first night I came to see you, and you couldn't even introduce us?"

Shame coiled through her. "I don't know why I didn't introduce you to Celeste, or tell you about my family. I'm sorry."

He stood, then retrieved the flowers. "It's hard not to accept your apology when you're lying in a hospital bed."

Not interested in fighting with Hudson, but more interested in understanding how the man ticked, she said, "How chivalrous of you."

After handing her the flowers, he said, "Looks like there's a note tucked between the stems."

She pushed the flowers apart, then retrieved the note. "It's probably from Will. My sister would have sent something with a gnome on it."

"Gnome?"

"Celeste's a bit...eccentric," she said, then opened the note.

She dropped the bouquet. Hudson caught the glass vase before it hit the tile, then set it on the floor.

"What's wrong? Who's it from?" he asked, and gripped her trembling hand.

She passed the note to him. "It's from the killer."

CHAPTER 11

HUDSON STOOD IN the corner of CORE's evidence and evaluation room, frustration tearing through him like a bad Mexican meal. Moments ago, during a conference call with Ian, he'd learned that the hospital security cameras hadn't identified who had delivered the flowers to Eden. While cameras had been positioned in the main corridors of the hospital, there hadn't been one near Eden's room. Plus, the people who were filmed by the cameras on Eden's floor either worked at the hospital or were visiting patients. When hospital volunteers, who brought flowers and gifts to patient rooms, had been questioned, not one remembered making a delivery to Eden's room. Another dead end.

"Quit pouting," Rachel said from across the room.

He shoved off the wall. "I'm not pouting. I'm pissed. The killer could have been in Eden's room. He could have…" He didn't want to think about what the sick son of a bitch could have done to Eden, or how the threat of his presence mirrored the Winters case. At least then there had been CORE agents in place to protect Eden. Damn it, he should have had Lloyd at the hospital to help keep her safe.

Last night they'd had a breakthrough, maybe even a second chance at a real relationship. Whether things between them worked out or not, he cared too much to let anything happen to her. "I'd only left the room for a few minutes. I should have never left you alone," he said, and looked to Eden.

She'd been released this morning, and while she'd said she felt better, the purple smudges of fatigue under her eyes, and the hollowness of her cheeks worried him. In his opinion, Eden needed to go home, have a big meal and then sleep for the next twelve hours. Not that it mattered to her. She wanted to come along with him to CORE to hear about Rachel's new leads. He just hoped being hospitalized for dehydration had been a wakeup call to make her realize she needed to take better care of herself. A body can only take so much...

He began pacing. "Damn it."

"It's not your fault," Eden said.

He stopped and turned to her. "It's not that. Don't get me wrong, I'll beat myself up for letting you down for the next hundred years. I...had a thought." He looked at Rachel. "Keep the smartass remark to yourself."

"He knows me too well," Rachel said, then pulled a pencil from behind her ear. "What are you thinking? And make it fast. I'm dying to show you what I've found."

"Remember when the killer said that Eden was tough, but a body can only take so much?" he asked.

Rachel nodded, while Eden looked away.

He walked to Eden, and placed a hand on her shoulder. He hadn't meant to upset her. He only wanted to brainstorm a few ideas. Knowing Eden liked her privacy, he decided to leave this discussion until they were alone.

"Never mind," he said, sat next to Eden, then nodded to Rachel. "Before you burst, tell us about your new leads."

"Wait," Eden blurted, and reached for his hand. "It's okay. I remember the killer saying that, and not understanding why. Now I get it."

Rachel tapped the pencil on the table. "Maybe I'm a bit slow today, but I *don't* get it."

Eden tightened her hold on his hand, and some of his earlier frustration disappeared. While a strong woman, she'd let her guard down and reached out to him. For support? For strength? He didn't know. He just hoped this meant her trust in him had started to grow. He'd meant what he'd said at the hospital last night. He didn't want to tiptoe around their past anymore. Not if they had any shot at a future.

"I didn't dehydrate from the flu. It didn't help, of course. The main reason is because I don't eat...much." Eden paused, then cleared her throat. "Rachel, can you go back to that second DVD, to where the killer addressed me?"

"Hang on," Rachel said, then a few seconds later she had the DVD running.

"Here," Eden said. "Listen."

"You demand perfection from yourself," the killer said. "Yet surround yourself with flawed people and animals. And yes, I realize you have flaws of your own, but you don't let anyone else see them, do you? You're tough, but a body can only take so much. Of this I know too well. It's also the reason why I'm here." He raised his hands and slowly spun in a circle. "In my private OR."

"Of this I know too well," Eden echoed after Rachel paused the DVD. "Either he's had an eating disorder or someone he knows has gone through the experience."

Hudson nodded. "Possible. But what would that have to do with torturing and killing those two men?"

Eden shrugged. "Maybe nothing at all. Maybe he just worries about me. You read the note he left."

He had, enough times to memorize the damned thing. "Look at what you're doing to yourself," he quoted. "I watched someone very dear to me suffer from the perception of perfection. Don't make yourself the victim. Be happy with who you are, and take good care of yourself."

"This 'perception of perfection' thing is starting to annoy me," Rachel commented as she reset the DVD. "I'm beginning to think it's a bunch of BS."

"Why's that?" Hudson asked.

"Check this out," she said, then hit PLAY on the remote. The start of the second DVD began, then just as quickly, Rachel hit PAUSE. She tapped at the keyboard a few times, then looked back to the now enlarged still shot. "Do you see it?"

Hudson squinted at the screen. "I see a close-up of the victim's duct-taped ankle."

"Oh my God," Eden gasped. "I see it."

He rose, then moved closer to the TV. "What the hell are you two looking at because I don't...holy shit." A portion of a tattoo peeked from beneath the victim's pant leg where the duct tape had hiked up the material.

"It gets better," Rachel began. "The little bit that we can see of this guy's tattoo matches..." She tapped the keyboard again, then pointed to the adjacent screen. "This one."

The hairy, tattooed calf of the first victim filled the TV.

Hudson glanced back and forth between the two screens, then rested his ass on the table. "Our victims knew each other."

"They could have been in the same fraternity together," Eden suggested.

"True," Rachel agreed. "But through my research of the Sigma Alpha Mu fraternity, I've found hundreds of alumni in the Chicago area alone. We couldn't see our second victim's face, and the way he'd been...mutilated, there's no way of knowing his identity let alone his age. He might be younger than our first vic. They might have gone to different colleges and don't know each other. This is why I'm beginning to think our killer's ranting about perception of perfection is crap."

"Maybe I'm the slow one," he said with a deep sigh. "Because I'm not following."

"I think I am," Eden said. "You think this is a hate crime."

Rachel bobbed her head and waved her pencil. "Exactly. Both of these men had, at one time, belonged to a Jewish fraternity. Isn't it possible that the killer is targeting either the fraternity alumni or Jews in general?"

"Not all Sammys are Jewish," Eden countered.

"True," Rachel responded.

Hudson folded his arms across his chest. "I don't buy it."

Rachel shrugged. "It would probably help if you had the

name of one of the victims. You could ask their family if they're associated with any fellow Sammys or if they'd received any threats recently."

After spending hours comparing drivers license photos to Rachel's composite of the first victim, and continuously coming up empty, he'd begun to think they were running into another dead end. If anything, they were moving backward instead of forward on the case, and the killer was already two steps ahead of them. At this point, all they had to work with was the suspicion that the killer's OR was in the country, matching tattoos, and a disturbing as hell film festival. Without a solid lead, he worried they wouldn't be able to stop the killer from torturing and murdering his next two victims.

More frustrated than when he'd first arrived, he walked over to Eden, then grabbed his coat off the chair. "I'm taking Eden home. She needs her rest."

As he helped Eden with her coat, Rachel waved a piece of paper. "You might want to make a phone call first."

"To who?" Hudson asked.

"Rita Elliot, ex-wife to *Doctor* Thomas Elliot, a former Sammy and, drum roll please, a practicing plastic surgeon specializing in breast augmentation."

Eden held her gloved hands in front of the heater. "Rachel's a piece of work. Why wouldn't she tell us she'd found out about Elliot's identity when we first arrived?"

Hudson turned the Trans Am onto the busy street. "Because she lives for drama and because she's a pain in the ass."

She smiled. "She's good at what she does, though."

"No doubt. I don't know what any of us would do without her." He reached over and took her hand. "Warm yet?"

"Getting there." Instead of pulling away, she held his hand. After their talk last night in the hospital, she liked the idea of lowering her guard and opening up to him. Considering she'd never allowed herself to dwell on emotions such as really strong like, taking baby steps with their relationship was a must, though. After spending years shouldering her demons and secrets alone, she needed to be sure she could fully trust Hudson, and her own feelings for him.

"Why don't I take you home so you can rest?" Hudson asked. "I can have Lloyd hang out with you while I pay Elliot's ex-wife a visit."

She shook her head. "I don't want Lloyd babysitting me again. Actually, I'm embarrassed to see him."

"Because he held a trash can while you puked?"

Rolling her eyes, she stared out the passenger window. "So, we're going to try and be open and honest with each other, right?"

"I thought that was the plan."

Her cheeks burned with mortification. "I...ah, after I started singing the Pina Colada song to Lloyd, I kind of said something about him banging my brother."

Hudson burst into laughter. "That's hilarious. I'm sure Lloyd realized you weren't yourself."

"Um, yeah. Except he really is banging my brother." She looked at him when he didn't respond, and began to wonder if she'd pegged him wrong. Maybe he was more judgmental than she'd thought. If he had issue with Lloyd and Will being gay, their relationship problems would be solved. There wouldn't be one. She might not have been the best sister, but she refused to associate with a bigot. "I take it you've got a problem with that," she finally said.

He shook his head. "No, actually. I could care less who Lloyd sleeps with, or...bangs," he finished with a grin. "You just surprised me."

"When Will told the family he was gay, it surprised us, too. When he was in high school, all the girls were crushing on him, and he always had a date." She shrugged. "I'm glad he's out, and happy, and with the right partner."

"Are you disappointed Will and Celeste didn't make it to the hospital last night?"

"No, not at all. Relieved is more like it. I...haven't been the best sister to either of them. Actually Celeste and I have been arguing more and more lately."

"Why's that?"

"Long story."

"We've got a thirty minute drive to the former Mrs. Elliot's house, so I've got the time."

Which meant Hudson wouldn't make her stay home with a babysitter. Thank God. Although embarrassed by her remark to Lloyd, if he had come to the house to stay with her, she would have apologized. And while she had confidence in Lloyd as a pseudo bodyguard, she preferred Hudson's company. With him, she knew she'd always be safe. Hudson didn't like to lose, and, at any cost, had always achieved his objectives.

"Thank you," she said and squeezed his hand.

"For the record, I'd prefer if you were at home resting. But I also know, Ms. Investigative Reporter, how important it is for you to be part of this case." He lifted a shoulder. "Besides, I like your company."

She gave his arm a light punch. "You wouldn't have said that two days ago."

"You wouldn't have given me the chance," he reminded her. "Now tell me the deal with your sister. The few times I met her, she seemed nice."

"She is nice. She's everything I'm not. Pretty—"

"I think you're prettier."

She grinned. "Thanks, but Celeste is pretty inside and out, where I'm not as...nice."

"Don't sell yourself short."

"I'm not. It's just that Celeste has always put everyone else first before taking care of herself, where I have always taken care of me."

"Eden," he began, and took her hand again. "If you don't take care of you, who will?"

She thought about him alone in a basement cell somewhere in the jungles of Columbia. How vulnerable and scared he must have felt. Her heart ached for him. She might have disposed of their relationship, and had acted flippant about her feelings for him, but deep down, she'd never stopped caring about him.

"Speaking from experience?" she asked.

"Absolutely."

"While I agree with you, Celeste sees things differently. She's been hard on me lately for being a control freak, and for not keeping in touch with the family. She just doesn't understand that I'm extremely busy with my career. I can't drop everything to meet for lunch or gab on the phone. I text and email. It's quick and easy, and—"

"Keeps you from having to have real contact."

So much for a truce. She pulled her hand away, then peeled off the glove.

Hudson blew out a deep breath. "I'm not trying to start an argument, only pointing out the facts. Your sister is different from you. She needs that human contact, whereas you don't. Maybe you can make an exception for Celeste and Will. You know, I don't have any siblings, but I would have loved a brother or sister. Growing up might not have been as hard and lonely."

Wow. All of this truth-telling crap exhausted and upset her. She didn't want to think about Hudson as a lonely little boy. How he might have lain in his childhood bed wishing for an older brother to soften whatever blows he'd been delivered as a kid. Thinking about any pain he'd endured made her heart ache. Thinking about the pain she might have caused Celeste and Will created a well of guilt. Still, she couldn't help the resentment toward Celeste, how she'd always been favored by their mother. How Celeste and their mom hadn't been able to help save her from the nightmare that still haunted her.

"I understand what you're saying," she began. "And I think you're right. Celeste isn't like me, and I think I need to keep reminding myself of that. I'll call her tomorrow and schedule lunch for sometime next week."

"Why not call her today?"

"Because I'm busy trying to find a killer. And after we meet with the ex-wife, I was hoping you'd take me to the station. I promise it'll only be an hour," she said before he could argue. "I really have to get this last segment for my show done."

He glanced at her, then shifted his focus back to the road. "One hour."

"Promise."

"Good," he said, then pulled the car into a driveway. After turning off the ignition, he faced her. "How'd we do for our first major truth-telling conversation?"

She thought about a couple of major points of interest she'd neglected to share. The Trans Am hadn't been the ideal place to blurt out that she'd been gang raped as a teenager, and that her sister and mom had claimed to be psychic, but hadn't been able to help her. At times, when she'd thought about the reasons behind her resentment for Celeste and her mom, she'd questioned her rationale. If she'd sometimes thought her actions and motives had been illogical, what would Hudson think? She needed time to consider how she'd word this portion of her past. Hudson might not be judgmental, but she didn't want to lose his respect. Even when she'd been angry with him, even when he'd made a huge mistake that had cost them their relationship, she'd always respected him as a person. Hudson's intentions had always been pure. Protect the innocent. Fight the bad guys.

"For a start, I think we did pretty good," she answered him.

"Dr. Phil, good?" he asked with a grin, then opened his door.

"I don't know if I'd go that far," she said, as he helped her from the Trans Am. "But it's a start."

He drew in a deep breath. "Are you sure you're up to this?"

She nodded, then rubbed her arms to ward off the cold, brisk wind.

"Then let's introduce ourselves to our victim's ex."

Pudge woke from a deep, dreamless sleep to Mama banging on

her bed tray.

bitch ungrateful bitch

"Yes, she is." Pudge climbed out of the bed. "I'm coming, Mama," Pudge shouted, then began to dress. Once clothed, Pudge left the bedroom, then headed for the living room.

"It's about time," Mama yelled. "What's wrong with you? It's almost noon. Are you sick or something?"

Pudge hadn't realized the hour, and wanted to hurry up with Mama. They needed to see the news and find out how popular Dr. Dread had been today.

"Don't you have to work?" Mama asked.

"I'm on the afternoon shift at the factory," Pudge lied. Mama had no clue there wasn't, and never had been, a factory job. While Pudge did earn an income, it came from WBDJ-TV. Mama didn't need to know about their aspirations, or the job at the station. Disclosing them would mean disclosing the disguise Pudge had perfected during the past two years. The people who worked at WBDJ didn't know Pudge as Pudge. And Mama wouldn't recognize her own child, even on the evening news.

"Whatever. Just make me something to eat. I'm starving. Damn near slept the day away yesterday," Mama griped, then gave her food order.

Pudge made the frozen pizza, eggs, waffles and bacon the bitch had demanded. After changing Mama's colostomy bag and checking her bedsores, Pudge took the remote off the bed.

"Gimme that," Mama commanded. "It's mine."

Pudge held the remote out of reach and walked toward the TV. "Just hang on a second. I want to catch the twelve o'clock news and see what the weather's going to be like today."

"It's frickin' November," Mama said over a mouthful. "Don't take a genius meteorologist to know it's going to be cold."

sleep sleep put mama back to sleep hate her hate her

Pudge hid a smile, and ignored the voice. With the TV set on Channel 5, Pudge watched and waited with anticipation.

Thirty minutes later, confused and concerned, Pudge

dropped the remote on Mama's fat belly. "Need anything else before I leave?"

"Where you going? I thought your shift don't start until later."

"It doesn't, but I have a few errands to run beforehand."

"Leave me enough food and soda to get me by 'til you come home."

Pudge took care of Mama, then went to the bedroom. "I don't understand. Why wasn't it on the news? They should have found the body by now."

dont worry dont

"You're right. It's stupid to worry. Maybe Nurse Gretchen wasn't supposed to work today, and that's why no one has searched for her."

yes yes smart so smart

Pudge dressed, then stood in front of the mirror and applied the necessary hair and makeup. "Poor Eden won't get the scoop on Nurse Gretchen when she's finally discovered. That dumb ass, Ryan Anders, won't either."

black ball blackity black ball

Pudge smiled. That fool, Kyle Edwards, had fallen for the bait, and had proceeded to force the Chicago police to black ball WBDJ from the CPD inner circle. Once Eden and Ryan were out of the picture, Pudge would rectify that situation and receive the promotion that had long been denied. "Richard Jeffries will be kissing my ass when it's all said and done. After he's finished paying his respects to Eden."

departed dearly departed

Pudge laughed. "Yes, my love. They should have never messed with us."

Michael Morrison stood against the brick wall, waiting for his next patient to emerge from his newly renovated, eight thousand square foot mansion. The plastic surgeon had paid nearly three million for the home, then had dropped another million for the renovations. Business had been very good for Dr. Leonard Tully. The money the doctor had made off of Eliza's surgeries could have paid for the upgrade to one of the mansion's seven bathrooms.

Twenty minutes passed and he began to worry that today might have been a waste of time. Tully should have left by now. Michael had researched his schedule and knew Tully came home for lunch twice a week, stayed for an hour, then left for the plastic surgery clinic he'd joined after Cosmetic Solutions and Med Spa had disbanded. Today was one of those days. He should have left by now.

The door to the mansion opened. Michael pushed off the wall as a short, rotund man kissed a beautiful woman on the lips. The man slipped on a pair of sunglasses, and began to walk down the steps.

Michael recognized Tully immediately, and also noticed the man's girth had grown since he'd last seen him. Ironic, considering the doctor performed liposuction for a living. In his opinion, if you're pushing your wares, you should look the part.

He also recognized the woman waving from the door as Mrs. Tully. Although in her early forties, she had the body and face of a twenty-year-old woman. Being married to a plastic surgeon did have its merits, he supposed. Too bad it wasn't a happy marriage. Lonely Mrs. Tully, Michael had discovered, had a penchant for young Latin men. Of course her husband didn't have a clue, and if he had, Michael assumed the man didn't care. Dr. Tully had his share of extra marital affairs as well. Wouldn't Mrs. Tully be interested to know that her husband also enjoyed the company of young Latin men?

Michael casually walked to the minivan he'd parked on an adjacent street. Once inside the van, he checked the review mirror, and waited for Tully to drive his Mercedes from the garage. Seconds later, Tully passed him. Michael switched the van's gear into DRIVE and began to follow.

Taking Tully during the day had its risks, but the timing worked. Mrs. Tully had planned a ladies weekend in Arizona, and would leave this evening. No one would be home to miss the doctor when he didn't arrive. Plus, Michael had a schedule to meet. There were also the coyotes that needed to be kept fat and happy. He didn't want to hear about them threatening his neighbors to the point that the animal warden had to become involved. Once he closed his OR, he could care less. The animal warden, the local sheriff, hell, even the FBI could roam his land and pick up the bits and pieces of the doctors that even a coyote wouldn't eat. He would have accomplished his mission, his promises to his daughter. Besides, he planned to be long gone before anyone set foot on his land. He had a one-way ticket to a place where no one could extradite him.

Tully slowed, then turned the Mercedes into a parking garage located next to the plastic surgery clinic. Michael followed, and keeping his baseball cap low, paid the parking attendant, then drove the van to the level where the doctor usually parked his Mercedes.

Michael had been in this garage several times, and knew where the security cameras were located. Unfortunately for Dr. Tully, the owners of the garage had installed cheap units, and only placed them at the entrance of the garage and at the elevator and stairwell.

Michael parked the van shy of the elevator and its camera, while Dr. Tully parked in his reserved spot near the middle of the garage. Knowing Tully would soon pass him in order to reach the elevator, Michael readied the syringe, crawled into the back of the minivan, then slid open the passenger side back door.

His heart pounded as he edged toward the back of the van and waited. The distinct click of the doctor's expensive Italian shoes echoed off the cement. Closer. Closer.

Michael watched the ground. When one leather shoe tip passed the van's bumper, he chop blocked the man in the esophagus. Tully dropped, clutching his throat and gasping. Michael jabbed the syringe into his neck, directly into the man's carotid artery.

Tully looked at him, his eyes already drooping and glassy.

"Why?" he mouthed, still unable to speak due to the blow to the esophagus.

Michael ignored the doctor and shoved him into the van. Tully resisted. Shoved back and planted one Italian shoe on the van's floorboard, and the other on the ground.

Considering Tully's weight, Michael wondered if maybe he should have used a stronger dosage. Worried someone might exit the elevator, or drive through the garage and see them, he opted for plan B.

Using all of his weight, Michael pushed Tully harder, then swept the other man's foot with his boot. One Italian shoe dropped to the ground as Tully fell forward into the van. Before the man could push himself up and offer more resistance, Michael grabbed the bat he'd used to subdue his first victim, and hit Tully on the back of the head. The man dropped and remained still.

Catching his breath, Michael picked up the shoe, tossed it next to Tully, climbed into the van, then closed the door. He checked the man's pulse.

Alive.

Good.

After going through all of this trouble, he'd hate to have killed Tully before he gave the man a taste of his own medicine.

CHAPTER 12

EDEN STEPPED UNDER the spray of hot water and released a sigh as she washed the lingering hospital scent from her body. When she realized the hair on her legs rivaled Fabio's, she reached for the razor and shaving cream.

Just in case.

Not that she planned on seducing Hudson.

Okay, so she did. Maybe.

Like her, he acted as if he wanted to explore their relationship. Based on some of the things he'd said and done the past few days, she suspected that exploration went beyond the emotional. She thought back to the other day, when she'd lied about having a date. Thought back to the way he'd shoved his big hands through her hair, and drew their mouths together until their lips were only inches apart. Remembered his words, how he'd boldly reminded her of the way she'd cried out his name when she'd come for him.

Flashbacks to when they'd been together, in his bed or hers, having hot sex on the kitchen counter or the living room floor, collided together into a pornographic kaleidoscope of naked skin, frenzied kisses, and rapturous caresses. Sucking in a deep breath, she dropped the razor and pressed her palm between her thighs. She needed to come, to release the pent up sexual frustration that had been driving her insane since Hudson walked back into her life.

Although tempted to take care of herself in the shower, she retrieved the razor and finished shaving. Since she'd broken up with Hudson, there had been a couple of bad lovers, and masturbation had become a necessity. Only now, the man she'd fantasized about during those lonely nights was in her home.

Down the hall.

Only a shout away.

She rinsed, then toweled off her hair and body while contemplating how and if she should attempt to seduce Hudson. The how really wasn't the difficult part to plan. The *if* was the problem. If she had sex with Hudson, there would be no turning back, and no easy way to remain as aloof about their relationship as she'd pretended two years ago, or even now. She did have an easy out should things go to hell again. The trip scheduled to New York and the Network job would be an excellent way to soften another break-up with him.

What was wrong with her? She was contemplating sex and a fast, easy break-up at the same time? She couldn't help herself, though. Yes, she loved to take risks, but not with her heart. And having an easy out was comforting, safe.

As she finished blowing her hair dry, she looked at her reflection in the large mirror. Her hair lacked the luster it used to have, and her body…

She quickly wrapped the towel around her, then rushed to the bedroom in search of anything to cover herself. The sight of her bony ribs, small tits, concave belly and flat ass horrified her. Being slim and fit had always been important to her. She controlled how she looked, no one else. But looking as if she'd been recently released from a prison camp hadn't been part of her strict diet and exercise regimen.

To think she'd considered seducing Hudson. She couldn't even hide her lack of curves in the dark. Hell, her bony ribs would stab him.

Dropping the towel, she pulled a pair of jeans out of the

closet. She slipped them on and looked in the mirror. She couldn't wear these. They hung from her hips and bagged around her legs and ass.

"Damn it," she muttered, as she shoved off the jeans, and then stepped into a pair of yoga pants. An oversized t-shirt and sweatshirt completed the horrible ensemble. She fought tears of frustration as she viewed her reflection again. She'd allowed herself to not only become too skinny, but so nutritionally unbalanced that she'd become dehydrated. Even more frustrating, she wanted to have sex with Hudson, but feared his response to her pathetic, scrawny body.

Sick of looking at herself, she left the bedroom and headed for the kitchen. The aroma of Italian sausage and pepperoni made her mouth water and her empty stomach grumble. She checked the oven. A pizza box sat on the warming rack, begging to be opened and devoured.

Pizza would be a good start on the road to regaining a few of her curves. Now that she thought about it, cheesecake would work, too. Her sister made awesome cheesecake. After Celeste opened the bakery, she'd have to buy a slice or two. Oh, and some chocolate chip cookies. She hadn't had her sister's cookies in years.

Although her mouth watered, rather than dive into the pizza, she decided, considering Hudson had obviously ordered it, she should wait for him as he had for her. She walked into the living room, then sat in the chair when she realized he was on his cell phone.

"Okay, Rachel," he said, looked at her and held up one finger.

A few minutes later, he ended the call, then set his laptop on the coffee table. "Rachel's in full pout mode," he said as he leaned back into the sofa.

"Because Elliot's ex had nothing to give us? She shouldn't be surprised. Those two are exes for a reason."

"True, but I'd hoped they'd been on good terms."

"A cheating husband does have a way of scorning a woman. At least she got a big set of boobs out of the bad marriage."

He grinned. "Also true."

"So the ex-wife ended up being no help. I'm sure your little brainiac has come up with some other ways to find information about Elliot."

"She has. She's found a way into his email account." He held up a hand. "Don't even ask. She's compiling a list of his contacts as well as trying to find any threatening emails. So far we know he was working out of a couple of satellite medical centers. One in Oak Park, and the other in Western Springs."

"Will we be heading to the Burbs to meet with his associates?"

"Not today. The procedures Elliot performs are outpatient. It's almost five, his offices will close soon. We can head there tomorrow, but I'm not sure how much good it'll do. Rachel called both of his offices, and was told that Elliot was on vacation until next week."

"Did she happen to ask when he'd left for this vacation?"

"Last Saturday."

She sucked in a breath, then nodded. "Timing works. We had bad weather Sunday. When we watched the DVD we could see lightning through the windows. The killer could have kidnapped him Saturday or even Sunday, then tortured and killed him that night."

"That's what I'm thinking."

"What's next?"

"Pizza."

She smiled. "For sure. I'm starving."

"Music to my ears," he said, and stood. He offered his hand, then helped her from the chair. In an instant, he wrapped his arms around her. "I think your sweatshirt has swallowed you."

"I'm cold," she lied, and squirmed out of his arms before he could feel every one of her bones. "Now tell me our next move. I didn't have a chance to go to the station today, and really need to make it in tomorrow." After their interview with Elliot's ex, she'd been too tired to work, and had longed for a hot shower.

He followed her into the kitchen. "We'll go to the station in the morning, then to Elliot's offices. By then Rachel should have a list of people we could meet. She's also running a background check on him. Considering he does have a medical license, I doubt she'll find anything criminal, but his finances might give us another route to explore."

"Perfect," she said as she pulled the pizza from the oven. "Tomorrow I can finally put my segment to rest, then give my full concentration to this case."

"I'd rather you concentrate on your health," he said as he searched for plates.

She moved past him, opened the cabinet above his head, then handed him the plates. "I told you I'm fine, and I promised that I'd take better care of myself. Watch and witness," she said, and grabbed a piece of pizza. "I haven't had pizza in almost four years." The doorbell rang. She dropped the uneaten pizza on the plate. "Are you expecting someone?"

He shook his head. "No. Stay here. I'll see who's at the door. And don't touch that pizza until I get back. I want to witness the miracle," he said with a grin.

When Hudson left the kitchen, Brutal pawed at her leg. She looked at the dog, then to the cat sitting expectantly by its dish.

"I guess you guys want to eat, too," she said, then began filling their dishes. As she turned to stow the food into the pantry, she froze.

"Hey," Celeste said, as she moved into the kitchen with her arms open wide. "How are you feeling?"

Eden set the food aside and hugged her sister. "Good, thanks. Is John with you?"

"Yeah, he's in the living room with Hudson. I'm sorry I didn't make it to the hospital yesterday."

After closing the pantry door, Eden shrugged. "It's not a big deal. I wasn't there long."

"I know, but Will didn't make it, either. One of us should have been there for you."

She'd told Hudson that the lack of her brother and sister's

presence at the hospital hadn't bothered her, but it had, and still did. Other than Hudson, no one had given a damn about her condition. Well, except for the killer. Even he'd left her a note and flowers.

She had no one to blame. She'd alienated herself from her family, and hadn't bothered to work on her relationship with Celeste. Hudson was right, she and Celeste were two different people, but more importantly, they were sisters. She loved Celeste, and was determined to set things straight between them. Starting today.

"It's okay," she said, then stowed the pizza back into the oven.

"I still feel bad. At the same time, I think your being hospitalized might have been a good thing."

Eden turned, and frowned. "Oh?"

Celeste slipped out of her coat, then rested it on the chair. "Well, you've had an obvious eating disorder for years, and have gotten way too skinny. Just look at yourself. You're swimming in that sweatshirt, and your legs look like sticks."

"Thanks for your concern." Although irritated with Celeste's comments, Eden kept her tone light. Damn it, she *would* keep the peace and take every effort to make amends with her sister. She did eye Celeste's abundant curves, though. She'd always been jealous of her sister's big boobs, tiny waist, full hips and butt. Even at her heaviest, Eden couldn't attain an hourglass figure. Built more like her dad's side of the family, she'd been forced to deal with long, thin legs and a flat chest. She suddenly wondered if Hudson preferred Celeste's body type over hers. As a wave of jealousy hit her she added, "And I don't have an eating disorder."

"So you're not making yourself throw up anymore?" Celeste asked.

Her sister had known? "No."

"Okay, then you're just anorexic now."

Celeste wasn't making things easy. Eden wanted to blow up at her, and tell Celeste to kiss her ass. But she could be the better person. She *would* be the better person. "Are you just about ready to open the bakery?" she asked, hoping a change of subject would help.

"Don't avoid the obvious, Eden. You have a lot of issues you need to deal with before you really cause harm to your body. I think you should see a psychologist."

"I was just thinking about your cheesecake before you and John got here," Eden said, ignoring Celeste's ridiculous suggestion. "I haven't had any of your bakery in forever."

"Stop it," Celeste shouted. "I've called Dad, and told him about you being hospitalized, and my concerns. He's flying into Chicago next weekend. When he gets here, Will's going to join us and we're going to have a long talk."

"Are we? Is this some sort of intervention you're planning?"

"If that's what you want to call it, then yes."

"Too bad you couldn't make it to the hospital yesterday. This pep talk of yours has been very inspiring," Eden said, then took a step forward. She'd tried to make amends, but Celeste had crossed the line. "Anything else you want to comment on before I make you leave?"

"*Make* me leave? Little juvenile don't you think?"

"How do you expect me to react when you walk into my house, full of apologies, then turn on me with all this bullshit?"

"I expect you to have the decency to listen," Celeste responded, and folded her arms over her ample chest.

"You *expect*? Here's what I expect. I expect you to respect my privacy. I also expect you to act like my sister, not my mother. One of the reasons I don't call or want to get together with you is because when we do talk, you spend the entire time telling me what I'm doing wrong with my life. Get your house in order before you come in and judge mine."

"My house is in order," Celeste said.

"Oh, that's right. I'm sure you have no daddy issues."

"That was a little low, don't you think?" Celeste asked, and fisted her hands to her sides. "And for the record, I'm fine with Ian being my biological father. My relationship with our dad hasn't changed. Got anything else you want to throw at me?"

"No, Celeste, I don't. You're perfect. Got yourself a Mr. GQ fiancé, the bakery, a couple of daddies...just perfect." Eden turned away, hating the bitterness of her tone. She couldn't help herself, though. Being near Celeste reminded her of how imperfect her life was sometimes. Yes, she had a nice home. Yes, she had an awesome career. But she couldn't help longing for what Celeste had...security. Her sister oozed confidence, was secure with herself, and had the love of a man who would literally kill for her.

Celeste placed a hand on her shoulder. "I never said my life was perfect. And I'm sorry you feel the way you do. I do wish you'd try to get to know John, though."

Eden moved to the counter. "The first time I met him, he made his opinion of me clear. Sorry if I don't feel like wasting my time impressing your fiancé."

Hudson let out a soft whistle, and looked at John. "Do you think they realize we can hear every word they're saying?" he asked, still shocked by Eden and Celeste's argument. After listening to Celeste berate Eden over her eating issues, when she'd acted as if she'd come to the house out of concern, he'd begun to understand why Eden didn't talk with her sister.

"I don't think they care," John said, then winced when a cabinet door slammed shut.

"Now you're going to tell me how to handle my love life?" Eden asked, her voice carrying from the kitchen to the living room.

"While we're at it, I might as well," Celeste answered just as loudly. "I know all about the affair you had with Hudson, and I hope you don't plan to make the same mistake twice. You could do better if you bothered to try."

"Kiss my ass. And by the by, did you find out about Hudson through office gossip or did you get that out of your crystal ball again?" Eden asked.

"Uh-oh, first me, now they're talking about you," John said. "Maybe we should take that dog outside before we hear something we shouldn't."

170

Hudson shook his head. He wanted to hear what Eden had to say about him. Hell, he wanted to hear her defend him against Celeste. Eden tended to flip from hot to cold, and he needed to know where he stood with her. The emotions ping ponging through his head and body whenever he thought of her, or was near her, sometimes left him in a weak position. Vulnerable. He wanted Eden in every way. To open his heart and mind to the idea of commitment, monogamy, love, and then have it squashed again? No way would he leave the room when he had a ringside seat, and could hear everything between the sisters.

"Stop with the jabs about my ability," Celeste shouted. "I'm sick of it."

"Your ability. God, Celeste, you make yourself sound like a fricking superhero."

"And you sound like a bitch."

"Now who's being juvenile?" Eden countered. "Look, thanks for stopping by. As stimulating as this conversation has been, Hudson and I were about to eat, then we planned to have a lot of really hot sex."

Hudson bit the inside of his cheek to keep from laughing. Sex hadn't been on the agenda—not that he wouldn't rearrange the evening's schedule to accommodate her. He'd never stopped wanting Eden, but hadn't planned to push the physical part of their relationship yet. Making a move on a women just released from the hospital bordered on tacky.

"Um," Hudson began. "You realize Eden's just trying to get at Celeste. I don't want word getting back to Ian that we're—"

John waved a hand. "What you do is your business."

Before Hudson could thank him, Eden stormed into the room. "You know where the door is. Use it."

Celeste trailed behind clutching her coat. "This is so typical of you," she said to Eden. "When you don't want to hear—"

"Obviously your psychic abilities aren't helping you understand me," Eden interrupted. "So let me clue you in on something. I'm a grown woman. I don't need you to tell me how to run my life. If I choose to starve myself, that's my business. If I choose to have hot monkey sex with Hudson, I will. So back off."

"How eloquent and classy," Celeste said, then she turned to Hudson. "I'm sorry. I assume you two heard our conversation."

He nodded as John said, "Yeah, pretty much every word."

"I see," Celeste said. "Again, Hudson, I'm sorry. You seem like a nice guy. But, no offense, I think what you two are doing is a mistake."

"Oh my God, Celeste," Eden shouted. "Listen to yourself. Why can't you let it go?"

"Come on, Eden," Celeste countered. "Do you honestly believe you and Hudson can have a real relationship like John and I have?"

Eden looked at him, and Hudson sucked in his breath. He'd seen Eden dressed in her finest, her hair and make-up perfect. But now, wearing a ridiculously big sweatshirt that hid her body, no make-up, and her hair falling from a slack ponytail, she'd never looked more beautiful to him. The fire in her eyes and the color in her cheeks had nothing to do with the obvious anger she harbored for her sister. Not with the way she slowly trailed her hungry gaze from his shit kickers, up his legs, to his chest, then to his mouth. When she settled her eyes on his, she released the door knob, then with seductive grace, moved toward him.

She took his hand, placed his palm on her back, then reached her arms around his neck. His eyes riveted on the heat radiating from hers, everything and everyone in the room disappeared from his mind. His sole focus lay with the beautiful woman tantalizing him with her inviting lips and intoxicating scent. Before he could clear his head from the sensual fog she'd induced, and gain a moment's worth of sense, her lips parted and he gave into temptation.

Eden kissed him hard, fast and without passion, then abruptly turned to Celeste, leaving him at a loss. Had the kiss been nothing but another way to needle her sister? He'd sworn there had been longing in her eyes. More than that, he'd sworn he'd seen pride and admiration. For that brief moment, before she'd walked across the room and kissed him, he'd honestly thought she cared about him, about them. That she believed, as he did, they already had what John and Celeste had, maybe even more.

"If you don't mind," Eden said to Celeste, and trailed a finger along his chest. "We'd like to get to that pizza and hot monkey sex."

Celeste shook her head, and sent Eden a half-smile. "Thanks for the show. I'm sure that's all it was," she finished with a shrug.

Eden stiffened in his arms. With her body taut, Hudson worried she was preparing for another scathing remark that would only continue this useless argument. "John," he said, and led her to the couch. She veered away, and headed for the kitchen instead. He watched her go, then turned to the other man again.

John had already moved to the front door, which stood open, letting in the cold, November air. Celeste no longer remained in the foyer, and must have decided to leave. With his hand on the door knob, John said, "I'm going to pretend the whole evening never existed."

Hudson cracked a smile. "I doubt the girls will."

"Right. I'm sure I'll have to listen to Celeste rehash the entire argument for the rest of the night. For the record, whether she's right or wrong, I'm always going to have Celeste's back."

Hudson nodded. "After seeing firsthand how things are between them, I think I understand why Ian didn't ask you to handle this case."

John pulled the coat collar around his neck. "That and he wanted us to focus on the wedding plans. You know what's funny about tonight? Celeste had planned on asking Eden to be her maid of honor." He released a sigh, his breath a puff of vapor against the cold. "I better go before she freezes to death."

After Hudson closed, then locked the door, he headed for the kitchen. When he didn't find Eden there, he moved to the bedroom. She sat on the bed stroking Fabio's long blond mane with one hand, and Brutal's scrawny little body with the other. When she looked up at him, the sizzle that had been in her eyes earlier had faded to shame.

"I'm sorry you had to witness that," she said.

He folded his arms across his chest, then leaned against the door jamb. "Just tell me one thing. And please, no lies or no half-truths."

She nodded. "Of course. What is it?"

"When you kissed me...was it like Celeste said? Was it just for show?"

CHAPTER 13

EDEN STARED AT Hudson as anger, shock, and mortification tore through her and blended together like a potent, toxic cocktail. She could blame her sister. Celeste *had* goaded her, belittled her relationship with Hudson. Instead of simply coming to his defense and leaving it at that, she'd kissed him in order to prove to her sister that they had something passionate and good together. In doing so, she'd made a fool of herself, and a mockery of their relationship. Now Hudson stood in the doorway of her bedroom questioning the authenticity of the kiss.

Rubbing a shaky hand across her forehead, she held his gaze. "No. The kiss wasn't for show."

Still holding his arms across his chest, he shifted his stance. "I don't believe you."

Tears welled in her eyes. She blinked them back, shocked by the sudden wave of sadness. The last time she'd cried had been when she'd ended things with Hudson. Was this the beginning of the end already? Had she screwed up bad enough that he might have changed his mind about her, about them?

"No lies or half-truths," she reminded him, and wiped a stray tear. "The kiss wasn't great, but it was real."

He shook his head. "Bullshit."

"What? How could you—?"

With hurt and anger darkening his eyes, he pushed off the door jamb, and in two strides hauled her from the bed. Holding her by the upper arms, he crowded her. Then, with a touch that belied the hardness of his face, he caressed her lips with the pad of his thumb. "It's been a while, but I know...I remember your kisses. This one, though. This one...there was no passion." He released her, then turned away. "No nothing."

Another tear escaped as he headed for the door. "Where are you going?"

"I'm not leaving if that's what you're wondering. I can't."

"Because I'm an assignment?"

He didn't answer, and instead, took another step toward the door. She couldn't let him go, not without knowing the truth. She realized it was time to pull on her big girl panties. Hudson had to understand her reasons for the kiss. He had to know how she felt about him, and for once, she had to stop looking for ways to sabotage their relationship in order to prevent the hurt she'd assumed would eventually come, and take a chance. She'd wasted two years away from him. There had been many lonely nights during those years when she'd thought about what could have been if only she'd tried. Would they have fallen madly in love? Married? Had a child? While she wasn't sure if she was necessarily marriage or mommy material, she was sure that she'd once loved Hudson. Damn it, she never stopped. Now she had to fight for them.

"You're right," she blurted. "The kiss wasn't real."

He turned. The shock and anger widening his eyes made her want to take a step back. Even Brutal and Fabio jumped off the bed and fled the room. But she held her ground.

"When Celeste said she thought we were making a big mistake, then acted as if only she and John had something good going, I...I wanted to show her she was wrong."

"I see," he said then tightened his jaw.

She reached up, and placed her palm on his rough, hard jaw line. "I don't think you do. When I had turned to you in the living room, and saw the way you looked at me..." She blew out a deep breath, then smiled. "I hope I'm not mistaken, but I swear I saw pride, respect and passion in your eyes. For *me*. No one has ever looked at me like that before."

When he remained stoic, she held his face with both hands. "I wanted to kiss you so bad. All I could think about, even with Celeste and John in the room, was you and me. Your skin against mine, your body twined with mine. Your lips on mine. And when I finally walked across the room to kiss you, I realized it was all wrong. What I wanted to show you...I didn't want anyone else to see. I wanted it to be for just you."

Gently, he gripped her wrists. "What did you want to show me?" he asked, his voice raw, husky and oozing with need.

The sexiness in his tone grabbed her, held her enthralled, and propelled her past the edge of uncertainty. He deserved the truth. "That I'd never stopped caring. That I've missed you. That I wish...I wish things could have been different."

"Me too," he said as he released her hands, then ran his fingers through her hair. Her ponytail came loose as he gripped her head in his hand. "When you left me, it was one of the worst times in my life."

Her eyes clouded with tears of regret, but she mustered a smile. "Worse than being tortured in a jungle basement cell?"

His gaze darkened as he drew her closer. "Those wounds healed."

But the wound she'd created hadn't healed. The words hung in the air unsaid. Regret washed over her, for what they could have been, for what she'd denied them. Before she could respond, make excuses or apologize, his lips were a hair's breadth from hers.

"Now kiss me." He nipped her bottom lip. "Kiss me like you meant to."

She wrapped her arms around his neck, threaded her fingers through his hair and then slowly, leisurely, pressed soft, reverent kisses along his jaw and the corners of his mouth. Looking into his eyes, catching the heat simmering in their depths, she let her eyes drift shut, and pressed her lips to his. Leading the way, she coaxed his lips until they opened, then slid her tongue along his.

Holding her head steady, he wrapped his other arm around her and pulled her impossibly closer. He ground her hips against his hard erection, and the passion brewing inside her erupted. The slide of their tongues grew more fervent and eager. She broke the kiss to catch her breath, and remove his shirt.

She pulled the material up his lean torso and began pressing open-mouthed kisses along his scarred, muscular chest. While she feathered her fingers along his hot skin, he finished disposing of the shirt, then reached for the hem of her sweatshirt. She froze.

"What's wrong?" he asked, and cupped her cheek.

Insecurity was something new to her. Considering she'd always been proud of her body, and had never had a problem flaunting it in the past to Hudson, she wasn't sure how to explain her sudden lack of confidence. But after everything they'd discussed tonight, she decided honesty was the only viable route to travel. She trusted him. And without trust and honesty, there was no relationship.

She kissed his hand, and continued to caress his chest. "I...don't look like I used to."

He raised a dark brow. "Did you grow an extra nipple?"

Grinning, she gave him a quick kiss on the lips. "Sorry to disappoint you, but no. I'm, as you know, thinner."

"So."

"So my body isn't all that great."

He cocked his head and studied her for a second, then said, "You think I care whether you're overweight or skinny?" He touched the tip of her nose. "Or if you have a big zit on your nose?" He paused. "Okay, I might be grossed out by that."

She lightly pinched his nipple and laughed.

"Seriously," he began. "The only thing I care about is what's in here." He kissed her forehead. "And in here." He touched her heart. "You're beautiful no matter what."

Moved by his words, she kissed him. As their tongues began to tangle and dance, he took the hem of the sweatshirt and t-shirt, and began to push them up her torso. Along the way, he unhooked her bra, then released her lips and removed the clothes. He dropped them to the floor, and gazed at her naked chest.

She moved to cover her breasts, but he stopped her. "Uh-uh, you're just as pretty as I remembered."

"Thank you," she murmured and allowed her arms to relax. "But can we at least dim the lights?"

He edged her toward the bed. When the back of her knees hit the mattress, he pressed her back, then gripped the waist of the yoga pants. "No way. I've been fantasizing about making love to you for over two years," he said, then pulled her pants and panties over her hips and down her legs.

Naked, she lay on the bed and looked at him. The heat and excitement sizzling in his eyes sent her earlier insecurities fleeing. Her own excitement intensified as she let her gaze roam over his strong, beard-stubbled jaw, his firm lips, then to his muscular chest and tight abs. Fingers itching to touch the soft hair along his chest, to unbuckle his belt and remove his jeans, she licked her lips and reached for him.

He bent instead, and knelt between her legs. Propping herself on her elbows, she watched, mesmerized as he angled his head, and kissed her inner thigh. He ran his hands along her legs. Up and down, touching every inch of her skin, but avoiding what needed the most attention. She raised her hips slightly, inviting him, begging him for what she truly wanted.

He nipped her inner thigh, then licked the spot. Blew a shallow puff of air on her exposed sex, then moved to her other thigh and repeated the nip and lick. Her legs trembled with anticipation. She closed her eyes as her body coiled with need and desire. With each teasing nip and lick, and each stroke of his calloused hands along her skin, she grew wetter, hotter.

"Look at me," he demanded.

When she did, she sucked in a breath. His mouth hovered over her open sex. The heat and longing in his eyes devoured her, and matched the burning desire pulsating through her heart and body.

Then he licked her.

Slow.

Soft.

Over and over, until she begged him for more.

Using his fingers he spread her labia, then dipped his tongue. His cheeks hollowed as he devoured her. Penetrated. Stroked. When he honed in on her clit, swirling and flicking his tongue, the desire that had been coiling through her exploded. She gripped his hair, and wrapped her legs around his upper back. Held him in place as she rode out the glorious orgasm.

Breathing hard, she released her hold on him. When he stood, she reached for his belt, and in record time had it off and his jeans undone. She cupped his bulge. "My turn."

"Later," he said, and shucked the jeans to the floor. "I need to be inside of you. It's been too long."

Although disappointed she couldn't taste him, when she glanced at his arousal, so damn thick and hard, the throb between her thighs intensified. The desire to feel his skin and his hard muscles against her body drove her into a frenzy of need. She stroked his erection anyway, then kissed the tip. "Are you sure?"

He groaned, then scooped her up and laid her on the center of the bed. After he moved between her legs, he kissed her lips, her neck, then flicked his tongue against her nipple. She jerked at the delicious sensation and reached for him. As much as she'd love to have his mouth on her breasts, he was right, it had been too long. "Now. Please," she begged as the tip of his penis kissed her sex.

"Yes," he hissed as he pressed his lean hips forward and filled her.

She hugged him, clung to him, tried to make sure that every possible part of her body touched his. God how she'd missed him. Not just his touch, but the way he made her *feel*.

Secure.

Desired.

Loved.

Just as before, when she was with him, all of her troubles

and worries disappeared. The only thing that mattered was what was between them. Holding him again, feeling him inside her, she wondered why she'd allowed herself to walk away from him. Wondered why she couldn't have been braver and taken the chance, the risk of exposing what had lay deep in her heart and soul.

As he began to rock his hips harder, faster, she gripped the scarred slabs of muscle on his chest, and looked up at him. Her heart melted. Behind the heat in his eyes, deep affection lingered, and she hoped he saw that and more in her own eyes. In her heart, she knew she'd never stopped loving him, and that she'd lied to herself two years ago about never loving him in the first place. She reached for his head, and drew his mouth to hers. Kissed him with all of the love coursing through her body. Now that she held him again, she didn't want to let go of him.

While still inside of her, he leaned back, raised her bottom off the mattress, and held her hip. He trailed his free hand over her taut nipples, then down her stomach until his fingers found her clit. She released a groan. His wicked touch, his thick arousal, made her grow impossibly wetter.

"Come for me," he whispered, then gripped her hips with both hands and rocked harder. Deeper. "Come for me, baby. I need to hear you. I've missed you so damn much."

A shock of desire electrified every part of her body. The orgasm ripped through her with so much force she curled her toes and screamed his name. As wave after wave of pleasure seized her and held her enthralled in a sexual sanctuary she never wanted to leave, Hudson thrust once, twice, then pulled his length from her and came with a low groan.

Breathing hard, he released her hips then rolled off the bed and headed into the bathroom. Seconds later, he returned with a towel, and used it to wipe her stomach. "Sorry," he said. "I didn't have any condoms and wasn't sure if you were still on the pill."

Once he finished cleaning her, he climbed back onto the bed and lay next to her. She cuddled into the crook of her arm, then rested her head on his chest. "I'm still on the pill," she said. "But thanks for thinking of me." She kissed the scar that ran across his left pectoral.

"I never stopped thinking of you," he said, and pulled her closer.

She lightly grazed her nails along his abs. "I never stopped thinking about you, either." Loving this moment, loving him, she decided she owed him the truth. If she expected him to be open and honest, she should do the same. "I…regretted not giving us a chance the moment I walked away, and have been ever since."

He cradled his head with his free arm and looked at her. "Then why did you? I know you were mad, but—"

"I was pissed," she interrupted. "And hurt. I felt betrayed, like you didn't trust me. Then when I found out Winters was a serial rapist, and I was his bait, I…" Uncertain if now was the right time to tell Hudson about what had happened to her when she was sixteen, she hesitated. Telling your lover you'd been raped didn't make for fun pillow talk. At the same time, she honestly believed she owed him a proper and long overdue explanation for her initial over-reaction. They'd cared about each other, and she'd been the one to end the relationship when he hadn't wanted that for them.

"Eden, honey, you don't have to tell me anything you—"

"No, it's okay. I owe you an explanation." She twisted her body until they were chest to chest, drew in a deep breath then blurted, "When I was sixteen, I was raped by four guys from my high school."

Hudson stared at her, and hoped to God Eden couldn't see the rage, the helpless fury storming through his body. Killing was suddenly on his mind, and given the opportunity, he'd make sure those men paid the price. He'd take his time, too. Make them suffer. Make them understand the wrong that they had committed against his woman. Fuck. And he'd treated her as bait to catch a serial killer.

He used all of his energy to keep his hand steady as he smoothed the hair away from her face, and tuck it behind her ear. "If I had known, I would never have…" He smacked his head with his hand, then scrubbed it down his face.

She grabbed his hand, then turned it and kissed his palm. "I'm not telling you this to make you feel guilty. If you'd told me about Winters back then, I would have wanted to help you regardless of what had happened to me. The ones who…hurt me, they never paid for their crime."

While he understood her way of thinking, and some of his guilt abated, knowing those men had gotten away with rape— *Eden's rape*—caused the rage inside him to boil. His head began to pound as his heart ached for the girl who'd been stripped of her innocence.

"Did you go to the police?" he asked.

"No. You've got to understand, I grew up in an extremely small town in Wisconsin. I'm talking a population of about a thousand or so people. The one guy, his dad was county sheriff at the time. Another was the son of one of the deputies. All four of them played football and were stars on the team. Even then, I was smart enough to know what would happen if I told. They'd walk and I'd be accused of crying rape."

"Your family? Did they know?"

She shook her head. "There's something else I need to tell you."

Christ, he didn't know if he could handle any more of her secrets tonight. Knowing what had happened to her ripped a hole in him. Right now, he wanted to hold her and love her, and erase the images of her assault from his mind. Tomorrow, though, he planned to put aside their current case and ask Rachel to hunt down the boys who'd raped Eden. He had several ideas of how he could serve them some proper justice.

"What is it?" he asked.

Her breath fanned across his chest as she bent her head and released a deep sigh.

"Eden," he prompted.

She looked at him, then rolled her eyes and said, "My mom and sister claimed to be psychic, but they couldn't predict my rape. Okay, I said it and I know it sounds stupid—"

He touched her chin. "Are they psychic?"

"I did tell you my mom had passed away, right?"

"No."

Her head hit his chest again. She mumbled something he couldn't understand then faced him. "I really never told you anything about myself, did I?"

As he stared into her eyes, eyes he thought he'd never see again after they broke up, he realized that a person's past really didn't matter. Yes, the past shaped the person one would become, but the here and now was what really mattered. Their here and now, this moment, was—in his gut—the start of their future. What had happened to her infuriated him beyond measure. But she'd trusted him enough to open up, share her vulnerabilities, share a part of herself with him. He treasured her, respected and admired her for her bravery and honesty.

"It's okay, and I think I'm starting to understand some of your sister issues. If she was psychic, how come she couldn't predict your...rape?"

She winced. "Stupid, huh?"

Shrugging, he touched her cheek. "You're not a stupid woman, Eden. And I'm guessing at one time you probably believed in your sister. I imagine after everything happened, you felt...I don't know, betrayed."

Nodding, she gave him a tentative smile. "I did. It was easy to blame Celeste for not warning me about my future. I'll admit I was jealous of my mom and sister's psychic bond. I wanted a special bond with my mom, too. I was always doing goofy things to gain her attention. I know she loved me, but I also knew, deep down, she loved Celeste best."

"But your mom claimed to be psychic and you didn't fault her."

"I looked up to her too much. She was so smart and pretty..." Her eyes clouded with tears. "I miss her."

He had no good memories of his mother. The woman had either been drunk or yelling about everything and anything. While he didn't have any brothers or sisters, he'd had plenty of friends who had, and understood the family dynamic. In his experience, there always seemed to be a love/hate relationship between siblings. No matter what though, they were family. Eden's mom was gone, but she had her sister and brother. Regardless of how any of them felt toward one another, they were still a family. Something he didn't have any more, never really had, and now craved.

He'd been a husband and a son. Neither had worked out well for him. His mom had left, his dad...with the way he'd treated him, he wished he'd left, too. As for his ex, he blamed himself for that bad end. He'd been young and newly married when he'd joined the Marines. Too gung-ho and arrogant, he'd volunteered for the toughest tours, and had only thought of himself, not how his absence would affect his wife. She'd left him for an insurance salesman, and now lived in Florida raising three kids. While he was happy for her, he wished for a family of his own. Lying here with Eden, breaking the silence of her past, he wondered if they could overcome their dedication to their jobs and put each other first. Marry and raise a family of their own. Too soon to tell, and determined to enjoy this moment, he pushed aside the longing for more to focus on what was most important to him. Eden. Her comfort and her happiness.

"John mentioned that Celeste was going to ask you to be her maid of honor tonight."

She half-smiled and rolled her eyes. "She better not make me wear an ugly dress."

"You would be in her wedding?" he asked, confused that Eden would agree when she and Celeste had obvious issues between them.

"Of course. She might drive me nuts with all of her nagging and psychic stuff, but she's my sister. I know it doesn't show...much, but I love her."

He brushed her cheek with the back of his knuckles. "You do realize how *nuts* you sound, right?" he asked with a smile.

She scooted forward, then gave him a quick kiss. "Aren't you glad we've decided to start talking about ourselves? Now you get to discover exactly how nutso I truly am."

Grinning, he said, "I can hardly wait."

"I'm starving. Let's eat." She scooted off of him, then rose from the bed. After she retrieved her sweatshirt, she pulled it over her head. "If you're lucky I'll tell you about the time my dad caught me making out with our minister."

He sat upright. "Holy shit, Eden. A minister?"

Laughing, she flashed her bare ass as she headed for the door. "I'm kidding. It was the minister's son."

Her goofy laugh echoed off the hallway walls as she moved toward the kitchen. Chuckling, he put on his jeans and realized he was finally seeing the real Eden. He'd already had it bad for her, but now that he'd discovered this playful, candid, tender, and devoted version of the woman he'd longed to have in his life again, he realized he might truly be a goner.

Tonight, she'd managed to break every barrier, and had infiltrated his heart and soul. If she left him again, he'd no doubt need car therapy. He'd rather work on that Corvette sitting in his garage for pleasure though, instead of using it to erase pain.

After he made his way into the kitchen, he watched her flutter around, setting the table and plating the food. Her bare butt peeked from beneath the sweatshirt, her long legs reminded him of how they'd been wrapped around his back earlier, and he realized he'd just have to make sure there was no pain. They'd started something tonight, and he didn't plan to finish it for at least another sixty years.

CHAPTER 14

DOROTHY LONG LAY on the rented hospital bed eating sour cream and onion potato chips, and watching a rerun of *The Golden Girls*. The show wasn't as good as *Mama's Family*, but she did love that spitfire, Sophia. Always telling the other women how it was, and meddling in their lives. Speaking of meddling...

For the second time in days, Dorothy wished she could leave her self-imposed prison and haul her sore ass off the bed. She wouldn't mind looking around her house and seeing what Pudge had been up to. Drugs, she assumed. Why else would Pudge sleep until noon? The drugs would also explain the mood swings, the forgetfulness, the sneakiness. Pudge used to dote on her. When she'd asked for Happy Jax, Pudge would hand it to her on a Styrofoam platter. Now she had to practically beg for a damned snack cake.

Plus, Pudge had been keeping strange hours. Her darling child had also switched the ibuprofen yesterday and had given her sleeping pills instead. Pudge thought she was stupid, but Dorothy had figured out the deception earlier today after she'd asked for a couple more ibuprofens for her aching rear. The pills had been different from the ones she'd taken yesterday. Why Pudge would switch her pills, she couldn't be sure. She'd slept like the dead all day yesterday and throughout the night.

Had Pudge brought someone back to the house? Or had Pudge stayed out all night? Drinking, doing drugs…fornicating.

Lately, Dorothy had heard interesting and disgusting noises coming from both the bathroom and Pudge's bedroom. She'd sworn Pudge had been with another person, had even thought she'd heard someone other than Pudge talking, but she hadn't seen anyone else in the house.

She blew out a frustrated breath, set the chips on her stomach, then took a sip of her grape soda. Someone else could have been in the house and she wouldn't have known. Pudge could have let them in through the back door off the kitchen, then snuck them into the bedroom without Dorothy knowing or seeing them. Damn it. If only she could leave the bed and see for herself.

Determined to learn the truth, Dorothy set the soda aside, then glanced at the clock. Half past seven. Pudge wouldn't be home from the factory for hours. The agency that supplied her home nurse, Gretchen, closed at eight. After that, she would only be able to reach their answering service. She should call, and make sure Gretchen came by to see her tomorrow rather than next week. She liked Gretchen, and after she explained her suspicions of drugs and how Pudge had switched her pills, Dorothy was sure the nurse would snoop in Pudge's room for her. If anything, Gretchen could notify the agency, and they could inspect the house.

But if they did find drugs, Dorothy could end up in a nursing home. Again, she didn't want that. She'd lose what little freedom she had left.

Dorothy reached for the phone anyway. She'd have Gretchen come by, and explain the situation in confidence. Wasn't there such thing as nurse/patient confidentiality? She wasn't sure, but hoped her longstanding relationship with the other woman would help.

Minutes later, and satisfied with herself for taking the initiative and calling the agency, Dorothy reached for the bag of chips. The woman at the agency had assured her that

Gretchen would visit tomorrow, and had promised to call Gretchen personally to confirm.

Dorothy crunched a couple of chips, and decided Pudge didn't need to know about the call or Gretchen's upcoming visit. She smiled and used the remote to raise the volume on the TV. Pudge needed to learn Dorothy could be sneaky, too.

Yeah, no one messes with Mama.

Sweaty and panting, Michael Morrison stepped away from the opened minivan and tried to catch his breath. Even though he'd parked the van in the steel garage near his OR, trying to haul Dr. Leonard Tully from the van proved to be quite the challenge. The doctor had him by at least one hundred and fifty pounds, and because he remained unconscious, he was dead weight.

Michael propped his hands on his hips, then looked around the garage for something to help him remove the man from the van and onto the surgical table. The Mechanic's Creeper he'd bought from Sears a few years ago to change the oil on his minivan caught his attention. Michael brought it to the van. He set the Creeper next to the opened door, locked the wheels, then rolled Tully from the floorboard onto the contraption. The doctor hit the metal with a thud.

While the Creeper could hold up to a thousand pounds, it was only forty-four inches long and seventeen inches wide. As he used Tully's legs to roll the Creeper closer to the OR, the doctor's arms and fat hung, and dragged along the floor.

Once in the OR, Michael glanced to the doctor, who reminded him of a beached whale riding a surfboard, then to the surgical table. "This isn't going to work," Michael said to the unconscious man when he realized there was no way in hell he could heave him onto the table. "Considering our options, though, we'll just have to improvise."

Thirty minutes later, Michael had the doctor stripped to his satin boxers and duct taped to the Creeper. Between the blow to the head, and the sedative he'd given Tully, Michael wasn't sure how much longer the man would remain unconscious. Because time was of the essence, if he were to have the DVD on Eden's doorstep by morning, Michael rearranged his medical supplies to fit the new situation. The height of the Creeper could only be raised six inches. In order to ensure a smooth surgery, he made sure everything he needed had been placed at kneeling level. He then checked the Shop-Vac, the wet/dry all-purpose heavy-duty vacuum he'd tweaked especially for Dr. Tully's procedure. Once sure all was well in his OR, Michael rose, then headed for the office.

A fresh bottle of Wild Turkey sat on the desk. Before he reached for the bottle, he turned on the old TV and DVD player. After both devices came to life, he hit PLAY on the remote, then opened the Wild Turkey. He took a long swallow, then another, and another as the home movie began, and Eliza's short life played on the screen.

"Help," Tully screamed from the OR.

Michael shoved off the desk, and still holding the whiskey bottle, ran from the office. When he reached Tully, he stopped, then circled the man.

"What is this?" Tully demanded. "Who are you and where the hell am I?"

Michael took a long swallow of the whiskey, then bent down to Tully's level. "You doctors sure ask a lot of questions," he said, then stood. After setting the bottle on the regular surgical table, he reached for the duct tape. "I've got to finish my movie before we begin your procedure. So, if you don't mind, I'd like you to kindly shut the hell up."

As he was about to place the tape over the other man's mouth, Tully screamed like a two-year-old melting over a stolen cookie. When the doctor finished, Michael said, "All done?"

"No," Tully rasped. "I demand that you release me. I'm a very important person. People will search for me and you will—"

Michael slapped the man's fat face. "Stop," he shouted,

then stood and covered his ears as the other man blubbered and wailed. "Stop, stop, stop." He paced the OR. The guilt, the rage, the shame blended together and made his head spin. The image of Dr. Thomas Elliot, lying on the surgical table, with crudely sewn stitches covering his new, maggot-filled chest crowded his mind and mingled with Dr. Brian Westly's gory perma-grin. Running his hands through his hair, he gripped the strands by the roots and tugged. The pain didn't blot out the men's screams, the blood...oh God, what the coyotes had done to the bodies.

"Listen to me," Tully said in a now calm, soft, and understanding tone. "I'm sure you're a good person. If you let me go, I won't tell anyone about this. I promise you. Just let me go, and we'll get you the help you need."

Michael reached for the whiskey. He nodded, then took a drink. The Wild Turkey burned his throat, and calmed his nerves. He looked down at the doctor. The guilt and shame disappeared the moment he saw the lies in Tully's eyes. Had the doctor looked at his Eliza with those same deceitful eyes as he'd talked her into the unnecessary liposuction? Rage stripped him of any remaining shreds of decency. Morality might have a place in a hospital OR, but not in his.

His OR was for the corrupt.

For the depraved.

For the evil bastards who had stolen his daughter's will to live.

And Dr. Leonard Tully had been one of those bastards. Now it was his turn to understand the pain he'd caused Eliza.

Calmer and more clear headed, Michael knelt next to the doctor. "I appreciate your concern, Dr. Tully, but I'm okay now. Just a case of pre-surgery jitters."

"Surgery." Tully frowned, and his eyes widened with fear. "I don't understand. Whose surgery?"

"Yours." He slapped duct tape over Tully's mouth. "Now, I realize you're probably anxious to begin, but I really must finish my movie. So be a good patient and relax. I'll be ready for you in a few minutes."

He checked the doctor's restraints again, then grabbed the whiskey bottle and returned to the office. "Damn," he muttered when he realized he'd missed most of the home movies. He'd intended to watch the DVD before each surgery to help remind him of his purpose and his goals. The DVD had also helped him cope with the guilt and the shame of torturing and mutilating another human being. After his mini breakdown in the OR, he realized he didn't need the DVD to help him through *this* surgery, though.

Once he'd looked into Tully's shit brown, deceitful eyes, the regret had disappeared and had been replaced with hatred. The pig disgusted him. He'd told his daughter she was too heavy to even consider a modeling career, and that liposuction would take care of the fat pockets stored in her legs, stomach, and hips. By the time Tully had finished with her, instead of smooth skin, she'd been left with hollowed indentations and dimples along her thighs. Her stomach and hips had become lumpy and lopsided.

As the home movie moved to the end, Michael hit the PAUSE button on the DVD player. The still shot of the police photo, taken when Eliza had been found dead in her bedroom, filled the TV screen. She'd never shown him what Tully had done to her body. He stood, then moved closer to the TV. Only when he'd seen this picture had he understood. Only then had he witnessed the butchery Tully had performed.

He curled his hands into fists, then looked to Eliza's letter.

Make them pay, Daddy.

With vengeance on the brain, and three quarters of a bottle of whiskey in hand, Michael stormed from the office. When he reached the OR, he stared down at Tully.

The man's eyes widened and watered as he stared at him with terror. He whimpered against the duct tape and attempted to move his big body. The Creeper remained locked, giving Michael confidence that the contraption would stay secure during the operation.

Slightly buzzed, he set the whiskey on the regular surgical table. He'd have to wait to drink the rest of the Wild Turkey until later. After the surgery, he'd have to make the ninety minute drive to Eden's townhouse to drop off the DVD. Speaking of which...

Michael collected the video equipment, then moved it closer to the Creeper. After making the proper adjustments, he changed into his scrubs, put on the surgical cap, and then tied the mask around his neck. When he reached for the vial of paralytic, he hesitated. He had enough for two procedures if the patients were of an average weight. Tully's girth was beyond average, and his body would require more of the drug than Michael was willing to give. After all, he still had another surgery scheduled.

Skipping over the vial, Michael grabbed the scalpel, then the hose attached to the Shop-Vac. He knelt next to Tully, then ripped the tape for the man's mouth.

Tully released a girly scream, and tears rolled down his doughy cheeks. "P...please," he stuttered. "Let me go. I promise I won't tell. I promise I—"

"Grow a set of balls, Doctor," Michael ordered. "Now listen closely. I want to give you a head's up on what I have planned. In a few moments we will begin your surgery."

"M...mine? I..." He turned his head and started at the medical equipment Michael had set near the Creeper, then swallowed hard. "W...what kind of surgery?"

Michael pointed to the Shop-Vac he'd rigged for this occasion. "The vacuum doesn't even give you a hint?" he asked, then grabbed a handful of Tully's belly flesh. "C'mon, Doc, if you're going to tell your patients they need to be skinny, then go ahead and remove the fat from their bodies, don't you think you should follow your own advice?"

Tully looked between the vacuum and the surgical tools, then back to him. His face pale, and coated with sweat, his eyes bulging with realization and horror, he shook his head. "You're crazy," he screamed. "Crazy."

"No," Michael shook his head. "I'm not crazy, I'm angry. At you and your fellow colleagues."

"I. Don't. Under*stand*," Tully shouted.

193

"Then let me enlighten you. Do you remember Eliza Morrison?"

Tully closed his eyes and slowly nodded. "Yes. She had been a patient at Cosmetic Solutions and Med Spa. She'd taken her own life, and then her father…" He opened his eyes. "Oh my God, you're her father."

"So you do remember me. Good. Yes, I'm Eliza's crazy father who'd tried to sue your medical group for her death. And lost." Michael shook his head. "I'm kind of a poor sport and don't care for losing. I especially didn't like losing my daughter."

"But it wasn't *our* fault. She was an obviously unstable girl."

"Obviously," Michael echoed in a soft, quiet tone that belied the rage churning through him. "If her instability was so *obvious*, why would you, or any of your colleagues, perform her surgeries?"

Tully shifted his shit brown, lying eyes. "At the time, we—"

Michael punched Tully's rotund belly. "Shut up." He hit the doctor again. "No more lies. No more excuses. I only want the truth. Did you know my daughter wasn't in her right mind when she first came to you?"

Crying, Tully winced when Michael raised his fist again. "Wait," he begged. "Her mother was with her. She approved the surgeries, and gave us her permission."

"Her *mother*," Michael said with disgust. "That woman had no right. You had no right. Eliza was over eighteen, and not competent enough to decide what she should and shouldn't do to her own body. You knew that. Her mother knew that. And yet, everyone ignored what was best for *my* child. Why? So her bitch of a mom could ride Eliza's coattails, and you and your fellow *doctors* could make a fast buck. Now she's dead."

"By suicide," Tully reminded him. "We didn't kill her. She killed herself. I understand your grief, but you can't blame us."

Michael stared at Tully, shocked the crybaby had the nerve, considering his impending surgery, to argue. Either Tully had a bigger set of balls than Michael had first thought, or the man was plain stupid. He shook his head, then said, "You *can't* imagine my grief or my hatred for you and your buddies. As I see it, you might as well have placed the razorblades in my daughter's hands the night she slit her wrists." He cocked his head and looked to Tully's stomach, red and blotchy from the punches. "So, now I'm going to give you a little taste of her pain."

Tears streamed down Tully's cheeks. "You're going to...slit my wrists?"

"For a doctor worth millions, you're not all that bright." Michael tapped the Shop-Vac. "That would be too easy. Use your imagination, Doctor. I did. And I've come up with the perfect way to help you understand the pain you'd caused my daughter. So, what do you say? Ready to get this show on the road?"

Michael pulled on the surgical mask, then hit RECORD on the video camera. He reached for the duct tape to seal the man's mouth shut, then tore off a strip.

"Wait," Tully shouted. "Shouldn't I get a chance to say something?"

"You mean your final words?"

Tully nodded.

He looked over his shoulder at the camera, then back at the man. "You don't deserve it." He slapped the tape over the doctor's mouth. "This is the only thing you deserve."

Michael raised the scalpel, then stabbed it into Tully's gut.

Pudge had finished prepping for the ten o'clock news segment when the station manager, Rodger Jeffries, ran into the studio waving his arms and motioning to cameraman, David Ito. Curious, Pudge followed David.

ass nice ass

Pudge glanced at David's ass and agreed. But now wasn't the time to think about sex. Something had happened. Some big news story had broken, and Pudge wanted to be part of it. This could be their chance to make a name for themselves.

Timing and luck. That's all they needed.

luck luck good luck dr dread good luck

Pudge's skin prickled with excitement. Could the commotion be due to the discovery of yet another Dr. Dread victim? Maybe. Maybe not. Pudge needed to know. If Gretchen had been found, and they'd been given the opportunity to work the story...the irony of the possible scenario made Pudge want to laugh. To report Nurse Gretchen's murder on the nightly news, stand in front of the camera acting sad and sickened by the tragedy, while knowing every gory detail...*personally.* Fucking hilarious.

"What's up?" David drawled as the news anchor, Kyle Edwards, moved into their circle.

Looks like we've got another Dr. Dread murder," Rodger said to Ito. "The CPD's blackballed our station, but we still need to report the story. Calling Eden in is not an option."

"She's the reason for our police problem," Kyle said with a smugness Pudge loved.

Kyle hated Eden as much as they did, if not more. For over a decade, the anchor had been stuck behind a faux desk, reporting the news other people had written for him. Unlike Eden, he'd never been approached by Network, never had his picture on the cover of local and national magazines, never won an award for his reporting skills. While Pudge considered him a pathetic whiner who would rather complain about the wrongs in his life, than take the initiative and make a bigger name for himself, he served a purpose. With Kyle's help, they would go places.

Rodger ignored Kyle, then turned to David. "Ryan Anders is too far away to make it downtown in time to air this story on the ten o'clock news. Channel 3 broke the story, so we're already late."

us us send us

"I'll go," Pudge blurted.

Rodger looked at Pudge, then shook his head. "You're not experienced enough, kid."

"But I reported—"

"No. You're not ready," he said, then turned to Ito. "I called Les Sinclair. He's willing to come out of retirement and do it. Pick him up on your way to the crime scene." Rodger handed David a sheet of paper. "Here's both addresses. And make it quick. I want to lead with this story tonight."

"I'm on it," David said, and as he left the room, he gave Pudge's shoulder a quick squeeze. David had known about Pudge's aspirations, and while Pudge appreciated his concern, he could go fuck himself. They didn't need his sympathy. Sympathy was for pussies. Pudge was a doer. Doers went places. They didn't stand around with their thumbs up their asses waiting for an opportunity to land in their lap.

Losing *this* opportunity to Les Sinclair stirred Pudge's anger beyond control, though. The old fart had long retired, and had been diagnosed with dementia two years ago.

Jeffries had made a mistake tonight.

pay make him pay kill him kill him

Killing sounded like an excellent idea, but Pudge had a better plan. When Rodger walked away, Pudge turned to Kyle. "Can't you talk to Rodger for me? He respects your opinion. If you tell him you've been working with me, that I've improved, maybe he'll let me—"

He shook his head. "Not here. Come to my office."

wants he wants something

Pudge already suspected as much, but didn't care. They'd give Kyle what he wanted—again—if it meant a chance to report this story or any story for that matter. Pudge had allowed Kyle to think of himself as a mentor. But he was merely a means to an end.

When Kyle closed the office door, he walked to his desk, then sat on the edge. "I know you've been working hard, and I know you're disappointed, but this story in particular is sensitive to Rodger. After what that bitch, Eden, had done to me on air, Rodger had taken a lot of shit from the station owners, the Chicago police, and from our viewers. Honestly, Les was the right choice. Chicagoans love Les, he's respected and a familiar face. I'm sorry, honey, but I think Rodger made the right call."

Furious, Pudge turned away.

hurt hurt him he used us used us hurt him kill him

Although right, Pudge ignored the voice. Hurting or killing Kyle would only hinder their opportunity for advancement. He might be using them, but he didn't realize they were using him, too.

"I understand," Pudge responded. "I just wish Rodger would recognize my talent."

"He will," Kyle said. "Actually, I heard that Rodger needs someone to report the upcoming dog show. I know it's not the hardcore story you're looking for, but it's a start. Would you like for me to recommend you?"

A fucking dog show?

no no way tell him no

While reporting about a dog show wasn't exactly the same as the Dr. Dread story, it was a start. Pudge needed more on-air experience if they were going to earn Rodger's respect.

lying lying hes lying he wont help using us using us wont help

Pudge suspected the same, but nodded anyway. Until Rodger noticed their talent, they needed Kyle's influence and guidance.

"Good. I'll talk to Rodger about it tomorrow." Kyle glanced at his watch, then rubbed his palm over his crotch. "We've got about ten minutes before we need to be back in the studio. Why don't you come here, and let me make things better."

Pudge knew what he meant by *better*, even before he began to unzip his trousers and pull out his dick. But Pudge wasn't in the mood to give him a blow job. Not when the Dr. Dread story had been dangled in front of them, then torn away. Still, Pudge needed to maintain the ruse with Kyle in order to use him for their success. Besides, they'd enjoyed their time with him a few nights ago. Right?

The voice didn't respond, and Pudge hesitated. Maybe hooking up with Kyle had been a mistake. Did they really need him? Look at how far they'd come on their own.

Kyle held his dick by the base, then nodded to his crotch. "C'mon, baby, I know you want it. And if you swallow every last drop, I'll make sure I talk to Rodger about you tonight, right after the show ends."

The lure of on-air time forced Pudge to move toward the desk. Pudge stared at Kyle's dick then knelt in front of him.

"That's it," Kyle coaxed. "And next time, when we're not on a time crunch, I'll make sure I fuck you properly."

While Pudge would like to be fucked properly, Kyle wasn't the man for the job. Eden's boy toy came to mind, and with his image on the brain, Pudge demeaned them, and sucked Kyle's dick. With each suck and lick, Pudge formulated a plan. Once they no longer needed Kyle, he would pay a high price for using them. Leaking a video of him screwing one of his co-workers just might be the right start.

CHAPTER 15

EDEN SNUGGLED HER bottom against Hudson's groin, his erection pressing against her. She hadn't even crawled out of bed yet, and the day already seemed brighter.

He palmed her breast, gave her nipple a seductive tug, then slid his hand along her belly until he slipped his finger between her thighs. Yes, she thought as she sucked in a breath and spread her legs. Today would definitely be a good day. Waking up to Hudson's hard, hot body, and then morning sex...? Other than a strong cup of coffee and a gooey cinnamon roll slathered in butter, she couldn't imagine a better way to start the day.

After years of sleeping alone, after years of *being* alone, she loved this moment. Last night had been an awakening for her. The whole day had been, really. She'd realized she had health issues in need of attention. She had family issues that she also needed to tackle. Most of all, she'd realized all of the issues she'd thought she'd had with Hudson were of her own making. He'd been there for her in the past, willing and ready to explore a future. But she'd sabotaged their relationship out of fear. She'd been afraid of having her heart broken, afraid of becoming too close to him only to have him reject her once he came to know the "real" Eden.

After last night, those fears seemed ridiculous. Hudson had showed her he cared deeply for her, with his words and his touch.

With the way he touched her now, she focused on him, on their pleasure, and reached beneath the sheets for his thick arousal. Her body hummed with need and anticipation as she guided him inside of her.

His warm breath puffed against her neck, as he slowly, sensually rocked his hips. She pressed against him, eager to feel every hot inch of him. He grabbed her hip, then positioned her until she was on her hands and knees. Pressing on the small of her back with one hand, and cupping her ass cheek with the other, he quickened his pace.

Loving the way he filled her, she fisted the pillow and raised her bottom higher.

"You're so damn sexy," he murmured, and caressed her bottom.

She dropped her head into the pillow and groaned as a delicious ripple radiated through her body. When he reached beneath her and rubbed her clit, she raised her head and looked over her shoulder.

Their gazes collided. The heat and intensity in his eyes, the way he stroked her sex with his fingers and his thick arousal, caused the delicious ripple to strengthen into a flood of ecstasy. The orgasm ripped through her core. She bucked against him and rode each wave after wave of pure rapture until he came with a low groan.

They collapsed in a heap on the center of the bed. He cradled her in his arms, then kissed her forehead.

"Good morning," he said with a sexy grin.

"It's a *very* good morning," she responded, and stretched. "Hungry?"

He nipped her earlobe. "For more of you."

"Cheese ball," she teased.

"What can I say? You bring out the best in me."

She glanced at the window, and even with the blinds drawn, noticed it was still dark. "What time is it?"

"Don't make me move. I'm too comfortable," he said, and cuddled her closer.

"I'll tell you what," she said as she began to disentangle their bodies. "You can rest, while I fix us breakfast. I noticed you'd stocked my fridge. How does an omelet sound?"

"Awesome. And for the record, Lloyd did the stocking."

"I'll have to thank him."

"I did make the grocery list though, so it's me who deserves a proper thanking. I happen to have a couple of ideas of how you can do that, by the way."

"I bet you do," she said as she pulled the sweatshirt she'd worn last night over her head. As she was about to move toward the bathroom, her cell phone rang. She glanced at the clock on the nightstand, then frowned. "It's six fifteen. This can't be good."

He propped himself on his elbow. "Who is it?"

She checked the caller ID and not recognizing the number, shook her head. "Don't know," she said, then answered the phone.

"Good morning, Eden. I hope I didn't wake you and your friend."

She sat on the edge of the bed, still unsure of the caller's identity. "I'm sorry, but who is this?"

"My name isn't important. My message is, though."

Her skin prickled with unease as she looked to Hudson, who had already climbed off the bed and was pulling on his jeans. She mouthed, "It's the killer," then pointed to the dresser and motioned with her hands for a pen and paper.

"That was very smart of you to install the extra security camera. I've been worried about the person who's been watching you."

"Thank you for your concern," she said, and nodded to Hudson as he handed her the pen and paper. "Should I be concerned about you, too?"

Hudson sat next to her, and put his ear close to the phone. She angled the cell, and hoped he could hear the killer's end of the conversation. Considering she didn't have a way to record the exchange, she needed an extra set of ears.

"Me? No. I wouldn't do anything to hurt you. I'd hoped you realized that by now. Especially after the flowers and note I left at the hospital. Are you feeling better?"

"I am. Thank you. Do you work at the hospital?"

"I was worried about you," he said. "You're too hard on yourself."

"I appreciate your concern, and I also noticed you avoided my question."

"Did I? Sorry, no. I don't need to work at the hospital. As you know, I have my own, *private* OR."

Despite the heavy sweatshirt, goose bumps skated along her arms as images of the killer's victims moved through her mind. "Yes, unfortunately."

"The DVDs are rather...gruesome. I apologize for that, but I do have my reasons."

"Your message."

"Exactly. I knew you'd understand."

"Honestly, I don't." Knowing this might be her only opportunity to speak with the killer, she pressed him. "Why the torture? Why not just kill them?"

"Killing them would be too easy," he responded, his voice remarkably amiable for a man discussing murder. "Do you know what it's like to hate so much that it festers inside of you until you're infected with uncontrollable rage? To eat, sleep, and wake to nothing but thoughts of vengeance rivaling the wrath of God? While I'm obviously no god, I am judge, jury and executioner in my OR. And when I've finished with my plans, you will understand why."

While most people would consider this man insane, Eden didn't. She honestly believed, based on his words and his actions on the DVDs, that Hudson had been right all along. This wasn't about sending a message to the masses, but about plain old revenge.

"I wish you would explain your reasons to me now. Maybe if we talk, another...surgery won't be necessary. I'm sure you know I haven't gone to the police. Leave your last two…ah…patients alone and—"

"You're truly a good person, Eden. I've loved two women in my life. Both are dead. You remind me so much of one of them, your looks, the way you push yourself to be the best, only you're stronger. If only she had been, then none of this would have had to happen. I do appreciate your not going to the police, but chatting about my reasons won't save my patient."

"Patients," she reminded him.

"Hmm? Oh yes, back to the reason I called you. I know I told you that I'd planned to take a few days off, but something came up and it required me to change my schedule. I had to perform a surgery last night, and I have another DVD for you. Because of your new security cameras, and your male guest, I couldn't leave the DVD at your townhouse."

She gripped Hudson's hand. "How do you know a man is staying with me?"

"I drove past your townhouse yesterday and saw the two of you entering. When I drove past this morning, I noticed his ride still parked along the curb. Tell him I'm a fan of *Smokey and the Bandit*, please."

"I will."

"Thank you. Now, about that DVD." After he gave her the location of the DVD, he said, "I really do like you, and wish that we could have met under different circumstances."

"Can I ask you something else?"

"Hopefully I have an answer," he said with a chuckle.

"How does my beauty pageant series fit with what you're doing in your OR?"

He sighed, then said, "You're an excellent reporter, Eden. I'm sure if you think long and hard about your series and my patients, you'll begin to connect the dots. If you don't, no worries. My final DVD will give you all of the answers."

"I honestly don't know if I can bear to watch another one of your surgeries."

"The last DVD won't be another surgery, Eden. It will be an explanation. I have to go now. It was nice talking to you.

Take care of yourself, and watch your back. If I find out who's been sneaking around your townhouse, I will call you again."

"Wait. Can I reach you at this number?"

The call ended. Eden quickly redialed the number, but the call rolled right into a computerized voice messaging system.

"Don't waste your time," Hudson said. "I guarantee he's made sure the phone is untraceable."

Although frustrated, she knew he was right. The man had always been one step ahead of them. He wouldn't let something as simple as a phone call bring him down before he'd finished what he'd started.

When Hudson pulled her into his arms, she hugged him. Knowing another DVD awaited them disturbed her. She didn't want to watch another person being tortured. But having a slightly better insight into the man behind the surgical mask unsettled her even more. His hatred and need for vengeance had turned him into a cold-blooded killer, and yet he had been concerned about her health and well being, and had acted as if he…cared about her. He'd also been in love.

She'd considered the killer a monster, and hadn't thought of him as a human being, a man who might have had family and friends. A regular job with a 401k. What had happened to make him hate enough to kill? When he'd asked if she'd known what it was like to hate, eat, sleep, and wake to nothing but thoughts of vengeance, she'd thought about the men who had raped her. There had been a time in her life when she'd thought of nothing else but how she could even the score. To make those assholes suffer. As she'd graduated from college, then dove into her career, she'd realized they weren't worth the effort. While the nightmares still visited, she'd worried that if she reopened old wounds, they'd never heal, especially if those men ended up walking away from their crime a second time.

She gave Hudson another squeeze, then pulled away from him. "We've got to go. You heard everything, right?"

He nodded. "Yeah, you did a great job with him. I'm sure you had a million questions buzzing through your head, but you zeroed in on things that were important."

"Thanks," she said as she stepped into her yoga pants. "We need to leave. Can you let Brutal out before we go? I don't want to come home to a mess."

Before he left the bedroom, he stopped, and cupped her cheeks. "You okay?"

She touched his hand. "Yeah."

"I was looking forward to that omelet."

Smiling, she turned, then kissed his palm. "Even skinny people can cook. Wait until you try my lasagna."

He kissed her again, then headed for the door. "I can't wait."

She couldn't either. They'd started something big last night. While she wasn't sure how their relationship would play out, considering she had plans to move to New York at the end of the month, she was sure of one thing—they needed to find the killer before he made another DVD.

Pudge sat in front of the bedroom mirror. "Please talk to me."

No answer.

"I'm sorry about last night, but you know we need Kyle. I had to do it."

no no you didnt he used us used us used us used us

Relieved the silence had been broken, Pudge smiled. The love they shared was more important than their aspirations. They could create a new name for themselves if necessary, but they couldn't lose each other. Not after all that they'd been through.

The day after Mama had killed that scum of a husband and father, Rick, Pudge had found true love in—of all places—the family bathroom. To this day, Pudge could remember the encounter, the relief to have found someone to share the pain and burden Mama had created.

Pudge smiled. With the business end of a sharp hatchet, man oh man the crazy bitch had really given it to dear ol' Dad. After Pudge had suffered years of Rick's abuse, the beatings, the rapes, helping Mama dismember him, then scatter his corpse throughout Illinois had been disgusting, and yet disturbingly satisfying. The meeting in the bathroom afterward had come at a time when Pudge had needed a friend, someone to help cope with the murder, and deal with Mama. That friendship had blossomed into love quickly, leaving Pudge confident and ready to leave the cesspool Mama called home, and venture off into the world of fame and fortune.

Pudge needed to make things right between them. Without their love and friendship, Pudge had no interest in fame and fortune. Success wouldn't be as fun without the partner Pudge had come to love more than life.

"I know he's using us. But we're using him, too. Don't worry. I have an idea of how we can get even with Kyle. Don't even think of bringing up killing him. What I have in mind for him...put it this way, he'll wish he were dead."

promise promise me

"I promise. Now, speaking of promises, I remember promising you that Eden would be dead by the end of the week, and it's already Friday."

yes yes kill her kill her

"On the way home last night, I went past her house and noticed the boy toy's car out front. If he's spending the night with her, we're going to have to come up with a way to catch her off guard during the day. We don't have to work, so I thought maybe we could play dress up and follow Eden around today."

Pudge reached into the closet and pulled out an unused disguise bought weeks ago. "Remember this?"

yes yes clever clever

"I know. Who would suspect a pregnant woman?" Pudge strapped on the faux belly, then chuckled. "Wouldn't I make a great mom?"

mama mama

"Don't call me that. It's not even funny. I would never be like that bitch."

no no mama yelling mama yelling

Pudge stopped and listened. "Damn it."

As they entered the living room, Mama began rattling off her breakfast order. Pudge went into the kitchen, retrieved a frying pan, then set it on the stove. Pudge was about to grab the eggs from the fridge, when the phone rang. Pudge glanced at the caller ID, then quickly answered.

Minutes later, Pudge hung up the phone. "That stupid bitch," Pudge whispered. Apparently, Mama had called the home nurse agency last night and requested a visit from Nurse Gretchen. The agency had called to inform them that Gretchen would no longer be available, but they had a replacement they could send by today. Of course they'd never said why Nurse Gretchen had been out of commission. They didn't have to.

hello dr dread hello

"Shh," Pudge hissed. "I don't ever want to talk about Dread again. Not after last night's bullshit."

yes precious so sorry so sorry

"It's okay. It's funny, actually. I was Dr. Dread. Dread killed Nurse Gretchen. Mama called to have Nurse Gretchen come over today, and because of that call, they probably found her body. This is good karma, don't you think? The only way I could have planned it any better would be if I'd been the one to report Gretchen's murder." Pudge cracked an egg. "But this means we'll have to wait until later to spy on Eden. I told the agency we didn't need a new nurse after all."

hello nurse nancy hello

Michael Morrison sat inside the diner, sipping a cup of black coffee. He pretended to watch the pedestrians pass the large glass window, while his true focus remained on the old homeless man sitting on a bench by the bus stop. The man had been the perfect choice. Blind in one eye, an obvious, bad case of cataracts in the other, he wouldn't be able to give Eden and her friend a description of him. Even if he could describe him, between the sunglasses, ball cap and thick scarf Michael had worn, the man wouldn't be able to give them much.

He'd given the man the manila envelope containing the DVD, and two hundred dollars for his effort. Michael had then told him he'd better not think of running off before handing the envelope over to Eden, otherwise he'd find him and kill him. The man had showed no fear, and Michael assumed death, to the old man, might seem a better route to take than the life he currently lived. Either way, Michael wouldn't kill the man. He wasn't a murderer. He was a crusader with a cause.

The waitress set a plate of scrambled eggs, bacon and hotcakes in front of him, then refilled his coffee. As he dug into the eggs, he glanced out the window again. The old man remained at his post, but now he had company. Eden and her friend, the man he'd seen leaving and entering her hospital room, stood next to the homeless man. While Eden talked to him and took the envelope, her friend scanned the area, likely looking for Michael. The guy could look all he wanted. The old man hadn't seen Michael enter the diner. The minivan had been parked a half dozen streets away. There were hundreds of people milling along the sidewalks, and dozens of shops and businesses on this block alone. Michael had become the proverbial needle in Chicago's haystack.

After stowing the envelope into her purse, Eden leaned down and said something to the old man. He nodded, then stood with her and her friend's help. They began walking together, crossed the street, and then approached the diner.

While his heart galloped, Michael poured syrup over the hotcakes. Eden entered the diner first, then helped the old man to a stool at the counter. She spoke to the waitress, then said something to her friend. As Michael finished his hotcakes, he noticed the waitress bring the old man a mug of coffee, as well as two Styrofoam cups. Eden handed one of the Styrofoam cups to her friend, placed money on the counter, spoke to the old man again, then nodded to her friend. Seconds later, they exited the diner, leaving the old man at the counter, a large plate of breakfast assortments in front of him.

Michael sipped the coffee, then wiped his mouth with the

napkin. While they'd been on the phone, he'd told Eden he'd thought she was a good person. After witnessing her small act of kindness to the old man, he didn't just think it, he knew it. Guilt shoved aside his breakfast and crawled into his belly. He honestly liked Eden, and almost regretted forcing her to watch the gruesome DVDs. Hell. He didn't even like reviewing them…much. Although he gained sick satisfaction from watching his patients suffer all over again, another part of him couldn't be more disgusted.

With himself.

With the men who had brutalized his daughter until she'd lost the will to live.

Regardless, he thought as he pulled out his wallet, checked his breakfast bill, then laid money on the table, Eden would be rewarded in the end. When he finished his death wish list, and gave Eden the last DVD, she would have a story that would seal her career. And he would have fulfilled his promises to Eliza.

Without looking at the old man, he left the diner. As he was about to turn the corner to head for his minivan, a display, located in the store window next to the diner, caught his attention. A pretty, dark-haired, life-like doll stared back at him. Eerily resembling Eliza as a child, the doll drew him closer to the window.

Eliza's birthday was coming up and while making the doctors who had hurt her pay for their crimes had seemed like the most fitting gift, he decided she deserved something not tainted with blood or death. He smiled as he remembered Eliza's past birthdays, how her eyes had lit up and her smile filled her face while she'd opened his gifts. As a child, she used to collect dolls. With the doll's fancy, pink dress and black patent leather shoes, he knew in his heart that she would have loved this particular one.

He entered the store, bought the doll, then headed for his minivan. He would give her the doll on her birthday. After he took care of his final patient and delivered the DVD to Eden. For now, though, he needed to head home. Last night had been a long night. Dr. Tully's procedure had proven more difficult than he'd anticipated. Liposuction wasn't as easy to perform as You Tube had made it look. He'd wing it on the next surgery.

After breast implants, veneers and now liposuction, rhinoplasty should be a piece of cake.

CHAPTER 16

"ONCE AGAIN, NO prints," Rachel said as she entered CORE's evidence and evaluation room.

Hudson blew out a breath. "We figured as much."

"What about the guy who gave you the DVD? Could he describe the killer?" Rachel asked.

Eden took the seat next to him, and shook her head. "He was old and half blind. The killer picked the right person for the job."

Hudson thought about the old man, how Eden had treated him with kindness and concern. When it came to her career, she was ballsy and cutthroat, but when it came to people in need...

He loved and admired the compassionate woman Eden kept hidden beneath the tenacious reporter veneer. Even more, he loved that she'd trusted enough to expose her softer side to him. Last night he'd come to an epiphany, the striking realization had grabbed him by the balls and made him truly comprehend the complexity of his emotions.

When he'd met Eden, the first time around, he hadn't been thinking about finding a place to belong. He'd already had that security through his career. What had been missing, though, was someone he could share every aspect of his life with—his dreams, hopes, fears. While he'd made solid friendships during his time in the Marines, CIA, and CORE, he couldn't turn to those men and express his intimate feelings. Even thinking about the words "intimate feelings" made him feel like a pussy. He'd been raised by a man who believed what you felt wasn't anyone's business, that you kept your emotions in check, and never let your guard down for anybody.

That philosophy hadn't worked too well for his dad. After a major drinking binge, he'd choked on his own vomit, and had died alone. His dead body hadn't been discovered until almost two weeks later, and that had only happened because the neighbors complained to the city about the tall grass that had grown around his dad's small bungalow. At his dad's funeral, aside from himself, only two other people had attended. One had been the minister, the other, the funeral director. That day, as the minister said a few words, Hudson had sworn he'd never end up like his father. Cold, ruthless…alone.

When Eden entered his life, he thought he'd found the woman who could soften him, help make him a better man. Even though she'd left him, he'd believed that their time together had changed him for the better. He'd begun to realize that while he'd liked his career path, he wouldn't mind something a little less dangerous. He'd started to think about moving out of the city, taking up golf or some such shit.

"Hello, earth to Hudson," Rachel sang.

He glanced at her, then to Eden. "I was just thinking about the old guy who gave us the DVD," he lied. Now wasn't the time to talk about his dad or his thoughts about the future. "I hope he keeps his mouth shut about the two hundred dollars. He'd be an easy target for druggies looking to score."

Eden winced. "I didn't think about that."

"Maybe the killer did, and figured someone else could clean up his loose end," Rachel suggested.

"I don't know about that," Eden said. "I don't think the killer has any interest in harming anyone other than the men he's going after. I also think your theory about this being a hate crime is wrong. No offense."

"Of course." Rachel tapped the pencil against her chin.

"And you suspect this because…?"

"When I talked with him on the phone, I asked him why he didn't just kill these men instead of torturing them first. He answered me with a question."

"Do you know what it's like to hate so much that it festers inside of you until you're infected with uncontrollable rage?" Hudson quoted, then looked to Rachel. "I agree with Eden. This is definitely vengeance. For what? We need to figure that out before he kills his last victim."

Rachel took the copy of the DVD. "I agree with both of you," she said as she turned on the DVD player. "I'll explain why after we watch our morning matinée."

"You can explain now," Eden said. "I don't have a problem postponing."

Hudson reach for her hand, then gave it a squeeze. "You don't have to watch this at all."

"I know," she said. "I also know I need to. He sent them to me for a reason, and I want to help stop him. It's just…after talking with him, I started thinking about what he might have been like before he snapped and decided to mutilate these men. Whatever happened to drive him to such a level of depredation had to have been horrific."

"Don't tell me you feel sorry for him," Hudson said, shocked by Eden's reaction. He'd met plenty of soulless murderers during his career. In his book, there was no such thing as a kindhearted killer.

"Hardly," she said, and looked at him. "I'm simply saying that I can understand the killer wanting to get even if these men had hurt him, or someone he loved, and had gotten away with it."

He thought about Eden's rape, how angry he'd been, and still was, that the men who'd assaulted her had never paid for their crime. He also thought about his plans to set that straight, and nodded. "I get what you're saying. Only his vigilante act won't make any sense until we understand why he's killing."

"Let's just watch the damned thing instead of trying to psychoanalyze this guy," Rachel said. "Hopefully he'll give us some new leads."

When Rachel turned her back to adjust the DVD and the volume on the TV, Hudson brought Eden's hand to his lips, and kissed her knuckles. Knowing the killer had probably watched them while they'd retrieved the DVD, and that he'd had intimate knowledge about Eden, scared the hell of out him. He wanted to keep touching her, reassuring himself that she was safe.

As he turned to face the screens again, he caught Rachel staring at them. She cocked a brow, then picked up the pencil she'd been toying with earlier. "Here we go," she said as she hit PLAY, then she chomped the pencil like a dog would a bone.

The TV screen came to life. "Wait," a large, very overweight man shouted. "Shouldn't I get a chance to say something?"

Dressed in the usual hospital scrubs and cap, the killer kept his back to the camera. "You mean your final words?"

The killer looked over his shoulder at the camera.

"This guy is a frickin' whack job," Rachel mumbled over a mouthful of pencil.

Hudson agreed as he stared at the killer's latest surgical mask. He'd drawn buckteeth on the first mask, a jack-o-lantern smile on the second. For this mask, he'd drawn a simple smile, but had added a set of sharp fangs to it, giving his face a devilish look.

"You don't deserve it." The killer held up a piece of duct tape. Between the angle of the video camera and the man's large stomach, Hudson couldn't see the victim's face, and assumed the killer had slapped the tape over the man's mouth.

"This is the only thing you deserve," the killer said, as he grabbed a scalpel, then stabbed it into the victim's stomach.

Even with his mouth sealed shut, the victim's scream pierced the room. Blood wept from the fresh wound. Another scream followed as the killer made another incision, this one larger, deeper.

"What the hell is he doing?" Rachel asked. "The other methods of torture were obvious, but this one..." She trailed off when the killer set the scalpel aside and stood.

"He's not on the surgical table," Eden said. "I thought the room looked different, but didn't know why. Now I can see it, can't you?"

Rachel hit PAUSE. "Yeah, and look," she said as she moved to the TV and pointed to the corner of the screen. "Wheels. Wherever he's performing his surgery, the building is big enough to hold a car."

Hudson studied the screen. He'd been restoring cars for years, and recognized the makeshift table the killer used for his victim. "He couldn't lift the man onto the surgical table, so he used a Mechanic's Creeper."

"Those things you use to roll under a car? I didn't realize that's what they were called. Creeper *is* rather fitting, don't you think?" Rachel asked, as she started the DVD again.

"Definitely," Eden said, and tightened her hold on his hand as the killer came onto the screen.

He loved that she wasn't afraid to lean on him for strength or support. The way she continued to let down her guard gave him hope that they had a shot at a future together.

Hudson glanced back at the screen. The killer held what looked like a hose for a vacuum cleaner, only the tip had been retrofitted. The wide mouth of a funnel had been duct taped to the end, and it looked as if a small razor blade had somehow been fastened to the narrow tip.

"I know my equipment isn't state of the art, but for our purposes, I think it will work," the killer said as he pressed the sharp tip against one of the victim's wounds. "Hmm, this isn't going to fit. I guess I should have made a larger incision."

He reached for the scalpel again, stabbed it into the open wound, then sliced it across the man's stomach.

More screams filled the room, and when the killer had finished, he leaned back on the heels of his shoes. "That should do it."

Rachel tossed the pencil on the table. "Frigging sick."

Hudson couldn't agree more. The gash along the man's stomach had been carved into a bloody smile.

The killer grabbed the vacuum hose again, and tugged it closer to the victim. The actual vacuum cleaner appeared on the screen.

"What is that?" Eden asked.

"It looks like a Shop-Vac," he answered. "They're a heavier duty vacuum that can be used for both wet and dry jobs."

Rachel paused the DVD again, stood, then paced in front of the TV screens. "This is going to be bad." She reached for her chewed pencil. "Really, really bad."

Hudson glanced at Eden. She rubbed her palm along her temple and nodded.

"Am I missing something?" he asked, not sure what Rachel and Eden knew.

Rachel stopped chewing the pencil. "Liposuction."

He looked to the screen, to the heavy man lying on the Mechanic's Creeper. The full realization of what the killer was about to do caused his stomach to roll.

"If the Shop-Vac's more powerful than a regular vacuum, and could hold...liquid." Rachel crossed her arms. "I don't get this guy. Why is he performing—?"

"Plastic surgery," Eden interrupted. "He's performing plastic surgeries *on* plastic surgeons."

"Makes sense," Hudson agreed. "But we only know for sure that the first victim was a plastic surgeon."

"Right," Eden began. "His specialty *happened* to be breast implants, and the killer just *happened* to give him a new set of maggot breasts. The killer told me today that he was judge, jury, and executioner in his OR." Eden pointed to the screen. "These men did something to him or someone he loved, and now they're paying for it."

"Or," he countered. "These could be random surgeons who simply represent what the killer doesn't like."

"Air brushed images on magazines. The perception of perfection, yadda yadda," Rachel said, and rolled her eyes. "I agree with Eden."

"So do I," Hudson said to Rachel. "None of this matters until we ID the other vics, though, unless you found something new on first victim."

"I've got a few interesting things to share about Dr. Thomas Elliot, but I'd rather get this over with first," Rachel said, then hit PLAY.

The killer slapped the top of the Shop-Vac, and waved the vacuum hose. "I love the internet. You can learn so much. It's where I learned how to navigate through your procedure. Really, though. How hard can this be? A little suck here, another there. It's not like I have to worry about vacuuming up organs or muscles, or damaging any nerve endings, right?" He cocked his head. "Wait a sec. I *do* have to worry about those things. Now that I think about it, I've seen the damage that can be done if a surgeon isn't careful." He elbowed the man's stomach. "Don't worry. I'll take good care of you. When I'm done, you won't even recognize your own body."

"Oh, no," Eden muttered as the killer reached over and turned on the Shop-Vac.

Hudson's stomach lurched as he viewed the torturous scene. He was certain the man probably screamed. But any sound made in the killer's OR had been drowned out by the Shop-Vac.

Seconds later, the killer turned off the vacuum. The victim's muted cries now filtered through the room.

"Well, this isn't working, is it?" The killer checked the tip of the funnel. "No problems with this, but maybe I should have used something wider to extract the fat. I guess we'll just have to improvise." He picked up the scalpel again and sliced the man's stomach. Blood oozed from the new wound and pooled on the cement floor. After he hacked through skin and layers of fat, the killer flipped the slab of flesh, exposing yellow, fatty tissue.

"Oh my God," Rachel gasped and turned away from the screen.

Eden gripped his hand. When he looked at her, she'd already closed her eyes and used her other hand to cover her mouth. He wanted to look away as well. Hoping the killer made a mistake, or gave them something they could use to find him or his next victim, he continued to watch.

"That's better," the killer said as he set the scalpel aside, and retrieved the vacuum hose. "Now we can attack those problem areas of yours. You know, if you'd lay off the sweets and hit the gym a few times a week, this wouldn't have been necessary. Actually, if you had a conscience, you might be at home—quite a nice place, by the by—or maybe playing with your Latin lover at that fancy hotel you seem to enjoy. Instead, you're stuck in my OR. Literally." He jabbed the tip of the vacuum hose into the fatty tissue. "You probably won't believe me when I say this, but I'm not enjoying myself. If only you and your buddies had listened to me."

"See," Eden said, her gaze now riveted on the screen. "He does know the victim."

Rachel turned around, and watched the screen, too. "And he just told us that the victims are all connected."

The killer turned on the Shop-Vac, and began scraping the razor-sharp tip along the inside of the skin that had once lined the victim's stomach. The hose sucked the victim's fat. Small pieces bounced off the plastic hose. The sound of chunks of tissue being swallowed by the vacuum, and mingling with all the blood and fat, caused bile to rise in Hudson's throat.

He fought the urge to vomit, and noticed that Eden and Rachel had once again looked away from the atrocious sight. After several minutes, the killer shut off the vacuum. The man didn't make a sound, and Hudson wondered if, like the last victim, he'd died. Then he noticed a slight rise and fall of his chest. Like with the first vic, he'd probably passed out from the pain.

"That didn't go as well as I hoped," the killer said as he pushed the vacuum aside. "So much for making him look...svelte." He glanced at the blood staining the cement. "And look at the mess he made."

With a shrug, he turned to the camera. "Sorry, Eden, this was probably a rough one to watch."

"That's putting it mildly," Rachel said, and took a seat.

"As I said before," the killer continued. "He gave me no

other choice." He stripped the bloody gloves from his hands. "Don't feel sorry for this man. For any of my patients. Justice comes in many forms. Unfortunately for this piece of shit, he had to endure my philosophy of what true justice entails. Before you judge me, think of the many people out there who've lost a loved one to a violent crime, only to have the justice system fail them and set the offender free. Personally, *obviously*." He smiled. "I believe in an eye for an eye."

While Hudson shared the killer's beliefs, he didn't think the extent of torture and mutilation he'd made his victims endure was necessary. A quick shot to the head with a .44 would have taken care of the job. He'd witnessed violence, unfathomable carnage, during his years with the Marines and CIA. Those assignments had made the cases he'd worked for CORE look more like child's play, like a frickin' playground brawl. He'd been the victim of torture at the hands of a sadistic madman, too. His torture, though, had been given to gain information. As a Marine, the shit he'd seen while serving in Afghanistan had hardened his heart and had made him question the ethics and morality of the human race. During that time, though, he'd been in a war-torn country. Inhumanity, brutality had been common and expected. His missions with the CIA hadn't been much different. Assassinating ruthless warlords and drug lords had been a dominating part of his job.

Like their killer, he hadn't enjoyed snuffing the life out of his assigned targets. Unlike their killer though, Hudson hadn't made his targets suffer. There had been times when he would have liked to drag out their impending deaths, subject them to atrocities similar to the ones they had committed against innocent people.

But, just because you'd like to do something, doesn't mean you should.

Hudson would like to kill the men who had raped Eden. He wouldn't though. He had morals. While he also knew, like their killer, that the justice system didn't always work, he wouldn't torture Eden's rapists, at least not physically. The 'eye for an eye' ideology, although enticing, didn't work. Whatever vengeance their killer sought, would only, if caught, send him to prison for life. Sure, the killer had served his justice, but at what cost?

"Well," the killer said, and rapped the Shop-Vac with his knuckle. "I guess I should tend to the mess." He looked at the victim's disgusting stomach, then winced. "I'd sew him up, but I really don't see the point. Do you hear that?"

Rachel raised the volume. "Howling. Just like what we heard during the last DVD."

"Sounds like my dinner guests have arrived. Yep, no point in wasting my time stitching my patient's stomach when they're only going to tear him apart. Gotta run. Three down, and only one more to go. Expect the last DVD on your doorstep Monday. Until then, please take care of yourself, Eden. "

When the DVD ended, Rachel hit PAUSE, then turned to them. "Oh my God," she said on a gasp. "He *is* feeding them to dogs."

"Or coyotes," Hudson reminded her. "Did you ever run the baying we heard during the last DVD against coyotes?"

"I did, and while I can't be sure, the sounds were similar."

"Coyotes, Chihuahuas, Poodles...does it matter?" Eden asked. "He's either purposefully slipping in leads, or he doesn't care."

Hudson realized Eden was right, and nodded. "He mentioned the victim's Latin lover, referred to the other victims as his buddies, he also made it clear that the victim, and I'm assuming the others, too, had done something to someone close to him. Now he's telling us he's feeding the victims to dogs, coyotes, or whatever."

"So let's think about it. If this is an 'eye for an eye' thing, what could four men have done, and evidently gotten away with, to deserve this kind of torture?" Rachel asked. She moved to the dry erase board that had the list of the leads they'd developed after they'd viewed the last DVD. "I think we can definitely assume his OR is in the country, and he's feeding the victims to...something. The building he's using to perform his surgeries is big enough to hold a car, but that wouldn't help us narrow his location. I'm sure there are plenty of farms with large barns within a two hour drive to Eden's townhouse."

Eden blew out a deep sigh. "I think we should focus on the victims. That's where we're going to make the connection. When I spoke to the killer today, he said he loved two women, and they were both dead. Could the men, these victims, have killed those two women?"

"Death by plastic surgery," Hudson said, then raised a shoulder when both women looked at him. "It's just like Eden said earlier. He's performing plastic surgeries on plastic surgeons."

"Again, like *you* said, we only know for sure Elliot was a plastic surgeon," Rachel reminded him. "But I like where you're both heading with this."

"When you researched Elliot, did you find out where he'd worked in the past?" Eden asked Rachel. "I'm wondering if maybe the victims were part of a surgery group."

"The dentist—if the second vic was a dentist—throws me, though," Hudson said.

"True." Rachel hit a few buttons on the keyboard. "Let's not forget that vic number two had a tattoo that matched Elliot's. A little coincidental, don't ya think?" A few more strokes to her keyboard, and one of the TV screens now showed the information Rachel had compiled on Dr. Thomas Elliot. "Okay, meet our first vic. Forty-five. No kids. He graduated from the University of Michigan, was a member of Sigma Alpha Mu fraternity, as we suspected. Although he did have a hefty alimony check to write to his ex each month, his finances are in order. No major debt. No glaring, large bank deposits that might raise some red flags."

"Can you get a list of men who graduated with Elliot and were also in the same fraternity?" Hudson asked. "See if any had gone into dentistry, and live in the Chicago area."

"Already done," she said, and with a few strokes to the keyboard a short list of Chicago area dentists appeared. "I also checked if any other men Elliot graduated with, whether they were in his fraternity or not, went into plastic surgery."

"How nice of the college to hand over that information,"

Hudson said with a smile, knowing Rachel likely had hacked into their computer system.

"Ah...yeah, that's right. They were most helpful. Anyway, believe it or not, I came up empty on that route."

"What about Elliot's current and past places of employment?" Eden asked.

Another few clicks to the keyboard and the victim's information filled the screen. "He's worked at only three places. After finishing his residency at Lakeview Hospital, here in Chicago, he stayed on there for about eight years. Then he worked at Cosmetic Solutions and Med Spa, which is also in Chicago, for three years, left there and then began his private practice out of the two medical centers in Oak Park and Western Springs."

"Maybe he worked with the other victims," Eden suggested, then furrowed her forehead. "I still can't see what these men did that would cause the killer to go to such extremes." She drummed her fingers on the table. "Why don't we start with the list of dentists? I can make those calls when we're finished here."

"I'll take care of it," Rachel said. "I'd planned to, but didn't have the chance yet. I just got all of this info early this morning." She tapped the keyboard, and seconds later the printer spat out a piece of paper. "Wait here. I'm going to run to my office and call the dentists' offices."

When Rachel left the room, Hudson gave Eden's hand a squeeze, then released it and rose. "According to this information," he said as he studied the data on the screen. "Elliot began practicing breast augmentation a little over eighteen years ago. During the first DVD, I remember the killer saying he'd been planning this a long time. I'm wondering how long."

Stuffing his hands into his pockets he thought back to the night he'd viewed the first DVD. At the time, he'd tried to talk Ian out of assigning him this case. He didn't investigate. He'd always been given a name, then told to hunt and track, and bring the assignment down by any means possible.

Ian had told him that hunting and tracking criminals was just another side to investigating. Right now, Hudson didn't agree. After spending years as a successful reporter, Eden probably had better investigating skills than he did, and Rachel had spent several years in Army Intelligence. Compared to these women, he felt more like the kid who used to lick the chalkboard back at his old elementary school, rather than an agent.

Frustrated with himself, with the inability to put a stop to the killer, he released a deep breath. "After Rachel's done with her calls, I'll take you to the station."

Eden rose, then moved across the room. When she reached him, she wrapped her arms around his waist. "Afterward, do you think we should go to Elliot's offices in Oak Park and Western Springs?"

He rested his chin on the top of her head, and smoothed his hands over her back. "I doubt the other victims would have a connection to him through his private practice. If they knew each other, my guess is that they'd worked together at either Lakeview Hospital or Cosmetic Solutions and Med Spa."

"Makes sense," she said as she stepped back and studied him. "What's bothering you?"

"Oh, I dunno, maybe watching a guy get liposuction with a Shop-Vac," he said, and looked away.

She grabbed his chin and forced him to look at her. "And?" she prompted.

He looked down at her. Riveted by her penetrating, knowing eyes, he held her gaze. She'd trusted him enough to disclose her past to him. He needed to trust her enough to share his insecurities. After everything she'd told him, and all of the things he hadn't bothered to disclose about himself, he owed her as much. He owed her the truth. "I'm worried I won't be able to stop him before he kills his next victim."

"*We,*" she corrected him. "This isn't just your burden. We all have stake in this." She cupped his cheeks. "And I believe in you. In us. We'll find him."

She believed in him. In them.

With her faith in him, in what they could accomplish together, he was no longer the chalkboard licker. He held her head, and brought his lips close to hers. "Thank you. I needed to hear that. Sorry I was having a...moment."

"It's called self-doubt," she said with a small smile. "You can't be a badass all the time, you know. You're allowed to have a...moment."

He stole a quick kiss, then asked, "Speaking from experience?"

"Me? No. I said *you* can't be a badass all the time. I'm always a badass," she finished with a grin.

"How could I have forgotten?" he murmured, then kissed her again.

"I can remind you later. I'm assuming you have a set of handcuffs."

Before his body went into sexual overdrive, he stepped back, and held his hands in the air as if surrendering. "I do. But let's not discuss them or what I'm *not* going to let you do to me. Well, at least not until we're alone. The last thing I need is for—"

"Holy shit," Rachel shouted as she burst through the door. "You're not going to believe this. I just found our second victim."

"Who is it?" he asked.

"Dr. Brian Westly, DDS."

CHAPTER 17

PUDGE TENDED TO Mama. Changed her colostomy bag, cleaned her bed sores, then gave the bitch a large snack consisting of barbeque chips and chocolate chip cookies.

choke choke choke on it

Hiding a smile, Pudge ignored the voice, then said to Mama, "I need to do some shopping. The new nurse should be here any minute. Hopefully I'll catch her before I go. I hate to leave the front door unlocked while I'm gone. You never know what kind of crazy person might walk in."

Mama shook her head. Her cheeks jiggled as she frowned. "What new nurse?"

"The agency called and said you'd asked for Gretchen to stop by today. But Gretchen isn't available any longer, so they're sending you someone new."

Mama shifted her focus to the TV. "Why didn't you tell me before?"

"Why didn't you tell me you'd called and changed your scheduled appointment?"

scheming scheming mamas up to something scheming

Pudge agreed. Mama rarely changed her appointments, and when she had, she'd always made Pudge do it for her. For Mama to have taken the initiative herself led Pudge to believe the woman was up to something.

money money inheritance mama will take away the money

"Aren't you going to answer me, Mama?" When Mama didn't respond, Pudge slammed a couple of cans of grape soda on the bed tray. "If you don't need anything else, I'm going to change and get ready to leave."

Pudge left Mama to her snacks and TV show, gathered supplies from the bathroom, then once in the privacy of the bedroom, reached into the closet for the uniform they'd purchased a few days ago.

Holding the scrubs in front of the mirror, Pudge smiled. "This is going to be fun."

yes yes hello nurse nancy hello

Michael Morrison dropped the hose. Water splashed his jeans and boots, then spread along the old brick pad behind the steel garage. Eyes watering, stomach churning, he used one hand to steady himself against the garage, then bent his head and retched. The whiskey he'd drunk before he'd begun rinsing out the Shop-Vac burned his throat. The wretched smell of vomit caused him to gag. He threw up again. Breathing hard, he wiped his mouth with an old bandana, then retrieved the hose. Angling the spray, and holding the bandana over his mouth and nose, he rinsed the vomit, along with the remaining contents from the Shop-Vac, into the old drain pipe.

Once the brick pad had been cleaned of any debris, he checked the Shop-Vac. The vacuum had cleaned up well. If anyone were to look at it, they wouldn't see Dr. Leonard Tully's flesh, fat, or blood. Of course a DNA test would find evidence of Tully's body, but that didn't matter to him. By the time they'd discover his identity, Michael would be long gone.

Gravel churned along the driveway. Surprised and half-drunk, he stumbled. He fumbled the hose, and the steady stream of water running from it soaked more of his jeans and boots. Then he remembered his neighbor, Larry Hollister, had left him a message last night about dropping off the tools he'd borrowed from Michael a few weeks ago. He relaxed, glanced down at his pants and chuckled. He looked as if he'd pissed himself. Shrugging, he moved to the faucet, then turned off the water.

He didn't bother trying to blot the water with the bandana as he walked from behind the barn toward the driveway. Larry would probably think his soaked jeans were funny, and if he didn't, at this point Michael didn't care. He'd had a hell of a day, and it was barely noon. After he'd bought Eliza the doll, then made the ninety minute drive back to the old farmhouse, he'd had a couple of shots of Wild Turkey. Last night, after he'd used the Mechanic's Creeper to roll Tully's body into the back fields, he'd cleaned the mess he'd made in the OR. He hadn't had time to clean the Shop-Vac, though. Knowing the contents of the vacuum, he'd needed alcohol to fortify him before he washed it. Unfortunately, no amount of alcohol could help him stomach the putrid matter that had coagulated and stuck to the inside of the vacuum. Even years of working in a hospital couldn't have prepared him for the smell.

His stomach churned. After last night, and then today, he might consider becoming a vegetarian. He didn't think he could ever look at the fat on a steak—or any piece of meat— without thinking of Tully's repulsive belly fat.

As he made his way toward the driveway, he slowed and instantly sobered. Larry wasn't alone.

"Hey, Larry," he said, then nodded to the deputy rounding the front of the SUV parked behind Larry's Ford. "Forgot you were coming by today."

The farmer grinned as he glanced at Michael's jeans. "I think I'd rather walk around with my fly hanging open and my Jockey's showin'."

Michael smiled. "Little mishap with the garden hose. I'd almost wish it was piss, water's damn cold."

Laughing, Larry nodded to the deputy. "This here is Deputy Darren Cooper."

Michael shook the deputy's hand. "Any relation to Sal

Cooper?"

"He's my dad," the deputy said.

"Sal's a good guy. He helped me with a tractor purchase, and didn't steer me wrong. I got it up and running yesterday," he lied. The tractor had been working for months, but Michael had remembered telling Larry, when he'd stopped by the other day, he'd been repairing it.

The deputy looked to the overgrown fields adjacent to the house. "That right?"

"I said I got it running." Michael leaned against Larry's Ford to support his legs. Having a deputy in his driveway, while the remains of his patients littered his back field, made his knees grow weak. Having stayed up most of the night didn't help, either. "I just haven't had time to brush hog. I'll get to it next week."

"Better if you're sober, anyway," the deputy said.

Larry laughed. "Yeah, buddy. I could smell the whiskey on you. I'm damn jealous, too. Nothing like startin' the day with a cup of coffee and a shot of Jack Daniels. Since I retired, the wife's up my ass all the time about my health and all that nonsense. I gotta sneak around like a kid stealing liquor from his old man."

"What you smell is left over from last night. But I've got some Jack if you're interested," he offered Larry. Michael wouldn't mind having a drink and BSing with the farmer. A little friendly conversation might help take his mind off of the dead men in the field, and the surgery he planned to perform tomorrow.

"Wish I could," Larry said with a sigh. "I gotta take the wife into town for some shopping, though. I told her to take herself, but she says shopping is a great way for us to *bond*. I've been married to the woman for nearly forty years. How much more bonding does a man need?"

Michael chuckled, then figured they'd made enough small talk—time to find out why the deputy dropped by for a visit. "So, Deputy, what brings you by? Or did Larry's wife hire you to keep an eye on her husband and make sure he made it home in time to bond?"

The deputy laughed, then relaxed against the fence post near the house. "I could think of a few wives that might hire me to do exactly that," he said, then his smile fell. "Larry told me he'd mentioned my dad's coyote issues."

"Yeah, that's right," Michael said. "Don't tell me they came after him again."

The deputy nodded. "My dad was letting his dog out when about five or six coyotes came up to the house. He shot and killed one when it snatched the dog. Two others came after him, and while he struggled to fend them off, or shoot them, the rest pulled apart the dog. According to my dad, once his dog was torn to shreds, the two coyotes attacking him joined the others. He started shooting them, and when they ran off, he climbed on his four wheeler and went after them."

Michael released a low whistle, then said, "Damn. Is Sal okay?"

"He ended up with about forty stitches on his hands, arms and legs, and had to start the rabies vaccine. With how aggressive the coyotes have been acting, there's no point in taking any chances."

Michael wished he would have found another way to dispose of the bodies. He hadn't anticipated a coyote infestation, or how feeding the scavengers might have caused harm to the neighboring farmers.

"I can't believe the old fool went after them coyotes." Larry shook his head. "He's a crazy son of a bitch. You must have gotten your smarts from your mama."

The deputy smiled. "That's what she tells me. Anyway," he continued, and turned his attention on Michael. "Dad said he chased the coyotes onto your property."

"Mine?" he asked, confused. Sal's property didn't butt up to his.

"Yeah, Dad said it was around eleven thirty or so." The deputy pointed west. "He took the four wheeler off his land, chased them through Larry's, then stopped at your fence line. When he couldn't go any further, he headed home, then to the

ER. He said he did try calling you. He figured you were up because the lights were on at the house and in the garage," he finished and nodded to the steel garage.

Michael thought back to last night. He'd heard the coyotes baying, calling for their next meal just after he'd finished Tully's liposuction. When he'd wheeled Tully's body into the field, he hadn't seen any of them, but he'd sworn they were out there. Prowling behind trees and overgrown bushes, creeping around the tall grasses, he knew they waited for him to serve them dinner. After he'd dumped the body, he'd rushed back to the safety of the steel garage. He'd had no desire to listen to the coyotes rip the flesh from Tully's body, or as they'd ended up doing to Sal, turn on him. Had he already dumped the body by the time Sal had taken the four wheeler to his fence? He must have, otherwise Sal would have heard the coyotes feasting and fighting over Tully.

"I was up around that time, working in the garage," Michael began. "I was doing some cleaning and had the Shop-Vac going. That thing is so loud. I probably wouldn't hear a freight train running through my back field, let alone a handful of coyotes."

"Ain't that the truth," Larry said. "And why the hell are you cleaning at eleven thirty at night? I'm out like a light by nine. The wife says I need my beauty sleep."

Michael half-smiled. "It's not working," he said, then he let his smile fall, and looked away. "A guy I've known for about seven years died yesterday. With his death on my mind, I couldn't sleep and needed to keep myself busy."

After both men gave him their condolences, Michael pushed off Larry's Ford. "Speaking of sleep, I think my late night and last night's whiskey is finally catching up with me. If there's nothing else, I'm going to head to my bed. Deputy, give my best to your dad. If I see any coyotes on my property, I'll take them out in his honor."

The deputy smiled. "Appreciate that. Actually, that's one of the reasons I stopped by. After what happened to my dad...the sheriff is worried these coyotes are getting too aggressive. We were wondering if you wouldn't mind if we came out on your property with the animal warden and a few other men, and hunted these sons of bitches down."

Oh, hell no.

Michael had one last name on his death wish list. He couldn't have a bunch of people traipsing around on his property. No doubt they'd find what little remains were left of his previous patients. After he finished his last surgery, the sheriff and animal warden could move around his land as they pleased. Until then, he needed to keep his cool, and his privacy.

"That's fine," Michael began. "But I'm going to need you to give me a few days before you start. I'll call the sheriff when I'm ready for you."

The deputy narrowed his eyes. "Now's as good a time as any. Maybe if you saw what my dad looked like, you'd understand the urgency of the situation," the deputy replied, his tone no longer friendly.

Michael knew, all too well, what the coyotes were capable of doing to a person. They'd had a hell of a good time with Tully. He'd told the bastard he wouldn't recognize his body when Michael had finished with him. While the liposuction hadn't gone as planned, the coyotes had taken Tully's waist size from a sixty-six to a thirty-two in a matter of a few hours.

He picked up the tool box Larry had borrowed, then moved toward the stairs leading to the house's mudroom. So much for catching a few hours of sleep. With the sheriff's interest in coming onto his property, he'd need to change his surgery schedule. "I do understand. Sorry, Deputy. Now's just not a good time for me. Thanks for returning these, Larry," he called over his shoulder. "See you around."

"What the hell do you have all over the back of your pant leg?" Larry asked.

Michael released the door handle, then twisted his leg. He looked at the back of his jeans. Bile immediately rose in his throat when he eyed the dark bloodstain and small chunks of Tully's fat and flesh.

Maintaining his composure, he glanced between both men,

caught the curiosity in their eyes, and shrugged. "Puke. After my friend died...I had too much to drink last night. I was too embarrassed to say this earlier, but I was using the hose to clean up the puke when you two stopped by."

With sympathy in his eyes, Larry nodded. "I understand. When's the funeral?"

There's a memorial service this evening. I'm heading into Chicago in a few hours to pick up another guy to join me," Michael said, and thought about his final patient, Dr. Victor Roth. "Together, we're going to pay our final respects. Then he's going to stay with me a night, which is why I'd like some privacy. Once he's gone, you can kill every coyote you can find. It's not like I'll have any use for them."

Dorothy Long flipped through the TV channels. After passing over a dozen different stations, she finally settled on the Sylvester Stallone movie, *Stop! Or My Mom Will Shoot*. Not necessarily an Oscar winning movie, she did like the mom, Estelle Getty, who also played that spitfire, Sophia, she loved from the *Golden Girls*. Plus, Sly Stallone wasn't too hard on the eyes. Not that she'd fantasize about him, or any other man. She hadn't had sex in over fifteen years. Not since the night Rick had raped her.

She chuckled. Not because of Estelle Getty's antics—the movie really wasn't all that funny. Thinking about Rick's last moments always cracked her up. While the rape had been miserable, the beating had been the worst he'd ever given her. She remembered looking in the mirror after he'd passed out, naked and drunk, on their bed. The left side of her face had doubled in size, and her eye had swollen shut. He'd split her lip, and knocked two teeth out of her mouth. She'd probably had a couple of broken ribs, but hadn't bothered going to the hospital. For what she'd planned while he'd raped her, she would have to maintain a low profile.

Her smile grew. God, she'd have to admit, she'd definitely

been off her rocker that night. But, damn it, she'd had enough of Rick's bullshit and had sworn he'd never touch her again. She'd learned her lesson about running to the police the hard way. *Rick* had made her understand. With his fist and his belt.

Not that night.

No, that night, she had set him straight.

Straight to hell.

Dorothy laughed. God, the look on his face when he'd woken up from his drunken stupor and saw her standing over him, wielding a hatchet, had been absolutely priceless. Even now she wondered what had been going through his mind just before she slammed the blade into the middle of his face.

The movie went to commercial. Rather than learn about feminine products, she kept thinking about that night. She didn't know why. Maybe because Pudge had been reminding her of Rick? Not that Pudge had physically abused her, but there was just…something off lately. Had to be drugs. Hopefully she'd find out soon enough. She would have to check her new nurse out before mentioning her concerns. Dorothy didn't want her snooping to come back and bite her on her sore ass. Living in a nursing home would be hell compared to living with her Pudge. Again, she wondered if nursing homes, at least the ones they could afford, had cable.

Pudge came into the room, just as the commercial had ended and the movie began again. "You leaving?" Dorothy asked.

"I told you I had errands to run. I don't want to sit around waiting on your nurse. I have plans this evening. I'll be back in a couple of hours."

"I thought you said you didn't have to work today."

"I don't," Pudge answered. "Not that it's any of your business, but I thought I'd go out with some friends."

Friends? Pudge didn't have any friends. Never had. Rick had seen to it, abusing her child, physically, sexually, emotionally until Pudge had become so introverted, the high school counselor had wanted them to seek professional help. Rick, of course, wouldn't allow such a thing. If people found out what he'd done to his own child…

"If you're going to the store, pick me up some ice cream. Either chocolate chip cookie dough or cookies and cream. Hell, just buy them both. Oh, and some onion rings. I know they give me heartburn, but I've had a taste for them lately."

Pudge nodded, then said, "I'll leave a note on the door for the nurse. Call my cell phone if there's a problem."

When Pudge left, Dorothy quickly glanced at the clock. She had a couple of hours before Pudge came home. If she arrived soon, that would give the nurse plenty of time to check through Pudge's things.

A stress eater, Dorothy plunged into the bag of barbeque chips Pudge had left her. Thirty minutes later, she crumpled the bag, and tossed it to the floor. Anxious and worried her plans would be spoiled by a tardy nurse, she dabbed the sweat coating her forehead. She lowered the volume on the TV and considered calling the nursing agency.

The door bell rang.

Dorothy muted the TV, then yelled, "Come in."

Seconds later, a middle-aged, plump woman entered the living room. "Dorothy Long?" the woman asked.

"That's right. You must be my new nurse."

The woman gave her a warm smile as she approached, then patted Dorothy's arm. "Yes, I'm Nancy Flannery."

Nancy immediately put Dorothy at ease. Although a few years younger, Dorothy liked the motherly way Nancy treated her. Unlike Pudge, Nancy fussed over her with a gentle touch and demeanor. She talked about how she was going to be a grandma soon, about her other children, and her dog. For some reason, Dorothy felt as if she'd known Nancy for years.

After Nancy finished checking Dorothy's blood pressure, heart and temperature, she moved to her bed sores. "Oh my," she said as she inspected Dorothy's bottom. "This must be very painful. It was my understanding that you have someone living with you. They should be treating these several times a day."

After Nancy finished cleaning and dressing the sores with

fresh bandages, Dorothy flopped back. Holding on to the bedrails, while Nancy had taken care of her, had exerted Dorothy. Drawing in deep breaths, she nodded. "That'd be my Pudge. I've done everything for that child, and what do I get in return?" Dorothy waved a hand. "I'm living in filth, and treated as if I'm an inconvenience."

"You poor thing," Nancy said. "If you're unhappy here, we could look into alternative living arrangements. There are nursing homes that—"

"I don't want to leave," Dorothy interrupted. "A nursing home isn't the right place for me. I'm comfortable here. It's just that lately…"

Nancy gazed at her with concern and compassion. "You can tell me, Dorothy. What we discuss will stay between us."

The sympathy in Nancy's hazel eyes, the kindness in her smile, washed away any concerns Dorothy had about her new nurse. "Well," Dorothy began. "As you can see, I can't exactly get out of bed and move around the house."

Nancy smiled. "What's important is the person you are on the inside. Don't look at your weight as a burden. Embrace the woman you are. I know we just met, but I can tell you're a bright, considerate woman."

Dorothy decided she liked Nancy more than Gretchen. Gretchen had always harped about what Dorothy ate, her lack of exercise and hygiene. She'd made her obesity sound like a sickness or disease, whereas Nancy didn't focus on the fat, she focused on Dorothy's feelings and her needs.

"Thank you," Dorothy said. "I appreciate you saying that. I don't get many compliments around here. Anyway, I've been worried about my Pudge."

"How so?"

"I…I can't be sure, but I think Pudge is using drugs, and bringing people back to the house at strange hours of the day and night. I can't be sure because I…" She looked down at her bulging stomach. "I know it's a lot to ask, but would you mind going into Pudge's bedroom and looking around. If my child has a drug problem, I want to know if we need to get professional help. I love my Pudge, you see. I don't know what I would do without my baby."

Nancy sighed and took Dorothy's hand. "From one mother to another, I understand completely."

"You do?"

Nancy nodded.

"If you do find drugs, will you report Pudge to the nursing agency? Like I said, I don't want to be forced into a nursing home if Pudge has to go to rehab or something."

"It'll be our secret. But, out of good conscience, I couldn't leave you alone all the time with Pudge. I'll make extra visits— no charge." She gave Dorothy's hand a pat before rising. "Which room is Pudge's?"

Dorothy pointed toward the hallway. "Check the bathroom, too. It's off the hall, just before the bedroom."

When Nancy walked away, Dorothy grinned. She couldn't believe she'd found a confidant in her new nurse, and could picture Nancy visiting her. Maybe they'd watch TV together or play a game of cards. She hadn't played cards in years. Releasing a wistful sigh, she conjured different scenarios. All of which included a clean house and Nancy. The filth Dorothy had been living in suddenly bothered her. Having this kindred spirit in her house made Dorothy yearn for change. Between Dorothy's disability check and Pudge's income, she wondered if they could afford a cleaning service. She'd love to see the house fixed up a little nicer, if she were to have Nancy visiting more often. Hell, she'd love to do the job herself.

Dorothy realized she no longer wanted to be chained to the rented hospital bed. She hadn't had a friend in so long. Nancy, with her sweet demeanor, and understanding eyes, made Dorothy want to walk, to move around, to clean her own damn house...to be a good friend.

Smiling, Dorothy laid her head against the pillow and waited for Nancy. At this point, if Pudge came home and found the nurse snooping, Dorothy didn't care. Nancy would fight for her, and Pudge wouldn't hold the cards any longer.

With friendship and long-needed companionship on the

brain, Dorothy was determined to make a comeback.

When Nancy entered the room carrying a large duffle bag, Dorothy said, "Before you tell me what you've found, I want you to know that I'm really excited you're here. It's been a long time since I've had a...friend to talk to. You've inspired me, Nancy. I want to lose the weight and get out of this bed. Go for coffee, go for a run." She chuckled. "The only time I'd ever think I'd want to run is if someone was pointing a gun at me. But not any more. I'm ready to get healthy."

Nancy laughed as she brought over the duffle bag. Hell, she didn't just laugh, she cackled, the sound eerily familiar and unsettling. Dorothy couldn't put her finger on her sudden edginess, but then she shrugged off the feeling. This was Nancy. Her new friend.

"Very touching," Nancy said as she unzipped the bag, then dumped the contents on Dorothy's legs.

Shackled to the bed by her weight, Dorothy panicked and made several attempts to roll and dislodge the disgusting things lying on top of her legs. Years of not using her muscles had her sweating and panting. Fear of what Nancy had discovered had her heart beating out of control and her mind racing.

Pudge had been very bad.

"Oh my God," Dorothy gasped. "W...what is all of this?" Shocked, she stared at the bloody clothes and sharp medical instruments. "This has to be part of a costume. Why else would Pudge have—?"

"I doubt this is," Nancy said as she held up a dildo. "Or this." She showed her more clothes stained with what appeared to be a lot of dried blood.

Sickened, Dorothy mumbled, "Dear Lord."

"Praying won't help you," Nancy said, her tone no longer sweet and compassionate.

Frowning, Dorothy glanced away from the filth on her bed, and looked to the other woman. "You're right. We should go to the police. If Pudge has hurt someone..."

Dorothy knew in her heart that this was Rick's fault. He'd screwed up Pudge's head. Dorothy had witnessed Pudge's beatings, and the night Rick had died, she'd learned the bastard had been raping his own child for years. Something he'd told Dorothy as he'd punched her in the head. Told her she couldn't do anything about it. But she had done something. She'd killed Pudge's tormentor, then laid him to rest in pieces.

But what if they did go to the police and report Pudge? Would the cops investigate their family's past? If they did, or if Pudge went under psychological treatment, they could find out what had really happened to Rick. Dorothy would go to jail. She couldn't allow that to happen. Between Rick and her weight, Dorothy had grown tired of being a prisoner.

"Let me see that," Dorothy demanded, and grabbed what looked to be a maintenance worker's uniform shirt. She checked the size, then sighed with relief. "It's a double XL, Pudge would swim in this thing." She tossed it aside. "I told you I thought I heard other people at the house. I bet Pudge is holding onto these things for someone else. Did you find any drugs?"

Nancy shook her head, and Dorothy swore the other woman eyed her with perverse amusement. No, not Nancy. Nancy was helping her. The thought of Pudge being involved in something that could drag them down had her paranoid.

"Okay, listen," Dorothy began, a plan formulating in her mind. "Why don't you put this stuff back where you found it? I don't want Pudge to know we were snooping."

"So you expect me to allow you to live alone with a murderer?" Nancy asked.

Dorothy shook her head, and answered Nancy honestly, "Pudge isn't exactly the sharpest tool in the shed, if you get my meaning, and couldn't pull off killing a person and getting away with it. That child is and always will be a door mat. Murderer." She shrugged. "I'll take my chances."

Nancy leaned over the bed and began stuffing the stained clothes in the bag. When she held up the scalpel, light glistened off the sharp edge. "Are you sure about that? If I were you, I'd be afraid."

"I'm not afraid of my own child."

Still holding the scalpel, Nancy grabbed her hair, then tugged. "You should be."

"Pudge?" Dorothy whispered, and began shaking. She stared in utter disbelief as Pudge tossed the wig to the floor. "I...I..."

"I, I, I," Pudge mimicked. "Did you really think I would be stupid enough to allow you to have access to my things? When you threatened my inheritance, I knew I had to make sure Gretchen didn't come see you...ever."

When Pudge sent her a vicious grin, Dorothy asked, "Did you...hurt Gretchen?"

"I did more than hurt her. You needed a new nurse. Honestly, I planned to just fill her shoes to make sure you didn't change your will or beneficiary."

"Pudge, honey, I wasn't going to do that."

"No? Then you were just going to have her snoop through my things?" Pudge shrugged, then put the scalpel in the duffle bag. "I guess it doesn't matter now. But what *does* matter is that you can't be trusted."

Pudge peeled off the nurse's nose, and then the plump cheeks. After dropping them on the bed tray, Pudge pulled the shirt off, and tossed it aside. "Look who's the stupid one now," Pudge said, and showed off the padding that had once been Nancy's ample breasts, thick stomach and hips. "You couldn't even recognize your own child. So here's what I'm going to do with you."

Shaking, Dorothy couldn't stop the tears streaming down her face. What had happened to her baby? "Pudge, I'm sorry. Please don't kill me. Please," she begged.

"If I was going to kill you, you'd have been dead a long time ago. Do you really think I enjoy feeding your fat face, wiping your ass, changing your disgusting colostomy bag? Do you think I like living here with you? That I'm living the fucking dream? Hell, no. But I want your money, and to get it, I need you to die...naturally."

Relief washed over Dorothy, until she caught a wicked glint in Pudge's eyes. "What are you going to do with me?"

"The better question is what am I going to do to you?" Pudge replied, and snatched the TV remote and phone off of Dorothy's bed tray. "Guess what that is? Absolutely nothing."

"I don't understand."

"And you thought I wasn't the sharpest tool in the shed. Let me lay it out for you. I will no longer take care of you. Those bed sores can fester until they're infected and reek as much as your colostomy bag, which I refuse to change—ever. Your food demands...well, I won't starve you, but kiss your snack cakes good-bye. As for your phone and TV privileges, all gone. I own you, *Mama*."

Dorothy stared at the TV remote Pudge held. Without TV, what did she have? Because she had no friends or family worth speaking to, she didn't have much use for the phone. But her TV...she'd go crazy without it. Panic bubbled from within the depths of her soul. She couldn't imagine lying in the hospital bed all day, alone, with nothing to do. "Please," she begged Pudge. "At least let me keep the TV."

"Seriously? The TV is your only concern?" Pudge chuckled. "You're pathetic. If I were you, I'd be more concerned about—"

A phone rang. Pudge reached into the bag that had been part of the nurse disguise and pulled out a cell phone. Dorothy thought about screaming with the hope of alerting the caller to her dire situation, but Pudge answered the call in the kitchen.

Seconds later, Pudge returned. "I've got to leave soon. I don't trust you to be quiet while I'm showering, or even when I'm gone, so..." Pudge opened the nurse's bag and pulled out a roll of duct tape and a set of handcuffs.

Her earlier panic morphed into raw terror. "Please don't do this," she begged as Pudge tore tape off the roll. "I'll be good. I promise. I'll be good."

Pudge cuffed Dorothy's hands around the bedrail, then pressed the tape over her mouth. "I know you will. You have no choice."

CHAPTER 18

EDEN SLUNG THE computer bag over her shoulder, then turned to Hudson, "Ready?"

He pushed off the wall of one of WBDJ's editing rooms. "That's it?"

She smiled. "I told you it wouldn't take me long to finish this last segment. Thanks for your help," she said to David.

The cameraman nodded his head. "My pleasure. I'm sure gonna to miss working with you. Don't forget about us little people when you get all big and famous," he said, then gave her a hug.

She looked over David's shoulder, and met Hudson's gaze. While his eyes didn't hold even a hint of jealousy, the disappointment she saw in them made her stomach drop, and her heart race with indecision. She'd rekindled her relationship with Hudson on the cusp of beginning a new career change—in another state. Now she wasn't sure if she even wanted to move. Yes, she wanted the Network job. Going national, with the opportunity of syndication, would take her career to a level she'd never imagined. Only her drive to be on top would cost her Hudson. He had a life, and his position with CORE, here in Chicago. What would he do in New York? Would he even consider moving for her? Was she even ready to take their relationship to that level?

As David released her and then spoke with Hudson, she realized she had some serious thinking to do. The realtor had left her a voice message this morning with regards to showing her townhouse to several potential buyers. Plus, her agent had emailed her the itinerary for next week's trip to New York, along with the Network contract to review. Weeks ago, she'd been ecstatic over the upcoming career opportunity. Instead of enthusiasm over the new move and job, her attention, her excitement now revolved around Hudson and what their future could hold.

Damn, him holding her, filling her body, her heart, her soul with the love she'd denied herself for too long. She knew in her gut she loved him. Even when she'd ended their relationship two years ago, she'd loved him. The fear of rejection, of failing, of allowing their relationship to step in the way of her career, had driven her to end things with him. Now she'd trade those lost years, maybe even the Network job, to have the chance to discover what their life together would have been like if only she'd taken the risk.

Risk. She'd taken on the pseudonym because she was a risk taker when it came to her career. Could she risk her heart *and* her career for Hudson?

Instead of focusing on the uncertainty of what their relationship would eventually become, she forced her attention to something less complicated—the killer and his DVDs. The investigation, while frustrating and gruesome, was straightforward when compared to the complexity of her heart. Find the identity of the third victim, as well as the possible fourth, and stop the killer. Only they didn't have much time. Another DVD would be on her doorstep by Monday morning.

David shook Hudson's hand, then waved to her. "See y'all," he said, and left the room.

"Do you want to go back to my place, or to CORE?" she asked Hudson.

He rubbed the back of his neck. "Rachel sent me a text while you were working. She's emailing me everything she's found on the dentist."

KRISTINE MASON

"I've been thinking. Now that we have Dr. Brian Westly's ID, maybe we should go to the police. I know the killer said no cops, but—"

"We still don't have a body. And according to his receptionist, Westly went on vacation."

"Permanently."

He half-chuckled. "That was bad. I'm worried Rachel's dark sense of humor is rubbing off on you."

"I wish her smarts would." The girl really was a brainiac. Nudging him with her bag, she breezed past him and into the hallway. "So, back to my place?"

"Yeah, hopefully we'll—"

David rounded the corner, his dark eyes bright with excitement. "Feel like reportin' one more story, ya know, for ol' time's sake?"

After she'd received the offer from Network last month, Eden had told the station manger she'd finish the beauty pageant series, but she wouldn't take on any other assignments. Aside from her relationship with Hudson, when it came to her job, she didn't like to leave things unfinished, and she'd worried the possible WBDJ assignments might overlap with her move to New York.

She shook her head as she followed David into the newsroom. "Give it to Ryan. He's replacing me. If he's going to build a fan base in Chicago, he needs the air time."

"Ryan's on assignment. Rodger wants someone on the scene ASAP."

"Didn't Les fill in last night with the Dr. Dread report? Have him do it."

David rubbed his jaw with his knuckles. "I'm assumin' you didn't see Les's report, otherwise you wouldn't have suggested him."

"That bad?" she asked, then looked around the newsroom for someone else who could handle the assignment.

"Rodger swore that if he didn't have anyone else next time, he'd send Pete."

"The meteorologist? Damn, must've been *very* bad."

244

"Speak of the devil," David said as Rodger approached them.

"Eden, I'm glad to see you," Rodger said.

The man hadn't spoken to her since Monday, the night she'd had the on-air tiff with Kyle, yet now he was glad to see her. Prick. Like Kyle, he'd been pissed off about her promotion to Network. While Rodger's reasons had been different—he'd been forced to replace one of his star reporters—he hadn't made the transition any easier for her. Avoiding her calls, cancelling meetings, blowing off any input she'd had on her replacement. None of this mattered anymore. She'd had a nice run with WBDJ, but it was time to move on to better things.

"Nice to see you too," Eden said, then grabbed Hudson's arm and began walking out of the room.

"Hold up," Rodger called. "I need someone to head to West Adams and South Jefferson. It's a parking garage not too far from the Chicago Union Station. It's also the last place anyone has seen Dr. Leonard Tully."

"Tully?" she echoed, and tightened her grip on Hudson's arm. Her stomach somersaulted with a mixture of hope and dread.

"Don't tell me you don't know who the guy is," Rodger said with exasperation.

"Of course I do." Her mind raced to come up with everything she'd ever heard about Tully. "What happened to him?"

"Missing. Police suspect he was kidnapped from the parking garage. Apparently he'd driven into the garage but never came out, not even to go to the clinic next door. His wife was supposed to go out of town last night, but her trip had been cancelled. When Tully didn't show up at their house, and she'd found out he'd never made it into the clinic, she called the police. We're trying to get a copy of the parking garage surveillance tape, but aren't having any luck. Maybe you can sweet talk the garage owners into giving you a copy." He nodded to David. "Ito will take you. Keep in mind, Tully is best buds with one of the station owners."

Eden wanted to drag Hudson out of the station and run to the car. There was no way in hell she could waste time reporting this story. Not when they'd just been handed the identity of the third victim.

"Look, Rodger," she began. "I—"

"Rodger," Tabitha Wilkens called as she rushed into the room. "I heard you need someone to report the Tully kidnapping."

Rodger glanced over Tabitha's head and looked at Eden. He nodded, and said, "I did, but Eden volunteered."

"No, I didn't. Quite frankly, I don't have the time. Let Tabitha go."

Tabitha turned to face her. The shock and appreciation in the other woman's eyes gave Eden the warm fuzzies. While she and Tabitha hadn't always had the best relationship, the young reporter deserved a chance. There had been a time, early in her career, when a senior reporter had given Eden a shot at a story. That story had been the start of her successful career. Eden didn't know Tabitha too well, but she had glimpsed the fire and hunger in the other woman's eyes and believed Tabitha would, like her, find success as a reporter.

"Yes," Tabitha said, then turned to Rodger. "Let me go."

Rodger ran a hand over his balding head, then blew out a sigh of resignation. "Fine. Don't screw up," he said, then walked away.

Tabitha didn't thank or acknowledge her as she followed after David and Rodger. Eden didn't care. She had more important things to deal with right now.

Holding onto Hudson's arm, she directed him out of the newsroom.

"Are we running from something?" he asked as she led him from the building and into the parking lot.

When they reached the Trans Am, she climbed into the car and closed the door. After he did the same, he asked, "What's going on?"

"Dr. Leonard Tully."

"Yeah, I heard what the bald guy said about him."

"But you've never heard of him?" she asked as she used her smart phone to pull up a picture of Tully. He'd recently donated time and money to a new clinic in Chicago, helping people who didn't have insurance with reconstructive plastic surgery. She'd sworn there had been an article about him in the *Chicago Tribune*. "Wait, got it."

After starting the car, he took the phone from her. When he glanced at the screen, he quickly snapped his gaze to hers. "Holy shit. This could be our guy."

"His physique definitely matches the third victim. We need to call Rachel. Tully could be our link to Elliot. I'm still not sure where the dentist fits in, but Tully definitely does. He's a plastic surgeon. Wanna take a guess at what he specializes in?"

He handed her the phone. "Liposuction."

"You got it," she said, then gripped the door handle as Hudson hit the gas and raced out of the parking lot. "Slow down, Speed Racer."

"Sorry," he said, and eased off the accelerator. "Would you grab my phone from my jacket pocket and call Rachel?"

She reached into his front pocket and quickly found the phone. If she hadn't been so eager to discover whether or not Tully had, at some point, worked with Elliot, she would have liked to have taken her time frisking Hudson. Scars and all, she loved his body, and would never grow tired of touching him.

Minutes later, Rachel was on the other end of the line, pulling up information on Tully and his work history. She crunched on a pencil as she searched. Although irritating to listen to, Eden didn't care if the woman chomped on a broomstick. Miss Smarty Pants had proven her skills time and again, and Eden had faith that she'd help them bring this case to a swift end.

"Got it," Rachel said.

Eden pressed the speaker phone button. "I've got you on speaker so Hudson can hear. What'd you find?"

"Tully worked with Elliot at Cosmetic Solutions and Med Spa during the three years it was open."

"How many other doctors worked at this place?" Hudson asked.

"One. Dr. Victor Roth," she said, then blew out a breath. "This is going to be bad if we don't get to him before the killer."

A chill swept over Eden. "What was Dr. Roth's specialty?"

"Rhinoplasty."

Michael Morrison parked the van in front of Dr. Victor Roth's brownstone, and killed the ignition. He hadn't planned on taking Roth today, but he also hadn't planned on the sheriff and his posse of coyote hunters' eagerness to tromp around on his land. Moving Roth's surgery up a day actually worked out quite well. While he'd been confident that he could complete his death wish list by Eliza's birthday, he'd been cutting it close. Now, though, he'd have an extra day. A little wiggle room, just in case things didn't go to plan.

Originally, Michael had intended to take Roth when he went for his usual morning run. Unlike Tully, Roth maintained a fit physique. Like Tully, Roth also had extramarital affairs. Only he didn't go for Latin men. On numerous occasions, Michael had followed him to an upscale gentlemen's club where Roth had enjoyed the company of many young women. He'd often take them to the adjacent hotel. Sometimes there'd be one girl, other times, two. Roth obviously didn't respect his wife of two years, or his young stepchildren. In his opinion, Mrs. Roth was better off without her doctor husband.

Cheaters were assholes who broke vows of trust and monogamy without a thought for their partner. Never, while Michael had been married, had he cheated on his wife. Even when their marriage had begun to crumble, he hadn't wandered into another woman's bed. Although his wife had become a raving bitch, he'd been raised to value commitment and keep promises.

Make them pay, Daddy.

Eliza's last plea filtered through his thoughts as he glared at Roth's brownstone. Michael definitely knew how to honor a commitment, the corpses in his field proof, and as the door to the brownstone opened, he silently promised his daughter that Roth would pay.

Roth wasn't alone. His pretty wife, and her equally pretty daughters, exited the home. While the young girls raced down the steps laughing and squealing, Mrs. Roth kissed her husband on the lips. She then turned, called to the girls, then ushered them into the Lexus parked along the street. Once she drove off, Roth closed the door.

Michael's stomach tightened with anticipation and anxiety. He'd kidnapped Tully during the day, but in a quiet parking garage that he'd studied and inspected months prior. While familiar with the general layout of Roth's home, he wasn't particularly enthusiastic about breaking into the man's house. With the exception of Dr. Roth, he didn't plan on stealing anything. Still, he'd rather Roth's wife and stepchildren not endure the fear and violation that often followed a break-in, which meant he'd have to make sure he was careful. The house would have to look as he'd found it. Mrs. Roth couldn't suspect that her husband had been kidnapped, at least not until Michael had finished his surgery and given Eden the final DVD.

He'd worked hard to make the doctors from Cosmetic Solution and Med Spa pay for their crimes against his daughter. The prize, the gift he'd promised Eliza, was only one surgery away from completion. No slip-ups, no screw-ups, no last minute jitters.

His confidence bolstered, Michael started the van, then shifted gears. He maneuvered until he backed the van into Roth's narrow driveway. When the driver's side back door was parallel to the house's back stoop, he killed the ignition.

Heart beating hard, adrenaline racing through his veins, Michael climbed out of the van and closed the door. He surveyed the small backyard, and both of Roth's neighbors' six foot privacy fences. Listening for a moment, he heard nothing but the bitter wind whistling through the naked trees.

Pulling his cap low, he walked up the few steps leading to Roth's back stoop, then knocked on the door. He counted to thirty, then knocked again. Harder. Louder.

"Coming," Roth said as he unlocked the door. "Can I help you?"

"Dr. Roth?"

"That's right," Roth said as he eyed the van.

"I'm from Morrison Heating and Cooling. Your wife called about tuning up your furnace."

Roth furrowed his forehead. "She must have forgotten to tell me." He blew out an impatient breath, then muttered, "Stupid ditz."

Michael looked away as if he hadn't heard the man, his hatred for Roth intensifying. Roth had no respect for women. Not Eliza, not the pretty Mrs. Roth, not the women he used from the gentlemen's club.

"You want to reschedule?" Michael asked, knowing there would be no change in plans. He did want to sound accommodating, though, to keep Roth at ease and without suspicion.

"No. It's fine. Are you going to be long?"

"About an hour."

"An hour?" Roth echoed with melodramatic outrage. "I have somewhere to be later, can't you do whatever it is you need to do any faster?"

Michael shrugged. "You willing to help me haul the tools out of my van?"

With an exaggerated eye roll, Roth nodded. "If it'll help," he said, and without a coat or shoes, he jogged down the steps to the van. "I don't know why she couldn't have had you come out during the week. I swear the woman doesn't have a brain sometimes."

Michael pulled the syringe from his coat pocket, and hiding it in his palm, used his other hand to slide open the door. He climbed inside and pretended to struggle. "Damn it," he shouted.

"What's the problem?" Roth asked. "It's freezing out here, give me what you need me to carry inside and let's get the ball rolling. I can't stand it when people waste my time."

"Sorry, sir. The one tool box I need is wedged between the seats. If you could climb inside and pull from your end..." Keeping the syringe out of sight, Michael continued the pretense of struggling. Once Roth entered the van, he'd make his move, then leave.

Roth crouched inside the van. While not a large man like Tully, he crowded the small space. Michael reconsidered the syringe. For him to stab the tip into Roth's neck, he'd need more room to move. Now he wished he'd removed the seats from the van.

Too late now, time to improvise.

"I don't know what the hell kind of operation your company runs," Roth began as he looked around the van. "But if this is any indication, be prepared for me to file a complaint with your superiors. Now what in the hell can't you seem to remove from this piece of shit van of yours?"

Michael slipped the syringe into his pocket, then reached under the back passenger seat. He grasped the bat he'd used to subdue Tully, then pointed to the small tool box. "That box," he said.

"Seriously? My eight-year-old stepdaughter could lift that thing out of here. You know what? I'm done with this. Get the hell out of here. I'm cancelling the appointment."

As Roth turned to jump out of the van, Michael hit him over the head with the bat. Roth dropped to the floorboard. Unfortunately still conscious, Roth moaned and writhed between the seats. Michael took the syringe from his pocket and stabbed Roth in the neck. Once he sent every drop of the sedative into the man's veins, he quickly restrained Roth with duct tape, then climbed over him and into the driver's seat.

He glanced at Roth's house and realized the man had left the back door open. Not wanting to draw alarm should his wife come home, or a neighbor stop by, Michael raced up to Roth's back stoop, closed the door, then ran back to the van.

After he started the ignition, he drove out of the narrow driveway, then onto the quiet street. When he reached the intersection, he stopped at the red light before making a right turn, and heading toward the freeway on ramp. As he momentarily idled at the stoplight, a car approached from across the intersection, then stopped.

Anxiety tore through his stomach. Tightening his grip on the steering wheel, he clenched his jaw. As he made the turn, he looked into his review mirror just as the light turned green and a black Trans Am sped through the intersection.

CHAPTER 19

EDEN STROKED FABIO'S soft hair, while Brutal snuggled on her lap. A sense of hopelessness, dread and foreboding ran through her mind and body. They'd been too late. The killer, once again, had been one step ahead of them.

Pocketing his cell phone, Hudson entered her living room, then sat on the couch next to her. As Brutal crawled from her lap into his, he said, "Stop beating yourself up, we don't know for sure that the killer took Roth. Could be the guy is out with his family."

"No. Roth's gone."

"Are your sister's psychic powers rubbing off on you?"

Pinching his leg, she narrowed her eyes at him. "Try a gut feeling. Thank you very much."

He sent her a tired smile, then used his thumb and forefinger to rub his eyes. "The killer said the next DVD would be on your doorstep Monday. It's Saturday. I guess it's possible he'd kidnapped Roth already, but that would mean he's killing these guys back to back." He dropped his hand, then began petting Brutal. "The guy's got to be exhausted."

"Why do you say that?"

"He's driving at least two hours to Chicago to kidnap these doctors, driving another two to wherever he performs his surgeries, kills the victims, then turns around and drives back to Chicago to drop the DVD. Either he's a machine or he's running on caffeine and hate."

Eden considered the killer's state of physical and emotional exhaustion, and became optimistic. "If he's tired, he might slip up."

"Doubtful. Even if he does, this is his last kill. He could feed Roth's body to the dogs or whatever, then disappear off the grid. Considering he's willingly exposed himself to you with his DVDs, and has always been one step ahead of us, I'm guessing he has a solid plan of escape."

She gave Fabio a final pat, then stood and began pacing. "We have to do something. I can't stand just sitting around, waiting for something to happen."

"We *are* doing something. We've left a message for Roth's wife to call us, and Rachel is pulling up everything she can on Cosmetic Solutions and Med Spa."

"I know," she said, and hugged herself. "I'm just so damned frustrated. I can't believe Bob blew you off." Because she'd been blackballed by the Chicago police, she'd asked Hudson to call Detective Bob Mallory. Now that Tully had been kidnapped, and CORE had plenty of evidence of foul play against the other two victims, she'd been certain Bob would want to become involved with their investigation.

"He didn't necessarily blow me off. He's all over the Dread murders right now. Besides, he said he'd forward our info to the lead detective working the Tully kidnapping."

"Who's the detective?"

"Ron Vincent."

"That guy will never call you back."

"Why wouldn't he?"

"He's one of those guys who doesn't like outside help." She'd seen Vincent in action, when she'd been reporting a story about a woman who had been kidnapping, then selling kids to people looking to adopt. When the FBI had stepped in, Vincent had done everything in his power to thwart their efforts. In the end, while all of the kids had been recovered, the woman had disappeared without a trace. "Trust me. We're on our own."

Pacing again, she asked, "Did you give Rachel my suggestion?" She'd recommended they focus on Med Spa's clientele. Considering the killer's focus had been on the doctors from Med Spa, maybe one of the two women the killer had spoken of, or perhaps both, had had plastic surgery through the medical group.

"Yes. She's working on it now. Although Med Spa has been closed for the past six or so years, they still have a website. She said it hasn't been updated since the place closed, but she somehow hooked into the server Med Spa had used. All of Med Spa's data is on this server, their financials, the list of their former clients. Anyway, she said it might take a while to…hell, I don't know what she called it. According to Rachel, I'm technically challenged, so I'm not going to pretend I know how she's working her magic."

"Technically challenged," she repeated with a chuckle, then shrugged. "I'm right there with you. I'm just happy that she's able to work any magic at all. With the privacy laws, I was worried she wouldn't be able to find any information on Med Spa's clients."

He grinned. "One would think, but apparently those laws don't apply to Rachel. Anyway, she said she'd email the list once the download is finished. Could be one hour, could be five."

Dropping her arms, she realized Hudson was right. They were doing all that they could for the time being. Still, she hated to sit and wait.

Yes, she could find something to do. Calling her realtor back would be one thing, responding to her agent, another. But doing those two things would only aggravate and frustrate her more. She didn't want to think about leaving Hudson. With the way he sat on her couch, cuddling Brutal, all she wanted to think about was them. They did have time to kill. Maybe she should bring up the move to New York. Ask him how he felt about her leaving Chicago.

Or maybe she should take a shower. Although avoiding the inevitable wasn't usually her style, with the way the day had been going, she didn't want to make it any worse. She loved Hudson, and honestly wasn't ready for any answers he might have for her. If she brought up the move and he told her to keep in touch, she'd be more than devastated. She'd be heartbroken.

After taking a chance and opening up her heart and soul to him, she didn't think she was ready for the foreseeable rejection. He had a life and job here. While she'd been honest with him about her past, she hadn't had the courage to tell him she loved him. He hadn't said the words either. Even if he did love her, would that love be enough to sacrifice his career for her? The bigger question, did she love him enough to sacrifice hers?

She needed a moment to gather her thoughts. "Well, if we have to wait, I might as well do it clean. I'm going to take a shower."

Setting Brutal on the couch, he stood, then moved toward her with a sexy swagger that had her heart rate climbing. He settled his big palms on her hips. "A shower sounds good," he said, his voice thick, husky.

The sudden intensity in his gaze caused an instant ache between her thighs. She curled her fingers into his shirt, and brought him closer. "I don't remember inviting you," she teased, while conjuring the image of his slick, hard, naked body rubbing along hers.

Running a hand through her hair, he released her ponytail and massaged the back of her head. "I can wash your hair," he suggested, and kissed her temple.

"Mmm. That might be nice," she murmured, and loving the way he kneaded her scalp, she let her eyes close.

With his other hand, he squeezed her butt, then dipped his fingers between her thighs. "Very nice," he whispered into her ear, before nipping her earlobe.

The little sting sent a shiver of anticipation through her body.

"Cold?" he asked as he placed soft kisses along her neck and jaw. When his mouth was a hair's breadth away from hers, he curved his lips into a sexy grin. "I can think of a few ways to warm you up."

She burst out laughing, and cupped his face. Still smiling she said, "Seriously cheesy. Do these lines of yours usually work with the ladies?"

"I don't know. I've never tried them before."

"Oh? So you've been saving them for me?"

He ran his hand over her breast, and gave her nipple a light squeeze. "That depends on whether or not it's working."

"Yeah, it's working," she said, her breath hitching as he manipulated her nipple with sensual finesse. With the exception of Hudson, every man she'd ever dated, or who had tried to date her, had been very polished metrosexuals. Successful businessmen who had spent equal amounts of time at the office as they had the gym and salon. While a couple of these men had been appealing, none of them could compare to Hudson. With his sense of humor and honest charm, he'd captivated her mind, heart and body from the start. And she loved his cheesy lines. She loved that he wasn't afraid to use them, to be himself around her. She loved that he didn't try to be anything more than Hudson Patterson, a trustworthy, honorable and incredibly sexy man.

When he began to move his hands under her sweatshirt, she pulled away. Gaze locked on his, she removed the sweatshirt, then dangled it from her fingertips. "I can use some help washing more than my hair." She cupped her breast, then slid her palm down her stomach to between her legs. "I'm feeling *very* dirty," she added, and tried to keep from grinning. She could bring on the Velveeta, too.

Another slow, sexy smile tugged at the corner of his mouth. His eyes heated and darkened to gunmetal gray as he swept his gaze from her black, lacy bra to the hand she rubbed along her sex. He took a step forward. "I like dirty," he said, his voice oozing with raw sex.

"Oh?" She slid the yoga pants over her hips, then kicked

KRISTINE MASON

them onto the hardwood floor. Wearing only the black bra and matching thong, she headed down the hall. When she reached the bedroom door, she turned. "Then maybe I should forget about the shower," she said over her shoulder.

Before she took another step, he was behind her, palming her breast with one hand, while pressing her hip against his erection with the other. "I promised I'd wash your hair," he murmured against her neck. "And I always keep my promises."

Hudson released her breast and hip, then turned her to face him. "Take off your bra and panties."

Eyes bright with excitement, she took a step back, and reached behind her. Her breasts thrusting forward, she slowly let the lace bra slip to the floor. Keeping her eyes on his, she turned, hooked her fingers around the thong. With an exaggerated sway of her hips, she bent and slid them down to her ankles, giving him a tantalizing view of her perfect ass.

Still fully clothed, he kept his eyes on her tempting backside and waited for her next move. He loved the way she teased him. Sex between them had never been a problem, and had always been hot and explosive, but never, like now, playful. While he loved hot and explosive, he *really* loved playful. He'd told her he'd never used his dumb lines on a woman, and had meant it. Never having been comfortable enough to let his guard down and simply be himself, he'd always gone the route of the badass lover. With Eden, he could be himself. He could play, laugh...love.

She finally turned. The hunger, the desire and the honest affection in her eyes had his heart jumping and his dick throbbing. And he knew. Knew without a doubt that he wanted to look into those eyes every day for the rest of his life. He wanted to experience every form of passion and pleasure with Eden. Not only physically, but emotionally.

Man, did other guys think like this? He didn't know, and at this point, he didn't care.

He was in love with Eden.

And she was completely naked.

She cocked her head and eyed him. "You're a little

258

overdressed, don't you think?"

Sucking in a breath as she moved toward him, he nodded. He'd been ready to say...something. Something sexy, or fun, or whatever, but her nearness, her nakedness, and the wicked, mischievous gleam in her eyes had him tongue-tied.

"We should rectify that, don't you think?" she asked as she slipped a finger through his belt buckle.

In record time, she had his belt undone, and his zipper down. She glided her hands inside his jeans, captured his boxer briefs, then tugged. His dick bobbed as his clothes puddled around his ankles. As he kicked them toward the bed, she pushed his shirt over his head, then tossed it to the floor.

Her gaze moved over his chest, then down his stomach, and settled on his erection. "*Much* better," she murmured as she dropped to her knees.

"Eden," he said, then caught his breath as she lightly grasped him. "I...want this to be about you."

Stroking his penis, she stood and snared him with her probing gaze. "What if I want this to be about you? What if I want to show you..." She trailed off, and looked away.

He cupped her chin, and forced her to look at him. "Show me what?" he asked, hoping she'd say the words. Eden, like him, had always kept her emotions in check. And as much as he wanted to tell her that he loved her, he hoped she'd say it first. After how things between them had ended two years ago, and how hard it had been for him to cope with that loss, he didn't want to face another rejection. Especially at this moment, when they were both naked and...vulnerable.

She smiled, nothing seductive, but the warmth of that smile, how it reached her eyes, had him hardening by the second. "I...wanted to show you how much I love your body," she said, and while still stroking his arousal with one hand, she caressed his scarred chest with the other.

Even when they used to date, he'd noticed her fascination with his scars. Laying his hand on hers, he helped her trace the scar that ran along his collar bone. "They're ugly."

Without looking at him, she moved their hands to the scar

along the right side of his chest. "They're not ugly. They're a part of you." She removed their hands, then kissed the scar. Her breath fanned along his skin as she said, "I love that you've never tried to hide them from me. Our scars, even the ones we can't see, make us who we are. Until now, I feel like all we've ever done was hold back from each other."

She raised her head. The tenderness in her eyes made him weak in the knees. Scarred, flawed, she cared about him. Her acceptance of him only deepened the love he felt for her.

He cupped her face, then brushed his lips along hers. "All I've ever wanted was to know you. Every part of you."

Drawing her closer, he kissed her. He'd meant to go slow. Show her how much he cared about her. But the moment she parted her lips and swept her tongue along his, a potent combination of love and lust exploded inside of him. He claimed her mouth, rubbed his hands along her back, loving the soft texture of her skin, until he grasped her bottom.

He lifted her, forcing her to release his erection, and wrap her legs around his back. Still kissing him, she feathered her fingers through his hair and held his head. Holding him locked in place, she took over their kiss. She nipped and licked his lips, pressed open-mouthed kisses along his jaw, until she brought their mouths together. Their noses and teeth collided. She blistered his lips with a kiss so hot that he swore he was going to self-combust if he didn't bury himself inside her heat.

Setting her butt on the edge of the mattress, he broke their kiss, then brushed his mouth along her neck and chest until he reached one incredibly taut nipple. While sliding his hand between her thighs, he drew the hard tip into his mouth, and sucked. She held his head to her breast as he slipped two fingers inside of her. Warm, wet and inviting, he ached to feel her hug his length. Loving the way she writhed and moaned, the way her body reacted, he needed to taste her first.

After giving her other nipple attention, he kissed a path down her flat belly, then gripped her hips and swept his tongue along her plump sex. Still holding his head, she rocked her pelvis against his mouth, and spread her legs wider. Her body began to tremble. Her breathing quickened. Knowing the signs, knowing she neared orgasm, he pressed his fingers between her thighs again, and with fierce determination, began flicking his tongue along her clit.

Her inner muscles suddenly gripped his fingers. Arching her back, she released a husky, sexy moan.

Kissing a trail along her inner thighs, he worked his way up, over her soft belly, until he reached her breasts. He scraped his lips along one nipple, while grazing his palm along the other. Another shiver tore through her. Her breathing slightly labored, she half-chuckled, then ran her thumb along his lips.

"So good," she said, then leaned forward and kissed him.

Before things became sexually out of control again, he grasped her hand, and bringing her with him, he stood. "How about that shower?" he asked, and rubbed his hands along her lower back and ass.

Without a word, she settled to her knees, and wrapped her hand around his cock. She looked at him. A wicked gleam heated her eyes as a small, sexy smile curved her lips. Then she took him in her mouth.

His breath caught as she sucked and licked him. When she grazed her nails along his balls, then followed with her tongue, it took everything in him to keep his knees locked and remain standing. Without inhibition, she gave him the purest pleasure. But if she didn't stop, he would explode soon. He wasn't about to allow that to happen without giving her one more orgasm, or missing the scorching sensation of burying himself between her sexy thighs. He'd fantasized about moments like this for two damn years. Now, he couldn't imagine that fantasy not being a reality.

She's leaving.

Even on the cusp of exploding in sheer ecstasy, the words filtered through his mind. He didn't want her to go. Two years without her had been two too many. He'd only just rediscovered the woman he'd denied loving, and regretted, more than ever, not fighting for her. Regardless, when she walked away from him again, he'd make sure she knew how he felt. Right now wasn't the time. Right now was about their pleasure. He didn't want to think about the lack of their future, only the present. He wanted to think about coaxing another orgasm from her, and feeling her slick heat around his erection.

Touching her chin, he reluctantly eased her mouth from him. Holding his gaze, she gave the head of his penis one last kiss, then stood.

"How about that shower?" she asked, and ran her hand along his ass.

Instead of answering, he moved forward, crowding her until she fell back onto the mattress. The shower could wait. He wanted her now, and as many times possible, before she left him.

Rather than allow his mind to drift down that depressing road, he spread her thighs, and climbed onto the bed until they were chest to chest. Her nipples pressed against him as she wrapped her arms around his back. Gazes locked, he slid inside of her, then held himself still.

They were making memories, and these memories would be all that he'd have once she left him.

Running her fingers through his hair, she kissed his temple. He captured her lips, and rocked his hips. The slow friction, the feel of her soft, naked skin, the taste of her lips, aroused him beyond measure.

As their tongues tangled, and their kiss intensified, he rocked his hips. Faster. Harder.

Breaking away, she gasped, spread her legs wider, and dug her nails into his back. The pleasure/pain stimulated every nerve ending running through his body. Like a piston, he pumped his hips. She scraped her nails along his back, then cupped her breasts. Whispering his name, she pinched and tugged her nipples. Then she reached a hand down, and touched her clit.

The sight so damn sexy, he wanted to come, but not until she made it there first. Determined to pleasure her, he reached beneath her and grabbed her bottom. Massaging her ass, as she rubbed herself, he thrust.

"Hud, I…" She gasped, then gripped his bicep. Her entire body shook. Her sex clenched him, drew him deeper into her body. As she rode out her orgasm, he thrust once, twice, then exploded.

With a ragged breath, he gently rolled their bodies until she lay sprawled on top of him. His heart beating fast, he laid his hand along her hip, and released a sigh. He was in some serious trouble. He'd fallen in love with Eden all over again, and she would leave him by the end of the month. As much as he wanted to stop her, he wouldn't try. He couldn't ask her to give up her dream job to stay in Chicago.

While he'd been thinking about leaving CORE for a line of work that wouldn't require worrying about someone shooting at him, he hadn't made any plans to change careers yet. He liked working for CORE, the people there were solid, and his friends. He also enjoyed an excellent salary and benefits. And although he'd been considering moving, he'd planned on heading to the Burbs, not another major city. He wanted a house in a quiet neighborhood, a yard to mow, bushes to trim. He wanted normalcy.

As he stroked her hip and his heart rate slowed, he wondered if he should tell her what he'd been considering. Better yet, should he tell her he loved her? If he did tell her, and she decided to stay for him, what would happen if they broke up again?

Running her hands along his chest, she shifted her body, leaned in and gave him a lingering kiss. "I'm ready for that shower now."

"Yeah, we kind of got a little distracted."

"A little," she said with a smile, then scooted off the bed, and headed for the bathroom.

Seconds later, he heard the spray from the shower beat against the tiles. Not about to miss an opportunity to continue to be naked with Eden, he climbed off the bed and followed her.

"No more fooling around," she said with a wag of her finger. "I'm hungry."

"You know what I'm hungry for?" he asked as he joined her in the shower.

"Let me guess, more of me?"

Pulling her close, so both of their bodies could enjoy the hot spray, he gave her butt a squeeze. "No. I already used that line this morning. But I'll use it again if it'll work."

"That'll depend on how well you wash my hair and body," she said, then turned and rubbed her bottom against his thickening erection.

Thirty minutes later, his hands slightly shriveled from too much water exposure, he dressed, while Eden blew her hair dry. He wasn't normally a fan of shower sex. There never seemed to be enough room in the stall to do as he pleased. But he was damn well pleased with the results this time around. If he wasn't hungry, he would head into the bathroom, remove her towel, then bend her over the counter and sink himself deep inside her. Maybe later.

He glanced toward the bathroom just as Eden dropped the towel and began to slip on a hot pink thong.

Definitely later.

Although Rachel might have the files downloaded by then and they'd be stuck in front of a computer. Searching for any leads to help them identify the killer.

In the meantime, he could bring up her move to New York. Maybe he could tell her about how he'd like to eventually leave CORE, Chicago, and buy a home in the suburbs. He could also tell her how he felt about her. Was now a good time, though? Even if it was, he still wasn't sure where to begin. He could just blurt out the words. Eden was used to his bluntness and probably wouldn't expect anything less from him.

"Considering we've been having marathon sex," Eden said as she stepped into the room. "I expected you to be either sleeping or smiling. Instead you look as if someone just died." Her eyes widened. "Oh my God. What happened? Did you hear from Rachel? Did the police find Dr. Roth?"

He moved to her, then held her by her upper arms. "Nothing. No. And I don't know."

"What?"

"Nothing's happened, I haven't heard from Rachel, and I don't know anything that you don't about Roth."

Frowning, she shook her head. "Then what's wrong?"

He no longer had to worry about how to start the conversation about his feelings, her move, and his plans. She'd just given him an opening.

Cupping her cheeks, he said, "I've never owned a Weed Whacker."

CHAPTER 20

EDEN GAVE HUDSON a quick kiss, then took his hand and led him out of the bedroom. "Hinting at what you'd like for Christmas?" she asked, amused by his random admission. "Subtlety never was your strong point. What would you weed whack anyway? The dead plants in your apartment?" As they entered the kitchen, her stomach grumbled. "I'm starved. How about you?"

He sat on the stool at the kitchen island. "I could eat. We missed breakfast and lunch. I know you gave me one of those stupid granola bars, but that doesn't count as a meal unless you're a squirrel."

Grinning, she opened both doors of the side-by-side refrigerator. When she spotted frozen tuna steaks, she said, "After that last DVD...I'm kind of grossed out at the thought of eating anything with meat. You don't happen to do fish, do you?"

"Maybe if its beer battered and deep fried, and there's no actual fish involved."

"Okay," she chuckled. "No fish."

"I could go for that omelet you were going to make this morning, unless you're going totally vegan on me."

She grabbed the carton of eggs. "Not quite. I couldn't imagine life without bacon...well, except for today. This will be a veggie omelet." After pulling a bowl from the cabinet, she cracked an egg. "Okay," she began, curious about Hudson's crazy urge to own a weed whacker. "So you want Santa to bring you a weed whacker. What else?"

"A lawn mower, snow blower, wheel barrel, shovels, brooms, garbage cans…"

She glanced over her shoulder. "I haven't seen most of those things since I'd been in my dad's…garage." Heart kicking up a notch, she wiped her hands on the kitchen towel, then faced him. "Are you moving out of the city?"

"Not anytime soon," he answered. "But you are."

No way to avoid the inevitable now.

Drawing in a deep breath, she leaned against the counter. She'd been dreading this discussion, but they'd made a pact to stop tiptoeing around the truth. Whether he loved her or not, they shared a special bond and he deserved to know her plans for the future. Only she didn't quite know herself. Torn between loving Hudson and her career, she didn't want to make a mistake, or lose either opportunity.

"At the end of the month," she finally said. "What does 'not anytime soon' mean?"

He lifted a shoulder. "I've been thinking about getting out of the city, maybe buying a house."

Hudson would move to the suburbs? Good Lord, did he plan on trading in his Trans Am for a minivan, too? "What about CORE?"

Another shrug. "I love my job, but sometimes I get tired of dead bodies and bad guys. Sometimes I think that I just want to work a boring eight to five office job, then come home to a house on a quiet street and mow the lawn."

Shocked into silence, she stared at him. With his shaggy hair, beard stubble, and worn jeans, she couldn't imagine Hudson sitting in an office cubical or BSing around the water cooler.

"I'm not going anywhere anytime soon. But what about you?" he asked. "Do you ever think about what it would be like to live a quieter, less chaotic life?"

"No," she answered honestly. "I did the small town thing,

and have no desire to go back."

Living in Wissota Falls had been unbearable and boring, even before the rape. With no diversity, no museums, concert halls, swanky restaurants…shopping, she hated small town life. When she'd had the chance to leave, she chose Chicago—the polar opposite of Wissota Falls. Here, she'd found herself, her career. Damn, even the man she loved.

"I understand," he said. "So, are you nervous about the new job?"

"A little. I'm more nervous about the move. I haven't spent much time in New York and don't know my way around. I'll probably have to carry a map and look like a tourist for the first few years I live there."

"You're one of the smartest women I know. I have no doubt you'll do just fine."

She smiled. "Yeah, I'll be fine," she said, then turned around and reached for another egg.

Before she cracked the egg, Hudson's strong arms surrounded her. He pressed her back against his chest, and she leaned against him. She loved when he held her, loved knowing that when she was emotionally exhausted or physically drained, he would be there to give her strength. After years of living on her own, and depending on only herself, she hadn't realized the thrill, the joy of having someone she could depend upon. She'd realized that it was okay to lean on a friend, and even relinquish some control.

After the rape, control had become very important to her. That night, and during the weeks and months that had followed, she hadn't had the power to fight her attackers or their continuous taunts. She'd become an introvert, and had hidden behind a fragile shell, until the end of that school year, when all of her tormentors had left town for either college or the military. She still had one more year of high school, and had understood that if she wanted to escape, she needed to grow a backbone and create a career plan. By the time she prepared to leave for Chicago to attend Northwestern University, she'd not only gained total control of her future, but the utter powerlessness, the vulnerability she'd once endured, had abated. For some reason, though, as she leaned into Hudson's strong arms, those feelings she'd thought no longer existed, began to surface.

Telling him she loved him, that she didn't want to leave him, would leave her vulnerable, especially if he didn't return her love. She obviously couldn't control his emotions, and had a hard enough time trying to manage her own. As for being powerless...she could change her future. She could stay in Chicago and forego the Network job. She had that power. But what if she stayed and their relationship failed? Or what if she stayed, their relationship blossomed, and Hudson decided to quit CORE and move to the suburbs? Living in the burbs, doing yard work, dealing with soccer moms and nosey neighbors, didn't appeal to her in the least. Not that she wouldn't consider having Hudson's kids, but when she pictured a future with children, she'd always pictured a life in the city, too.

She hadn't even told Hudson she loved him, and she was already trying to dissect the future of their children. And Hudson considered her smart. If only he knew. She should stop being a wimp and just tell him. Drawing a deep breath, she decided she'd blurt everything out and tell him the truth.

Before she opened her mouth, he rubbed a hand along her arm, kissed the top of her head, then turned her. His eyes unreadable, he held her hands, and said, "When I heard about the Network job...I was so proud of you. You set out to achieve something, and you did it." He looked away. "At the same time, I felt...selfish. I didn't ...I don't want you to go. But I'd never do anything to stop you."

When he met her gaze, the fierce determination in his eyes stole her breath. For the first time, she honestly believed he did love her. She knew Hudson, knew and understood the man behind the dominating, and sometimes arrogant, veneer. He would never sway her decision, not because he didn't want her around, but because it was *her* choice. And it was a choice she didn't want to make.

Tears welled in her eyes. She dropped her gaze to his chest, gripped the front of his shirt and fisted the material. "I'm feeling pretty selfish, too. I want the job." She rested her forehead on his chest. "But I need you."

He tipped her chin, and with the pad of his thumb, swiped a tear from her cheek. With apprehension in his eyes, he cupped her face. "What are you telling me?"

Heart beating fast, stomach somersaulting, she laid her hands on his, and said, "I love you."

His gaze turned molten as he crushed his lips to hers. Holding her tight, he kissed her. With intensity. With passion. She met each stroke of his tongue and clung to him, as if this might be one of their final moments together.

Breaking for air, she placed open-mouthed kisses along his jaw, then gripped his shoulders. "I don't know what to do."

"Shh," he soothed. "We'll figure this out together. We...you, don't have to make any major decisions just yet. Who knows? You might get fired on the first day, and be back in Chicago on the next flight."

Laughing, she hugged him again. "You're right. I might not even like having my own show. Or the series could flop and get cancelled."

"What have you done about your townhouse?" he asked.

In need of a tissue, she stepped away from him and grabbed a napkin from the cabinet. "I have a real estate agent, but I haven't returned any of her phone calls."

"Maybe you should think about leasing instead of selling. Just in case."

"I hadn't thought about that," she said as she tossed the napkin in the garbage, then washed her hands. "I didn't plan on buying anything in New York right away. As it is, the real estate agent in New York is having a hard time finding me something suitable, as well as dog and cat friendly. Leasing my townhouse might be a good option."

Her heart lightened with hope and optimism. Maybe they could, somehow, make this work between them after all. Everything didn't have to be black and white, and set in stone.

Hudson was right. She might hate New York, or even her new job.

"I can keep Fabio and Brutal for you until you get settled," he suggested.

With a few quick steps, she fell into his arms, then gave him a soft, lingering kiss. Taking a step back, she smiled. "I'll need to visit my babies. And if I lease the townhouse, I'll need a place to stay."

Grabbing her rear, he hauled her to his chest. "I have a pullout couch in the living room."

She twined her arms around his neck. "How generous of you, but I think I'd rather sleep in your bed."

"The pullout's for your animals, because we'll be doing more than sleeping in my bed."

Rising on her tiptoes, she brushed her lips along his, then murmured, "Sounds x-rated."

His mouth curved into a smile. "*Very* x-rated. Maybe after we eat I'll give you an example...or three."

"Are you dropping a hint that you're hungry?"

"For that omelet."

"What about me?"

"Always." He gave her rear a gentle squeeze. "But I didn't want to sound predictable. Remember, I've already used that line today."

After a quick kiss, she moved back to the counter, and reached for another egg. "I'm so glad we finally talked about my move. It's been weighing on me."

"Trust me. I've been thinking a lot about it, too."

She cracked the egg into the bowl. "Maybe you'd like to come to New York with me next week? I mean, if we're finished with this case."

"I was hoping you'd ask me. And I'd go even if we haven't caught the killer. Don't forget, we still aren't sure if there's someone else involved."

"You mean the phantom stalker," she said, and looked over her shoulder. "Other than those few phone calls last month, and the word of a killer, there's been no evidence that anyone is stalking me."

"I agree. I wonder if maybe the killer brought up the stalker thing to help take some of the focus off of him."

She nodded. "Good point. Still, maybe we should stick with this twenty-four/seven protection for a while. My animals would miss you if you left."

"Just your animals?"

"Look at you fishing for an ego boost."

"I know something that doesn't need a boost," he said, then nodded to his zipper. "Get it? I don't need any enhancement."

"Oh, I got it alright." After wiping her hand on the dish towel, she tossed it at him. "I also just realized I should have never laughed at your first line. Now I'll be forced to suffer—"

The doorbell rang.

He set the towel on the counter, gave her butt a pinch, then said, "I'd like toast with my omelet."

Before she could throw the towel at him again, he left the room. Seconds later, she heard her sister's voice from the foyer.

Damn it. Eden turned off the stove burner, then set the frying pan aside. She wasn't in the mood to deal with Celeste, especially after their argument last night. She wanted to make things right with Celeste, and had for a long time. If only her sister would stop nagging and harping.

Then she remembered Hudson mentioning that Celeste wanted her to be the maid of honor. Maybe that's why she'd stopped by tonight. And if that was the case, Eden needed to be the bigger person. Shove aside their differences, and support her sister. After finally discussing the move with Hudson, she might as well fix her family life, too.

When Celeste entered the room, Eden immediately pulled her into her arms. "Oh my God, Celeste, what happened?"

Sobs wracking her body, Celeste hugged her. "I'm so sorry."

Eden leaned back, and held Celeste's shoulders. "Is Dad okay?"

Celeste nodded, then waved her hand as she moved to the counter and ripped a paper towel from the roll. "Everyone's fine." She hiccupped. "Everyone but me," she said, then blew her nose.

"I don't understand. Is it the bakery?" She narrowed her eyes and thought about Celeste's arrogant fiancé. "Did John do something to you?"

"God, no. He's in the living room with Hudson."

"Then what's wrong? You're kinda freaking me out."

"Last night," Celeste said, her chin trembling and fresh tears springing from her eyes. "I can't get it out of my mind. How I treated you after you were just released from the hospital. How I treated Hudson." She crumpled the paper towel. "I'm so sorry, Eden."

Guilt crashed into Eden's heart. "You aren't the only one with regrets. I…haven't been the best sister."

"You've been fine. It's me. I had no right to butt into your life. Last night, after John and I left your place, I called Will and told him about our fight. You know what he said?"

Eden shook her head as she grabbed a napkin from the cabinet, and handed it to her sister. If Celeste was going to keep blowing her nose, she wanted her to do it in comfort.

"He told me that I was wrong. That I needed to stop mothering you. What's funny is that I didn't even realize I was doing it. I'm sorry, E. I…I just worry about you and——"

Eden hugged her. "Stop. I know you're just looking out for me. And I also know that I haven't exactly been…forthcoming with regards to what's going on in my life."

Gripping Eden by the shoulders, Celeste leaned back and gave her a watery smile. "That's an understatement. We used to be close. It seems like after I left for college, you wanted nothing to do with me. If I did something wrong, I'm sorry. Whatever it was would have been unintentional. I love you and would never do anything to hurt you, despite how I acted yesterday."

Another wave of guilt surged through her as she stared at her sister. The rape had occurred two months after Celeste left to attend the University of Wisconsin. Celeste was right, Eden hadn't wanted anything to do with her sister, or her mom, or anybody for that matter. The humiliation, the pain and misery from the rape, and the crude taunting afterward had forced her to withdraw from everyone. But Celeste had been an easy target for her anger. As their mom's golden child, and so-called psychic, it had been easy to fault Celeste for not warning her about the rape. Stupid. Even as an adult, she knew the whole idea of resenting her sister for something Celeste couldn't control was ridiculous.

While she still didn't believe in Celeste's alleged "gift," her sister deserved better treatment. She'd always been good to Eden. Celeste had been her best friend. Now that she thought about it, she hadn't had another, true friend—other than her sister—since the night of the rape. She missed Celeste. When they were teenagers, they would stay up late dreaming about the future...what kind of job they'd have, house...husband.

Determined to set things straight with her sister, Eden took her hand. "There's something I need to tell you."

An hour later, after Eden explained the rape, the internal and psychological fallout that had followed, as well as her eating disorders, Celeste blew her nose. She crumpled the napkin, then pulled Eden into her arms. "I wish you would have told me. I'm so sorry that happened to you. The thought of what those boys did...my heart aches."

Eden held her sister's hand. "I didn't tell you all of this to make you feel worse. I told you because I wanted you to understand why I've been such a bitch all of my adult life."

Celeste half-laughed, and squeezed Eden's hand. "You were kind of a bitch even before that," she teased, then sobered. "Thank you for telling me. Please don't hide from me anymore."

"Promise."

"Promise? Then tell me about Hudson and what's going to happen when you move to New York."

Eden leaned back in the chair. "I think we're going to play things by ear. I don't want to end what's between us—at all, and I don't think he wants to, either. But, damn, this is my dream job."

"I know, honey, you've worked hard for this opportunity," Celeste said, then cocked her head to the side. "Would he consider moving for you? I'm not saying right away, but maybe after a while."

Eden shook her head. "I wouldn't dare ask him. He's already made it clear that he would never try to sway me into staying in Chicago, and I appreciate that he knows this is my choice."

"He gets you," Celeste said with a grin.

Eden thought about Hudson's concern about her animals, his cheesey lines. The way they'd both tried to hide from each other, only to realize they couldn't. How he'd handled learning about her past and eating disorders. The touch of his hands along her body... "He does. And you know what? I not only get him, but I'm in love with him."

"Really? I'm so happy for you."

"Yeah, I'm happy for me, too. Hopefully we can work through my move to New York."

"If you love each other, you'll make it work."

Eden smiled. "True. Speaking of love and all that gooey junk. I heard a rumor that you were looking for a maid of honor."

Moments later, after promising her sister that she'd go dress shopping with her before leaving for New York next week, Eden stood, and said, "The guys have been awfully quiet. They didn't even try to raid the refrigerator for a beer."

Celeste stood, too. "Were you making dinner?" she asked and pointed to the frying pan on the stove.

"Yes, but that's okay. This conversation was way more important. I'll finish making it when you leave."

"I'm leaving right now," Celeste said, and walked out of the kitchen.

Eden followed her, then smiled when she saw John and Hudson sitting on the couch watching college football. Fabio had draped himself over John's outstretched legs, while Brutal had curled into a ball and lay on Hudson's lap.

"Look at how adorable our men are," Celeste said to her.

Hudson looked over his shoulder. "We're too badass to be adorable."

John removed Fabio from his legs, then stood. "Everything good?"

Hudson rose, too, but cradled Brutal in his arms. Eden smiled as she watched him. Whether he liked it or not, the sight truly was adorable.

"Everything's great," Celeste said, then looked to Hudson. "I'm sorry for how I treated you yesterday. I was dead wrong. You make my sister happy, which makes me happy."

"First you call him adorable, now you're getting sappy on him," John said. "We better go before he has to show you what a badass he really is."

Laughing, Celeste hugged Hudson, then moved to Eden and did the same. As they embraced, John shook Hudson's hand and said, "We could save Ian a lot of money if we made this a double wedding. You up for taking another walk down the aisle?"

Another walk down the aisle? Her mind racing, Eden stepped away from Celeste, and stared at Hudson.

"Ian's got plenty of money," Hudson said to John. "You should hit him up for the honeymoon, too."

When he didn't deny or confirm John's reference to remarrying, Eden assumed John's comment had been a simple slip of the tongue, and relaxed. She and Hudson were in a sort of good place. They hadn't exactly hammered out the details of the future, but both were willing. To her, that was a good start.

"Come on, John," Celeste said as she opened the front door. "We've interrupted their dinner again. Let's go home. I have several sample books of wedding invitations I want us to go through tonight."

"Can we scrapbook when we're finished?" John asked just before he shut the door behind him.

Once Celeste and John left, Hudson set Brutal on the dog bed, then rubbed his stomach. "I'm so hungry. I'd eat another one of your gross granola bars. C'mon, I'll make the toast, while you cook the omelets and tell me what happened with your sister."

Holding his hand, she followed him into the kitchen while trying to decide if she should ask him about John's marriage comment. Because she knew not knowing would bug the living shit out of her, she blurted, "What did John mean by another walk down the aisle?"

He blew out a deep breath, and ran a hand through his hair. "I...I was married a long time ago."

Stunned, she stepped back, and narrowed her eyes at him. "Any children I should know about?" she asked, disgusted with him, and with herself. How could she have been stupid enough to believe Hudson had changed? Now that she thought about it, other than the little bit he'd told her about the time he'd been held captive in Columbia, he hadn't said anything about himself, or his past. She'd foolishly allowed her heart to rule her head. All his bullshit about tiptoeing around the past or the truth, had been just that—bullshit.

"No," he said, and approached her. "Jen and I were only married for a few years, and ninety percent of the time I was overseas."

She took another step back until her hip hit the counter. "Jen," she echoed. "And you didn't think you should have mentioned *Jen* to me?"

"I honestly didn't think it was that important," he answered. "I'm sorry, Eden. I guess I screwed up."

Utter betrayal sliced through her heart. He hadn't trusted her. To think that she'd thought she knew him. She didn't—at all. What she knew of him had been superficial and only what he'd wanted her to see. Like when they'd been together before, he had to control every aspect of their relationship. God, she'd even allowed him to convince her to lease her townhouse in case she decided to move back to Chicago. He'd told her he wouldn't ask her to stay, but he'd manipulated her anyway, and had swayed her into thinking they might have a shot at a future together.

Not anymore.

Not ever again.

"You guess?" she asked, shocked that he could sum up his lack of trust so flippantly, as if he'd forgotten something off the grocery list. She hurt. Bad. She didn't have many people in her life she could trust, and she'd trusted Hudson. She'd trusted that they'd become close enough that they could share private thoughts, emotions…their past. "God, Hudson. You gave me so much crap for never talking about myself and avoiding the past. Then I went and opened up, and told you about my rape. Something I'd never told anyone, by the way, not even my own family. And you didn't think to even mention an ex-wife. I mean, it's not like you haven't had plenty of opportunities."

"I know, but after you told me what happened to you, I realized our pasts really didn't matter. It's who we are now that counts."

"Gee, how poetic," she said, laying the sarcasm on thick. How convenient that he'd come to this miraculous conclusion *after* she'd been the one to open herself to him. Figuratively and literally. "When you quit CORE, maybe you should consider writing greeting cards."

With his eyes full of concern and apology, he crowded her against the counter. "You're right. I should have told you about my ex. I'm sorry. I shouldn't have expected you to tell me about yourself, then not do the same in return."

Shoving his chest, she moved away from him. Although thoroughly pissed, she couldn't forget that a short while ago they'd made love. He'd held her in his arms and had loved her body, had filled her heart and soul with hope for a future. She needed to distance herself from him. Lust would not cloud her judgment again.

"Eden, please. What can I do to make this up to you? Tell you about Jen? How I married her out of high school because all I ever wanted was a family of my own. That my mom had left me when I was about nine, and that I wished my dad had left me, too. He was a bastard who used me as his occasional punching bag, especially when he was drunk." Shoving his hands in his pockets, he looked to the floor. "I can tell you about my tour in Afghanistan, the horrible things I saw, or better yet, the horrible things I did during my years with the CIA. I can tell you—"

"Stop." Holding up a hand, she shook her head. "I need space."

She didn't want to hear any more, not now. At this point, she couldn't figure out his agenda. He'd had plenty of opportunities to tell her these things. For him to hurry up and lump them all into one big confession didn't work for her. She didn't want a forced confession. She believed relationships were about give and take. Only she had been the one to give. All he'd done was take.

Tears filled her eyes. Throat tightening as she fought to control her emotions in front of him, she moved past him.

He snagged her hand. "Eden," he said, his tone thick, quiet...pained.

He tilted her chin, but she refused to face him, to allow him to see the hurt. She'd already shown him too much. "I want to be alone."

With the tip of his finger, he traced her jaw. "I love you," he said, and tucked a lock of hair behind her ear.

Her heart and stomach ached with insult. Pushing past him, she rushed to the bedroom, then slammed the door. In the privacy of her room she let the tears fall. She'd wanted to hear him say the words, but not like this. Not as a way of apologizing.

Falling onto the bed, she hugged the pillow. Hudson's scent lingered on the linens, and she shoved the pillow across the bed. Hiding in the bathroom wouldn't work either. She'd only be reminded of the way he'd held her, coaxed her body with his rough hands and—

"Eden," Hudson called from the other side of the door. "I just heard from Rachel. We have the clientele list from Med Spa."

She'd been so focused on Hudson, she hadn't even thought

about the killer or Dr. Roth.

Damn. She didn't want to be anywhere near Hudson. He'd broken her heart. Now she had to spend the rest of the evening sitting next to him, searching for any link to the killer.

CHAPTER 21

WITH DUSK FAST approaching, Michael Morrison pulled into his gravel driveway. He drove the minivan to the steel garage, climbed out, then opened the door. As he waited for the garage door to finish rising, he headed toward the van, then stopped.

Movement in the overgrown fields caught his attention. He scanned the tall grass. The head of a coyote surfaced, followed by another, then another. With caution, he glanced to the other side of the property just as another coyote crept from the grass onto the gravel.

They're waiting for their next meal, and I'll deliver it. Soon.

As he climbed back into the van and drove into the garage, he realized the coyotes weren't much different from his patients. Like the doctors from Med Spa, coyotes were opportunistic hunters. Only the coyotes hunted their prey for survival, while the doctors preyed on insecure, young women for profit.

Once he parked the van, Michael quickly closed the garage door. He didn't want to become his dinner guests' appetizer.

Sealed in the building, he slid open the driver's side back door.

Dr. Victor Roth glared at him.

Michael jerked back, then relaxed when he saw that the

duct tape he'd applied earlier had stayed intact. His hands and feet bound, and held together behind his back with triple layers of tape, Roth remained hogtied. Still, the doctor had woken too early. Michael needed time to prep him for his surgery, and he couldn't do it while the man was awake.

Time to improvise.

Michael went to his office and retrieved the varmint rifle. He rushed back to the OR, grabbed a hunting knife, then moved toward the van.

Roth's eyes grew big and round as he darted his gaze from the knife to the OR. He attempted to talk, but the duct tape kept him mute.

Holding the rifle in one hand and the knife in the other, Michael eased toward the doctor, then leaned into the van and severed the tape that held Roth's arms and legs together and behind him. "Get out," Michael ordered, and raised the gun.

Hands still taped behind his back, and ankles bound, Roth inched like a worm toward the open door. When he reached the edge, he stopped and looked up at Michael.

"Do it." When he realized Roth's head would take the majority of the fall, he added, "It's not that far of a drop, and if you're worried about messing up your face...maybe breaking a nose, don't. I was planning on fixing that big ol' honker of yours anyway."

Instead of moving forward and out of the van, Roth began to shift his body backward.

Michael set the knife on the roof of the van, then raised the rifle and took aim. "One way or another you're coming out of that van. You can do it with a bullet in your ass, or you can cooperate and follow my directions."

Roth's face grew red and his eyes watered. The veins in his neck strained as he tried to speak.

Lowering the rifle, Michael leaned into the van, and ripped the tape from Roth's mouth.

"You son of a bitch. I'll kill you for this. I'll fucking kill you," Roth raged.

"Big threats for a guy who's bound up and has a rifle

pointed at him. But I understand. It's like I said, though, you either get out of the van now, or you can get out of the van later…with a bullet in you."

Roth spat on the floorboard. "Fuck you. Go ahead and kill me. I don't take orders from you."

"Oh, I'm not going to kill you. That's the coyotes' job. But I will start shooting. First your ass, then your leg, then maybe your hand…I'm trying to remember. Are you a lefty or a righty? I'd hate to shoot the wrong hand. I know how critical it is for you to be able to use your hands when performing surgeries."

"You sick bastard," Roth shouted.

"All of this name calling isn't necessary. Just do as you're told." He raised the rifle and aimed at Roth's ass. "You've got ten seconds to get out of the van. One, two, three…"

Michael pulled the trigger.

The shot echoed throughout the garage, along with Roth's scream.

Raising the rifle again, Michael aimed for the man's leg. "One, two—"

"Don't," Roth wailed. "Please. I'll move. I'll move." He cried as he heaved his body toward the opened door. "See. You don't have to shoot. You *didn't* have to shoot. If you'd given me to ten, then—"

"I still would have shot you."

"Why?"

Michael shrugged. "I don't like you."

Roth dangled his head over the concrete. "The feeling's mutual. I fucking *hate* you."

Tired of Roth's potty mouth, Michael grabbed the man by the belt, then hauled his ass out of the van. When he landed face down, Michael pressed the butt of the gun into Roth's bullet wound.

More wailing and blubbering ensued. Michael rolled his eyes. "Crybaby," he said, then grabbed the back of Roth's belt again, and lugged him closer to the OR. Once he reached the surgical table, he forced Roth to his feet.

Roth resisted. Twisting his body and throwing himself to the concrete.

With a schedule to meet, and in no mood for Roth's bullshit, Michael smashed the butt of the gun into Roth's kidney. The man rolled to his side, and raised his bound ankles. Before his feet could connect with Michael's legs, Michael swung the rifle like a golf club.

Blood spurted from Roth's nose. Wincing, he released a groan, then closed his eyes. His body limp and unmoving, Michael gave his stomach a swift kick. No reaction. Good, now he could prep Roth for surgery.

Within twenty minutes, Michael had Roth on the surgical table, his arms and legs bound. Sure Roth could not escape, he went to the office. He eyed the bottle of Wild Turkey on the desk, but didn't give in to temptation. He needed to stay sober. For what he had planned afterward, his head needed to be clear.

He'd love nothing more than to be half-drunk when he performed Roth's nose job. Mutilating a man's face, even if he hated the guy, was not something he looked forward to doing. The blood, the screams…they would follow him into hell and live with him for an eternity.

He'd crossed the line of morality the day he kidnapped Dr. Thomas Elliot. Even then he could have stopped, released Elliot, untouched, somewhere far from his farmhouse. Never having harmed a creature in his life, he'd wanted to stop.

His daughter had deserved justice, though. Whether his brand of justice was right or wrong, it was justice nonetheless.

Ignoring the whiskey, he moved toward the TV, then stopped. Roth's groans drifted into the office. "Damn it, why can't he stay the hell asleep," Michael mumbled, then an idea appealed to him.

After unplugging the TV and DVD player, he carefully pushed the TV cart from the office and into the OR. After plugging all the cords into the socket, he adjusted the cart at an angle in which Roth could have full view of the movie. Once satisfied that he'd given Roth access to the TV screen, he moved to the surgical table, then twisted the man's head.

"Unless you want me to bind your head to the table, face the TV."

"Fuck you," Roth said, then spat.

Michael wiped the phlegm from his face, and shook his head. "You shouldn't have done that," he said, then walked to the van and retrieved the hunting knife he'd left on the roof. When he returned to the surgical table, he waved the blade, then shoved it into the sole of Roth's foot.

Roth screamed, high and loud.

Leaving the knife imbedded in his foot, Michael clamped a hand over Roth's mouth. "I dare you to swear at me again."

Roth shook his head.

"Be good," Michael said as he released Roth's mouth. He removed the knife. "Or else this blade will find its way into your other foot. After that, maybe I'll go for your groin."

Sweating and panting, Roth lolled his head. "Please, if it's money you're after…"

"I don't want your money. But I do want you to watch something. Now that I think about it, I regret not showing this DVD to the others."

"Others?" Roth echoed.

"Mmm-hmm, you know, Tom Elliot, Brian Westly, Leo Tully…"

Tears streamed through the blood on Roth's cheeks. "Did you…?"

"Kill them? Not really." When Michael noticed Roth's body relax, he added, "With the exception of Westly, the coyotes did that for me."

The man's prone body tensed. "Why? What did we do to you?"

Michael hit PLAY on the DVD remote. "Watch."

The home movie began with Eliza in her pretty purple dress, and as it moved forward through the years, he glanced at Roth. His bloodied face contorted in confusion, then with realization as the final still shot of Eliza appeared on the screen.

"Any of this making any sense, Doctor?"

"Yes," he hissed as more tears streaked his face. "I remember you now. And I remember your daughter. *She* came to us, and we did what she asked."

"Right." Michael nodded. "She asked you and your doctor buddies to scar her body."

Wincing when he raised his head, Roth said, "She still looked good enough."

Arching a brow, Michael blew out a deep sigh. "Good enough," he repeated. "There was nothing wrong with her in the first place. Do you agree?" He waved the hunting knife. "And I suggest you tell me the truth."

"I...I think the rhinoplasty enhanced her face."

"And the other surgeries?"

Roth glared at him, then glanced away. "No."

"No? Interesting." He set the knife on the workbench. "Personally, I think you're full of shit and are trying to save your sorry ass. Look at my daughter." He pointed to the TV screen. "You know damn well you screwed up her nose when you were trying to *enhance* her face. You tried to narrow the tip, and removed too much cartilage. Her nose began to collapse, and her nostrils become distorted."

"She still didn't look that bad," Roth, the arrogant prick, argued. "And I told her I could fix it."

"In a year, and for more money," Michael said with disgust. "You, Elliot, Westly, and Tully are all nothing but a bunch of egotistical blood suckers. You preyed on my daughter, on her money and insecurities, just like you'd preyed on other young women."

"That's not true," Roth whined. "We were only trying to help women appreciate their faces and bodies."

"Is that why you gave Westly a nice bonus each time he sent you a new patient?"

"A referral fee, that's all that was, and there's nothing illegal about it."

"No, not illegal, but immoral. I've researched some of your clients, the young women who endured the same botched-up surgeries as my daughter. Some of those girls still need psychiatric help, while others had to endure multiple surgeries to fix what you bastards had done to them."

"Immoral? Who are you to judge what's immoral? Look what you're doing to me, what you've done to my colleagues."

Roth's impertinence, over what he and the others had done, and the way he dared to accuse and judge, spiked Michael's temper. He gripped Roth's broken nose, and squeezed. "Don't you dare scream. Don't even utter another word."

The man winced and opened his mouth.

Michael squeezed harder. "Not a word."

Roth nodded, but Michael didn't release him. Of all the men, he wanted Roth to suffer the most. While the other surgeries had been bad, Roth's had been the worst. At least Eliza could cover the disfiguring lumps and scars on her body with clothes. But she couldn't cover her nose.

And although the botched surgeries could have been fixed eventually, the doctors at Med Spa, specifically the lead doctor, Victor Roth, had expected Eliza to pay for them. She'd seen an attorney, but the contract she signed with the doctors had stated, in much more eloquent and bullshit legal jargon, that basically all sales were final. If only her stupid bitch of a mother had paid better attention to the contract Eliza had signed. Instead, she'd kept her head in the clouds. She'd looked at dollar signs rather than consider her daughter's health. Sarah had been convinced these surgeries would take Eliza to the necessary level of perfection, and would lead to a multimillion dollar modeling career. Because of Sarah's selfish stupidity, and Roth and his colleagues' greed, Eliza was dead.

Michael released Roth's nose. After wiping Roth's blood on the man's shirt, he walked to the video recorder, angled the camera in order to have Roth's face in the frame, then pressed RECORD. "I want you to tell me everything," he said. "I know you spearheaded the surgical group, Cosmetic Solutions and Med Spa. Now tell me how you ended up putting Westly on the payroll."

The defiant son of a bitch remained mute. With a shrug,

Michael slipped on the surgical mask and cap. For this occasion, he didn't bother to draw a mouth on the mask. Instead, he created a large pig's snout in honor of the pig about to experience the butchery of plastic surgery.

"Nothing to say?" Michael asked as he picked up the scalpel from the workbench, and then waved it in Roth's face.

Weary, and emotionally drained, Michael had lost the desire to drag out Roth's torture, but for Eliza, he'd endure. Pinching the bridge of Roth's nose, he pressed the tip of the scalpel against the man's swollen nostril.

"Wait," Roth shouted. "Please wait. I'll talk."

Michael took a step back.

"It's true," Roth blurted. "I met Elliot and Tully at our country club, and together we formed Med Spa. Business hadn't been that great. About a year after we opened, Elliot brought Westly to the club to play golf. Elliot and Westly had gone to college together and had been in the same fraternity. When I found out Westly was a dentist, I started asking him about his clients. When I found out how many of his patients were going to him for veneers, I...I started thinking that if those people were willing to shell out that kind of cash for their teeth, maybe some of them might be interested in fixing other parts of their face and body."

He drew in a deep breath through his mouth, then looked away.

"And?" Michael prompted.

"And I suggested he talk up Med Spa. If he sent a patient to us, they'd get a ten percent discount on their procedure, and Westly would get a bonus from us."

"Those patients really didn't get any discounts, did they?"

"No, we just raised the price."

Those lying bastards. Michael kept his temper in check. An outburst might shut Roth up before he finished giving the world his confession.

"And did you or any of the other doctors, Westly included, suggest unnecessary surgeries to your clients?" Michael asked, and hoped the man answered honestly. If Roth lied, holding his temper under control would become dangerously difficult, especially because he knew all about the lies they'd spewed to Eliza.

When Roth didn't answer, Michael moved toward him with the scalpel. "If you're finished talking, we'll just go ahead and—"

"Yes," Roth blurted with a sob. "We all did. Okay? Is that what you wanted to hear?"

Aware of the video recorder, Michael shook his head, and kept his emotions under control. Although he wanted to choke the life out of Roth, and kill the others all over again, he also didn't want to appear as the violent villain, either. Conning their clients out of money, encouraging them to have avoidable and excessive surgeries, had been unethical and criminal. They were the villains.

"I didn't want to hear that you lied and manipulated your patients," Michael began. "I didn't want to give your colleagues their personal procedures, either. But I also didn't expect to bury my daughter because of your lies and manipulations. You *did* lie to her, didn't you?"

Chin trembling, Roth nodded. "I'm sorry," he sobbed. "We knew she was insecure and impressionable, but—"

"Impressionable," Michael echoed, the fury now slowly bubbling to the surface. "My daughter's IQ was *eighty*. According to her psychiatrist, she was borderline intellectually functioning. But she pushed herself, and had even enrolled in the community college. Was she impressionable? Absolutely. Did she deserve to be preyed upon...?"

Clenching the scalpel, he turned away before he stabbed Roth in the chest. From the time Eliza had been a toddler, and he and Sarah had realized she would face challenges based on her intellectual disadvantages, he'd warned Eliza to never trust anyone. Especially after Sarah had begun entering Eliza in beauty pageants. With a world filled with sexual predators, Eliza's naivety, her inability to truly think through a situation and read the pros and cons, he'd worried. When Sarah had divorced him, and he was only able to see Eliza alternating weekends, his worry had deepened. Eliza had always known she wasn't the brightest kid, but when her mother had filled her fragile, adolescent mind with dreams of a modeling career, his daughter's insecurities had grown. If she couldn't be the smartest kid, then she would be the prettiest. No matter the cost.

"Impressionable," Michael repeated. "Did her mother happen to tell you just how impressionable Eliza was?"

More tears streamed down Roth's face as he nodded.

"So you knew Eliza wouldn't understand your instructions regarding her procedure or any of the contracts she'd signed?"

Another pitiful nod. "But her mother was with her when any of us explained the surgeries and when we'd given her the contracts."

"I don't doubt that. Trust me. I blame her as much as I blame you." Michael shrugged.

"It's a shame she put a bullet in her head before I had the chance to show her how much she disgusted me." He moved toward Roth again. The man had confessed enough, and Michael wanted to move on with his procedure. While he didn't look forward to the blood and screams, he did look forward to finishing his promise to Eliza.

"Wait," Roth shouted. "I told you everything you wanted to know. You have it on video. I'm ruined." He sobbed. "My name, my reputation, I...I'm ruined. Please, think of my wife and my daughters."

Michael glared at Roth. "Like you thought of your wife and stepdaughters when you took women to your hotel room? Trust me. I am thinking of your family. I'm thinking that they're better off without you. Even if I did let you go, you'd be worth more dead than alive. Don't you think?"

Roth grew silent. The tears stopped. He no longer struggled against his restraints. Instead, he drew in a deep breath, then said, "You're right. I deserve to die for what I've done. Go ahead and kill me. I don't want to live anymore."

The sobbing began again. Amused by Roth's acting skills, Michael smiled. "Playing the martyr won't work on me.

Besides, I told you I wasn't going to kill you," he said as he approached Roth with the scalpel. "The coyotes will, after I fix your nose."

Roth screamed and raged. The veins at his temple and neck bulged. Spittle flew from his mouth. He swore and threatened Michael. Bowed his body against the restraints.

Tired of all the noise, and ready to complete his death wish list, Michael ripped a piece of duct tape from the roll. He pressed it against Roth's opened mouth, then reached for the scalpel.

Pinching the bridge of Roth's nose again, Michael drew the blade close to the man's flaring nostril. "We'll just take a little off the tip of your nose."

Although prone and secured to the surgical table, Roth fought, jerked his body and head. The scalpel slipped, and Michael sliced through Roth's nostril. Even with the tape over his mouth, Roth's scream reverberated off the steel walls.

Wincing, Michael shook his head. Roth already leaked a lot of blood. This could be extremely messy, and he didn't feel like dealing with a mess. Then again, what did he care? After he delivered the DVDs to Eden, he would not return to the farmhouse. He had bigger, better plans for his future.

"Look what you made me do," Michael said. "I guess I'll have to take off the other nostril as well. We can't have you all lopsided."

After removing the other nostril, Michael began to cut into Roth's nose. As the man screamed and cried, sick satisfaction bled into self-loathing. Torture, mutilation, murder...never in his life had he thought he could sink to this level of depredation. He might not have been a saint, but he'd always upheld high, moral standards for himself. When Eden watched this DVD, when she heard Roth's confession, would she understand? Would the rest of the world? Or would everyone think he was insane?

His sanity had never been the issue. His sorrow, his need for retribution had been what had fueled him. Everything he'd accomplished in his OR had been for Eliza.

He didn't expect many people to comprehend the depths of his grief, or his need to right the wrong committed against his daughter. He also understood that what he'd done to the other men, and what he was currently doing to Roth, would be construed as monstrous. But in his OR, monster or not, he was judge, jury and executioner.

Today marked the end of seven years of planning, researching, and preparing. The day they'd touched Eliza, Roth and the others had unleashed a dark, sinister hatred Michael hadn't realized he'd been capable of carrying. The others had paid for their crimes, and so would Roth.

As he was about to finish removing the cartilage from Roth's nose, he realized the man had passed out.

Thank God.

Slicing Roth's face had been beyond grotesque. Like with Westly's dental surgery, Michael had been too close to Roth, had been able to see the pain, misery and regret in his eyes. While he didn't feel sorry for Roth, or any of them, he mourned for not only Eliza, but for the honorable, moral, respected man he'd once been.

He couldn't allow himself to dwell on what he'd done, or all that he'd lost. Time was ticking, and he had an agenda to keep.

After quickly undoing Roth's restraints, he flipped him over, then hogtied him. He retrieved the wheel barrel, shoved Roth's unconscious body inside, then grabbed his varmint rifle. Wheeling Roth through the wide service door, he scanned the gravel driveway.

In the distance a coyote bayed.

He pushed the wheel barrel over the gravel, then onto the dirt path leading deep into the woods. With each step he made, the hatred that he'd carried for seven long years began to dissipate. He imagined that hate scattering amongst the naked trees, or being carried into the distance on the cold wind.

And smiled.

CHAPTER 22

STARING AT THE closed bedroom door, Hudson ran a hand through his hair, then scratched the back of his head. He'd messed up—big time.

Riding on a high from when Eden had admitted she loved him, he'd barely paid attention to John or the football game they'd been watching. When John had mentioned the whole 'another walk down the aisle' thing, Hudson hadn't thought anything of it. The only thing he'd been thinking about was Eden, how they were going to make their relationship work. Well, and that omelet she'd promised him.

Now the only thing on his mind was trying to find a way to make things right.

Heading toward the living room to open the files Rachel had sent them, his stomach tightened into a ball. He couldn't wipe away the image of Eden—the hurt and disappointment that had clouded her eyes with tears and sadness. He couldn't remove the dull ache that had taken root in his chest, the moment he'd realized he'd hurt the woman he loved.

When she'd said she loved him, he'd been stupid to not tell her that he loved her. But he'd been overwhelmed and ecstatic that Eden—one of the smartest, strongest, sexiest women he'd ever had the pleasure of knowing—actually loved him. His family certainly hadn't, his ex-wife had, just not enough. But

Eden *did* love him, flawed, scarred, she loved him. She'd showed him with her body, with her trust. What did he give her in return?

Jack shit.

While he honestly believed their pasts didn't matter, Eden had thought otherwise. She'd given a part of herself the night she told him about her assault. She'd given him her trust. Instead of returning the gift, he'd unintentionally trashed it. Knowing Eden, her need to control, her need to have a plan of escape, he worried that if he didn't rectify the situation, she'd leave for New York and never come back to him.

He'd fight for her this time. Loving her, being a part of what they had together, was the best thing he'd ever done. Letting her go wasn't an option. He wouldn't beg her to stay. He'd told her that before, and had meant it. She needed to explore her career opportunities and make her own choices. That didn't mean he wouldn't continue to support and love her.

When she'd told him she loved him, his plans to move to the suburbs and take a different, safer job had suddenly sounded...boring. While he'd been ready to take a less chaotic route, he realized that if Eden wasn't along for the ride, his life wouldn't be the same. He would rather have the chaos that followed her busy career, and even the hectic lifestyle of New York, than live without her. Now he had to find a way to make her understand his mistake, and believe in him again.

Her slippered feet brushed against the hardwood. He turned and caught the contempt and hurt in her eyes before she bent and picked up Brutal.

"Have you opened the files yet?" she asked, then sat on the couch next to him.

"Eden, honey, I—"

"Don't." She glared at him. "Let's just work on the clientele list."

With a nod, he opened the file. She wanted to stick to business. He could do that...for now. Eventually she'd have to listen to him, and when he was given that opportunity, he'd lay everything on the line and hold nothing back.

"Rachel sent us the clientele list from the approximately three years Med Spa was open, along with before and after photos. We'll review A through M, and she'll work on N through Z." He sighed, and shook his head. "I'm still not sure what good this will do without a name though."

She scratched Brutal behind the ears. "The killer mentioned two women that he'd loved. I think we should keep our focus on the female clients who had both liposuction and breast implants."

He stared at the list that contained over three thousand names. "It's too bad Rachel couldn't use her computer magic to narrow the list by procedure."

"She tried?"

"Yeah, with the way the files were set up, she couldn't. As it stands, we're lucky she was able to download the list and pictures." As he opened the file with the before and after photos, a thought occurred to him. "When the killer called you, he said you reminded him of one of those women. That you even looked like one of them. Maybe we should look for someone who resembles you, too."

Setting Brutal on the cushion next to her, she leaned forward and hugged herself. "It's a long shot, but you're right. I just hope we're not chasing our tails. There might still be a chance to save Dr. Roth."

"Rachel checked to see if the wife filed a missing persons report." He shook his head. "Nothing yet." He stood, and moved toward the kitchen. "I'm going to call Rachel again and tell her how we're going to attack the list and photos."

After he talked to Rachel, he returned to the living room. Eden had already started looking through the photos. When he sat next to her, she didn't look at him. He glanced at the clock on the screen. Already close to ten, he planned on pulling a late night. "If you want to go to bed, I've got this," he said, and hoped she'd take him up on the offer. Spending hours sitting next to a severely pissed off Eden didn't appeal to him. He'd rather work alone than deal with the complication, or the reminder that he was an asshole.

"I'm not going anywhere. Let's just get this done."

By one in the morning, they'd found thirty-four female clients who had a slight resemblance to Eden, and had had both liposuction and breast implants. And that short list had been made from clients A through C. They still had thousands of more names and photos to review.

Stretching, he glanced at Eden. Although she sat upright and facing the computer, her head rested against the back cushion of the couch, and her eyes were closed. Good, he'd rather she slept. Sitting next to her during the past three hours had been hell. Not once did she look at him, or make any conversation other than to point out a client. She acted as if they'd never kissed, touched, made love. The way she'd detached herself from him, treated him as if he were a stranger, cut deep and reminded him of what a fool he'd been. The memories of their last break-up surfaced, along with the anger, pain, and regret that had followed.

He scrubbed a hand down his face, then stood and stretched. Needing a break, and something to eat, he went into the kitchen. The frying pan still sat on the stove, the bowl containing a few egg yolks remained on the counter, along with the carton of eggs. He cleaned up the mess, tossed the warm eggs in the trash, then made himself a sandwich. He also realized the animals hadn't eaten and fed them, too.

Plate in hand, he headed back into the living room. Eden hadn't moved. As he ate his sandwich, he continued to work.

By four-thirty in the morning, he'd made it through the L's. At this point he had compiled a list of one hundred and thirteen women who slightly resembled Eden, and all had had both breast implants and liposuction. Damn, and he still had about six hundred M clients to review.

He rubbed his eyes, and laid his head against the cushion...

Eden woke with a jerk. She blinked several times and glanced next to her. Hudson's long legs were stretched, his feet propped on the coffee table. He had one hand on her thigh, and the other draped over Fabio, who had curled his big body on Hudson' lap.

A part of her wanted to shove Fabio aside and take his place. Although still hurt and pissed, she couldn't deny the way her body and heart ached for him. Not in the mood to go there, she looked from Hudson to the notes he'd made. Slipping his hand off her thigh, she reached for the notebook.

Impressive. While she'd slept, he'd made it all the way through to the M's.

She glanced at the clock. Not quite six, she decided to let Hudson sleep, and began reviewing the M clients' photos and surgical procedures. When she came across a woman who had long black hair, breast implants and liposuction, she jotted down the name next to the others Hudson had written. After they completed the client list, Eden hoped Rachel could run the names they'd noted against death records. The killer had said he loved two women, both were dead. Based on the killer's obvious need for vengeance, his hatred for the plastic surgeons, she firmly believed they would make their connection to the killer through one of these women on the list.

Thirty minutes later, she'd gone through another one hundred and fifty clients. She stared at the screen when another woman with black hair caught her attention. This client had had breast implants and liposuction, but beneath the list of her procedures was a set of double asterisk marks sandwiching the letter W. Beneath the asterisks and W was ten percent.

Unsure of what the W and ten percent indicated, she made a note next to the woman's name, then continued to scan through the list. Twenty women later, she discovered another set of the asterisk, W, and ten percent combination. As she was about to look at the next client, Hudson stirred, then woke.

Rubbing his eye with his palm, he said, "Sorry, I didn't mean to doze off. What time is it?"

She glanced at the clock on the computer. "Quarter to seven. I'm the one who's sorry for conking out on you. I can't believe how many names you got through."

"I'm just amazed at how many people get plastic surgery." He stretched, then added, "How far are you into the M's?"

"I think I've looked at around a hundred and seventy. One thing I've found...when you were going through these, did you happen to notice this beneath any of the procedures?" she asked, and pointed to the asterisk, W, and ten percent grouping.

Leaning forward, he looked at the screen, then nodded. "Yeah, I remember seeing it a few times, but assumed it was some internal office code for pricing."

"Which makes sense, but why only for some clients?"

"I don't know, maybe they were running a special, or maybe the clients who received the discount knew the surgeons and got a friends and family deal."

"Didn't you say Rachel had their financial records as well?"

He tapped at the keyboard, then pulled up the file containing Med Spa's financial records. After a few minutes, Hudson said, "Nothing looks out of the ordinary, but I'm not an accountant."

As he browsed through another screen, she touched his hand. "Wait. Look at that."

"Holy shit."

A column titled "Westly" contained hundreds of names with dollar amounts next to them.

"I think we've just found the dentist's connection to Med Spa," she said, excited that they'd made excellent progress. "My guess is that the ten percent is what Westly had received for client referral. He knew Dr. Thomas Elliot. What if Elliot offered a kickback for every client Westly sent to Med Spa?"

"Which would mean that the woman, or women, we're looking for had also seen Westly."

"A patient who had gotten veneers," she said, then picked up the notebook. "Let's narrow our list, starting with Sheila Abbot."

Hudson opened up the clientele list, then scrolled back to the A's. When he stopped on Sheila Abbot's information, he smiled. "There's a W."

"Good. So she stays on the list. Next up, Natalie Anderson."

By the time they'd finished going through all one hundred and fourteen women on their list, they'd discovered that fifty two of them had been, if their hunch was correct, referred by Westly. With the list narrowed, and the rest of the M's to tackle, Eden suggested that they still make note of the women who held a resemblance to her, and had had both breast implants and liposuction, even if they didn't have a W beneath their procedure record. In case they were wrong about Westly.

"I can use some coffee," Hudson said. "Brutal probably has to go potty, too. If you want to take a break and wait for—"

"No. I want to get this done," she said, and didn't look up from the screen until the front door clicked shut. Releasing a deep breath, she leaned back into the couch. While she was still angry at Hudson, when they'd discovered the possible Westly connection, she had been so thrilled, she'd wanted to give him a victory kiss. Bad idea. At this point, she didn't see the purpose in salvaging their relationship. Yeah, he could be sweet—he had an obvious affection for her animals— considerate, thoughtful, sexy...

Needing some caffeine herself, she stood, and decided to head into the kitchen to make the coffee anyway. While she knew Hudson was a good man, he had trust issues. Not that she was one to talk. With Hudson, though, she'd realized she had wanted to trust him, that she could trust him. She still did. The problem they faced wasn't about her lack of trust and commitment, but his. She couldn't be with a man who remained on constant guard. Sure, after she'd told him off, he'd been ready to talk. He'd even told her he loved her. Unfortunately, the damage had already been done. While the betrayal had lessened, she worried if they did try to stay together, she would always wonder if he was keeping secrets.

As she poured the coffee into a mug, the front door slammed shut. Seconds later, Brutal raced into the kitchen on three legs, his tail wagging as he nudged his dog bowl.

"I'll feed him. Although the little piggy ate around one this morning," Hudson said when he entered the kitchen. "When you were in the hospital, I noticed you were low on cat food. I hope I had Lloyd buy the kind Fabio likes." He showed her the box.

Damn. He would be the perfect man if he lost some of his emotional baggage. His thoughtfulness toward her and the animals tempted her to stop the icy attitude and make things right between them. Only she felt like a fool for having told him personal, private secrets, and being so caught up with loving him that she hadn't noticed he'd kept himself, his personal private secrets hidden. Some investigative reporter she turned out to be.

"That's the right kind of food," she said, and only because he was feeding Fabio and Brutal, she poured him a cup of coffee. "I'm going to get back to work."

Her cell phone rang. She quickly glanced at the kitchen clock, then at Hudson. Her pulse quickened. Was the killer giving her another wakeup call?

She grabbed the phone off its charger, then checked the caller ID. "It's work," she mumbled, disappointed and relieved. A part of her had hoped she'd have the chance to talk with the killer. If he hadn't already taken Roth, maybe she could have talked him out of it. Doubtful, based on his need for vengeance, still, she would've at least liked to have tried.

"Morning, Rodger," she answered.

"Eden, I know you said you wouldn't take any more stories, but I need you."

Rolling her eyes, she leaned against the counter. "It's twenty after seven on a Sunday. What's so earth shattering that you can't have Ryan or maybe Tabitha take care of it?"

"There's been a shooting at Saint Mark's Catholic Church on Westminister. Ryan Anders can do it, but with this kind of situation, I need another person there. Someone with experience. Tabitha's too green." He paused, then said, "Look, we just heard on the police scanner that anywhere from twelve to seventeen people are dead or injured. The gunman is still in the church and holding the parishioners hostage. You know I don't kiss ass, Eden. But you're this city's most popular reporter. I need someone Chicagoans trust."

She didn't care if Rodger was kissing her ass or not. Her heart ached for the people who had died or had been injured by the assailant. For the parishioners being held hostage, their families, and their whole community. Violence had been on an upswing. For this type of violence and devastation to happen during Sunday morning mass…

"I'll do it," she said as she made her way to the bedroom.

"Thanks, Eden. I owe you. David's gearing up the van. Your place is on the way to Saint Mark's, plan on him picking you up in about thirty minutes."

Eden dropped the suit on the bed, and began undressing. "Sounds good."

"Kyle just got here, and is going live in a few. He'll be your contact person once David has you and Ryan set up. I don't want any of the bullshit that happened on Monday."

The bullshit hadn't been her doing, but now wasn't the time to go there. She had thirty minutes to make herself presentable. "As always, I'll be nothing but professional," she replied, then ended the call before she said something that might bite her on the ass. Kyle was a douche bag. She'd love to tell Rodger that. She'd love to tell Kyle that. What did it matter at this point? This would be the last and final story she'd cover for WBDJ. Right now her concern lay with the innocent people at Saint Mark's, their families, as well as giving Chicagoans some peace of mind.

She finished buttoning her blouse, then slipped on her suit coat. Rushing into the bathroom, she released her ponytail. After she brushed her hair, she realized fixing it would take too much time. Besides, the blisteringly cold November weather called for warm accessories. Once she'd brushed her teeth, then applied her makeup, she grabbed a warm, knit hat, gloves and boots from her closet.

"Eden," Hudson shouted from the living room. "I found her."

She finished zipping her tall boot, and hurried from the

room.

Hudson met her in the hallway. "I've already called Rachel," he said as he grabbed her hand and rushed her into the living room.

"How do you know this is the woman we're looking for?" she asked as he sat her on the couch in front of the computer.

"Look for yourself."

She glanced from him to the laptop screen, then gasped. "Oh my God," she whispered as she stared at a young woman with long, straight black hair and green eyes. The resemblance uncanny, she could have been Eden's younger sister or cousin.

"Read the procedures," Hudson prodded, and pointed to the screen.

"Breast implants, liposuction, and...rhinoplasty." She shook her head. "I can't believe I didn't think about checking for patients who had nose jobs, too. Especially considering it was Dr. Roth's specialty."

"I didn't think about it either. But it doesn't matter. Scroll down."

She did, then covered her mouth and looked at him.

"Scary, huh?"

"Horrifying," she said, her stomach and chest tightening as she gaped at the after photo of Eliza Morrison. "She doesn't even look like the same person."

"I know. They butchered that poor kid. I don't even understand why they performed any of these procedures on her in the first place. She was a beautiful girl. Hang on," he said when his cell phone rang. "It's Rachel." He answered the call, put the phone on speaker, then set it on the table in front of them. "I've got you on speaker. What'd you find?"

"Hopefully our killer," Rachel said. "Okay, I'm looking at Eliza Morrison's death certificate."

"Damn," Eden muttered, and despite the wool suit and lined boots, a chill swept through her.

"Right," Rachel said. "She committed suicide seven years ago. Her parents are...were Michael Adam Morrison and Sarah Marie Morrison."

Eden glanced at the clock. David would be by to pick her up in about fifteen minutes. Now she wished she hadn't agreed to cover the shooting. If Eliza ended up being the link to the murders, she wanted to finish what the killer had started, and hopefully save Roth.

"Sarah Morrison...this is weird, she died days after her daughter. Suicide."

"And the father?" Hudson asked.

"Michael Morrison, age forty-four. Interesting...he has a couple of Illinois certifications, one as a registered nurse, the other as a nurse anesthetist, which might explain his access to the drugs. Okay, last known address is 2650 Old Mill Road in Oregon, Illinois which is...oh my God, one hundred miles from Chicago. Hang tight, I'm going to pull up an aerial view of his property. Gotta love Big Brother sometimes, and...presto. I'm forwarding the link. But it looks like Morrison owns an old farmhouse and it has a large barn on the back of the property."

"This *has* to be our guy," Hudson said. "Rachel, can you call the local sheriff, explain the situation, and have him head out to Morrison's with a few deputies. Give him my number, and send his to my cell phone. We'll leave now and be there in ninety."

"Got it," she said. "One other thing I just found. Morrison had filed a civil suit against Cosmetic Solutions and Med Spa a few months after his daughter committed suicide."

"What happened?" Eden asked.

"He lost."

She looked to Hudson.

"If this is our guy, he definitely still got even," he said. "Rachel, I'll call you from the road." After he disconnected the call, he stood, then rushed to foyer.

"I can't go," she blurted, even though she wanted to be there when they apprehended Michael Morrison. But she'd made a commitment. If the news story hadn't involved a church shooting that would impact the city, she'd call Rodger back and tell him to let Tabitha do the story. Rodger was right about Tabitha, though. She'd done all right with the Tully story, but she *was* still green.

"Damn," he muttered as he shrugged into his coat. "With all this, I…forgot. Sorry. I can wait for you and let the sheriff deal with Morrison."

"No. You go." She stood and moved toward the door. "You know what the inside of his barn looks like, and what to look for."

"Yeah, but—"

"You've got to go. Now."

He looked away. Rubbed his beard-stubbled jaw against his shoulder. "I don't want to leave you alone."

"I won't be alone. David's going to be here in…" She glanced at the clock. "In about ten minutes. I'll be fine."

Within a split second, he crowded her. "We still don't know about this stalker."

Heart beating fast from his nearness, from the intense possessiveness brightening his eyes, she drew in a deep breath, then said, "Remember what we discussed? Could be the killer said something about the stalker to try and divert us from him. We've had no evidence anyone's been stalking me."

"The phone calls and text—"

"Happened last month."

He looked away again. "Maybe I don't like the idea of you going on an assignment where there's a guy with a gun randomly shooting people."

"Please. I'll be fine. It's not like I'm going to go into the church."

He rubbed his chin. "What if Lloyd goes with you?"

"Again. David's on his way. I think I can manage to be by myself for the next ten minutes. But if makes you feel better, have him meet me at the church. Tell him to text me, and I'll give him my location."

"That'll work." He turned, then hesitated at the door. "I can stay until David gets here."

"It's a ninety minute drive to Morrison's house. The sooner you leave…"

Nodding, he reached for the door knob.

Brutal brushed past her, tail wagging, and went straight to Hudson. When the dog pawed at Hudson's leg, he picked him up and scratched his ear. "Watch your mommy for me," he said, then set him back on the floor.

As Brutal made his way to the dog bed, she hesitated, then took a step. "You'll call me, right? About Michael Morrison, I mean."

"I knew what you meant," he said on a deep sigh. "Even if I was hoping for something else."

Meeting his gaze, she caught the longing, the regret in his eyes. She looked away. Between her upcoming move and his lack of trust, as much as she loved him, ending things between them now would save them both from a lot of future battles and heartache.

Still, a part of her didn't want to see him go. They'd been joined at the hip for a week. She'd come to rely on him, his strength, the way he could make her smile during the worst situations. The way he made her body hum, and her soul come alive...

"Hud, I..." She took another step. "Be careful."

In two strides, he crowded her again. Cupping her face, he smashed his lips against hers.

Although she couldn't resist kissing him back, torn between wanting to cling to him and wanting to shove him away, she fisted her hands. He'd hurt her. While she couldn't deny loving him, that hurt remained buried in her heart and mind.

When he pulled away, he swept his thumb along her bottom lip. "We have some serious talking to do."

"I don't know if there's anything else to say."

With a sigh he moved to the door, grabbed the knob, then looked over his shoulder. "You sure about that?"

She nodded, even though she wasn't feeling sure about anything at the moment. Her relationship with Hudson was in shambles, they were potentially on the fringe of apprehending the killer, and she was about to report a terrible church shooting.

Shrugging, he opened the door. As the cold November wind swept into the foyer he said, "I love you, Eden."

When the door snapped shut, she hugged herself and fought back the tears filling her eyes. She loved him, too. While she liked taking risks, in order to keep her heart intact, and her life under control, she'd still leave him. At this point, she didn't see any other option.

CHAPTER 23

PUDGE RUSHED INTO the WBDJ studios, turned down the hall, then hurried into the busy newsroom. Normally quiet on a Sunday morning, the newsroom exuded an unusual amount of commotion. Smack in the middle of all the chaos stood the station manager, Rodger Jeffries. The one man Pudge couldn't seem to impress.

No matter how hard Pudge had tried, Rodger had been nothing but negative. Even when co-workers, like Kyle, had given Pudge high recommendations, Rodger always had a bullshit reason to give assignments or edgy breaking news stories to someone else.

Not today.

no no todays our day today we show him we show them all

When Kyle had called this morning, Pudge jumped at the chance to be part of the news team Rodger planned to send to Saint Mark's. While Pudge could care less about the victims or the church's parishioners, having the opportunity to work a story that would make national headlines only made Pudge hungrier. The carrot had been dangled in front of them too many times, only to be snatched away. This time, they'd chomp on that carrot, and if need be, even the hand dangling it. Pudge would not take no for an answer.

As Pudge moved toward Rodger, Kyle stepped in the way.

"I don't have time, Kyle," Pudge said, maintaining focus on the station manager.

Kyle took Pudge by the elbow and maneuvered them toward the exit and into a quiet hallway.

"What the hell, Kyle. I told you I don't—"

"Stop," Kyle said. "Listen to me. Rodger's already given the story away." He glanced around, then massaged Pudge's upper arm. "I'm sorry, honey. I tried to talk him into using you, but he wouldn't budge. You know this story is going to make national news. He needs to have someone with more experience. I have faith in you, and I really tried…I know you're disappointed. Maybe we can meet later, and I can make it up to you."

liar liar hes using us using he didnt try he doesnt care he wants sex sex sex

Disappointment didn't come close to describing Pudge's emotions. Hate worked. Right now, Pudge hated Rodger for not giving them a chance. But Pudge hated Kyle even more. The man was a user. He'd given them hope too many times. Had tried to convince them that he would take them places. Pudge realized that the only place Kyle would take them to was a cheap hotel. He'd fuck, demand a blow job, all with promises of a bright career. They had no career here at WBDJ. Not until Rodger took notice of their talent. Not until they removed a few people who stood in their way.

Pudge eyed Kyle, and decided ruining the man might prove beneficial. He'd never help them. While Pudge didn't necessarily want his job, after his humiliating, demeaning treatment with nothing given in return, he deserved punishment.

kill kill him kill him

Death would be too easy for a man like Kyle. The bastard wouldn't be let off that simple. Besides, for now, he was their link to Rodger. Pudge would wait, and when the time was right, Kyle would pay dearly.

"Maybe I can go as a backup," Pudge suggested. Whoever was working the story might have an accident that would render them unconscious or too hurt to report.

yes yes slip on the ice slip break a limb break a neck

Hiding a smile, Pudge asked, "Who's Rodger sending?"

"Ryan Anders and…Eden," he said with disgust, and narrowed his eyes. "Apparently a Network contract isn't enough. Greedy bitch wants all the glory and attention. She isn't supposed to do any more reporting for the station, but you *know* she saw national headlines the moment she heard about the shooting."

enough enough of eden risk you promised you promised to get rid of her do it do it now now before she steals your job do it now

In an effort to conceal the hatred and rage from Kyle, Pudge looked away. "Who's working the cameras?"

"David and that intern…I can't remember his name. They're leaving in a few, if they haven't already, to pick up Eden, then head to the church."

"Kyle," one of the assistant producers said as he leaned out the newsroom door. "You're on in one minute."

When the door closed, and they were alone in the hallway, Kyle gave Pudge's arm a squeeze. "I've got to go. Will you meet me later?"

no no tell him no

"I'm really upset about all of this. Call me, but I can't make any promises," Pudge said, and forced a smile.

Kyle looked around, then leaned in and licked Pudge's earlobe. "I can promise to fuck you until you come, then I promise to fuck you some more after that." He pinched Pudge's nipple, then with a smug grin, turned and headed into the newsroom.

As soon as the door shut, Pudge ran down the hallway, out of the building, and into the parking lot. Pudge reached Mama's 1985, rusted out, piece of shit Buick Skyhawk, opened the trunk, then grabbed the backpack.

precious what are you doing

Pudge opened the backpack, checked its contents, then slammed the trunk. "What I should have done a long time ago."

no precious no not now not now wait wait

With a half-laugh, Pudge ran across the parking lot to the garage where the WBDJ news vans were stored. "What happened to 'kill kill kill'?" Pudge asked. "You've been the one telling me kill every person that screws with us. Did you suddenly grow a conscience?"

love love you worried so worried youll get caught this time we need to plan first

Pudge slowed near the garage entrance. "Hush," Pudge hissed, peered around the corner and watched as David loaded the van. Ryan Anders and the intern approached with additional equipment, and Pudge knew it was now or never.

"Hey," Pudge shouted, and clutched the backpack. "Glad I caught you guys. Rodger told me to tag along in case you need an extra hand with the equipment."

David smiled. "Awesome, love to have you on board. Climb on in, we're ready to go."

Pudge nodded, entered through the back passenger door, and took a seat next to the intern. Knowing the garage contained security cameras, Pudge waited to make a move. Other than vacant cars, the parking lot, though out in the open, would work to Pudge's advantage.

David started the van. The horrible twang of some shitty country song blared from the speakers as he pulled out of the garage, and slowly wound the van through the parking lot.

Pudge opened the backpack. With one hand, carefully searched, then gripped the handle of the scalpel. With the other hand, Pudge grabbed the Taser gun.

Adrenaline pumping, pulse rate quickening, Pudge nudged the intern. "Want a mint?"

"Sure," he said, turned his head, and opened his hand.

Pudge slammed the scalpel into his throat, then sliced. Blood splashed over the intern's hands as he wrapped them around his throat. Coughing, sputtering he jerked his body and kicked his legs. His foot made contact with the back of David's seat.

Pudge caught David's gaze in the rearview mirror. Saw his

eyes widen as he slammed on the breaks. "What the hell?" he shouted over the music.

Ryan turned. Pudge aimed the Taser and fired. His body jerked and jumped, strained against the seatbelt. As volts of electricity wracked Ryan's body, David shoved the van into PARK and leapt toward Pudge. The seatbelt held him back. As he quickly moved to unlatch the seatbelt, Pudge jumped forward and sliced the bloodied scalpel through the air.

The razor-sharp edge connected with David's cheek, but the good ol' boy still managed to unbuckle the seatbelt. Grabbing the headrest with one hand, he shot out his fist.

Pudge ducked, then shoved the scalpel up, catching the soft spot under David's chin. As he screamed, Pudge dug the scalpel deeper until the blade pierced David's tongue.

With a grunt, Pudge ripped the scalpel from beneath his chin. Blood poured from David's mouth. He clutched the gash with one hand, narrowed his watery eyes and pushed his way into the back of the van.

Knowing Eden would be expecting David, Pudge didn't have time for a brawl. Pudge sliced the air again. Once. Nothing but air. Twice. Air again. Third time around, Pudge slit his nose. When he used his free hand to shield his face, Pudge jabbed the blade into the back of his hand. Plucked it out, then slashed his stomach.

He swung, while Pudge anticipated he'd clutch his bleeding torso. His fist connected with the side of Pudge's head.

hurry hurry kill him kill him

Driven by rage, hatred and need, Pudge punched the button securing the intern's seatbelt, then shoved him to the floor of the van. David, the pathetic, wannabe cowboy looked down at the intern, and raised his leg over the dead man's body. Pudge took advantage of David's concern for the man and thrust the scalpel into the cowboy's gut. Twisted, then gripped the handle with both hands and dragged the blade. David didn't drop.

"Fucking die," Pudge shouted. Ripped the blade from his gut then aimed for his throat.

The scalpel connected.

David's eyes widened.

Pudge pulled the blade free. When he fell forward, landing on top of the intern, Pudge quickly flipped him over, and slashed his throat.

Ryan moaned.

Before the man regained full mobility, Pudge reached around his headrest and slit his throat, too.

Panting hard, Pudge unbuckled Ryan's seatbelt, grabbed under his armpits, and pulled him over the van's center console. Once the bodies were piled in the back, next to the camera equipment, Pudge dragged in deep breaths.

The country music streaming from the speakers continued to play. The van's engine still hummed. Pudge glanced out the window, checked every direction, then reached for the backpack. After setting the bag on the passenger seat, Pudge checked the rearview mirror.

Blood splatter covered Pudge's skin. "Damn it." Pudge looked around the van. "I need to make myself pretty for the bitch."

will anders use will anders

Pudge climbed into the back of the van. Although Ryan's crisp, white shirt was covered in blood, his black over coat appeared clean.

Moving fast, Pudge pulled the coat off the dead man, and slipped into it. A little big, but better big than bloodied. Eden couldn't be alarmed. She couldn't know or suspect. She was the next to die.

Shrugging into Ryan's overcoat, Pudge spied a blanket next to the equipment and the dead bodies. A water bottle, likely David's, sat in the cup holder by the driver's seat. After dumping water onto the blanket, Pudge wiped the blood spatter, then checked the rearview mirror again. Neck and face clean, Pudge smiled, then tossed the blanket over the bodies.

amazing amazing precious amazing

"I was kind of badass, wasn't I?" Pudge asked.

yes yes i want you so bad so bad feel you fuck you

Desire ran through Pudge's body. Three kills in a matter of minutes. A new record. One that definitely required a good fucking. "Maybe we should see Kyle later," Pudge suggested.

only only if you promise to kill him too kill him

"So greedy. It's one of the things I love about you. Won't Eden be enough?"

mama mama too please please

Pudge glared at the rearview mirror. "You know the rules. She dies naturally."

you you can come up with an excuse excuse

"I can for these guys," Pudge said, and nodded toward the back of the van. "I left the studio, my car wasn't working. I walked home or paid cash for a bus or cab."

your prints bloody bloody your prints

"I've been in this van a million times. I'll wipe stuff up, but my DNA was in here long before today."

no no check your hand blood so much blood.

"Shit." Pudge stared at the deep, three inch gash. Blood oozed from the wound, and trickled into the cuff of Ryan's coat.

what what will we do now what now

Pudge moved to the back of the van again, ripped the shirtsleeve off of Ryan's arm, then used the material to cover the hand wound. Once in the driver's seat, Pudge buckled the seatbelt, turned off the shitty music, then shifted the van into DRIVE.

"Slight change of plans," Pudge said, and drove the van out of the parking lot. "I've got to make sure my blood isn't in this van or on any of the bodies. Fuck." Pudge punched the passenger seat. Blood began to stain the material Pudge had used to tend to the wound. "I didn't want to have to do this, but I'm taking Eden home to meet Mama."

why why mama cant see cant know she will talk she will talk

"To who? Mama's arms are cuffed to the bed, her fat mouth is sealed shut and she has absolutely no access to the phone. Keep your cool. I don't need you screwing this up for us."

worried worried so scared worried

"Knock it off," Pudge shouted. "You're the one that wants everyone dead."

sorry sorry plan tell me the plan

"We're going to keep it simple. We'll take Eden back to Mama's, kill her...I dunno, maybe in the kitchen."

good good big knives knives big

"Sicko." Pudge smiled, then said, "After Eden's dead, we'll clean up any of my blood, clean the van, throw her inside with the others, then ditch it somewhere far away from the house. I just wish I could remember which one of these dicks I cut myself on...had to be David. He put up a fight. The guy just wouldn't die."

clothes clothes take his clothes

"Yes. You're so brilliant." Pudge grinned. "I'll take all of their clothes and not have to worry about my blood being on any of them. Even if they did find my blood, they still wouldn't know it was mine. Unless...what if they force all WBDJ employees to give a DNA swab?"

we we will leave quit the job wait for mama to die then leave start fresh fresh start

Pudge nodded. "Another brilliant idea. It's obvious that prick, Rodger, isn't going to give us a chance. We'll quit before the shit hits the fan, and find something else to do while we wait for the fat bitch to die. Then where will we go? California? Florida?"

warm warm somewhere warm anywhere with you precious i love you

Pudge released a deep sigh. They'd been through so much together, and Pudge couldn't wait until they were alone, in the privacy of their bedroom. After they screwed each other silly, they could plan, dream and fantasize about the future.

"I love you, too," Pudge said, then glanced at the van's clock. "We're close to Eden's townhouse and only a few minutes off schedule. It'll be at least another thirty minutes before anyone from the station starts looking for David, Eden and the others." Anticipation coiled through Pudge's belly. Plenty of time to take care of business.

Pudge slowed the van along the curb in front of Eden's place. Glancing at the townhouse, Pudge caught Eden looking out the family room window. Seconds later, Eden exited, then hurried down the front steps.

boy toy dont forget edens boy toy

With everything that had happened, Pudge *had* forgotten all about him. Hopefully he wasn't in the house. Even if he was, what did it matter? Pudge drove the WBDJ van. Eden worked for the station. Fuck it.

want want to fuck him

"So do I, now hush," Pudge whispered as Eden waved and approached the van.

When Eden opened the passenger door, she climbed in and smiled. "Hey, Rusty. I wasn't expecting you. I thought David was picking me up."

"Rodger thought it'd be best if David and Ryan went immediately to the church. So, you're stuck with me."

"No hardship there," Eden said. "It's been a while since you've worked the camera for me. I love working with David, but I also love the way you capture everything that's going on when we're working a site."

minion minion she treats you as her lowlife lackey minion

"Well, I hate working for you," Pudge said, then punched Eden in the face.

Her head snapped back, and connected with the window. Before she could gain her bearings, Pudge hit her again, unbuckled her seatbelt, then reached over the center console. Grabbing Eden's hair and overcoat, Pudge shoved her toward the back of the van. Once Eden lay on the floorboard, Pudge climbed over her, then grabbed the backpack.

Eden moaned, and shook her head. She opened her eyes wide, then twisted her body.

Pudge kicked her in the gut. Once. Twice.

Coughing, Eden hugged her waist, and curled her legs. "Stop. Please, Rusty. Stop," she cried, then raised her head. "Oh my God." Her eyes grew wide as she gaped at David's bloodied cowboy boot. "David?"

"He's dead," Pudge said, and snapped a handcuff around her wrist.

Eden quickly jerked her arm. Pudge was faster, and clasped the other cuff around the metal rod holding the headrest.

The bitch fought against the cuffs. She pulled and tugged at the headrest to the point Pudge thought she might actually rip the metal rod out of the seat.

kill kill her now dont wait kill her now

"Two great minds think alike," Pudge said. "I was thinking the same thing."

Pudge grabbed the bloody scalpel from the backpack, then glanced out the van's back window. A car approached, slowed, then parked along the curb. Although the car idled some thirty feet behind the van, Pudge didn't want to take any chances killing Eden just yet.

After slipping the scalpel back into the backpack, Pudge reached inside for the Taser gun. "I need you to stay still, and be quiet for a little while. If you don't, I'll just keep doing this."

Pudge shot Eden with the Taser gun. Her body bowed, violently jerked, twitched, then she collapsed.

Satisfied, Pudge moved back into the driver's seat, shifted gears, then headed for home.

Michael Morrison gripped the steering wheel, and clenched his jaw. Heart beating erratically, he waited until the news van turned the corner, then stepped on the gas pedal.

Moments ago, when he'd turned the corner to reach Eden's townhouse, he'd seen the WBDJ news van. At the time, he'd thought the situation perfect. He hadn't noticed Eden's boyfriend's Trans Am along the street, and assuming she'd entered the news van, he figured she'd be gone for a while and he could deposit the DVDs at her front door.

He hadn't anticipated Eden being kidnapped in broad daylight, though.

At first, he wasn't sure if Eden had been taken against her

will or not. He hadn't been able to see much through the news van's back window. When he'd seen the electric, blue light dancing, and caught the brief iridescent glow of Eden's horrified face, he panicked. He'd tested Taser and stun guns in the past, and had even considered purchasing one to subdue his patients. With his access to sedatives, he'd realized he didn't need the weapon. Now he was glad he'd researched them and had actually shot several models. If he hadn't, Eden would have been taken, without anyone's knowledge.

But he knew. Now he needed to tell someone before something terrible happened to Eden.

He didn't want to call the police. Not yet.

"Damn it," he muttered, and slammed his fist against the steering wheel. He'd completed his death wish list, and had only one last thing to do.

As he followed the news van, he considered his options. If he called the police, and gave them Eden's location, they could apprehend the stalker. At least he assumed the person driving the van was the stalker. Considering he'd seen someone lurking around her house one time too many, how could he not? It didn't matter at this point. What mattered was Eden's safety. While he needed her to tell the world his story, he also wanted to keep her safe. He hadn't been able to protect Eliza. Her mother had brainwashed his *impressionable* daughter, and while he'd tried to stop Eliza from going through procedure after procedure, Eliza hadn't listened. She was dead, but Eden was still alive. He could be the one to make sure she remained that way.

Deciding he'd call the police, Michael reached for his cell phone, then hesitated. The phone wasn't one of his disposables, it was his personal phone. Traceable, the police would know he'd made the call. Eden would learn his identity. She would eventually, but that was to happen when he was ready. He wasn't ready yet.

He could stop at a payphone. Then again, he couldn't remember the last time he'd even seen a payphone.

The boyfriend.

Yes. He could contact the boyfriend, and *he* could call the police. Unfortunately, Michael only had Eden's cell phone number.

As the news van made another turn, Michael caught a street sign indicating he wasn't far from St. Mary's Medical Center. The boyfriend had been at the hospital. If he'd brought Eden to the ER, and she wasn't lucid due to the dehydration, he would have left his contact information. How long would it take him to look up her medical records? Minutes, once he reached a computer. At that point, though, he could call the police from a hospital phone. Again, the police could trace the call back to him. He knew too many people at the hospital, and today was his day off.

"Shit," he muttered, and blew out a deep breath. He wanted to do the right thing. After what he'd done to his patients, he needed something to remind him of the conscientious, decent man he had once been. Still, he refused to deviate from the final part of his plan. He would do the right thing, but without handing himself over to the police.

The boyfriend was the only option.

The news van slowed, then turned into an old neighborhood just minutes from the hospital. As a short cut to the freeway, he used to drive through this neighborhood. Over the years, the neighborhood had become dangerous, and he'd opted for a longer, safer route. Built after World War II, many of these small, cookie cutter ranch homes had been nailed shut with boards and plywood, the rest were rundown with the effects of the economy and unemployment. Rusted, dented older model cars lined the streets and narrow driveways. Garbage littered the tree lawns. Combined with the bare trees, dismal landscape, as well as the cloudy, grey sky, driving through this small neighborhood gave him a sense of desolation.

And dread.

Whoever had kidnapped Eden likely didn't have money, or a means of escaping a life of poverty. Michael understood desperation. When he'd formulated his plan against the doctors from Cosmetic Solutions and Med Spa, he'd been desperate to right the wrongs that had been committed against his daughter. He'd learned, the hard way, that educated professionals would go to any length for money. His butchered, dead daughter the proof. He hoped to God Eden's kidnapper wasn't desperate enough to kill, or some psychotic without a conscience.

When the van turned into a driveway, Michael made a mental note of the address, and continued down the street. As he drove, he checked the rearview mirror, in case the kidnapper had been onto him, and had backed the van out of the driveway. If that had happened…

He wasn't going to go there. At this point, he needed to stay focused, and keep his head clear. For Eden's sake.

Five minutes later, he parked in the employee lot outside of St. Mary's Medical Center, then rushed into the hospital. Fortunately, Sunday mornings were quiet, and ran on a skeletal staff. He passed a housekeeper mopping the floor, nodded, then headed into the stairwell. When he reached the second floor, he hurried toward the nurse's station. Empty.

He quickly moved behind the counter, then sat in front of the computer. Within seconds, he accessed Eden's medical records, then jotted down Hudson Patterson's cell phone number. After closing her file, he stood, then headed into the hallway.

"What are you doing here?"

Michael turned. Laurie, the receptionist from the OR stood outside of the second floor break room. Shoving Hudson's information into his pocket, Michael said, "I'd left something in my locker."

Laurie frowned. "You're locker's on the fourth floor."

Drawing on his acting skills, he looked around the ward, then shook his head and smiled. "That explains why I couldn't get into my locker. I guess I should have had that third cup of coffee this morning. I must still be half asleep. What are you doing here?" he asked. Although he wanted to sprint out of the building and to his car, he also didn't want to blow Laurie off and raise her suspicions.

"I've got a wedding to go to next weekend, so I switched shifts...and floors."

Although his heart raced with anxiety and concern for Eden, Michael forced a yawn, then said, "If I don't see you, have fun at the wedding. I've gotta head to my locker." He grinned. "On the *fourth* floor. I have a feeling I'm not going to live this one down." He shook his head and wagged a finger at Laurie.

She laughed and waved. "My lips are sealed."

Once Michael stepped into the stairwell, he ran down the steps. He reached the first floor, then glanced around the hallway. When he didn't see a soul, he tore down the hall, out the door, and into the parking lot.

CHAPTER 24

HUDSON'S CELL PHONE rang as he shifted the Trans Am onto the Kennedy Expressway. He quickly checked the caller ID, then answered.

"This is Ogle County Sheriff, Jim Wilson."

Easing the Trans Am onto I-290 Hudson said, "Jim, thanks for calling me. One of COREs agents, Rachel Davis, said she spoke with one of your deputies, Darren Cooper, and filled him in on our situation. Will you send—?"

"Son, I'm standing in the middle of Michael Morrison's steel garage as we speak. Trust me. I've been more than filled in on the situation." The sheriff sighed, then said, "I've never seen anything like this before. This garage looks like something out of a horror movie."

"What about Morrison? Were you able to apprehend him?"

"We've checked his house from top to bottom. He's not here. Neither is his van."

"Rachel told Deputy Cooper about the missing doctor, Victor Roth. Any sign of him?"

"Not in the house or garage. I've got men combing through Morrison's back fields. How long before you get here?"

Hudson glanced at the clock. Due to the church shooting, he'd lost a lot of time. Several routes to the freeway had been clogged by traffic or blocked by the police. "According to my GPS, about ninety minutes."

"Okay, we'll see you in a—hang tight," the sheriff said, his breathing growing labored. Dogs barked in the background. Men shouted.

Alarmed by the sudden commotion, Hudson gripped the phone tight. "Jim, what's going on?"

"Oh my God. Oh my God," the sheriff said, his voice laced with revulsion.

"Damn it, Sheriff. What the hell is it?"

"I think we found your doctor...at least what's left of him. Christ Almighty, this explains the coyotes."

Hudson's stomach tightened. He'd hoped they'd been wrong with regards to how the killer had been disposing the bodies. During his career, he'd seen some messed up shit. Feeding human beings to animals hadn't been one of them. "What about the coyotes?"

The sheriff explained how the coyotes had attacked one of Morrison's neighbors, and that the neighbor had chased the animals onto the killer's property. "Deputy Cooper actually went to see Morrison and ask him if we could hunt the coyotes on his property. Morrison told him we could head over in a few days. Said something about having to go to Chicago to pick up a friend for a funeral."

"When was this?"

"Yesterday."

The day they suspected Roth went missing. "Are there any other bodies?"

"I..." The sheriff blew out a deep breath. "Sorry, I...I'm having a hard time keeping my breakfast down. There are bones scattered all through the clearing, and...hang on a sec. Cooper, what's that over there?"

The wind whipped in the background, dogs whimpered, then a man shouted.

"We got a head," the sheriff said. "A fucking head. Sick son of a bitch. I can't believe...look, we're going to seal off the area and wait for you."

"Don't wait on me," Hudson said. "We've got to find Morrison. Have your men start going through his things. In the meantime, I'm going to have Rachel contact the FBI and see if they'll get involved. Call the State Police and have them send in their crime scene investigators."

After Hudson ended the call, he contacted Rachel. As her phone rang, another call came through on the line. "Patterson," he answered.

"Eden's been taken."

Hudson's skin crawled as fear gripped him by the throat. Recognizing the killer's voice he weaved the Trans Am onto the exit lane. "You son of a bitch, where'd you take her?"

Morrison chuckled. "So Eden told you about me. Did she show you the DVDs? Wait, you're not a cop are you?"

"No."

"Don't lie to me. If you couldn't tell from my DVDs, let me reiterate...I don't like liars"

"I'm not a cop. I'm Eden's boyfriend."

"You listed yourself as her fiancé when you brought her to St. Mary's ER."

"Is that how you got my number? Do you work there?"

"How I know what I do shouldn't be your concern. What you should be concerned with is who has Eden. I can assure you it's not me. I warned her several times that someone was watching her."

The stalker.

Hudson sped the car through a red light, then reentered the freeway and headed back toward Chicago. He shouldn't have left her. Damn it, he should have waited until she'd finished with the church shooting, and let the county sheriff and state police deal with what was at Morrison's house.

Then again, Morrison could be lying.

"Do you know where she is?" Hudson asked, and glanced at the clock. He could be at the church in twenty minutes.

"I do."

Hudson pressed on the gas pedal and took the Trans Am to eighty five. "If you didn't take her, who did?"

"I'm confused about that myself," Morrison replied. "I'll be honest with you. I finished my patient ahead of schedule and went to Eden's this morning to drop off the last DVD. When I pulled up to her townhouse, a news van was parked along the curb."

Of course a news van would be in front of Eden's place. David was supposed to pick her up to take her to the church shooting.

"Go on," he prompted as he wove the car through the light Sunday morning traffic.

"I didn't see her get into the van, but what I did see leads me to believe that she was possibly hit with a stun gun."

"There's equipment in the van, maybe what you saw—"

"Trust me. I know it was a stun gun. I almost bought one to help with my patients. At this point, instead of trying to put holes in my story, I suggest you listen. I followed the van and know where Eden's been taken."

Hudson didn't know what to think. Eden's safety met top priority, but what if Morrison was blowing him a bunch of bullshit?

He needed to call Lloyd. The plan had been for Lloyd to meet Eden at the church.

He could also call the TV station and find out if she'd made it to the church. But he didn't want to end the call with Morrison.

The man had always been one step ahead of them, and had always covered his tracks. Now that he'd finished killing the men he'd blamed for his daughter's suicide, Hudson doubted Morrison would go back to his farmhouse. Morrison had told the sheriff's deputy that they could hunt the coyotes on his property in a few days. Hudson believed Morrison had agreed to the hunt because he'd planned to be long gone by the time anyone discovered the remains the coyotes had left behind.

"Where are you?" Hudson asked.

"None of your business. But I will say this. I'm where I can keep an eye on the house. If the kidnapper leaves, I want to be able to follow. I don't want anything to happen to Eden."

"If you're so concerned about her, then why don't you just call the cops?"

"I still have one last thing to take care of, and I can't do that from prison."

Hudson glanced at the GPS. Less than a minute and he'd exit the freeway. "Okay, so you don't want to tell me where you are, then how am I supposed to get to Eden?"

"Where are *you*?"

"On the Kennedy Expressway about to get off at West Lake Street."

"Good. You're close. I know you know where St. Mary's Medical Center is located. Head in that direction."

Hudson merged into the exit lane. "Look, at this point, I don't give a shit about what you've done," he said, and meant every word. Right now, his concern focused on Eden. During the Winters case, while he'd made sure no harm could come to her, his sole focus had been on catching the rapist. While he'd successfully apprehended Winters, he'd still lost Eden. Because he had to win, prove that he was the victor, he'd lost her. He wouldn't let that happen again. She was too important to him. Even if she refused to take him back, he would die before he'd allow anything to happen to her. No matter what, he loved her. This time around, apprehending the criminal wasn't as important as saving Eden.

"Honestly, you *should* care about what I've done," Morrison said. "You watched the DVDs, you witnessed their suffering. Because we've got a few minutes to kill, I'll let you in on something."

"What's that?"

"I hated every minute of it. I've never harmed a soul in my life until...well, until I performed my first breast implant. Unfortunately, I had to give these men a taste of their own medicine. I tried to go through legal channels, but the justice system doesn't always work."

"So you decided to play judge, jury and executioner in your OR."

"I take it Eden shared our phone conversation with you as

well. You two must be very close. Do you love her?"

"I'm three blocks from St. Mary's Medical Center. Where next?" he asked instead of answering Morrison's question. How he felt about Eden wasn't the killer's business.

"Please answer my question."

"Or?"

"Or?" Morrison echoed. "I'm the only person, other than your fiancée's kidnapper, who knows Eden's location. Do you really want to screw with me?"

He didn't. He wanted Eden safe, and in his arms. "Yes, I love her," he admitted.

"Good. Do you plan on marrying her?"

Damn it. Explaining his messed-up love life to a man who had tortured and mutilated his victims didn't sit well with him. Still, Morrison was right. He needed the man's help to find Eden. "It's complicated," Hudson said.

"What's so complicated? Unless she doesn't love you."

"She does, it's just...look, now isn't the time to get into my relationship with Eden."

"It's just what?" Morrison insisted.

Hudson made a turn, caught a street sign for St. Mary's Medical Center. "I'll be in front of the hospital any second. Where do I go from here?"

"Answer my question first."

Slamming his fist against the steering wheel, Hudson gripped the phone. "Why? What do you care?"

"I like Eden, and I want her to be happy. I wasn't able to give that same happiness to my daughter. Is it such a bad thing to care?"

The images of Eliza Morrison's before and after photos surfaced. A wave of empathy knocked Hudson in the chest. While he still didn't agree with how Morrison had handled his vendetta against the doctors from Med Spa, he sympathized with his loss. The man had lost his daughter, then his wife. For some reason, Morrison had made a connection with Eden. Considering the current situation, he decided there wasn't anything wrong with Morrison caring for Eden. Besides, if it wasn't for Morrison, he wouldn't have even known Eden had been taken, let alone her location.

"No," Hudson finally said. "I'm glad you care about her enough to help. For the record, we do love each other. As you know, though, she's moving."

"The Network job in New York," Morrison said. "Her ambitions have paid off quite nicely."

"She deserves the job."

"She deserves to be happy. I've seen the two of you together, and until you came along, I hadn't seen her smile much. Keep in mind, careers, jobs, they come and go." He released a sigh, then said, "Drive past St. Mary's, and make a right onto Ledge Road."

"I'm turning now."

"Good. Go down two blocks, then turn left onto Maple Street. Park the car in front of a white house with a bright red door. It's on the right side of the street. You can't miss it."

Hudson turned onto Maple Street, slowed the Trans Am, then abruptly swerved. "I'm here," he said as he parked, and stared at the house with the red door.

He jerked and swiveled when a rap came at the driver's side window. Hudson immediately recognized Michael Morrison from his driver's license photo. Holding the phone away from his ear, Hudson slipped it into his jacket pocket, then showed Morrison his empty hands. While he carried a gun, he didn't need Morrison to know and become skittish.

"I'm getting out," Hudson shouted.

Morrison nodded, and took a step back.

As Hudson exited the Trans Am, Morrison handed him a thick manila envelope. "Please make sure Eden gets this."

"Not planning on sticking around?" Hudson asked, and dropped the envelope on the passenger seat.

"The house is on the next street. If you look between the yards here," he said, and pointed toward the house with the red door. "You can see part of the news van."

Hudson craned his neck, then saw the van. "I see it."

"The address is 8753 Elm Street." Morrison took a step

back toward the other side of the road. "Eden's been in there for a little over fifteen minutes. I suggest you call the police."

"Wait," Hudson said, and withdrew his gun from his shoulder holster. "I'd prefer if you stayed."

Morrison narrowed his eyes. "So you *are* a cop. I told you I don't like it when people lie to me."

"I didn't. I'm a private investigator."

"How convenient for Eden," Morrison said, and took another step back. "What I'm wondering, though, is why you'd waste time on me, rather than rushing to save the woman you love? What do you think Eden would prefer? That you make sure you apprehend me or save her."

He'd always made it his mission to complete an assignment. No matter the cost. From the time he could talk, his father had pushed him to be the best. To always come out the winner. Morrison, no matter how heinous his crimes, wasn't worth losing Eden.

"Don't contact Eden again," Hudson said, then reaching for his cell phone, he sprinted between the yards. Before he closed in on the news van, he dialed 911, gave the operator the kidnapper's address, then pocketed the phone.

As he rounded the van's back bumper, he peered through the window. Empty. Stepping away, he hesitated, then looked through the van's window again. A cowboy boot stuck out from beneath a blanket. David.

Adrenaline pumped through his veins, along with raw fear.

This was no longer a kidnapping. Whoever had Eden wasn't afraid of murder.

The 911 operator had told him to hold his position and wait for the police. If he hadn't been on the phone with Morrison, he could have called CORE for backup. Right now, he was on his own.

He edged toward the back stoop, crouched, then crept up the rotted, wooden steps. When he reached the door, he ducked beneath the window, then slowly raised his head. He froze.

Eden lay on the floor, where a small kitchen led into

another room. Her right arm above her head, her wrist cuffed to the door knob.

Uncertain who he was up against, and running on hate and adrenaline, he jumped off the stoop, then moved toward the front of the house. A twig snapped. Gun raised, Hudson turned.

Michael Morrison shot his hands to the sky. "I saw Eden inside," he whispered. "I'll help you, but when I hear sirens, I'm gone."

Hudson lowered his gun. "I can use the help. Do you have a weapon?"

Hands still in the air, Morrison said, "I've got a tire iron stuffed in the back of my pants."

"Turn around." When Morrison pivoted, Hudson pulled the tire iron free, then handed it to him. "I'm going to check the front of the house. You hang out by the back stoop. If anyone comes out, run around the opposite side of the house and get me."

Morrison nodded. "Works for me."

As he was about to head toward the front yard, Hudson stopped, then said, "When you do hear those sirens, you better—"

"Run like hell?" Morrison smiled. "I can tell you live by a certain code. And I respect that. I'm here for Eden, not for you. Trust me. After tonight, I'll never see you again."

Although he didn't like the idea of letting a murderer go, he didn't like Eden being held hostage even more. He understood Morrison. The man had killed for revenge. Whoever held Eden...that uncertainty worried him more than setting a killer free.

CHAPTER 25

EVERY MUSCLE AND nerve ending in Eden's body ached. She knew the results and differences between a Taser and a stun gun from a story she'd reported a few years ago. Now that the gun had been turned on her, she realized its true effectiveness. The voltage had knocked her unconscious. She had no idea how long she'd been out, or where she'd been taken.

Forcing her heavy eyelids open, a wave of vertigo consumed her. She shut her eyes again, and clutched her nauseated stomach. Her right arm didn't cooperate. She tugged, shifted her aching head, then panicked.

Cuffed to a door, she fought the dizziness and forced her sore muscles to strain against the doorknob. Grabbed her wrist with her other hand and tried to free herself.

Muscles still screaming, Eden ignored the pain and swiveled. Now fully alert, she took in her surroundings, then gagged and fought the bile rising in her throat. It smelled as if someone had dumped the contents of a dozen Porta Potties in the room. TV guides, yellowed newspapers, soda cans, wrappers and dirt littered the wood floor. Across the dimly lit room stood a hospital bed, which had been piled high with pillows and blankets. The bed immediately reminded her of Michael Morrison's surgical table and his OR. Only Michael hadn't taken her.

Rusty.

She'd known him for several years. Adept as a cameraman and excellent with editing film, Rusty had been one of the few people she'd liked at WBDJ. Why would he do this to her? She remembered David, and her chin trembled. Why would he do this to any of them?

"Doesn't she look sad?" Rusty laughed as he walked down the short, cluttered hallway and entered the room. He knelt in front of her, and nodded. "You're right. Pathetic is the more appropriate word."

A muffled scream came from the hospital bed. Metal scraped against metal.

Eden turned and caught movement. Her skin prickled with fear. Those weren't pillows and blankets on the hospital bed. "Rusty," she said, making an effort to keep her voice calm. "Who's in the bed?"

"Mama. She doesn't get many visitors anymore, so I'm sure she'd love to meet you." He moved toward the bed, then turned on a lamp.

A morbidly obese woman lay prone on the bed. Duct tape covered her mouth. Her arms were stretched, and both of her hands had been cuffed to the bedrails. Eyes wild, the woman screamed against the duct tape again. Although sympathetic to the woman's situation, Eden's focus remained on survival, escape, on the hope that someone would look for her when she didn't show at the church. Once free, she'd help the woman. Until then, she had to find a way to keep Rusty from killing her.

"If you scream, I'll put the tape over your mouth again," Rusty said to the woman. "I know what I'm doing, quit nagging me. This will be over soon."

Confused, Eden glanced around the room again. Although it sounded as if Rusty had been talking with someone, she hadn't heard or seen another person.

He ripped the tape off his mother's face. "Be good."

The mother nodded, then began to cry. "Why, Pudge? Why

are you doing this? Who is this woman?"

"Mama, this is Eden Risk. Eden, meet Mama. The smelliest bitch you'll ever know."

"I only smell because you won't change my colostomy bag," Mama began, then looked at Eden. "I've been cuffed to this bed for almost two days. Pudge won't feed me, give me anything to drink or let me watch TV."

"I know, you were right," Rusty said with a shake of his head. "I should have kept the tape over her mouth."

"You're scaring me," Mama said. "Who are you talking to?"

Rusty shoved away from the hospital bed, and fisted his hands. "The only person who knows the real me."

"Who?" Mama asked. "This Eden person? How could she know you the way I do? You don't even look like you."

"Stop with all the fucking questions," Rusty yelled. "That pathetic, self-serving bitch." He pointed to Eden. "She doesn't know me. You don't know me. All you've ever done was use me."

Rusty paced the room, smacking his hands on his legs. He stopped. "I will. I'll take care of Eden. But I told you. Mama dies naturally. Let me clean the van first." He fisted his hands, then punched the air. "Fine. I'll kill her now," he screamed.

Face flushed, veins protruding from his neck and temples, Rusty grabbed a backpack off the floor.

Eden realized Rusty was obviously crazy. He'd murdered David, kidnapped her, held his mother prisoner, and ranted to himself. Terrified by what he might do next, Eden shifted her legs beneath her rear, knelt, then glanced around the filth and clutter, searching for something she could use to protect herself.

When she looked into the kitchen, she spotted a butter knife sitting on the kitchen table next to dirty plates and old food. While the dulled blade wouldn't offer much protection, she'd rather have that, than nothing at all.

Grabbing the knife wouldn't be easy. While the table was nearby, she would have to close the door to reach it.

Wait. If she closed the door, she could lock herself inside

the kitchen. Once she locked him out of the kitchen, though, Rusty could leave through the front, then come in through the back door.

"Is that blood? Oh my God," Mama shouted. "No, no, no. What did you do?"

Eden quickly looked, then covered her mouth and stared at the scalpel Rusty held.

"Shut up, Mama."

"Pudge, honey, you can't do this. They'll find you. And when they do, they'll find out about Daddy."

Rusty rushed to the hospital bed, raised his arm, then slammed down the scalpel.

Mama screamed.

Eden kept her mouth covered and held her breath.

Plucking the scalpel up, Rusty rolled the handle between his hands. "Next time, I won't miss," he said to his mother. "Don't ever talk about Daddy to my precious again. Got it? What you did to Rick is all on you, Mama. You killed him. Slammed a hatchet into his face, then made my sweet precious help you chop up the body and bury it all over the state of Illinois. If it wasn't for me, your Pudge would probably be locked away in a mental institution, drugged and drooling. Now, if you could please shut the fuck up, I'd like to help my precious finally take care of that scrawny little bitch over there."

Mama looked at her, and Eden swore she saw revulsion in the other woman's eyes. "Yes," Mama said. "You should take care of her. I know who she is."

Rusty, or whoever he'd become, chuckled. "You? Please, when have you ever watched the news? Every damn time I walked in the room, you were watching some shitty rerun or movie."

"I might be an invalid, and I might like my shows, but I do watch the news. She's one of those investigative reporter types," Mama said, and nodded to Eden. "And now she knows all about Rick. So, go ahead and take care of her, and whatever mess you've gotten my baby involved in, just make it quick.

Someone's gonna be looking for her."

Smiling, Rusty raised the scalpel. "For once, I agree with you."

Even if Rusty's mother could help her, Eden realized the woman wanted her dead. Rusty and his mother harbored some messed-up family secrets. And now she knew them. Knew that they'd killed a man.

Not ready to go easy, she jumped to her feet, and slammed the door shut. Rusty pounded on the door as she locked it, and reached for the butter knife. She changed her mind, then took one of the plates, and smashed it against the table.

Rusty stopped pounding.

Mama screamed, "Kill her."

A door slammed. Eden gripped the broken plate and held the sharp edge in front of her.

Gaze locked on the back door she waited.

Prayed.

Hoped.

Damn it, this shouldn't be happening. She wanted to see her sister marry, and give her a bunch of nieces and nephews. She wanted to see her brother and dad, tell them that she loved them. Most of all, she needed to see Hudson.

Regret coiled and mingled with adrenaline as she stared at the back door's small window.

His past, hers, none of it mattered. If he was willing to give them a chance, so was she. As for New York…she still wasn't sure how they'd make a long distance relationship work, but she was determined to try. She loved him. Needed him in her life. His love, support and friendship made her whole. As she stared at the door, waiting for Rusty to burst through and kill her, she realized she'd spent so many years pushing herself to be the best at her career. While she'd succeeded, that success had come at a lonely cost. She didn't want to be alone anymore. She wanted to surround herself with family, friends and Hudson's love.

Determined to survive, she crouched and prepared to lunge once Rusty rushed through the door. Seconds ticked. Nothing.

Her stomach twisted with dread and anticipation. Where the hell was Rusty? He should have been—

A gunshot ricocheted from outside.

Eden flattened herself against the locked door, and stared out the window. From the other room, Mama yelled and screamed.

Breath quickening, Eden clutched the broken plate, then jumped and cried out as Rusty crashed through the back door. Panting, and still holding the scalpel, he quickly shut the door, then leaned against it. Blood soaked the front of his shirt. His hair, a wig Eden realized, had slipped toward the side of his head revealing his shaved scalp.

Eyes wild, Rusty stared at her with hate, then his face crumpled as he touched his stomach. "Precious," he murmured, then he glared at her again. "This is your fault. If you would have—"

The back door smashed open, knocking Rusty off his feet. He rolled, then lunged. Shoved her in front of him, and pressed the scalpel to her throat.

"Drop it or she's dead," Rusty said, and tightened his arm around her waist.

Tears filled her eyes as she stared at Hudson. Blood trickled from the slice on his cheek, more blood dripped to the floor from the cuff of his leather coat, as well as the slash to his stomach. Rusty was right. This was her fault. Had she taken Michael Morrison and the anonymous, threatening calls more seriously, none of this would have happened. Hudson wouldn't be injured, and David wouldn't be dead.

Clutching the broken plate to her side, she decided to let the guilt consume her later. "Do what he says," she told Hudson.

"She's right," a man said as he came up behind Hudson. "He has the advantage."

Eden immediately recognized Michael Morrison from his driver's license photo. Confusion and betrayal fueled her anger. What was happening now might be her fault, but she hadn't expected Michael to conspire with Rusty. To think, even after the heinous crimes he'd committed, she'd felt sorry for the man and for all that he'd lost.

Hudson's face hardened as he slowly lowered his weapon. "I know," he said.

"Let's go," Michael said, and moved to leave.

Rusty laughed. "You two aren't going anywhere. Boy Toy, put the gun on the floor and kick it to me," he said to Hudson, then nodded to Michael. "You, get inside or I slit her throat."

Sirens sounded in the distance. Mama yelled from the other room.

"Sounds like you have a full house. Sorry I can't stay and enjoy the party," Michael said. "I have someplace else to be."

"Don't you move," Rusty ordered. "Don't you dare take a step. And you, Boy Toy, I told you to drop your gun and kick it to me."

"Pudge," Mama screamed. "Hurry, hurry, the police. I see them on the street."

"Shut up," Rusty shouted, then pressed the scalpel harder against her throat. "I'm handling the situation just fine without—"

Eden leaned into Rusty and turned the doorknob with her cuffed hand. Rusty stumbled back, the scalpel nicking her throat. As his rear hit the floor, she landed in his lap.

Mama wailed and cried.

The sirens grew louder.

Arm dangling from the doorknob, and still holding the plate in her other hand, Eden pressed her head back and bowed her body forward. She jammed the point of the broken plate beneath her.

Rusty grunted. The scalpel grazed her throat as he jerked his body and loosened his grip around her waist.

She released the plate, grabbed his wrist and bit.

"Bitch," Rusty snarled, and dropped the scalpel into this other hand.

"Eden, move!" Hudson shouted.

"Kill her, kill her. They're coming. Hurry," Mama cried.

Before Rusty gained hold of the blade, and hoping to hit his plate and gunshot wound, she elbowed him in the gut.

"Now!" Hudson demanded.

Holding the doorknob, she swung her body. Hudson fired. Once. Twice.

"No, no, no," Mama howled and sobbed.

Clinging to the door, Eden drew in deep breaths and looked over her shoulder. Hudson kept the gun trained on Rusty as he moved toward them.

"Are you hurt?" he asked, and checked Rusty's pulse.

She shook her head. "But you are. How bad did he cut you?"

He knelt in front of her, and touched her chin. His eyes darkened as he looked at the nicks and scrapes on her neck, then he narrowed them and glared at Rusty. "I want to kill him all over again," he said, his voice filled with hate. "If it hadn't been for Morrison—"

The Chicago police burst into the house through both the front and back doors. Hudson immediately dropped his weapon, raised his hands and identified himself. Mama continued to sob and babble. During the chaos that followed, the police and detectives' questionings, the arrival of the coroner and EMTs, Eden kept her focus on Hudson. Whatever had happened to lead him to Rusty's house didn't matter. What mattered was that they had a chance. How they'd make things between them work, she still didn't know.

At least they were both alive and able to give it a try. For now, that's all that mattered.

The next morning, Eden held Hudson's hand as they sat in CORE's evidence and evaluation room. Rachel had every TV screen on, each filled with information on both Michael Morrison and Chris Long, the man she'd known as Rusty Jones.

Owen Malcolm and Ian Scott filtered into the room. Owen had just flown in from Las Vegas after finishing an assignment.

Since he'd watched one of the DVDs, he voiced an interest in the results.

After each man took a seat, Rachel said, "The Chicago PD asked us for a little favor. They're hoping we might be able to track down Michael Morrison. I've pulled up everything I could find on the man, and have that info on these screens." She pointed to four of the six TVs. "These two screens contain the particulars on Chris Long, the man who kidnapped Eden."

"Can we start with Long?" Eden asked. At this point, she didn't want to discuss Michael's whereabouts. She didn't care. Yesterday, after the police had arrived, she and Hudson had spent the day, and most of the evening, either at the police station or the hospital, where Hudson had received stitches. Afterwards, they'd gone to CORE to make copies and view the two DVDs Michael had left for her. One had been the surgery he'd performed on Roth. The other DVD had been...heartbreaking. After she'd watched the home movies Michael had created of his daughter, she'd understood the full scope of the man's pain, grief and need for vengeance. Coupled with the fact that he'd risked his freedom to help Hudson rescue her, she realized, despite the severity of his crimes against the doctors, Michael wasn't a bad man. He was a distraught father who had made extremely poor choices.

Rachel nodded, and pointed to the screen with Long's information. "Okay, meet Chris Long, aka, Rusty Jones, Murugan Punjab, Nancy Flannery, and Dr. Dread. Police found fake IDs and disguises in Long's bedroom that linked him to all of these identities and the Dread murders. In total, they suspect Long is responsible for six murders, the three nurses from the Dread cases, and the three men from WBDJ."

Eden looked away, and fought back the tears. She hadn't known Ryan Anders or the intern, Steven Cline, well. But David had been her friend, a kind, funny, talented, unique person. She'd miss having him in her life.

"Do we know if Long had any metal health issues?" Ian asked.

"There's no record," Rachel responded. "But based on

what Eden witnessed, and the mother's statement, it appears Long experienced auditory hallucinations and bizarre delusions." She shrugged. "We'll never know for sure, but I wouldn't be surprised if Long's psychosis was triggered by what the mother did to the father."

"And that was…?" Owen asked.

"The father, Richard Long, physically and sexually abused both mother and son. One night, Mama had enough and killed him."

"With a hatchet," Eden added, remembering the argument between "Pudge" and Mama. "Then she made her son help her cut up the father and bury pieces of his body all over the state of Illinois."

"That'll definitely trigger something," Owen said.

Ian nodded, then looked to Eden. "I wonder what caused Long to go after you?"

Eden shook her head. "I have no idea. I worked with Rusty, I mean, Long, for several years. Never once did he show any sign of aggression or malice toward me."

"I met him," Hudson said. "Seemed like a regular guy."

"That's what Morrison's coworkers and neighbors are saying about him, too," Rachel added.

"Before we get to Morrison, what's going to happen to Long's mother?" Ian asked.

"She's made her confession and has already accepted the State's Attorney's plea bargain. Dorothy Long will spend the next ten years in prison. Based on her health, I doubt she'll ever leave." Rachel turned off the screens containing Chris Long's information. "Now on to Morrison. Eden, Hudson and I watched his last two DVDs yesterday. I've turned over everything, except our copies, to the police. According to Ogle County Sheriff, Jim Wilson, and the State Police crime scene investigators, the partial remains of four bodies have been found on Morrison's property. It'll take a while for DNA results, but based on the DVDs he'd sent Eden, and the fact that all four doctors associated with Cosmetic Solutions and Med Spa are still missing, every law enforcement agency involved in the Morrison case thinks the victims are Thomas Elliot, Brian Westly, Leonard Tully, and Victor Roth."

"Between Long and Morrison, that's a lot of dead bodies in one week," Owen said.

"Brilliant observation." Rachel rolled her eyes. "Anyway, one of the last DVDs Morrison had given Eden was Roth's torture and...confession."

"Confession?" Ian echoed.

"Yes," Eden said. "It turns out Victor Roth knowingly gave Eliza Morrison, Michael's daughter, unnecessary procedures."

"Wasn't she over eighteen when she opted for the procedures?" Ian asked. "Legally, she—"

"No one is questioning the legality of what the doctors at Med Spa did to Eliza," Eden began. "You're right she was eighteen, and her mother was present when she signed any contracts with Med Spa. The morality of what these men did to her is where Roth's confession comes into play."

"What do you mean?" Owen asked as he stood and moved toward the TV screens.

Physically and emotionally exhausted, Eden squeezed Hudson's hand, and looked away to hide the tears. Every time she thought about Eliza Morrison, her pretty before and horrifying after photos, and her intellectual challenges, Eden mourned for the young girl and her father. While she still didn't agree with how Michael had handled his retaliation against the surgeons, she understood how, in his grief, he could have rationalized his brand of justice.

"Eliza's IQ was eighty," Hudson answered for her. "And she was considered borderline intellectually functioning."

Owen ran a hand through his hair as he stared at the TV screen showing Eliza's before and after picture. "Poor kid had no idea what she was getting herself into."

"No," Rachel said, and wiped a finger under her eye. "But her mother did."

"The mother's dead?" Ian asked.

Hudson nodded. "During Eliza's funeral, Sarah Morrison stood in front of her daughter's casket, then put a bullet in her head."

"In front of over a hundred people," Rachel added.

Ian's cell phone rang. "I've got to take this. Hudson, Rachel, send me the full report once you've closed this investigation."

After Ian left the room, Rachel said, "As far as I'm concerned, this investigation is closed."

"I agree," Hudson said. "But we still need to confirm the IDs of Morrison's victims."

"And the Ogle County animal warden needs to hunt down the coyotes Morrison used to finish off his victims," Rachel added.

"Um, hello?" Owen rapped a knuckle on the table. "What happened to the investigation isn't closed until the killer has been apprehended?"

When no one answered, Owen said, "Michael Morrison tortured and killed four men. I had the unpleasant experience of watching one of his DVDs. I get that you three might feel sorry for the guy and his daughter, but he's still a murderer." He pointed to the TV screen containing Eliza's information. "And I think I have an idea where you'll find him."

"What?" Eden stood and moved toward the screen. When she looked to where Owen pointed, she shook her head. "With everything that happened, I didn't even think about..."

Hudson and Rachel crowded around the TV, too.

"I've got to go," Hudson said, and grabbed his jacket.

Owen headed for the door. "I'll come with you."

"Wait," Eden called, and shrugged into her coat. "I'm going, too."

Hudson rested his hands on her shoulders. "I'd rather you stay and—"

She brushed past him. "I'm going."

Thirty minutes later, Hudson pulled the Trans Am into Holy Cross Cemetery. Rachel had already texted Hudson the location of Eliza Morrison's headstone. After stopping at the cemetery office for a map, Hudson weaved the car through the cemetery's small lanes.

"Stop," Eden said, and grabbed Hudson's arm. "Look, there's a white minivan." She looked at the map. "And this is the area where Eliza was buried."

As soon as Hudson parked the Trans Am behind the van, Eden opened the car door.

"Wait." Hudson snagged her hand. "Let me and Owen check things out first."

She touched his beard stubbled jaw. "I need to go. I need to talk to Michael. If it wasn't for him…I might not be here right now."

Owen leaned forward. "What are you talking about?"

Even when the police had questioned her and Hudson yesterday, neither of them had mentioned that Michael had helped locate and rescue her. Or that Hudson could have actually cuffed Michael and handed him over to the police. Considering he was known to go to any length to apprehend a criminal, the decision to let Michael go hadn't been too difficult for Hudson. Last night, as they lay in bed holding each other, he'd told her that he owed Michael. That he'd rather watch a murderer go free than live without her in his life.

Thinking about that moment brought tears to her eyes. She couldn't imagine not having Hudson in her life, either. While she still wasn't sure how they'd make their relationship work, they were both committed to trying.

"Nothing," Hudson finally said. "Let's go."

The frigid, late November wind howled through the headstones and monuments as they walked up the small hill leading to Eliza's grave. Standing at the top of the hill was a small, family mausoleum. As they passed the corner of the mausoleum, Eden gripped Hudson's hand and ran.

"No," she cried as she slowed. Letting go of Hudson, she dropped to her knees. Tears blurred her vision as she touched Eliza's headstone, then the pretty life-like doll resting against the cool marble.

Hudson crouched next to Michael Morrison's dead body. "There was no other way for him."

She glanced to the gun Michael had used to take his life,

then back to the headstone.

"Happy Birthday, Eliza," she said, then fell into Hudson's arms, and wept.

EPILOGUE

Christmas Eve

GIDDY WITH EXCITEMENT, Eden hung up the phone, then checked the turkey roasting in the oven. The twenty-five pound bird still had a couple of hours to go, and their guests wouldn't arrive for another hour.

Plenty of time for Hudson's surprise.

She dropped the potholders on the counter, removed her apron, then hurried into the guest bedroom. After retrieving one of Hudson's Christmas presents she'd hidden in the closet, she headed into the living room. "Busy?" she asked.

Sitting on the couch, with both Fabio and Brutal draped over him, he looked away from the TV and grinned. "Very, can't you tell?"

"Then I guess you don't have time to open up one of your Christmas presents."

Using the remote, he turned off the TV, then gently nudged the animals from his lap. "I thought we weren't exchanging until tomorrow morning."

"Well, something came up today, and it kind of goes along with one of your gifts. This one in particular," she said, and set the beautifully wrapped, tall, rectangular box in front of him.

Eyes bright, his smile grew. He stood, then pulled her into

his arms. "Can I give you one of my presents, too?"

She slipped her hand between their bodies, then slid her palm over his zipper. "This is the only package I'm interested in...of course, after our guests leave," she murmured, and kissed his freshly shaven jaw.

Chuckling, he caressed her rear. "I could make fun of you for your cheesy line, but it's kind of hard when all I want to do is take you into the bedroom, lay you on the bed, push this tight little skirt up and—"

"Stop," she groaned, then moved away before he completely sidetracked her with hot monkey sex. "Hurry up and open your present."

His eyes darkened as he stared at her cleavage. "I'd rather open—"

"Seriously," she laughed, and shoved the box between them.

"Okay," he said as he began unwrapping the present. "But you better believe I plan on coming back to this conversation..." He glanced from the box to her. "You bought me a weed whacker?"

She grinned.

Smiling, he asked, "So I can weed whack the dead plants in my apartment?"

"Not exactly. I was thinking about that yard in the Burbs."

He grew serious, and stared at her. "I go where you go. And I know the suburbs aren't one of those places on your list."

Her heart rate skyrocketed with hope and anticipation. Since the night she'd been kidnapped, they had both made an effort not to hide their emotions from each other. One thing she had kept hidden, though, was her new possible career path. Uncertain as to how things would play out, she'd decided not to tell Hudson. She didn't want to dash either of their hopes with bad news.

"They could be," she began, and smoothed the front of his pressed, button down shirt. "You know how after the kidnapping Network decided to give me until after the first of the year before they'd need me to begin working on the show?"

He nodded.

"What I didn't tell you is that I came up with a way I can still do the job I love without moving to New York. Actually, I can do this job anywhere I want. Chicago, the suburbs, Palm Springs, Tahiti…"

"Maybe I'm a little slow…do you mind explaining what new job?"

She laid her hands on chest. "After Michael died, I kept reading through that last letter he'd left for me, and thinking about Eliza and what had driven him to do something that was the polar opposite of the man everyone claimed to know."

That letter had been almost as heartbreaking as the DVD containing the old home movies of Eliza. Michael's words had been compelling and sincere. He'd apologized for involving her in his pursuit to right the wrong committed against his daughter, and had gone into great detail as to how he'd brought his plans of vengeance to fruition. Later, he'd written about Eliza. Not her tragic end, but about the funny, adorable child and sweet, sensitive young woman she had once been.

Hudson kissed her forehead. "This case hit you hard."

"It did. I shouldn't sympathize with a murderer, and I don't, but I do sympathize with a grieving father. So, I decided Michael was right. This was the story of my career. But rather than exploit the victims, and tarnish Eliza's memory by showing clips of the DVDs on the show Network wants me to do, I decided to write about it."

"I'm starting to feel stupid. What are you writing?"

Smiling, she said, "My first true crime novel. I sent my agent a proposal for Michael and Eliza's story. She shopped it to several publishers and I just heard back from her. I have a contract, an excellent advance, and…" She toyed with the collar of his shirt. "I was thinking that with all the cases you guys have at CORE, I'll have plenty of stories I can write about in the future."

He cupped her cheeks, and gave her a quick kiss.

"Seriously? You just sold a book? And you're not moving?"

She grinned into his palms."Yep."

After kissing her again, he pulled back and held her shoulders. "First, congratulations on the book," he said, the concern in his eyes belying his words.

"What?" she asked.

"The Network deal was your dream job. If you decided not to do it because of…us, I guess I worry that—"

"There's nothing you need to worry about." She wrapped her arms around his neck and ran her fingers through his short hair. "Did I tell you I like the new do?"

"You're changing the subject."

"Maybe."

"If you don't want to talk about it."

"No, it's okay. When I was at Long's house, holding a broken plate and preparing for the worse, I decided that if I got out of his house alive, I wasn't going to let my career dictate my life anymore. I need you with me."

"Always," he murmured, and gave her a long, lingering kiss. "I can't imagine life without you."

Tears swelled in her eyes. "That's a line I'd like to hear every day."

He smiled. "Count on it."

THE END

OTHER CORE TITLES AVAILABLE BY KRISTINE MASON

SHADOW OF VENGEANCE
BOOK THREE OF THE
CORE SHADOW TRILOGY

Welcome to Hell Week. You have seven days to find him...

At Wexman University, male students will do anything to get into a top fraternity. They'll prove their worth during Hell Week by participating in various physical, psychological and even juvenile pranks. But those shenanigans aren't so funny when pledges start disappearing. What kind of evil has stalked this small Michigan university for the past two decades? Theories range from obscene scientific experiments to grotesque satanic killings...but they're all wrong. The murdered boys serve a single purpose...the ultimate revenge.

Rachel Davis, forensic computer analyst for the private investigation agency CORE, has been itching to leave her desk behind and work in the field. When her brother Sean, a student at Wexman, is found beaten and his roommate kidnapped during Hell Week, she gets her chance. Only her boss insists former U.S. Secret Service Agent, Owen Malcolm, helps her with the investigation. Owen is the last person she wants on this assignment. She'd been secretly half in love with him for over four years, until the night he'd crushed her ego and destroyed her hopes for any kind of future with him.

For his own reasons, Owen refuses to risk becoming involved with a coworker. Now that he and Rachel are stuck working side-by-side to solve this perverse investigation, he's having a hard time fighting his attraction to her...an attraction he's tried to deny from the moment they met. But time is ticking. They have seven days to find the missing pledge and catch a killer. Seven days before the body count rises and the pledge ends up another victim of Hell Week.

Enjoy an excerpt from Shadow of Vengeance...

SHADOW OF VENGEANCE
BY
KRISTINE MASON

CHAPTER 1

MONDAY

RACHEL DAVIS STARED at the ringing cell phone, at the Michigan area code. Panic clamped her heart and tightened her chest. Her brother, Sean, lived in Michigan, but only called her from his cell phone, which used a Chicago area code. She glanced at the alarm clock beside her bed. He also never called her at six in the morning. Hoping something had happened to Sean's phone and he was calling from the dormitory landline, she quickly answered.

"Rachel Davis?"

Not Sean.

Panic morphed into utter dread. "Yes, who is this?"

"Sheriff Jake Tyler. Dixon County, Michigan."

Mouth dry, mind racing, she reached into the nightstand drawer and grabbed a pencil. "Why are you calling, Sheriff?"

Please let Sean be okay.

"It's about your brother."

She closed her eyes. Not caring that she'd just finished her hair and make-up, or that she was dressed for work in a freshly laundered suit, she slumped onto the bed and curled into the fetal position. Sean was her only family. Whatever news the sheriff was about to give her, she'd take it lying down. Fainting onto the hardwood floor would hurt like a bitch.

"Ma'am?"

"Is Sean...?" She couldn't say the words. Hurt. Missing. Dead.

"Your brother is at Dixon Medical Center. He's been beaten, but the doc working on him says he'll recover without issue."

Anger suddenly surged through her veins. She shot off the bed. "Beaten? When did this happen? Where? At the university?"

Although she'd tried to encourage Sean to remain in Chicago and attend Northwestern, he'd chosen Wexman University, in northwest Michigan, instead. He'd liked the idea of going to a small school, loved the campus, the engineering program and the fat scholarship the school had awarded him for his academics. While she'd respected his wishes, and the scholarship had definitely been a Godsend considering she was paying for his education, she'd still wished he would have stayed closer to home. She loved his company and missed seeing his face on a daily basis.

Now he was lying in a hospital bed.

"Actually, we're not sure where the beating took place. The doc thinks, based on the way Sean's wounds have healed, that your brother was hurt sometime Saturday."

"Saturday?" Pinching the pencil between her fingers, she paced the bedroom. "In case you're not aware, Sheriff, it's Monday."

"I'm fully aware of the day, ma'am," he replied, his tone holding a hint of irritation. "But your brother wasn't found until last night around midnight. He had no ID and considered a John Doe until a couple of hours ago."

Rachel stopped pacing and snatched the picture frame off the dresser. Staring at the photograph of her and Sean at a Chicago Cubs game last summer, memories of the cheering crowd, the mouthwatering aroma of hot dogs and popcorn, filled her mind and made her want to cry. They'd had a great time at the game, then later pigged out on pizza and wings. He wasn't just her brother, he was her best friend. And she could have lost him.

Tears filled her eyes as she set the photograph back on the dresser. Swiping a stray tear from her cheek, she drew in a deep breath.

She needed to maintain control. Think. Obtain the facts. Analyze the situation. Leave emotion out of the picture—for now—and use every resource she had available to find out who had hurt Sean. She worked for CORE (Criminal Observance Resolution Evidence), damn it, and had helped the agency investigate and solve hundreds of cases. She'd solve this one, too. And when Sean was well enough to travel, she'd haul his ass home. Maybe even force him to be the next bubble boy. Anything to ensure he remained safe.

"Miss Davis? You still there?" the sheriff asked.

She tucked the pencil behind her ear, then rubbed her temple where a deep throb began to build. "Sorry, Sheriff, I'm still here and didn't mean to snap at you. My brother..." He was the only family she had left. After their mother had run off with a musician six years ago, she'd become Sean's legal guardian. Had she been old enough, the courts should have given her that right when he was born. Even at twelve she'd been a better parent than their mom. The woman had spent more time trying to land her next husband than paying attention to her children. Rachel loved Sean. Without him in her life...

Clearing her throat, she said, "I work for a private criminal investigation agency and we specialize in—"

"I'm aware you work for CORE. One of your agents recently helped the Detroit PD with a case. A few months back, another of your people helped bring down a serial killer in Wisconsin."

"That's right," she said, and headed into the kitchen to where she'd left her laptop running. "So, I understand that you might not be able to give me all the details while you're still running this investigation." She paused. "You *are* considering what happened to my brother as something worth investigating, correct?"

"Of course. Actually, I was hoping CORE might lend us a hand."

While she'd planned to use COREs resources to find out who had hurt Sean, the sheriff's hopes bordered on extreme. CORE didn't usually handle cases like this unless they were high profile or the client had deep pockets. Frowning, she said, "What about the Michigan State Police?"

"They...have no interest in what goes on around these parts."

"That doesn't make any sense," she said, and closed the case file she'd been working on before her shower and the sheriff's call. CORE had worked with the FBI, law enforcement in different cities around the country, as well as numerous state agencies. During the four years she'd been with CORE, she had the opportunity to work with the Michigan State Police a few times. In her experience, their personnel had been both capable and professional.

"It will once I explain. Now, the county can't afford to pay your agency—"

"We do plenty of cases pro bono." More concerned over her brother than the sheriff's issues with the State Police, she shifted focus. "Forget about that and give me details. It's the end of January. Last night the temperature dipped to fifteen degrees in Chicago, and I'm betting it was even colder where you're located. Did my brother suffer from exposure? Who found him and where? What are his exact injuries? Do you have any suspects or—?"

"Hang on, and slow down," the sheriff said on a deep sigh. "Let me start at the beginning. Your brother was found by a local guy. He was heading home from work and spotted his body on the side of the road. Sean couldn't have been outside for too long because his body temperature was normal. The guy who found him even said he was surprised your brother's skin was warm when he touched his neck to find a pulse."

Somewhat relieved that Sean hadn't been lying in the freezing cold for over twenty-four hours, Rachel began to type notes onto her laptop. "Who was the man who found my brother?" She'd like to thank the Good Samaritan. If he hadn't found Sean, he could have frozen to death.

"Hal Baker. After he brought Sean to the hospital, Hal took me to where he found your brother. Based on the way Hal described the state of Sean's body, the doc and I both think that he was thrown out of a vehicle. Something high off the ground—maybe an SUV or a truck—and that's how he suffered the concussion and broken arm. The broken ribs, and bruising to his face and body...I think that happened somewhere else."

She paused her fingers over the keyboard and fought back the worry, anger and grief. Whoever had done this to her brother would pay dearly. "Did you find tire tracks on the road, or any fibers or DNA evidence on Sean's clothes?"

"While there's snow on the ground, there's none on the road. There weren't any fresh tire tracks, and I didn't find any shoe imprints in the snow near where Sean was found. As for DNA evidence, we're small time here, Miss Davis. I did bag Sean's clothes and could probably send it to the Michigan State Police, but like I said, they really—"

"Don't have any interest in what's going on in those parts," she repeated what the sheriff had said earlier, and shook her head. "I'm still having a hard time wrapping my brain around that nonsense, Sheriff."

"Right. We...ah...had some past events that made the Michigan State Police look bad and my department look like a joke."

"Unless these past events are in any relation to what happened to my brother, I see no reason—"

"Miss Davis," the sheriff interrupted. "I'm afraid they do. Over the past twenty years we've had well over a dozen missing person reports in our county. Nineteen to be exact. Out of all of the cases, only five of those missing persons have been found. The couple of times the State Police came in to help investigate, the reports ended up being nothing but a hoax."

Shrugging, she said, "I don't see why that would keep the State from helping with future investigations."

"Look, I've got a meeting with our town council and honestly don't have time to go into the details right now."

"Fine, then you can explain when I get there," she said. "It's about a six hour drive from Chicago, and I'll need to stop by CORE on my way out of town." She glanced at the clock and did the math. "Will you be able to meet with me around three? I want to see my brother first."

"Sure. I'll meet you at my office in Bola. If you've been to the university, you would have had to pass through the town."

If Wexman University wasn't located near the town, and she hadn't had the best breakfast of her life there, she probably wouldn't have remembered the forgettable Bola, Michigan. Located near the Menominee River, the small town thrived on tourism during the summer, and the students and faculty from the university throughout the remainder of the year. Except for the small manufacturing company at the edge of town, and the place she'd eaten breakfast, she couldn't recall anything else about Bola, other than it being boring.

"I'm familiar with Bola," she said.

"Good, then I'll see you at three."

While the sheriff gave her his contact information, the missing persons he'd mentioned nagged at her. Bola's population—she remembered from the town's billboard—was around twelve hundred. Last fall, the university's enrollment had been almost equal to the number of residents living in Bola. Granted, those missing person cases had occurred over the course of twenty years, but with approximately twenty five hundred people living in the area nine months out of the year, the number of missing persons seemed...staggering.

"Before you go," Rachel said, and headed for the bedroom to pack a bag. "You mentioned that what happened to my brother relates to the missing persons you've had over the years. How so?"

"I planned on telling you when we met. It's also the reason why I was hoping CORE could help us." He paused, exhaled deeply, then said, "With almost every one of those missing persons, a note was left behind. Same writing, same message. Only this time, the note wasn't left behind. It was left *on* your brother, stuffed in the pocket of his jeans."

She stopped packing, and sat on the edge of the bed. "What did the note say?"

"Welcome to Hell Week. You have seven days to find him."

A chill swept over her and prickled the hair on her scalp. During fall semester, Sean had participated in the university's rush week, and had decided to pledge the Eta Tau Zeta fraternity. Over winter break, he'd told her he was excited to join the Zetas, that they were a great group of guys, but had worried about the expense. She hadn't worried about the money. The cost to join the fraternity and live at the frat house wasn't much different than that of the dorms.

What had worried her, though, were the hazing rituals that occur during Hell Week. Sean had assured her that the university didn't allow any form of hazing, that the school's policy was strict and if any member of a fraternity was caught or even suspected of hazing, they would be expelled. Although the universities no-tolerance rules had eased her mind, and she'd met most of the boys from the fraternity, she'd still worried about her baby brother. She'd practically raised him and couldn't help being overprotective.

Now he was six hours away, lying in some rinky-dink hospital.

"That note might make sense if you found it in Sean's dorm room," she said, more as a way to alleviate her unease. The missing persons, the note, Sean's beating, the way he'd been left along the road...something wasn't right in Bola.

"I don't think the message was meant for Sean. Have you met your brother's roommate?"

In an instant, the image of a handsome, athletic, blonde-haired, blue-eyed kid jumped into her mind. Although Josh

Conway was the polar opposite to her redheaded, brown-eyed, lanky, bookworm of a brother, the two boys had become close friends, and both were pledging the Eta Tau Zeta fraternity. "Yeah, I know Josh. What about him?"

"According to the dormitory residential assistant, both Sean and Josh were last seen leaving their dorm room Saturday evening. They were supposed to meet a few others at the library for a study session. Neither showed."

"Is Josh…?"

"We have no idea of his whereabouts."

And her brother had been beaten and left for dead.

Welcome to Hell Week.

Dread settled in the pit of her stomach as a grisly thought came to mind. "Sheriff, these missing persons your town has seen over the years…were any of them students at Wexman University?"

"Not all, but most of them. Nine to be exact. With Josh Conway's disappearance…we're now up to ten."

Ten? "The students, were any of them pledging a fraternity or sorority?"

"Fraternities. They were all male."

Rachel tightened her grip on the cell phone. "When? Was there a specific time of year when these boys went missing?"

"January."

"And their bodies?"

"They've never been found."

While she wasn't a criminalist like some members of CORE's team, her years spent with Army Intelligence, along with her hacking skills, had prepared her for the job and had made her valuable to Ian Scott, the owner of the agency. During her tenure, she'd been involved in some seriously twisted cases. Her mind worked quick and zeroed in on one thing.

"You have a serial killer in Bola."

"That's right, Miss Davis. Welcome to Hell Week. We have only seven days to find Josh Conway."

****

With a yawn and a stretch, he climbed out of bed and toed on his slippers. After shrugging into his robe, like a kid on Christmas, he raced down the staircase and into the kitchen. Eagerness and excitement hummed through his veins. Better than Christmas or a birthday or any other holiday, today marked a special day, a special beginning. The time of year he anticipated the most.

Hell Week.

As the coffee brewed, the strong, rich aroma of hazelnut and cinnamon wafted throughout the kitchen. While he waited for that first delicious cup, he did a mental checklist of today's schedule. Mondays were always a full workday, filled with meetings and preparations for the upcoming week. Pity. He'd love to play hooky today. He'd love to play with the pledge in his basement.

The pledge would have to wait until this evening. Work came first. Deviating from his daily routine was not an option. Besides, he knew in his heart, now, this moment wasn't the right time. In the past, he'd made mistakes with his pledges. In his overzealousness, he'd rushed things, which had made for some...deadly results. He couldn't rush anything with the new pledge. Twenty years ago, what had begun as therapy had now become legend. *He* had become legendary. No. There would be no rushing, no overzealousness. No more mistakes.

After what Junior had done on Saturday, there had better not be any more mistakes. He poured coffee into the mug, then blew on the liquid before taking a sip. Although still angry over Junior's screw up, he couldn't stay mad at his only child. Hell Week would become Junior's legacy. The gifts of dominance, control, power...definitely the kind of inheritance that keeps on giving.   And he wanted his child to feel, to truly understand, what it is to have power over another human being. Over their pledge.

Although Junior had been born a disappointment, he never wanted his own flesh and blood to experience what he had twenty-five years ago. The powerlessness, the helplessness, the utter degradation at the hands of monsters. While it had taken him years to battle the nightmares that still haunted him, he'd made his mark on the world. Well, at least in Bola, Michigan.

Chuckling, he shrugged and looked out the kitchen window. He glanced at the trees in his backyard, now naked save for the clumps of icy snow resting on their branches, then to the path that led to the Menominee River. When he'd been a child, that path had terrified him. His parents had warned him never to walk through the forest alone, to never go near the river, or bad things will happen. Too true, he chuckled again, then took another sip of his coffee.

He no longer knew what it was like to be afraid. The Townies knew. They knew and they feared him.

Just like his parents had done, the town folk of Bola had spun terrifying stories to their children in order to keep them from venturing too far into the dense forests surrounding Bola. The university students, most of them spoiled, coddled, little shitheads, didn't buy into the Townies fears and beliefs. They'd considered him a myth, akin to the celebrated Bigfoot many of the ignorant Townies had claimed to have seen roaming the area.

Fools.

He was no myth. But he should be feared. Every male student at the university should agonize and wonder.

Will he come for me this year?

While he'd bet there were a few young men who worried, they wouldn't have to concern themselves any longer. He'd taken his pledge. By noon today, word of the boy's disappearance would reach every corner of the campus and county. And so it would begin.

Seven days of torture.

Seven days of hell.

The front door opened, sending in a loud gust of wind, then quickly shut.

"Junior?" he called as he left the kitchen and moved down the hallway into the foyer. He stopped, leaned against the stair rails and eyed his favorite mistake. "What have you learned?"

"They found Sean Davis late last night. He's recovering at Dixon Medical Center. Depending on the severity of the concussion, he'll likely be released in a few days."

"And the note?"

"Sheriff Tyler didn't mention it, but it's obvious he found it. Around four this morning, he questioned all the boys at the Eta Tau Zeta house, as well as the RA and some of the kids living at the dorm."

He sipped his coffee, then said, "I wonder if our dedicated sheriff has tried to contact his family."

"Davis'?"

Waving his hand, he shook his head. "I don't care about that whiney, little skid mark. Idiot, I'm referring to our pledge."

"Yes, sir." Junior looked to the floor. "Sorry. I don't know. As you're aware, the university administration offices open at eight. I wouldn't be surprised if they receive a call from the sheriff then. Does he need Josh's parents to file a missing person report?"

The mug, filled with his delicious coffee, smashed and splattered on the tile. In an instant he had Junior by the throat and up against the door. "*Pledge*," he said, and tightened his grip. "*That* is his new name. *That* is what you will call him. Do you understand?"

Junior nodded, and whispered, "Yes, sir."

He reined in his anger and loosened his hold. "Josh Conway is dead, figuratively speaking of course," he began, calmer now, and stepped over the mess on the floor.

"Yes, of course."

Turning his back, he walked down the hallway toward the kitchen for a new cup of coffee, but stopped at the threshold. "Clean up the mess you caused and meet me in the basement."

"I thought we wouldn't begin with the pledge until this evening."

"You're right, we won't. But he must be given a taste of what's to come."

****

Owen Malcolm stifled a yawn and waited for Ian Scott, his boss and founder of CORE, to end his phone conversation. He glanced around Ian's luxurious, yet comfortable office, particularly at the large, leather sofa near the fireplace, and ached for a nap. Not about to curl up on his boss' sofa, he leaned into the plush office chair, instead.

The past couple months of travelling might have finally caught up with him. November, there had been California and Las Vegas. December had him in San Antonio for a few weeks, then from there he'd flown to Virginia to spend the holidays with his family.

While he'd loved visiting his parents, sisters and nieces and nephews, he couldn't count the trip as a vacation. If he hadn't been working odd jobs around the house for his mom and dad, his sisters had been ushering him, and his nieces and nephews, to the obnoxiously loud, germ and kid infested Play World. How many times can a kid go on the same humungous, inflatable slide without growing sick of it? Infinity, he assumed, because his sisters' kids never stopped until they'd left, then had begged to go back the next day.

He'd take the raucous Play World over this last assignment, though. While Miami in January had its perks, beautiful, warm beaches, wild nightlife, and even wilder women, he didn't have the chance to enjoy any of it. Instead, he'd spent three weeks helping the Miami-Dade police track down the man who'd been robbing, raping, then murdering elderly women. He'd found the guy. But the prick had put a bullet into his head before the police could arrest him. The suicide might not give the victims' families total closure, but it had made his part in the investigation easier. Now he wouldn't have to travel back to Florida for a long, drawn-out trial.

He looked out Ian's office window. Nothing but gray sky. Maybe a long, drawn-out trial in Miami wouldn't have been such a bad thing. Chicago plus January equaled snow and freezing temperatures.

Ian hung up the phone. "How was Florida?" he asked.

Owen straightened. "I didn't get much of a chance to work on my tan," he said, then leaned forward and handed Ian the case file.

As he glanced through the paperwork, Ian asked, "When did you get back?"

He looked at the clock. "My flight got in about an hour ago. I haven't even been to my condo yet."

Arching his black brows, Ian leaned into his chair and shrugged. "Go home then."

"I didn't mean to imply—"

Ian shook his head and offered him a slight smile. "I know you didn't."

"Then why are you sending me home without giving me my next assignment?" In the six years he'd worked for Ian, other than his annual holiday trip to see the family and the occasional vacation, he'd never ended a case without being handed another.

And he needed another.

When he visited his folks, they kept him too busy to think. When he took a vacation, he always made sure they had been well-scheduled trips, packed with a full itinerary. Downtime, lounging on the beach or poolside, didn't work for him. If he stopped moving, his mind would go into overdrive. Bringing up the past. His mistakes. His regrets.

Ian moved, as if to run his hand through his salt and pepper hair, then instead, scratched the back of his head. "I don't have anything for you."

During his time with CORE, he'd only seen one member of the team let go. And it had started with, "I don't have anything for you."

Flashbacks from his days with the U.S. Secret Service suddenly shifted through his head. The cover-ups. The bullshit. The lies and dismissal.

He'd been loyal to Ian because the man had helped him salvage his career. Although his boss could be manipulative, it was done with purpose. Not as blunt as he'd like, Ian was still an excellent employer. He didn't want to lose his job with CORE. Sure, with his background, he could find another position, with another private agency, but he had no interest in working elsewhere. CORE had become his life. He liked his fellow agents, his hefty salary, the bonuses and the benefits.

"Is this the start of your firing process?"

Ian's bark of laughter filled the office. "God, no. Why in the hell would I fire you? I can work you like a dog, and you never complain. *I* have no complaints." He grew serious, then said, "You've been working cases back-to-back, and I don't want you to burnout. I thought you could use a week to regroup. Paid, of course."

Most people would have jumped at the opportunity of paid time off. And while he appreciated Ian's intentions, he didn't want a break. He'd rather work. The assignments kept his mind busy, his thoughts focused.

"I appreciate the offer, but I'm good."

Ian eyed him, then nodded. "If you change your mind, just let me know. Meanwhile, I have an interesting cold case that needs solving." He pulled a file from the drawer and set it on the desk.

Owen liked cold cases, especially the older ones where modern day technology hadn't quite been invented. They were like puzzles. He enjoyed sifting through old paperwork, crime scene photos, and evidence. Seeing what fit and what didn't, then solving what no one else had been able.

A rap at the door caught his attention. As he turned, Rachel burst into the room. She came to an abrupt halt when she saw him, then looked to Ian.

"Sorry, Ian. I didn't mean to interrupt, but I…" She looked away, stared out the window, then reached for the pencil tucked behind her ear.

Something had Beaver upset. Not once, during the four years Rachel had worked for CORE, had Owen ever seen her at a loss for words. The woman always had something to say, and had an annoying habit of doing so over a mouthful of pencil.

"I can come back," Owen said, sensing Rachel might want a moment alone with Ian.

"No, actually, I wouldn't mind if you stayed. I might be able to use your help."

Interesting. Rachel never liked having him around, and rarely asked him for help with anything. Why, he didn't know. All he knew was that whenever he walked into the room, she threw verbal jabs, snarky uppercuts, and sarcastic hooks. He didn't care, and actually liked Rachel. Although a bit...mouthy, he couldn't deny her capabilities as CORE's computer forensics analyst, plus he admired her intelligence and her quick working mind.

"I'd be glad to help," he said, still dumbfounded that she'd willingly have him part of the conversation.

She moved to the leather office chair next to him, then sat. "Yeah, well, no one else is here yet, so I have no choice."

So much for thinking she'd been interested in *his* expertise.

"What's going on?" Ian asked her.

"It's my brother," she began. "Late last night, he was found on the side of the road just outside of Bola, Michigan, beaten and unconscious."

"My God, Rachel," Ian said, and leaned forward. "How's his condition?"

"He's okay. I'll know more when I see him."

Ian nodded. "Absolutely. Take all the time you need. It's a long drive to Bola. If you want to use the jet, feel free."

She smiled and shook her head. "Thank you, but I'm going to drive. I'm not sure how long I'll be gone, and I don't want to deal with a rental."

"Understood," Ian said.

"I'm sorry about your brother," Owen said, and meant it. He had three older sisters, and if anything bad had happened to them, he'd be devastated. And out for blood. While he doubted he'd ever have a family of his own, his parents, his sisters and their kids, meant everything to him. They accepted and loved him, faults and all. He knew Rachel had basically raised her brother, and couldn't imagine how she must be feeling. "Do you have any idea who did this to him?"

"The sheriff I spoke with doesn't have any leads. That's why I wanted you to stick around. I...ah." She paused and glanced to the ceiling. Seconds later she looked at him. "I'd like your advice."

Seriously interesting. Most times when he offered his opinion, she'd somehow find a way to either dismiss him or cut him down.

"When I get to Bola I plan to investigate my brother's beating," she continued. "I know where to start, and already have a list of the people I want to interview."

"Are you planning on running this investigation on behalf of CORE?" Ian asked.

She tapped the pencil to her lips. "Are you okay with that? If not, I can—"

Ian waved a hand. "Our resources are yours."

Blowing out a deep breath, she tucked the pencil behind her ear. "Thank you. I have a feeling I'm going to need it. Sean's beating...based on what the sheriff told me, I don't think it was random."

"Why's that?" Owen asked.

"The sheriff said they found a note stuffed in Sean's pocket. It said, 'Welcome to Hell Week. You have seven days to find him.'"

"But they obviously found your brother," Owen countered.

"Right. They found Sean. His roommate, Josh Conway, is missing."

"Could this roommate have gone home for the weekend?" he asked.

"No. Sean told me his parents are overseas."

"Didn't you tell me that Sean planned to join a fraternity?" Ian asked.

"Yes. The Eta Tau Zetas"

"Based on the Hell Week reference," Ian began. "Is it possible that this was a hazing gone bad?"

She nodded, and hugged herself. "I thought about that, only..."

"What?" Owen asked.

"The sheriff said that over the last twenty years, nine male students from Wexman University have gone missing. Josh makes ten. These students always disappear in January. And with every one of these missing boys, the same note is left behind."

Owen rubbed his jaw, both confused and disturbed. "You're telling us that nine guys go missing, the same time of year, with the same message left behind...have any of the bodies been discovered?"

"No."

"Does this sheriff realize he has a possible serial killer in his county?" he asked, dumbfounded that Bola, Michigan's local law enforcement, hell, even the university, hadn't pieced the obvious together and asked for outside help.

"He's well aware."

Irritated at the sheriff's ineptness, he leaned forward and asked, "Then why not bring in the Michigan State Police?"

"The sheriff tried that route. I'm still confused as to what happened when they participated in the investigation..." She faced Ian. "I have vacation time, and you said I can use CORE's resources. The sheriff can't afford to pay us, but if it's okay with you, I want to investigate what's happening in Bola and find Sean's roommate."

"Of course," Ian said. "But there's no need to worry about vacation time and fees. Not when family is involved. Besides, this is an interesting case."

"Very interesting," Owen said. "A possible serial killer who targets victims at a certain time of year...strange, too."

Ian nodded, and removed the cold case file from the desk. "Agreed. This cold case can wait a few more weeks. Rachel has just handed you your next assignment."

Excitement pumped through Owen's veins. He'd gladly take the case. What had and was happening in Bola sounded like a huge puzzle with a lot of missing pieces.

"I didn't *hand* him anything," Rachel said. "And I told you *I* want to conduct this investigation."

"You can." Ian smiled. "Only you'll do it with Owen."

SHADOW OF DANGER
BOOK ONE OF THE
CORE SHADOW TRILOGY

Four women have been found dead in the outskirts of a small Wisconsin town. The only witness, clairvoyant Celeste Risinski, observes these brutal murders through violent nightmares and hellish visions. The local sheriff, who believes in Celeste's abilities and wants to rid their peaceful community of a killer, enlists the help of an old friend, Ian Scott, owner of a private criminal investigation agency, CORE. Because of Ian's dark history with Celeste's family, a history she knows nothing about, he sends his top criminalist, former FBI agent John Kain to investigate.

John doesn't believe in Celeste's mystic hocus-pocus, or in her visions of the murders. But just when he's certain they've solved the crimes, with the use of science and evidence, more dead bodies are discovered. Could this somehow be the work of the same killer or were they dealing with a copycat? To catch a vicious murderer, the skeptical criminalist reluctantly turns to the sensual psychic for help. Yet with each step closer to finding the killer, John finds himself one step closer to losing his heart.

ULTIMATE KILL
BOOK ONE OF THE
ULTIMATE CORE TRILOGY

When the past collides with the present, the only way to ensure the future lies in the ultimate kill...

Naomi McCall is a woman of many secrets. Her family has been murdered and she's been forced into hiding. No one knows her past or her real name, not even the man she loves.

Jake Tyler, former Marine and the newest recruit to the private criminal investigation agency, CORE, has been in love with a woman who never existed. When he learns about the lies Naomi has weaved, he's ready to leave her—until an obsessed madman begins sending her explosive messages every hour on the hour.

Innocent people are dying. With their deaths, Naomi's secrets are revealed and the truth is thrust into the open. All but one. Naomi's not sure if Jake can handle a truth that will change their lives. But she is certain of one thing—the only way to stop the killer before he takes more lives is to make herself his next victim.

CONTEMPORARY ROMANCES BY KRISTINE MASON

KISS ME

When is a kiss...

After a series of bad relationships, Jenna Cooper wants a sex buddy—no-strings, no emotional involvement, and absolutely no expectations of commitment. She sets her sights on Luke Sinclair. A player and commitment-phobe, he'd make the perfect boy toy. Only Luke's tired of playing the scene and wants a serious relationship with Jenna, not a series of one-night stands.

...More than a kiss?

When Luke makes Jenna an offer she can't refuse, the sexual tension between them combusts and their emotional chemistry becomes too hard for Jenna to ignore. They both end up with more than either bargained for, especially when Jenna's wild past is exposed and threatens to tear their relationship apart. Now Luke will do anything to make things right between them, but knows it's going to take more than a kiss...

PICK ME
BOOK ONE OF THE
REALITY TV ROMANCE SERIES

For the chance of a lifetime...

To help save the TV reality show, *Pick Me*, from cancellation, Valentina Bonasera swaps her position as the show's Production Assistant, to play the role of Bachelorette, only to discover Bachelor Number One, rancher and sports agent, Colt Walker, happens to be her one and only one-night stand she'd snuck away from six months ago.

...Pick me.

Colt had never forgotten the hot, sensual night he'd shared with Valentina, or how she'd left him without so much as a note or her contact information. He'd spent months searching for the woman who'd given him a night he couldn't forget and thought he'd never see again. Now that she's in Dallas, he's determined to make her his...

LOVE ME OR LEAVE ME
BOOK TWO OF THE
REALITY TV ROMANCE SERIES

Love me...

Carter James, real estate agent for the hit reality show, *Renovate or Relocate*, has been crazy about the show's designer, Brynn Dawson, for years. He's been aching to take their friendship to a new level and when he gets his chance to spend a hot, sensual night with her and fulfill his wildest fantasies, he falls hard for Brynn. When the director of the show reveals that Brynn could possibly be fired, Carter knows he has to act fast before she's booted from the show. He'll not only jeopardize his reputation, but he'll go behind her back to help her keep her job. Knowing Brynn's pride is also at stake, he hopes his deception doesn't come back to haunt him in the end. He can't imagine life without the woman he loves.

...or leave me.

Brynn has been aware of Carter for years. How good he smells, his sexy smile, his lean, muscular body, his big, rough hands and what she'd like him to do with them. When she takes a chance by going from friends to lovers, she risks both her heart and their friendship, but discovers it's the best decision she could have ever made. Despite having her job on the line, she also knows that as long as she has Carter by her side, she can get through anything. Until she finds out what Carter's been up to. Hurt and betrayed, her emotions raw and her love for him tested, she'll have to decide whether she can move past the deceit and love him or if his lack of faith in her will force her to leave him.

ABOUT KRISTINE MASON

I didn't pick up my first romance novel until I was in my late twenties. Immediately hooked, I read a bazillion books before deciding to write one of my own. After the birth of my first son I needed something to keep my mind from turning to mush, and Sesame Street wasn't cutting it. While that first book will never see the light of day, something good came from writing it. I realized my passion and found a career I love.

When I'm not writing contemporary romances and dark, romantic suspense novels (or reading them!) I'm chasing after my four kids and two neurotic dogs.

You can email me at authorkristinemason@gmail.com, visit my website at www.kristinemason.net or find me on Facebook https://www.facebook.com/kristinemasonauthor and https://twitter.com/KristineMason7 to connect with me on Twitter!

CPSIA information can be obtained at www.ICGtesting.com
Printed in the USA
LVOW06s1759130514

385614LV00025B/1650/P